When Mercy Rains

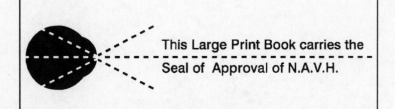

THE ZIMMERMAN RESTORATION TRILOGY, BOOK ONE

WHEN MERCY RAINS

KIM VOGEL SAWYER

THORNDIKE PRESS
A part of Gale, Cengage Learning

GALE
CENGAGE Learning·

Farmington Hills, Mich • San Francisco • New York • Waterville, Maine
Meriden, Conn • Mason, Ohio • Chicago

GALE
CENGAGE Learning·

LIBRARY OF CONGRESS CATALOGING-IN-PUBLICATION DATA

Sawyer, Kim Vogel.
  When mercy rains / by Kim Vogel Sawyer.
    pages cm. — (The Zimmerman restoration trilogy ; 1) (Thorndike Press large print Christian romance)
    ISBN 978-1-4104-7317-2 (hardcover) — ISBN 1-4104-7317-1 (hardcover)
  I. Title.
PS3619.A97W435 2014b
813'.6—dc23   2014029525

Published in 2014 by arrangement with WaterBrook Press, an imprint of the Crown Publishing Group, a division of Random House, LLC, a Penguin Random House Company

For Kaitlyn,
who forgives readily and
remembers the slight no more

Remember not the
sins of my youth,
nor my transgressions:
according to thy mercy
remember thou me for
thy goodness' sake,
O LORD.

PSALM 25:7, KJV

PROLOGUE

Suzanne
Spring 1994

The hiss of approaching tires on wet pavement broke the tense silence between the mother and daughter seated on the bus-stop bench. Suzy flicked a look at Mother and dared a timorous comment. "Here it comes." Now that her leave-taking was upon her, would her mother's disapproving demeanor soften?

The lines of Mother's mouth remained etched in a stern line, the furrows between her brows forming a V so deep it might never depart. Suzy hunched into her wool coat — a coat far too cloying for the damp May dawn but also too bulky to fit in her small cardboard suitcase. She'd be gone well into the winter months, and Mother insisted she'd need it so she should wear it. And she always did what her mother said.

Well, almost always. Who knew one foolish mistake could hold such far-reaching consequences? *I'm so sorry, God.*

The bus groaned to a stop at the curb, and Mother curled her hand around Suzy's elbow, forcing her to rise. Although Mother's grip was hard, impersonal, Suzy welcomed it. Her ordinarily demonstrative mother hadn't touched her even once in the past two weeks, as if fearful Suzy's stains would rub off. So she pressed her elbow against her rib cage, needing to feel the pressure of Mother's work-roughened fingers against her flesh. But the coat proved too thick a barrier. Suzy blinked rapidly.

"Get your case."

The moment Suzy caught the handle of the old suitcase, Mother propelled her through the gray drizzle toward the bus. The slap of the soles of their matching black oxfords sent up dirty droplets from the rain-soaked sidewalk, peppering their tan hosiery. The dark spots reminded Suzy of the dark blotch now and forever on her soul. She pushed the thought aside and looked into the opening created by the unfolding of the bus door.

The driver glanced from Mother to Suzy, seeming to focus on their white mesh caps and dangling ribbons — Mother's black, Suzy's white. Accustomed to curious looks from those outside her Mennonite faith, Suzy didn't wince beneath the man's puzzled scowl, but she battled the desire to melt into the damp concrete when Mother spoke in a strident tone.

"I am Abigail Zimmerman, and this is my daughter. She is traveling one-way to Indianapolis."

One-way . . . Suzy swallowed hard.

Mother gave her elbow a little shake. "Show him the ticket, Suzanne."

Suzanne. Not Suzy as she'd been tenderly called her entire life. She gulped again and drew the rumpled ticket from her pocket.

The driver eased himself from the seat and plucked the rectangle of paper from Suzy's icy fingers. He stared at it for a moment and then bobbed his head and waved a hand in invitation. "Come on aboard. Long drive ahead of you."

Suzy gritted her teeth to hold back a cry of agony. He didn't realize how long. She turned to Mother, silently praying the mother who had dried her tears and bandaged her childhood scuffs would reappear, would read the fear in her eyes and offer a hug. A kind word. A hint of forgiveness.

Mother leaned close, and Suzy's heart leaped with hope. "The people at the . . . in Indianapolis know what to do. You do what they say." Mother's harsh whisper raised a slight cloud of condensation around her face, softening the fierce furrows of anger etched at her eyes and mouth.

"I will." Questions Suzy had fearfully held inside pressed for release. What had Mother and Dad told Clete, Shelley, and little Sandra? Did the fellowship know she was leaving? Would she be allowed to call home?

"Afterward you can come to Arborville again. It will be as though this never happened." Mother took a step back, shoving her balled fists into the pockets of her lightweight trench coat.

Tears flooded Suzy's eyes, distorting her vision. The suitcase encumbered one arm, but she lifted the other, her fingers reaching fleetingly toward her mother. "Mother, I —"

"At least you will be able to bless your cousin Andrew and his wife. God will redeem your sin. Now go, Suzanne." Mother jerked her chin toward the rumbling bus. "Go and put this unpleasantness behind us."

Behind *us* . . . Suzy's shame had spilled over and tainted her entire family. She bowed her head, the weight of her burden too much to bear.

"I will see you afterward."

Mother's words sealed Suzy's fate. With a

heavy heart, she climbed the stairs, the unwieldy suitcase and her trembling limbs making her clumsy. She trudged down the narrow, dim aisle past snoozing passengers to the very last bench and slid in. Hugging the suitcase to her aching chest — to her womb, which bore the evidence of her shame — she hung her head and toyed with the plastic handle of the suitcase rather than clearing a spot on the steam-clouded window to see if Mother might wave good-bye.

The bus lurched forward, jolting Suzy in the seat. She closed her eyes tight as a wave of nausea rolled over her. Her thoughts screamed, *Wait! Let me off!* She didn't want to go so far away. She needed her mother. She would miss her father and sisters and brother.

And Paul.

Her mother's final comment echoed in her mind. *"I will see you afterward."* After Suzy delivered this child and handed it to others to raise. The ache in her chest heightened until she could barely draw a breath. She leaned her forehead against the cool glass and allowed the long-held tears to slip quietly down her cheeks. She would leave her home in Kansas, and she would count the days until she could put this nightmare behind her and go back to being Mother and Dad's Suzy again.

CHAPTER 1

Suzanne
Twenty Years Later

Suzanne Zimmerman balanced a clipboard against her hip and recorded the milliliters of antibiotic-infused solution administered via Mr. Birney's IV, then she checked the box next to "pain medicine dispensed" and confirmed the time on her wristwatch before writing it down. Her clerical duties complete, she slid the clipboard into its plastic pocket on the wall and moved to the side of the tall, railed bed.

The blinds were drawn against the night, and only one small fluorescent bulb glowed from a panel above the bed, but the dim beam of light was sufficient. To her relief, Mr. Birney's face had lost its ashen appearance and his breathing was much less labored than when he'd been admitted three days ago.

As she looked down at him, his eyes fluttered open. His gaze drifted around the room, confusion marring his brow, but then he fixed his faded gray eyes on her face, and his expression cleared.

She touched the man's wrinkled hand. "I'm sorry. Did I disturb you, Mr. Birney?"

"Call me Ed. 'Mr. Birney' makes me feel like some old man."

Suzanne swallowed a smile. According to his file, Mr. Birney had turned eighty-two a month ago. He spoke in a crusty tone, but she admired his spunk. And she was thankful for it. He'd need spunk to recover from his bout of pneumonia. "Ed then. Are you comfortable?"

"As comfortable as I can be in this crazy contraption. Hard as a rock and folding me in half like a pretzel. A bed like this belongs in a medieval torture chamber."

Reflecting upon the proverb about laughter being good medicine, Suzanne teased, "Well now, you guessed our secret. We purchase our beds from Torture Chamber Supply Company. After all, if you're too comfortable, you won't want to get well and go home."

Mr. Birney gave a brief snort of laughter that ended in a cough. He shook his head, the lines of his jowls shifting with the motion. "Torture Chamber Supply Company.

That's a good one." His eyebrows beetled, real concern chasing away the glint of humor. "About goin' home . . . I'll be doing that, won't I?"

Compassion filled Suzanne. She looked directly into Mr. Birney's watery eyes and spoke with great confidence. "You'll be going home. No need to worry."

He heaved a rattling sigh, then set his jaw in a stubborn jut. "Wasn't worried. Just wondering. Somebody's gotta keep the bird feeders filled, you know."

"That's true." Suzanne was glad he had a reason to keep living. So many of the elderly patients who came to Mennonite Manor Hospital and Recovery Home had no motivation to get better. Attitude played a significant role in recuperation, and she suspected Ed Birney would be back in his little home feeding the birds very soon given his plucky attitude.

Apparently reassured, Mr. Birney closed his eyes. Suzanne remained beside his bed for a few more minutes, watching the rise and fall of his chest, then sent up a quick prayer for his full recovery before stepping into the quiet hallway.

In less than half an hour, the day-shift workers would begin to arrive and the hospital corridors would buzz with activity, but night shift was quieter, peaceful. She'd worked the graveyard shift for so many years now, she had no trouble catching her sleep during the daytime hours and couldn't imagine any other schedule.

She rounded the corner to the nurses' station, the rubber soles of her white lace-up shoes squeaking on the freshly waxed tile. A familiar head of short black waves showed over the edge of the tall counter, and Suzanne gave a little skip to speed her steps. "Linda! You're back!" As she stepped behind the counter, the hospital's longtime bookkeeper rose and held her arms open. Suzanne wrapped her friend's bulky form in a hug.

" 'Course I am." Linda banged her thick palm against Suzanne's shoulder several times before pulling loose. "Counted down the days 'til my vacation was finally over and I could head on back here. Whole time I was gone I worried the place would fall apart without me, but look at this — the walls're still standing and nobody seems the worse for wear." She balled her fists on her hips and pasted a fierce scowl on her face. "But these files are a mess and nobody bothered to refill the candy dish. How'm I s'posed to get anything done if I haven't got any black cats to chew on?"

Suzanne laughed. "You and your licorice cats. I'll stop by Sarah's Sweet Treats on my way home this morning and pick up a bag for you." Surely Linda's purchases of licorice cats had kept the little candy shop open over the years.

"And that's why you're my favorite." Linda released a deep, throaty chuckle. She dropped back into the wheeled chair and began organizing the manila files scattered across the long desk.

Suzanne leaned against the edge of the counter and watched Linda work. "Did you enjoy your vacation? I bet the Caribbean islands were beautiful." Every year, Linda and her husband visited an exotic location for her retreat from work. On more than one occasion they'd invited Suzanne to join them, but the cost was always beyond her means. Even so, she wouldn't trade the years of raising her daughter for a hundred Caribbean cruises.

"Beautiful and *hot.*" Linda fanned herself with both palms, pretending to pant. "I told Tom next year we're going to Alaska. Polar bears instead of palm trees. Wanna come?"

A vacation with Linda and her teddy bear of a husband would be pure delight. She loved both of them — they'd become her surrogate parents over the years. But she

19

shook her head in gentle refusal.

Linda snorted and returned to her file sorting. "Girl, you've got enough vacation time saved up to take off for six months."

"Seven," Suzanne corrected with a smile.

Linda rolled her eyes. "But do you go anywhere? Huh-uh. Work, mothering, church, work, mothering, church . . . That's your whole life." She gave Suzanne's elbow a light smack. "You need to do something fun. Live a little. The Bible says, 'All work and no play makes Jack a dull boy.' "

Suzanne burst out laughing. "The Bible says that?"

"So maybe the good Lord Almighty didn't say it, but it's good advice all the same." Linda's round black face pursed into a worried frown. "You know I'm proud of you, Suzanne. Heavenly days, you beat all the odds, having that baby when you were hardly more than a baby yourself and then getting your nurse training without a family to support you. You raised Alexa right, and you made something of yourself. When I volunteer down at the crisis pregnancy center, I hold you up as an example of what those scared girls can be if they put their minds to it."

Suzanne lowered her head, both pleased and embarrassed. With God's help and the loving support of friends like Linda, she'd managed to carve a decent life for Alexa and herself. Even so, the stigma of once having been an unwed teenage mother still lingered. A part of her resisted accepting Linda's praise.

Linda went on in her husky voice. "But that girl of yours is old enough to fend for herself now. Why not take some time off? Do something for yourself for a change?" She leaned close, her dark eyes fervent. "You've earned it, Suzanne."

The mutter of voices and patter of footsteps signaled the arrival of day-shift workers. Suzanne bent forward and deposited a kiss on Linda's plump cheek. "I'll think about it," she said, then turned to greet the incoming nurse.

She updated the day nurse on medications prescribed to patients during the night, listened to one worker's complaint about the hospital's failure to change to computers in lieu of the old record-and-file system, and reminded her — as she'd done dozens of times before — of the small, mission-minded organization's limited budget, completed and initialed her reports, and then finally headed to the bank of lockers for her coat and purse.

As she pushed her arms into her trench

coat, Linda's suggestion to take some time off whispered through her mind. She'd promised to think about it, but thinking was all she'd do. She wouldn't take time away from the hospital. Here she was needed. Respected. And busy, leaving her no time to reflect on the past or how things might have been.

She slipped her purse strap over her shoulder and stepped out into the cool dawn. Beneath a rose-colored sky, she crossed the street to the small, graveled parking lot used by hospital employees and planned her morning. Breakfast with Alexa, a quick jaunt to Sarah's Sweet Treats for a half pound — well, maybe a pound — of licorice cats, then pajamas and bed.

She slammed the door on her late-model sedan, sealing away Linda's suggestion. Her friend meant well, bless her loving heart, but Suzanne was satisfied with her life of work, mothering, and church. God had gifted her beyond all deserving. She had no desire for anything more.

The alarm clock's buzz roused Suzanne from a sound sleep. She slapped it silent, then rolled over and stretched like a lazy cat. After tossing back the covers and slipping her feet to the floor in one smooth movement, she sat on the edge of the mattress for a few seconds and allowed herself to awaken by increments. Yawned. Rubbed her eyes. Yawned again.

Finally awake, she padded to the window and rolled up the blinds. Late-afternoon sunlight poured into the room, making her blink, but she welcomed the splash of brightness. During the winter months she often awakened to a black sky, making her feel as though the sun never shone. But now spring had arrived with its longer days and warmer evenings. Before long she and Alexa would be able to sit on their tiny balcony in the evenings, sip tea, and chat while watching the sun set over Franklin. One of their favorite activities. They'd always been content with little pleasures.

The clatter of silverware found its way past her closed door. Alexa was setting the table, so apparently supper would be ready soon. Knowing how her daughter disliked letting a meal grow cold, Suzanne quickly showered then dressed in a work uniform — flowered scrub top over a long straight skirt, anklets, and her comfortable oxfords. She brushed out her damp hair, braided it into a single plait, and then twisted it into a bun on the back of her head. After running a soapy cloth over her face and brushing her teeth, she made her bed and then headed to the kitchen.

Alexa looked up from chopping a red pepper into thin slices and smiled. "You're just in time to turn the chicken breasts on the grill."

Suzanne raised her eyebrows. "You started the grill? Kind of early, isn't it?" They'd only turned the calendar to April three days ago.

Alexa shrugged, sending her long ponytail over her shoulder. The silky tresses, as richly brown as a mink's fur, fell straight and sheeny down her slender back. "The sun warmed up the balcony, and I couldn't resist having our first cookout." She bobbed her chin toward the sliding doors at the far end of their small combination sitting and dining room. "Better go turn 'em before they scorch."

Suzanne grabbed the two-pronged fork from the end of the counter and stepped onto the balcony. The aroma that rose when she lifted the grill's cover made her stomach roll over in eagerness. She poked the thickest chicken breast with the fork, and clear juices ran out to sizzle on the hot grid. She stuck her head inside and announced, "They're done."

Alexa bustled over with a plate, and Suzanne transferred the chicken from the grill, then turned off the burner and closed the gauge on the propane tank. She entered the apartment just as Alexa carried the bowl of salad to the round table tucked in their tiny dining alcove.

"I hope you don't mind just having chicken and a salad." Alexa lifted a pitcher of tea from the middle of the table and poured it over ice cubes in two jelly jar glasses. "A light supper will leave room for what comes later." She waggled her eyebrows teasingly.

Suzanne slipped into her chair, smiling. She'd gotten spoiled over the past years since Alexa had taken on the responsibility of cooking. Her daughter was especially adept at creating delectable desserts. Fortunately all of her hallway walking at the hospital worked off the extra calories. "What did you concoct this time?"

"A triple-layer torte with both chocolate and strawberry fillings."

Suzanne nearly groaned. "Oh, that sounds rich. Where did you find the recipe?"

Alexa offered another glib shrug and plopped into her chair. Suzanne would never cease to be amazed at how Alexa could move so quickly and still appear graceful. "I sort of made it up. If it turns out, you can take the leftovers to work and share."

Suzanne had no doubt she'd be sharing with her coworkers. She held her hand toward Alexa, and her daughter took hold. They bowed their heads in unison, and Suzanne offered a short prayer of thanks for the meal. Alexa used a pair of plastic tongs to serve the salad — a combination of colorful chopped vegetables, walnuts, and dried cranberries that was almost too pretty to eat.

Suzanne lifted her knife and fork and cut into the tender chicken breast. At the first bite, she murmured, "Mm . . . how did you season this?"

Alexa swallowed a bite and took a sip of tea before answering. "I brushed them with olive oil, then sprinkled on dried parsley, basil, a little seasoned salt, and some garlic pepper. I was afraid the garlic pepper might be overboard, but it doesn't taste bad at all."

"It tastes great." Suzanne stabbed up another bite.

"I used the same seasonings and olive oil for the salad dressing but added some fresh-squeezed orange juice and a little bit of sugar."

"Sweetheart, everything is wonderful, as always." Suzanne gave Alexa's wrist a squeeze, pride filling her. "You're going to make a wonderful homemaker for a lucky man one day."

A wistful expression crossed Alexa's youthful face. "Well, you keep praying for my husband-to-be, Mom, and I'll keep my eyes open. So far he's stayed pretty well hidden."

Suzanne forced a light chuckle, but inwardly she cringed. If she'd raised Alexa in the Old Order sect, she'd probably already be published to marry. At nineteen, she was considered old enough to be a wife and mother. Although Suzanne prayed daily for a loving, God-honoring husband and faith-filled home for her daughter, she didn't mind waiting another year or two for Alexa to find the man God had planned for her. She liked having her close. As Alexa had grown older, she'd become more than a daughter — she'd become Suzanne's best friend. Would they be as close if —

She chased away her inner reflections by asking about Alexa's work. Alexa shared a few cute anecdotes about the children who came through the line at the elementary school where she helped prepare and serve lunch each day, then Suzanne told her about Mr. Birney and asked her to pray for his full recovery — as he'd said, someone needed to fill the bird feeders. Their supper hour passed quickly, and when they'd finished, Alexa carried their empty plates to the sink, then removed the torte from the refrigerator.

As Alexa sliced into the towering dessert, she said, "Oh, Mom, I almost forgot. You got a letter today. From Arborville."

"Really?" Letters were rare, usually arriving around Christmastime, the time of year when families were expected to contact one another.

"I put it on top of the daily newspaper." She shook her head, pursing her lips in a what-is-this-world-coming-to expression. "Read the article on page three about the abandoned baby a kitchen worker found in the Dumpster behind a restaurant. I can't believe someone would just leave a newborn in the trash that way . . ."

Suzanne experienced an inner jolt of reaction to Alexa's dismayed comment, but she didn't respond. She knew all too well how children were tossed aside by unfeeling or desperate parents. As she crossed to the far side of the room and picked up the long envelope, she offered a prayer for God to provide a loving home for the little foundling. Every child deserved to be loved and nurtured by caring parents.

Then she turned her attention to the envelope, and her hands trembled. The return address said Cletus Zimmerman in scrawling penmanship. Clete had never written before. Letters always came from Mother.

"Cletus is your brother, right?" Alexa slid a sliver of cake onto a dessert plate and licked a smudge of icing from her thumb.

Suzanne nodded woodenly.

Alexa snickered. "He should be a doctor with handwriting like that. What does he say?"

"I don't know. I haven't opened it yet."

"Well, don't just hold it. Open it, goofy." Alexa's teasing grin did little to calm Suzanne's rattled nerves.

Suzanne managed a weak smile. She peeled back the flap and removed two sheets of yellow notepad paper. Clete's messy scrawl covered the front and back sides of both pages. Mother's letters, which were meant to encompass a year's worth of news, never filled more than one sheet of paper. Comparatively speaking, Clete had written a book.

Alexa touched Suzanne's arm. She jumped in surprise, unaware Alexa had left the kitchen. A soft smile curved her daughter's lips. "Mom, sit down and read your letter. I'll put the cake back in the fridge, and we'll have it when you're done, okay?"

Suzanne cupped Alexa's smooth cheek in a silent thank-you. Then she sank onto the couch cushion, flicked on the table lamp, and angled Clete's letter toward the light. She read slowly, frowning at times as she struggled to make sense of her brother's sloppy handwriting, but eventually she reached the end. By the time she'd finished, her desire to sample Alexa's triple-layer torte had fled. She wouldn't be able to swallow a bite.

CHAPTER 2

Suzanne

"You mean to tell me nobody bothered to let you know your mama had been hurt bad enough to put her in a wheelchair?"

Suzanne held a Styrofoam cup of black coffee between her palms and nodded in understanding at Linda's incredulous blast, yet at the same time she felt the need to defend her family. "I suppose I shouldn't be surprised. After all, I didn't go home when my father died." She hadn't been able to. If she'd missed her boards, she wouldn't have received her nursing license. Alexa's and her future had rested upon her taking those exams. She sighed. "My siblings probably thought I wouldn't care."

"That's a bunch of hooey." Linda's voice rose above the chatter of three young aides taking their break at a table on the other side of the small cafeteria. Her dark eyes flashed. "You're one of the most compas-

31

sionate people I know. It's what makes you such a good nurse." She leaned in close, the spicy smell of licorice wafting to Suzanne's nose. "What are you going to do, girlie?"

In the three days since the letter from Clete had arrived, Suzanne had thought of little else, yet she had no answer. How could she go? Mother had been so adamant no one ever discover she'd become pregnant out of wedlock. She'd stayed away to protect her secret — to protect the family from finger-pointing and criticism. If she returned now, especially with Alexa in tow, it would open the door to questions and speculation.

She swallowed a lump of agony. "I don't know."

"You been praying about it?"

"Of course I have."

"And the Lord hasn't spoke to you one way or the other yet?"

Suzanne shook her head. Why did her prayers concerning her family seem to go no farther than the ceiling?

"Well, I sure won't be the one to tell you what to do —"

Suzanne tamped down a moan. She'd stayed late this morning and poured her heart out to Linda in the hopes the older woman, so practical yet so wise, could direct her.

"— but I will say you should do nothing until you hear from the Lord."

"And what if He remains silent?"

Linda reached across the table and took Suzanne's hand. Such a simple touch, but the warmth of her palm offered soothing comfort. Sometimes Suzanne wished Linda was her mother instead of her mentor and friend. She blinked back tears as Linda spoke tenderly. "Honey, sometimes God speaks best through silence. We just have to be close enough in tune to read His Spirit. Keep your heart open. You'll know what you're supposed to do when the time comes."

Linda withdrew her hand, and Suzanne lifted her cup to take a sip of the now-cool strong brew. She made a face and set the cup aside. "Will you pray for me?"

"Tom and I pray for you every day anyway, but we'll pray especially for God to direct your thoughts." Linda picked at the doughnut on the paper plate in front of her. "Did your brother tell you when they wanted you to come?"

"He didn't mention a specific date." Suzanne cringed, recalling Clete's strong wording. *"We need your expertise. None of us can do what needs doing for Mother."* "But the tone of the letter hinted at desperation.

33

I think he hoped I'd come right away."

"Well, at least you know you've got the time if need be. All that saved-up vacation — it could come in handy." Linda spoke in a musing tone, seemingly unaware of the turmoil her statement stirred within Suzanne's breast. Were all the years of stockpiling vacation days meant to give her the time to care for her mother? If only she knew for sure. "And since it's a family situation, the board of directors would probably give you a leave of absence if you asked. You've been a faithful employee for almost fifteen years. That counts for a lot."

Frustration built and spilled over. "So can't you see my dilemma, Linda? I have the time. I have the training. They really seem to need me. But I can't find peace about packing a bag and returning to Arborville."

To Suzanne's further aggravation, Linda had the audacity to laugh. "Well, honey, why would you? You've been away from there for more than half your life! And your leave-taking wasn't exactly under happy circumstances. Of course you've got apprehensions about going back."

Suzanne cringed. Linda only knew the half of it. And she couldn't bring herself to share the other half. After burying her secret for

34

twenty years, she wasn't sure she'd ever be able to bring it to the surface.

Linda checked her watch. "*Tsk*. Look at the time. I better get to my desk, and you should go home and put yourself to bed. Those circles under your eyes are darker than midnight."

Despite her flustered emotions, Suzanne released a soft laugh. Linda's wry forthrightness always managed to boost her spirits.

Linda pushed herself from her chair and shot a pointed look in Suzanne's direction. "Walk with me." They dropped their breakfast items in a trash receptacle and then ambled through the hallway. Linda threw her arm across Suzanne's shoulders. "What does Alexa think of all this?"

"I haven't told her."

"What?" Linda came to a halt, forcing Suzanne to stop, too. Her surprised expression changed to a disapproving glower. "Why ever not?"

"I told her my mother had been injured." Alexa had clapped her hand to her mouth in horror when Suzanne shared how the three-hundred-pound bale of hay rolled from the transport trailer and pinned Mother to the ground. They both agreed God's hands had sent the rains to soften the ground, giving the slight cushion that

35

prevented her from being crushed to death. Even so, her shattered bones and damaged nerves left her a paraplegic. "But I didn't mention Clete wanting me to take care of her."

"Suzanne, you've got to tell her." Linda shook her head, emitting a little huff. "Alexa isn't a child anymore. She's a young woman, and whatever you decide to do will affect her. Go home and talk to your daughter. Give her a chance to pray for you and with you. Give her a chance to offer you some moral support. After all these years of you doing everything for her, let her do a little something for you. It'll build her character." Taking Suzanne by the shoulders, she turned her in the direction of the lockers. "Go home, Suzanne Zimmerman."

Her head low, Suzanne began moving toward the exit.

Linda called after her, "And when you've finished talking to Alexa, get some sleep. Those raccoon eyes are liable to scare the patients."

Alexa

Alexa inserted her key in the apartment door and let herself in. Humming, she dropped her jacket over the arm of a dining table chair and leaned against the counter to flip through the few envelopes she'd found in their mailbox. Two bills, an invitation to change their television service to a different company — silly, since they didn't even have a television — and a coupon for a Mexican restaurant. Mom couldn't eat Mexican because the spicy food gave her indigestion, so Alexa threw away both the coupon and the TV-service advertisement, then placed the bills in the little basket on the corner of the counter where Mom would be sure to see them when she got up.

She headed for her bedroom to change her spaghetti sauce–stained T-shirt — somehow she'd gotten splashed above the bib of her apron — but before she took three steps, a quiet voice stopped her.

"Alexa?"

Spinning toward the sound, she let out a gasp of surprise. The end-table lamp snapped on, bringing her mother's form into plain view. Alexa pressed her palm to her chest and forced a laugh. "Mom, for heaven's sake, you nearly scared me out of my skin. Why aren't you in bed?"

Mom yawned. "I wanted to be where I'd hear you when you came in. Can you sit down for a minute?" She patted the sofa cushion beside her. "I need to talk to you about something important."

"Sure." After three days of near silence, Alexa welcomed the opportunity to talk. She seated herself sideways, tucking one foot beneath her, then placed her hand over her mother's knee and tipped her head. "Is it bad? You've been awfully quiet the past few days. You've worried me."

A frown pinched Mom's face. "I'm sorry. I've been deep in thought, but I didn't intend to worry you."

Alexa shrugged, eager to put Mom at ease. "It's okay. Maybe a little worry on my end is fair considering all the worrying you've done about me, huh?"

To her surprise, tears winked in Mom's eyes. "You've never given me a reason to worry about you, Alexa. Yes, I've worried about not doing right by you, but you have been a delight from the first moment I held you in my arms. I'm so proud of the young woman you've become. Anyone would be blessed to have you for a daughter."

Fear attacked, making her break out in a cold sweat. She gripped Mom's knee hard. "Are you dying?"

Mom's eyebrows shot upward. "Dying?"

"Are you sick? Is that why you've been quiet? Have you been trying to find a way to tell me? Well, I'm listening now — you can tell me. Please tell me." Her lungs seemed incapable of pulling in a full draft of air, so she heaved in panicked little puffs.

"Alexa, honey, calm yourself." Mom peeled Alexa's hand from her knee and held it between her palms. "I'm not sick."

"You're not?"

"No."

Alexa slumped forward. "Oh, thank goodness. When you said . . ." She forced herself to draw a big breath and let it out slowly. Her imagination had run away with her again. But this time she'd had help. Why had Mom given that glowing little speech if she wasn't sick or dying? "Then what is it?"

"Remember the letter that came from your uncle?"

Alexa sat quietly as Mom explained Uncle Clete's request for Mom to come to Arborville and assume nursing duties for their wheelchair-bound mother. While she listened, her heart began a rapid *thump-thump-thump* of excitement, and she found it hard to stay in her seat. Mom was going to Arborville? Then Alexa would finally have the opportunity to meet her grandmother, her uncle, her aunts, and the rest of the family Mom had left behind.

Alexa blurted, "When are you going?"

Mom's mouth dropped open. "You want me to go?"

Alexa threw her hands wide. "Why not?"

"I'd have to take a leave of absence from the hospital, give my church responsibilities to someone else, be apart from our friends, leave you here alone . . ."

Alexa drew back. "What do you mean, leave me here?"

"Your home is here. Your job is here. Everyone you know is here." Mom bit her lower lip, her brow crinkling in either confusion or consternation — Alexa couldn't be sure which. "You wouldn't want to go there, would you?"

All the longings Alexa had carried from little girlhood welled up. She caught Mom's hands and squeezed, trying to impress upon her how deeply she wanted this chance to know her family. Her father — Mom's best-kept secret — and his family would probably never be known to her. But now she could meet Mom's family and finally feel as if she belonged. "My job is just a job, biding my time until I can decide what I really want to do. This apartment is only home because you're in it. Sure it'd be hard to be away from our friends at church and from Linda and Tom — I love them. But they aren't family."

How could she make Mom understand without hurting her? "I'm curious about

40

your family. *My* family. I always have been. But when I asked you questions about them, I could tell it made you mad. Or sad."

Mom lowered her head. "I'm sorry, honey."

Alexa blew out a frustrated breath. "And now I'm making you sad again. Mom, please listen to me, okay?" She waited until her mother looked up and met her gaze. She spoke gently. "From the time I was a little girl, I've taken the . . . the snippets of information you've shared about your Old Order upbringing and painted these elaborate images in my head. Pictures of the farm, the people, the small, close-knit community." The imagined scenes paraded through her mind again, making a grin tug at her cheek. She wanted to find out what it was like to be a part of it.

"I love you, Mom. You're fantastic, and you've always given me security and love" — she pressed her hands to her aching chest — "but here, in the center of my soul, there's this empty spot only a complete family can fill." Her throat tightened and tears threatened. She didn't want to crush her mother, but she had to know. So she gathered her courage and dared to ask the question she'd held inside for far too long. "How did you do it? How did you leave them? You are so important to me. I could never walk away from you and not come back — not even for days, let alone for years."

Mom looked away, and the muscles in her jaw clenched. "You don't know everything that happened, Alexa."

Alexa's heart hurt for her mom. Obviously the pain, although decades in the past, was still very much a part of her. "Of course I don't. I wasn't there. But I do know this . . ." She tipped sideways a bit, trying to make eye contact with her mother. "You gave me life. You're my *mom*. No matter what, if you needed me, I'd be there." Minutes passed in silence while Alexa held her mother's limp hands and waited for her to speak.

Mom remained quiet so long she began to wonder if she'd fallen asleep sitting up. Then a soft chuckle left Mom's lips. She turned toward Alexa. Tears slid down her cheeks, leaving their tracks behind. A wry smile lifted the corners of her lips. "Linda was right."

"Linda's always right. About what this time?"

"You're growing up."

For some strange reason, the comment made her want to cry. She sniffed hard.

"And I guess, when I can get the arrangements made, we'll go to Arborville."

Alexa threw her arms around Mom and let out a cry of exultation. "It'll be great, Mom, you'll see." She could hardly wait to see her words proved true.

Chapter 3

Suzanne

Suzanne inched up the narrow aisle of the JetBlue aircraft, her carry-on bag bumping the backs of her knees as she went. From behind her, Alexa released a happy sigh.

"Wow, Mom, it almost feels like a dream, doesn't it?"

A dream? More like a nightmare. The past three weeks had been fraught with stress. She'd never imagined how many phone calls, written requests, and face-to-face meetings would be necessary to take a two-month leave from her life in Indiana. But she couldn't stomp on Alexa's happiness. Always much more bubbly than her reserved mother, Alexa had exhibited more enthusiasm about going to Kansas than anything else, ever. She flashed a quavery smile over her shoulder, which Alexa returned a hundredfold.

Suzanne passed the uniformed flight attendants who stood at the doorway thanking the passengers for utilizing their airline. Although she acknowledged their comments with only a slight nod, Alexa replied cheerfully.

"You're welcome. Thank you for a great flight — my very first."

The attendants laughed, and the taller of the pair said, "We hope it won't be your last."

"Me, too."

In the tunnel leading to the terminal, Alexa eased to Suzanne's side. Her shoulder bag swung wildly on its long strap, bumping Suzanne's hip. "Do you suppose there'll be a welcome committee waiting for us? After all, you haven't been home in . . . well, forever." Alexa's tinkling laughter spilled out. "Wouldn't that be amazing? Your whole family out there waiting, holding up a big sign and balloons or flowers or something."

Suzanne moved sideways to avoid another whack from Alexa's overstuffed purse. She should have taken advantage of their lengthy flight time and shared the entire truth with Alexa. Her stomach churned. If — and it was a mighty big "if" — her entire family waited, at least one of her long-held secrets would be revealed quickly and she could stop worrying about her family's reaction to

Alexa's presence.

She fixed a serious look on her daughter, one she'd perfected over the years in an attempt to squelch her abundant exuberance. "Don't get your hopes up, Alexa. We're arriving on a weekday afternoon. People have jobs and responsibilities. It's very unlikely any of my family is here. They've probably sent a driver to retrieve us."

"Oh." For a moment, Alexa's bright countenance dimmed. But then in typical form, she gave a cavalier shrug and grinned. "No matter. Once we reach Arborville, there'll be a reunion. I'm sure of it."

They rounded the final bend leading to the reception area, and Suzanne caught Alexa's arm, guiding her away from the stream of others making their way to baggage claim. She looked into her daughter's expectant face and feared her heart might break. Why hadn't she told Alexa the truth years ago when she began asking about the big family living on a farm in Kansas? Her mother's harsh command rang in her memory, stinging her anew. *I don't care what you want, young lady. You will give up that baby to your cousins, and no one besides you and me will ever know what you did!* Suzanne hadn't wanted to inflict pain on her precious girl, so she'd sidestepped Alexa's questions rather than divulge the events surrounding her leave-taking.

She'd always admired Alexa's cheerful outlook and active imagination, seeing them as gifts even if she sometimes wished her daughter would ground herself more in reality. For years she'd carried a boatload of regrets, but the biggest one at that moment was that she had not been completely honest with the most important person in her life. The truth would shatter Alexa.

She gently squeezed Alexa's elbow. "Honey, listen to me. I know how excited you are — how long you've wanted to meet your grandmother and uncle and aunts — but I don't think you fully understand how the Mennonites live."

A sheepish grin climbed her cheek. "Actually, Mom, I know more than you know I know. I kind of researched Old Order Mennonites when I was in junior high." She shrugged. "Curiosity . . ."

Suzanne cringed. "Well, you still don't know how my family lives. Please don't be hurt if there isn't —"

Alexa's gaze moved beyond Suzanne's shoulder. She jerked loose of Suzanne's light grasp and pointed. "Mom, look. That man over there has a sign with *Zimmerman* on it. Let's go!" Without a moment's pause,

Alexa looped her arm through Suzanne's elbow and headed for the waiting man.

He wore the Sunday garb of Suzanne's sect — white shirt buttoned to the collar and tucked into black trousers. A suit coat with no lapels hung open, revealing a sliver of navy-blue suspenders. The man appeared to search the crowd, but as Alexa and Suzanne approached, he pinned his focus fully on Suzanne. His gaze traveled from her face down the line of her simple sweater and matching cardigan, long skirt, and bottom four inches of her low-heeled slouch boots and then up again. His brow furrowed, but he appeared more puzzled than disapproving.

He dropped the crude sign with its block-letter printed name into a nearby receptacle and took two steps toward them. "Suzy?"

Alexa arched her eyebrows, her lips quirking into a teasing grin. "Suzy?"

Suzanne gave her daughter a brief frown, then turned to the man. "I go by Suzanne now, but yes, I'm Suzanne Zimmerman."

The man's puzzlement faded in an instant. He released a self-conscious chuckle. "I'll try, but it'll be pretty hard for me not to call you Suzy."

Only then did she notice the pale scar running from the outer corner of his left eye to his hairline, the result of a childhood encounter with the sharp barb on a neighbor's wire fence. The entire fellowship had praised God for allowing the barb to miss his eye and leave his sight unaffected. A buzzing filled her head and her jaw slackened. "Clete?"

He nodded, his blue eyes sparkling. "That's right. Welcome home, Sis."

And then Suzanne found herself wrapped in her brother's embrace. When she'd left, he'd been a gangly eleven-year-old, the top of his head barely reaching her chin. Now his chin pressed against her temple, and his firm hold spoke of a man's strength.

His deep voice — unfamiliar yet somehow known — filtered past the ringing in her ears. "It's been a long time. Too long." Did a hint of recrimination color his tone?

Suzanne extracted herself and peered into her brother's face. "I'm here now."

Perhaps he recognized the challenge she'd injected in her simple reply, because he gave a nod and his expression softened. "Yes, you are."

Alexa, who'd stood silently by and shifted from foot to foot during the brief exchange, now bolted forward. "Hello." Her greeting whooshed out breathlessly. She took his hand and shook it, her smile growing broader with every pump. "It's so good to finally meet you."

Clete nodded, his gaze zipping back and forth between Suzanne and Alexa. "Yes. Yes, of course it is. Um . . ." He withdrew his hand and scratched behind his ear, his confused glance landing on Suzanne. "Who is this?"

Befuddlement pursed Alexa's face. "Who else would I be? I'm —"

Suzanne slipped her arm around Alexa's waist. "This is my daughter, Alexa."

Alexa

Surprise widened her uncle's eyes, but as quickly as his startled expression formed, it disappeared, leaving Alexa wondering if she'd seen it at all. He reached for her, and she allowed him to tug her against his broad chest.

For years she'd anticipated this moment — being welcomed into a large circle of family instead of being the only child of a single mother. But now that her uncle's arms held her in what she could only define as an uncomfortable embrace, all the wonderful images of reunion she'd conjured faded. She pushed lightly against his chest, and his arms dropped.

He ducked his head briefly, as if collecting

himself, and then he aimed a wobbly smile at Mom. "We'd better get your luggage."

Alexa darted ahead, needing to gather her thoughts. She searched for a positive aspect to the situation. In moments her ready imagination served up a plausible scenario. Mom hadn't told her family she'd be bringing her daughter along. After all, they'd asked her to come to nurse Grandmother. They probably assumed Alexa had responsibilities keeping her in Indiana. So her arrival caught them by surprise. That would explain Uncle Clete's confusion.

She glanced over her shoulder, noting the firm line of her uncle's mouth. Mom appeared equally grim. Although he and Mom hadn't seen each other in two decades, they walked side by side in a tense silence. Shouldn't they be speaking over the top of each other in their eagerness to catch up on their lives? Unease sent a tingle down her spine. Something was wrong.

Most of the passengers had already claimed their luggage, so only a few bags remained on the slow-moving conveyor belt. Alexa snagged Mom's black bag and her own green-with-orange-polka-dots one. To her dismay the brand-new upright cases, purchased especially for their trip to Kansas, bore oil stains and scuff marks. Their damaged appearance too closely emulated the marred expectations of meeting her family for the first time.

Uncle Clete stepped forward and reached for the bags. "I'll get those. I left my truck in short-term parking, so we won't have a long walk. This way." He spoke kindly yet impersonally, the way one might address a stranger.

His tone raised a prickle of resentment. She followed her uncle from the terminal into a cool early evening. The leftover scent of a recent rain filled her nostrils, and she breathed deeply, willing the fresh essence to chase away the unwelcome emotion.

Mom often berated her to act her age, and now Alexa gave herself the same admonition. To expect instant affection was childish and whimsical. She and her uncle were strangers. After twenty years apart, he and Mom probably felt like strangers, too. Alexa would allow a few days for everyone to settle in and get comfortable. They just needed a little time.

Beside her, Mom shivered, and Alexa automatically slipped her arm around Mom's waist. Mom shot her an appreciative smile, and Alexa answered it with a bold wink. Poor Mom . . . She looked exhausted. She'd worked all night, honoring her responsibility to the hospital right up to the last minute, then traveled all day. Her reticence was probably more a result of tiredness than anything else.

"Here we are." Uncle Clete unlocked the door on a gray pickup truck with a double cab. "Suzy . . . er, Suzanne, why don't you sit up front and Alexa can have the back." Without waiting to see if they followed his directions, he moved to the bed of the truck and heaved their suitcases over the edge.

Alexa cringed, imagining the additional bumps and scratches his rough treatment would certainly inflict on their luggage, but she held her tongue and climbed into the backseat of the cab. Bits of dried grass and dirt clumps littered the floor, and the distinct aroma of cattle clung to the uphol-stery. She sucked in one last draft of the rain-scented air before slamming the door closed behind her.

A child's booster seat sat in the middle of the bench, and Alexa pushed it to the far side to give herself more room. Uncle Clete settled himself behind the steering wheel, then sent an unsmiling glance into the back. "Oops. Want me to put that in the bed with the suitcases?"

"It's not bothering me," Alexa said, unex-pectedly warmed by his offer. She clicked her seat belt into place. "Who does it belong to?"

Uncle Clete answered as he backed out of the narrow parking space. "My daughter Jana."

"How old is she?" Alexa couldn't quite temper the eagerness in her voice. The yearly Christmas letter coming from Arborville had never told as much as she wanted to know about Mom's family — her family. She wanted to know everything.

"Four."

"And she's your youngest, right?"

He pulled a curled-edge photograph from beneath the sun visor and handed it over the seat. "Youngest of three. Jana's the one on the far left. Jay's in the middle — he's eight. And then Julie's five."

Alexa examined the images in the grainy photo. The trio of children stood at the edge of a wheat field. The little girls wore knee-length gingham dresses, obviously home-made, and the boy's shirt seemed to be sewn from the same blue-checked fabric. Bright sunshine turned their fair hair into halos. Mom craned her neck to peer over the seat, so Alexa gave her the picture as she told her uncle, "They're real cute. Your girls look so much alike and are so close in size, they could be twins."

He stopped at the gate to pay the parking fee. As the truck merged with other cars leaving the airport, he said, "We get asked that a lot. Especially since we have a set of twins in the family."

Alexa leaned as far forward as the seat belt would allow. She searched her memory for details from Grandmother's annual Christmas letters, but she came up empty. "I've forgotten — which of your sisters has twins?" She shouted to make herself heard. Now revving at close to sixty miles an hour, the truck's engine roared like an angry lioness.

"Shelley and her husband, Harper." Uncle Clete yelled, too, turning his face slightly to send his answer into the backseat. "Girls — six years old. Their names are Ruby and Pearl."

Now Alexa remembered. She'd thought the names pretty but old-fashioned. "Does Mom have any new nieces or nephews?" She tapped Mom's shoulder with her fingertips, hoping to encourage her to ask these questions so she wouldn't feel so nosy.

"Our youngest sister, Sandra, and her husband, Derek, have a little boy named Ian. You probably know about him — he turned three last week — but they're expecting another baby midsummer." Uncle Clete flicked a quick look at Mom. "Just wondering . . . Wasn't your husband able to come with you?"

Mom turned her face toward the side window. Alexa frowned. Mom's family didn't already know she wasn't married? Although puzzled, Alexa found no insult in the question. She'd adjusted to not having a father, and she'd hardly been the only girl in school being raised by a single mother. Mom had explained long ago how a foolish decision to break God's instruction to save sex for the marriage bed resulted in her becoming pregnant.

Watching Mom struggle to provide for her and be both mother and father had been a good lesson for Alexa. She wanted a family someday, but she wanted the support of a husband both physically and emotionally. She'd promised her mother she wouldn't make the same mistake, and she intended to keep the promise.

Mom still hadn't answered, so Alexa piped up. "It's just Mom and me."

Uncle Clete's eyebrows descended. "I see." He aimed his gaze forward, his jaw set so tightly the muscle in his cheek bulged.

Mom stared out the side window at a landscape that looked so much like Indiana's, Alexa had a hard time believing they weren't still in their home state. Silence fell, making the truck's engine seem to increase in volume. Alexa wriggled uncomfortably, wishing someone would say something.

Uncle Clete cleared his throat. "Alexa, how old are you?"

"Nineteen."

Mom suddenly seemed to come to life, sitting upright and turning to face Uncle Clete. Her face glowed bright red, but she spoke in a strong voice. "How long will I be needed?"

He rolled his clenched fists on the plastic steering wheel. He didn't look at Mom. "Why?"

"Because I'd like to know."

Alexa wanted to know, too.

Uncle Clete swallowed, his Adam's apple bobbing. "I'd thought . . . for good."

Mom shook her head as if she hadn't heard right. "I only arranged for a two-month leave."

He pulled in a deep breath and released it, his big frame sagging a bit as the air left his lungs. "Mother is never getting out of that wheelchair. The damage to her spine can't be fixed. None of the rest of us know how to help her. You're the nurse. Our missionary nurse." His tone took on a bitter edge, as if he'd tasted something unpleasant. "Shelley, Sandra, and me . . . we figured you'd be happy to use your training to serve your mother."

Mom said, "Have you moved her into town?"

Uncle Clete snorted. "She won't leave her house."

"Of course she won't."

Although she'd never seen it, Alexa held a picture in her head of Mom's childhood home. A rambling farmhouse two stories tall with decorative gable trims, an attic, too many bedrooms to count, a spindled porch in front, and a screened sun porch off the kitchen. She'd dreamed about living in a century-old house exactly like the one in which Mom grew up, and even though Mom sounded dismayed, Alexa couldn't resist a rush of elation at the thought of staying, even if only briefly, in the old house out away from town.

"For the past four months, Tanya, Shelley, and Sandra have taken turns caring for her," Uncle Clete went on. "But they have to bring the kids along, and Mother . . ." He slowed the truck and turned right onto a dirt road. He held the speed to a crawl, but even so, the truck bounced over ruts, making Alexa grateful for the seat belt holding her in place. She hoped the suitcases in the back wouldn't fly over the edge.

"Mother lost most of her patience a long time ago, and now that she's hurting all the time, she pretty much has none. It doesn't work to have the kids underfoot. That's why we thought . . . We didn't know about . . ." He snapped his mouth closed again.

Mom sighed. A resigned sigh. "She shouldn't be on the farm. I can't imagine her trying to get around in a wheelchair out there."

"We're fixing that." He eased the truck around a bend. Up ahead, the farmhouse Alexa had envisioned in dozens of childhood daydreams materialized. She leaned forward and stared at the house as Uncle Clete continued. "It's taken a while for him to clear his schedule enough to do everything we need done, but we hired a local contractor to put in ramps, widen the doorways, and rebuild the kitchen and bathroom to accommodate Mother's wheelchair. You might remember him — Paul Aldrich."

A gasp escaped Mom's lips, and Alexa turned her attention from the house's white clapboard siding to Mom's colorless face. A chill wound its way up Alexa's spine. "Mom, are you all right?"

CHAPTER 4

Suzanne

Paul Aldrich. At the mention of his name — a name Suzanne hadn't heard spoken aloud since she was a girl of seventeen — memories flooded her mind. They came in such a rush, none took individual form but became a hodgepodge of images and feelings that left her dizzy. She closed her eyes and pressed her palms to her chest, willing the tidal wave of disjointed remembrances to pass.

"Mom?"

Alexa's worried voice penetrated her muddled thoughts. With effort, Suzanne opened her eyes and forced a smile. She patted her daughter's hand, which rested on the seat back, hoping neither Alexa nor Clete noticed how badly she trembled. "I'm fine, honey. I think my lack of sleep is catching up with me."

Concern glimmered in Alexa's brown

eyes, the golden flecks becoming more prominent as Clete opened his door and the glow from the dome light fell across her face. "Well, then, as soon as we're inside you're going to bed. You look so pale. I hope you aren't getting sick."

Suzanne laughed lightly, amazed at how much the expression of amusement revived her. "Since when are you the nurse?"

Alexa didn't laugh in reply.

Clete said, "My wife, Tanya, and the kids are here — they're expecting us."

Suzanne glanced at the house. If they'd been expecting guests, why hadn't someone turned on the porch light? Why were the rooms behind the panes of glass dark and forbidding? She eased out of the truck cab but stood in the triangle of weak light cast by the dome light, hugging herself.

"I'll get the suitcases. Just go on in. The door's unlocked." Clete slammed his door shut, startling Suzanne into dropping her pose.

She closed her door more softly, then moved across the damp, cracked sidewalk to the porch. But once beneath the robin's egg–blue porch ceiling, she couldn't bring herself to open the screen door. Its slam on her final morning here still rang in her memory. Her mother had lectured the children to always close the door gently — slamming it would weaken the hinges — but on that morning Mother had allowed it to smack into its frame with force. Suzanne shivered.

She shifted her attention to the ginger-bread trim on the old porch door. The top right fan bracket was missing one delicate spindle, and the door's green paint was crackled like alligator skin. Although dusk had fallen, encasing the porch in somber gray, she observed other evidences of neglect — chipped and peeling paint on the house's clapboard siding, a shutter hanging loose, porch boards curling, and clumps of winter-brown overgrowth hugging the stone foundation. Obviously her mother's accident had rendered her incapable of maintaining the house in the past few months, but this dilapidation was years in the making. Why hadn't the fellowship or Clete kept up with repairs?

Clete and Alexa stepped onto the porch, each pulling a suitcase. Clete frowned. "Haven't you gone in yet?" He sounded impatient. "It's still your home, Suz . . . zanne, even if you've chosen not to visit."

She could have snapped back that the "choice" to leave hadn't been hers, but weariness weakened her bones. And her spirit. "I was waiting for you."

He heaved a sigh and reached for the screen door. The hinges creaked, seeming to beg for a squirt of oil. He wrenched the brass doorknob on the solid oak door and gave it a push. Holding the screen door open with his hip, he gestured for Suzanne and Alexa to enter. Alexa headed in first, curiosity igniting her face. Suzanne followed slowly. Her feet turned clumsy — partly from tiredness, partly from an overwhelming sense of déjà vu that left her light-headed.

Alexa had moved to the middle of the front room, but Suzanne stopped just inside the door, her gaze bouncing around in confusion. Same sofa and chair arranged in an L in the far corner. Same afghan draped over the sofa's back. Same upright piano lurking on the opposite wall and same hymnal resting in the music rack. Same oak rocking chair in front of the window with a basket of yarn and half-completed projects on one side and a white-painted iron floor lamp standing sentry on the other. The sickening feeling of stepping back in time increased. In twenty years, had nothing changed?

Clete tugged the lamp's pull string, and light flooded the room. Tears sprang to Suzanne's eyes. Yes, things had changed. Everything was faded. Dusty. Tired looking. The house and its contents hadn't changed, but it seemed the joy that once filled its rooms had departed, leaving nothing but a soulless shell behind.

The thunder of galloping feet carried from the enclosed staircase, and a pair of little girls with blond braids and big blue eyes careened into the room. "Dad! Dad!" they chorused, their high-pitched voices the first glimpse of joy Suzanne had seen since she met Clete in the airport. They dashed straight for him, forcing Alexa to move out of the way or be run down. He captured the pair in a hug and then planted a kiss on the top of each little head.

As he straightened, he turned the girls toward Suzanne. "Julie, Jana, this is your aunt Suzanne. Say hello."

The older girl, Julie, offered a shy smile. "Hello."

But the younger one, who wriggled beneath Clete's restraining hand on her shoulder, pointed at Alexa. "Who's that?"

Clete pushed his daughter's hand downward. "It isn't polite to point, Jana."

Jana craned her neck to peer into Clete's face. "But who is that?"

Alexa rested her palms on her knees,

bringing her face level with the children's. "I'm your cousin Alexa. It's very nice to meet you, Jana and Julie."

"You're pretty," Jana blurted, then she caught her sister's hand, and the pair raced out as quickly as they'd entered.

Clete shook his head, an indulgent grin creasing his cheek. "Needless to say, they keep us hopping."

Alexa gazed after the little girls. "They're adorable."

Suzanne recognized the wistfulness in her daughter's tone, and remorse for all Alexa had been denied having been raised far from a large circle of family smote her once again. She'd never regretted keeping Alexa. Alexa was her God-given blessing. But she wished she could have given her gregarious child the things she desired most — a father, siblings, cousins.

Clete cleared his throat. "Tanya and Mother are probably in the kitchen. Did you want to go on up to your room, or would you like to meet my wife?"

Although sleep sounded heavenly, Suzanne said, "I'd like to meet Tanya." But after she'd made the decision, she realized he'd said Mother would be there, too. Her feet refused to carry her forward.

A hint of compassion softened her brother's expression. "It'll be all right. Tanya's wanted to meet you for a long time." He'd misunderstood her reluctance, but she didn't bother to enlighten him. "I think she was even happier than Shelley and Sandra when we got your letter saying you'd come."

Suzanne wanted to ask why Shelley and Sandra hadn't come out to the farmhouse to greet her, but she held the question inside, fearful of the answer. Her sisters had been so young when she left — only nine and five, not much older than little Jana. They probably barely remembered her.

Clete headed toward the kitchen, and Suzanne looped arms with Alexa and followed. Memories rolled like an old movie reel as she moved past the dining room's long trestle table and ladder-back chairs, then through the dim passageway lined with floor-to-ceiling cupboards. If she opened the first bottom cupboard, would she find the old marble game she, Clete, and Mother used to play when the chores were done on Saturday evening?

A bare bulb hanging on twisted wires from the middle of the ceiling sent glaring light throughout the simple kitchen, and Suzanne blinked several times, her eyes protesting the onslaught. When she could focus again, her gaze settled on the slender form of a young woman standing at the kitchen sink with her back to them. She hummed as she sloshed a soapy cloth over dishes, the bow of her apron bobbing with her movements. A white mesh cap covered her hair, and black ribbons trailed across the shoulders of her blue print dress.

The pungent aroma of spicy goulash permeated the narrow room, competing with the yeasty scent rising from a bowl on the back of the stove. The familiar smells combined with the image of the woman at the sink sent Suzanne backward in time. For a moment, she almost believed it was Mother standing there, just as she had hundreds of times during Suzanne's childhood, and her heart swelled as longing to go back to those simpler times nearly buckled her knees.

Then Clete said, "Tanya?" And the woman turned.

Suzanne's imagining was whisked away in a heartbeat. This woman's face — round, smooth, unfamiliar — wasn't Mother's.

Tanya broke into a wide smile. "Oh, my, I didn't even hear you come in." She came straight at Suzanne with wet, sudsy hands extended. Just before Tanya reached her, she seemed to remember what she'd been doing. She stopped and laughingly lifted her apron's skirt to dry her hands. Then she grabbed Suzanne and clung hard.

"Even if I didn't know you were a Zimmerman, I'd know you were a Zimmerman." Tanya laughed again and pulled back to smile into Suzanne's face. "You look so much like Shelley and Sandra!"

Clete put his arm around his wife's shoulders. "Tanya, Suzanne brought her daughter with her. This is Alexa."

Although Tanya didn't embrace Alexa the way she had Suzanne, she offered a smile of welcome. "Alexa . . . what a surprise. Welcome to Arborville."

"Thank you." Alexa glanced around, seeming to take in the white-painted cupboards, the ruffled red-checked curtain at the single window, the 1960s-style refrigerator, and the lumbering six-burner gas stove. "This room is great. It's so retro." She turned eagerly to Suzanne. "But where is Grandmother?"

Clete looked to Tanya, who shrugged sheepishly. "She often turns in early. She went to bed shortly after supper, and she won't rouse until seven or so tomorrow morning. You'll have to wait until then to meet her."

Alexa's shoulders sagged in apparent regret, but Suzanne couldn't deny relief at postponing their reunion. In her mind's eye, she could still envision her mother's stern face as she'd put her on the bus to Indianapolis so many years ago. Her disapproval had been palpable that day, and Suzanne had no desire to relive those heartbreaking minutes.

Tanya said, "Are you hungry? I could reheat the goulash, or you could have some ham spread on crackers if you prefer something light."

Alexa steepled her hands beneath her chin in an expression of delight. "Goulash? Oh, yum. I haven't had goulash since I was a little girl. This couple Mom and I stayed with before I started school fixed goulash, and I loved it."

"Well, then, goulash it is." Tanya moved briskly to the cabinets and removed a small saucepan. As she headed toward the stove, she spoke to Clete. "Would you go up and tell the children to put away their toys and get into their pajamas? As soon as I've fed Suzy and —"

"Suzanne," Clete and Suzanne chorused.

Tanya flicked a quick puzzled frown at Clete, then went on in a cheery tone, ". . . Suzanne and Alexa some supper, I'll be up to tuck them in."

Alexa followed Tanya to the refrigerator.

"You can go up if you need to. I'll heat the goulash. Just point me to the microwave."

Tanya laughed lightly. "We don't have a microwave. But it won't take long to heat on the trusty gas stove."

Alexa sent a wide-eyed look at Suzanne, which she decided to ignore. She moved to the cabinets and opened the upper one to the right of the sink. A stack of chipped pottery bowls waited on the second shelf. When she was younger, she'd had to climb on a little wooden stepstool to reach them, and as she lifted down the stack, she automatically peeked through the opening leading to the half bath. Sure enough, the battered little stool huddled in the corner like a sleeping cat.

Clete paused in the kitchen doorway. "Wouldn't you rather I take the children home so they can sleep in their own beds tonight? Now that Suzanne is here . . ."

Suzanne's pulse revved into double-beats.

Tanya shook her head, the ribbons from her cap swaying. "Let's stay tonight — give your sister a chance to sleep in tomorrow morning after her day of travel." A soft smile graced her face. "I think a few days of getting reacquainted would be welcome before she assumes duties for your mother, don't you think?"

Clete offered a brusque nod, then turned on his heel and left the room. In his absence, an uncomfortable silence fell for a few seconds. Then Tanya retrieved a ladle from the drainer beside the sink and began transferring noodles and tomato sauce from the large kettle into the saucepan she'd placed on an iron burner.

"Not too much." Suzanne pressed one palm to her jumping stomach. "It's late, and it might not settle well."

"Just enough to hold you over until breakfast." Tanya lit the burner beneath the pan, covered the kettle again, and carried it to the refrigerator. As she turned from the fridge, her gaze landed squarely on Suzanne, and tears filled her eyes. "Oh, Suzanne . . ." She rushed at her, arms wide, and wrapped her in yet another firm embrace. She whispered, "I'm so glad you came home. We've needed you for . . . so long."

Suzanne put her arms loosely around her sister-in-law's frame. Her years of nursing bid her to offer comfort, but how? If Tanya needed stitches or medication or even a sponge bath, Suzanne could give it, but she had no idea how to respond to her obvious emotional distress. She met Alexa's gaze over Tanya's shaking shoulders, and she read the same confusion in her daughter's eyes that filled her own head. *What is wrong in this household?*

CHAPTER 5

Alexa

"Amen." Her nighttime prayers complete, Alexa rose from her knees and turned to sit on the edge of the twin-size bed crammed into the corner of one of the upstairs bedrooms. The iron frame let out a low groan, and she cringed. She didn't want to disturb Mom. Poor Mom . . . She'd fallen, exhausted, into the room's other little bed less than half an hour ago and had drifted off to sleep almost at once. Alexa envied her. She wanted to sleep, but her restless mind refused to shut down.

With a sigh, she tiptoed to the window and pushed aside the simple panel curtain. Moonlight bathed the landscape in a soft glow, shimmering on the tin roof of the barn and turning several small outbuildings into lumbering beasts. A shiver of anticipation wiggled its way down Alexa's limbs. Tomorrow she would explore each of those buildings. Tomorrow she'd walk in the yard where her mother had played as a child. She'd count the chickens in the pen and maybe even collect eggs the way Mom had. Such intense eagerness gripped her it brought the sting of tears. Finally she would know what it felt like to live on a farm. And finally, finally she would get to know her family.

Alexa lowered the curtain with a gentle swish against the windowsill. She stood in the scant light afforded by the glowing face of her alarm clock, which she'd placed on the dresser between the pair of beds, and gazed down at her sleeping mother. Years ago, on the pretense of writing a school report, she'd looked up information on a library computer about Old Order religious sects and learned the women wore dresses and head coverings. Until then, she'd not understood why Mom twisted her long, dark-blond hair in a bun and always wore long skirts instead of jeans or trousers even though the majority of the women from the church they attended wore pantsuits and cut their hair in short, trendy styles.

"You can take the girl out of Arborville, but you can't take Arborville out of the girl," Alexa whispered into the quiet room, smiling at her private joke. With her hair loose around her shoulders and her face relaxed in sleep, Mom looked so much younger than her thirty-seven years. An unexpected wave of tenderness swept over her, and she bent forward to give her mother's temple a light kiss. Mom snuffled and Alexa froze, holding her breath. Convinced she hadn't roused her mother, she released her breath in a whoosh and turned toward her bed, but she wasn't ready to lie down.

She lifted her favorite purple zebra-print bathrobe from the end of her bed and, as soundlessly as possible, moved to the door and inched it open. A shaft of light filtered into the room, and Alexa quickly stepped into the hallway and closed the door behind her, sealing Mom in the dark bedroom. Light from the stairwell illuminated the square landing and turned the crystal doorknobs into glittering diamonds. She turned a slow circle, counting the doors. Five in all. Behind one was a bathroom where she and Mom had brushed their teeth at the pedestal sink before dressing for bed. The others were probably bedrooms.

When she and Mom had come up an hour ago, Uncle Clete had taken them directly to the room across from the stair opening. He apologized for not being able to put them in Mom's old room, but he'd already put Julie and Jana to sleep in there since the little girls liked sharing the double bed. Mom and Alexa had assured him they'd prefer their own beds, even if they were only twin-size beds. But she wished she could have at least peeked into Mom's room and seen what it looked like. She shrugged. She could always explore tomorrow.

A mumble of voices carried from downstairs. Apparently Uncle Clete and Aunt Tanya were still up. Good. She'd visit with them — pepper them with questions — until she was too tired to stay awake any longer. She shoved her arms into the bathrobe, tied the belt, then made her way downstairs, taking care to move quietly so she wouldn't bother the sleeping children or Mom. When she was halfway down the stairwell, the voices lost their mumbling quality and Alexa made out their words.

"— don't know how Mother will take it." Uncle Clete sounded distressed. Alexa paused, uncertain as to whether she should continue down or return to her room.

"Give her a chance to explain before you jump to conclusions, Clete." Aunt Tanya's reply came, her voice low and soothing. Alexa envisioned the pair on the sofa together, probably holding hands, the way couples in the romance novels she checked out from the library sat for serious talks. "It's possible she's adopted. After all, they look nothing alike."

"That's true. But if so, why not just come right out and say so?"

"Well, think about it. Do your cousins Andrew and Olivia call Anna-Grace and little Sunny their adopted daughters, or do they call them their daughters? They've raised the girls, which makes them theirs in every sense of the word, so of course they don't qualify their relationship with them." Tanya spoke so reasonably Alexa found herself nodding in agreement even though she wasn't part of the conversation.

A heavy sigh carried around the corner, followed by Uncle Clete's defeated voice. "I understand what you're saying, but I've seen the letters she sent to Mother over the years. She never mentions having a daughter. Why not tell us?"

Alexa jolted. They were talking about her.

Uncle Clete's voice turned anguished. "I can't help worrying she's an out-of-wedlock child. What will the fellowship say?"

Although she was well aware of her illegitimacy, Mom had always assured her she needn't feel ashamed — she hadn't sinned by being born, and her birth hadn't taken

God by surprise. She'd been raised to believe she had a purpose in the world and that she was loved unconditionally by both God and her mother. Thanks to Mom's gentle teaching and the acceptance of her church family, Alexa had never experienced even a tiny smidgen of disgrace over her fatherless state. But in that moment shame smacked down on her with such force it bent her forward. And something else became very clear.

Mom was embarrassed about her. She must be. She'd kept Alexa's existence a secret from her family. The realization hacked away at the foundation of Alexa's security. She didn't want to hear anything else, but her legs felt rubbery and weak. If she tried to move, she'd surely collapse. So she remained in the stairwell, holding to the wooden rail with both hands and silently praying for the strength to return to her bed.

Tanya's voice drifted to Alexa's ears. "Whether she is or not, we can't send them away. Your mother requires constant care, and Shelley, Sandra, and I can't keep coming out here. We have other responsibilities that are being neglected. It isn't fair to our children. We can't hire another nurse — it's too costly on top of what it will take to make this farmhouse wheelchair friendly. And she'd probably just run the nurse off anyway." A hint of desperation entered Tanya's tone. "We don't have any other choice. She needs Suzanne. *We* need Suzanne."

"I know. I wouldn't have contacted her if there'd been any other option. But how will we hold up our heads if —"

"Shh, Clete, the shame isn't ours to carry."

A long pause, and then Uncle Clete spoke in a grating voice. "*I just wish she'd come alone.*"

At last Alexa found the courage to move. On trembling legs she climbed the staircase, placing her feet so carefully not even a mouse would have been startled by her progress. She entered the room, slid into her bed, and pulled the covers to her chin. Dry-eyed and aching, she stared into the dark room.

"*I just wish she'd come alone.*" Her uncle's words and anguished tone tormented her. She pressed her fist to her quivering lips, hurt beyond description. Uncle Clete had wondered how he would hold up his head if his sister had given birth to an illegitimate child. Now how could Alexa possibly face him?

The family she'd wanted for as far back as she could remember didn't want her.

■ ■ ■ ■

Suzanne

Suzanne awoke with a jolt in a dark, too-quiet room on a badly sagging mattress. Her pulse raced as confusion smote her. Where was she? Then, remembering, she dropped back against the lumpy pillow. She stared into the room until her eyes adjusted enough to make out the line of the electrical cord reaching from the plug-in at the base of the overhead light bulb to the dresser where it met Alexa's alarm clock. A faint yellow glow outlined the black plastic box, but Alexa had turned the face toward her so Suzanne couldn't see the digital numbers. But she didn't need to see the time to know it was very early.

The house was completely quiet. No traffic noise filtered through the windows. No neighbors' voices rumbled through the walls. No trash-can lids clanked or dogs barked or sirens blared — all sounds that had become familiar during her years of living in the city. When she'd first moved to Franklin, it had taken her weeks to learn to sleep through big-city noises. Now their absence held her awake.

Her back ached, too. She shifted onto her

side, cringing at the intruding twang of bedsprings. The new position eased the fierce ache in her lower spine but a twinge in her hip kept her from fully relaxing. Her body, confused by the change in her sleeping routine, felt tense and restless. Should she get up? It might be nice to have some time alone downstairs to reacquaint herself with her surroundings before everyone else awakened.

She made herself lie still for several long minutes, hoping she might drift back to sleep, but when her hip began throbbing in protest at the uncomfortable mattress, she decided to give in and go downstairs. She draped her bathrobe over her arm, ducked beneath the electrical cord, and crept out to the landing. When she was young, Mother had always left a small lamp burning on a table in the landing. But no guiding light directed her now. With no windows allowing in a touch of moonlight, the landing was black as pitch. So black Suzanne suffered a momentary attack of dizziness.

Pressing her palm to the wall, she felt her way to the staircase, then inched her way down, counting the risers as she went. She remembered counting them the night she'd sneaked out to meet Paul Aldrich. Fourteen in all. Fourteen chances to turn around and go back to her room. Fourteen steps to a night that changed her life forever.

She stepped from the staircase into the front room where the lace panels shrouding the windows let in faint, murky light. She paused to tug on her bathrobe, then moved past Mother's rocking chair to the sofa. She sat at one end and pulled up her knees. The room held a chill, and she considered draping the afghan over herself, but it felt wrong to use it without asking permission. So she tucked her bare feet under the flap of her robe instead.

The old pendulum clock hanging above the piano softly and rhythmically ticktocked, a comforting sound. Like a heartbeat. At least something seemed alive in the deathly quiet house. She squinted at the round yellowed face and scrolled hands. Five fifteen. Or thereabouts. The old clock, although faithful to count the minutes when someone remembered to wind it, had never kept true time. Dad had always moved the minute hand a few positions when he rewound it. Forward or backward? Suzanne couldn't remember. The clock hung high on the wall. Mother couldn't reach it there. Who wound it for her?

One question released a parade of others. Did her siblings really expect her to stay here forever, caring for Mother? How much help did she require? Why did the house look so forlorn and weary? If Suzanne stayed beyond her planned leave of absence, how would she cover expenses when her vacation pay ran out? Would Alexa choose to stay here with her, or would she go back to Indiana alone?

Curled there in the corner of the sofa, her cheek against the tufted velvet scattered all over with earth tone–colored daisies — when Mother and Dad bought the set, she'd laughed at the strange color for daisies — she sent the questions to the One who never slept.

God, I wouldn't have come if it hadn't been for Alexa. When she said she would always be there for me, the way You've always been there for me, I felt as though You were talking through her, encouraging me to reach out to my mother. But now that I'm here, I'm not sure I should be. Her dry throat began to ache, the desire to give vent to tears tightening her chest. *How do we ignore the years of separation and the hurts that have been left to fester? How can I be here without them discovering the truth?*

The secrets she'd carried for so many years bore down on her. She pressed her forehead to her raised knees. *God, forgive me, but I can't tell them everything. I can't ever let Alexa know what I stole from her. I know it's wrong to ask this of You, but . . . oh, please, Lord . . . let me keep my secrets while I'm here. The truth will only hurt them and Alexa. And me. I'll stay two months. Long enough to determine the extent of Mother's needs and locate a nurse who can provide care. And then I'll go back to Franklin and leave my family in peace.*

Overhead, floorboards creaked. A door clicked open and closed, then water spattered against the side of the porcelain tub. Tanya? Probably. The others would be up soon, too. The day was beginning. In the next hour, she and Mother would be face to face. Mother and Alexa would be face to face. Her stomach rolled with apprehension and she pressed tighter into her huddling pose. *Dear Lord, help . . .*

CHAPTER 6

Suzanne

Breakfast turned into a chaotic affair, and Suzanne wished she'd stayed upstairs. Little Jana bumped Jay's glass of milk with her elbow, dumping it into Julie's lap. Julie set up a howl that surely was heard all the way into town. Jana, out of pity for her soggy sister, added her wails to the mix. Tanya took Julie upstairs to wash away the stickiness and change her clothes, and while they were gone, Jay ate the last piece of toast, which Julie had wanted. Consequently another storm erupted. By the time Clete left with all three children in tow — to drop Jay and Julie at school and then take Jana to Shelley's for the day — Suzanne's head ached from the tumult. How had her mother slept through such a clamor?

As soon as the door closed behind them, Tanya turned to Suzanne with an embarrassed grimace. "Aren't you glad you won't be taking care of *them*?"

If she were to answer honestly, she would hurt Tanya's feelings. "They're young, away from their own home and routine. They're bound to be a little rambunctious."

Tanya's smile thanked her for her understanding. She grabbed the dishrag from the corner of the sink. "I'll get this table cleaned up so Alexa won't have to sit in our crumbs when she eats breakfast. Do you think she'll be down soon?"

Suzanne had awakened Alexa when she went up to dress, and she'd expected her to come straight down. Maybe their day of travel on top of her weeks of being almost too excited to sleep had caught up with her. "I'm not sure. But don't worry about fixing her anything. She's quite self-sufficient in a kitchen."

Tanya paused in scrubbing up the milk rings left from the children's cups. "She's a very pretty girl, Suzanne, and so polite. You must be proud of her."

Suzanne crossed to the stove and poured herself a cup of coffee. She chose her words carefully. "I am. Alexa is the best thing that ever happened to me. I can't imagine my life without her."

"I feel the same way about our three. Even though they wear me out sometimes!" Tanya rinsed the rag and hung it over the sink's edge. She leaned against the counter and fixed Suzanne with a pensive look. "I noticed both you and Alexa wear skirts, but neither of you have head coverings."

Subconsciously Suzanne touched her heavy braided bun with trembling fingertips.

"I hope I'm not being intrusive, but I wondered . . . Have you left the Mennonite faith?"

"Alexa and I attend a Mennonite Brethren church in Pleasant View, a small town near Franklin, where we live. The hospital where I work is supported by the MB church." She deliberately used the present tense when referring to church, work, and home.

"I've heard of the denomination, but I'm not familiar with the Mennonite Brethren. Are they similar to Old Order in their beliefs?"

Suzanne sought the best explanation. "The church is very scripturally based, but they don't follow specific dictates concerning attire or forbid using worldly conveniences. Those things are left to the individual conscience." She glanced down at her lightweight hunter-green sweater and khaki skirt and offered a short laugh. "Although I've been away from Arborville for more years than not, I feel more comfortable in a skirt, and Alexa has chosen to respect my preference."

"May I ask . . . How did you come to join their church?"

If Suzanne were to give Tanya a complete answer, it would take hours. And open the door to far more questions than she wanted to field. "We stayed with an MB couple in Indianapolis while I attended nursing school. Had it not been for their help with Alexa, I wouldn't have been able to earn my license as an RN. I'm very grateful to them."

"I'm glad you had people to help you. It must have been hard when Alexa was small."

Memories rose to torment her. Of those baby days when Alexa cried and Suzanne cried, too, frightened she'd taken on more than she could comfortably bear. Of the happy times when Alexa learned to roll over or sit up or took her first toddling steps. And even though the Martens celebrated with her, she'd longed to share the milestones with her mother. The mingled joy and pain had tied knots in her heart. *Hard* didn't begin to cover it, and Suzanne had no desire to revisit those days. "As you said, children can wear you out sometimes. But they're always worth the effort."

Tanya gazed at Suzanne for a few seconds, her lips pursing in indecision, then she turned toward the dirty dishes stacked beside the sink. "I'll get these washed and put away. Mother Zimmerman will be getting up before too long, and I —"

"Tanya!"

"Oh, that's her now." Tanya lifted her apron to wipe her hands. She flung an inquisitive look at Suzanne as she headed for the passageway to the dining room. "Do you want to come in and let your mother know you're here, or would you rather wait until she's dressed?"

Suzanne swallowed a hysterical giggle as she envisioned her modest mother's chagrin at being caught in her nightclothes by someone who was now a stranger. "Go ahead and get her dressed first. She'd probably rather not become reacquainted while she's wearing her nightgown."

"Tanya!"

Tanya darted out of the kitchen. How long would it take her to help Mother into her clothes — five minutes? Ten? Unable to simply stand still and wait, Suzanne busied herself by running a sinkful of water. She washed, dried, and put the items back in the cupboards. Just as she finished placing the silverware in their drawer, she heard

Tanya speaking.

"All right now, Mother Zimmerman, close your eyes. No peeking! Do you promise? I have a surprise waiting for you."

Suzanne turned from the silverware drawer in time to see a wheelchair bearing a gray-haired, haggard-looking woman roll through the passageway. If Tanya hadn't been pushing it, she wouldn't have known the wheelchair held her mother. She drew back in shock. How had her mother aged so rapidly? She appeared closer to eighty than her true age of almost sixty. Her startled gaze bounced to Tanya, and her sister-in-law frowned, shaking her head in silent warning. Suzanne closed her eyes briefly, silently praying for strength, then met Tanya's gaze once again. She mouthed, *I'm ready.*

Tanya curled her hands over Mother's shoulders. "Okay, open your eyes!"

Abigail Zimmerman's eyes opened slowly, as if her eyelids were too heavy to lift. Her watery gaze traveled across the kitchen to Suzanne, who stood rooted next to the open silverware drawer. Her heavy brows descended in obvious bewilderment.

Hardly aware of what she was doing, Suzanne slid the drawer closed and then approached the chair. She held her breath as she walked slowly, deliberately, the stiff fabric of her skirt chafing the bare expanse of her shins above her anklets. As she moved toward her mother she felt the years dropping away, and suddenly she was seventeen again, afraid and uncertain and so in need of assurance. Her breath wheezed out on a prayer. *Dear God, help me . . .*

Her mother's eyes never shifted from her face the entire distance, and when she reached the chair she dropped to her knees and took one of Mother's blue-veined hands between both of hers. "Mother?" Her voice cracked. She swallowed and tried again. "It's me, Mother — Suzanne."

Mother's frown deepened. She pulled her hand free of Suzanne's light grasp. "Of course you're Suzanne. Did you think I wouldn't recognize my own daughter?"

Suzanne zipped a glance at Tanya, who stared at the back of Mother's head with wide, appalled eyes. She licked her lips and looked at Mother again. "Well, I —"

Mother angled her head, peering up at Tanya. "Did you bring her here?"

Tanya put her hand on Mother's shoulder and spoke soothingly. "Clete and the girls asked her to come."

"Why?"

"Because she's a nurse, Mother Zimmerman. And you . . ." Tanya pinned Suzanne with a pleading look.

Suzanne touched her mother's knee. The sharp contour of the bone startled her, and her tongue turned clumsy. "C-Clete said you needed a nurse's care." She certainly needed something. This gaunt, ancient frame couldn't possibly belong on her independent, stalwart mother. "That's why I came. To take care of you."

Her mother huffed out a heavy breath. "I have three people already taking care of me. Why do I need yet another?" She aimed her glare at Suzanne — the same glare she'd worn when Suzanne confessed she'd missed her monthly period. "I thought you had a nursing job in Indiana. Did they fire you?"

"No, I asked for time off. So I could . . ." Suzanne hung her head. Why bother to explain? Her mother hadn't wanted her twenty years ago, and she didn't want her now. She pushed to her feet. She'd performed her duty. She'd come at her brother's request. She'd tried, but it was pointless. The hurts were too deep to heal, the chasm too wide to bridge. She gave Tanya a pointed look. "Maybe it would be best if I returned to Franklin immediately."

Tanya shook her head, dismay playing on her face. "No. Please, Suzanne. I'm sure she just needs time to —"

"Don't talk about me like I'm not in the room!" Mother snapped out the command so harshly, both Tanya and Suzanne drew back. She glowered at Tanya. "I won't take Suzanne away from the mission hospital. She loves her work. In every letter, she told me she loves her work. She's already given up enough for —" She clamped her jaw closed and hunched low. Although Suzanne and Tanya waited in silence for her to continue, she kept her lips set in a firm line.

Tanya sighed. Her sad gaze met Suzanne's. "I suppose we —"

"Mom?" Alexa entered the kitchen. She'd brushed her sleek hair into its familiar ponytail. The simple hairstyle along with her straight denim skirt and white blouse gave her a mature appearance. But in Suzanne's eyes she was a little girl again — a helpless child in need of protection. She couldn't subject Alexa to her mother's venomous rejection.

She hurried to Alexa's side and turned her toward the entryway. "Go upstairs, honey," she whispered. "I'll be there in a minute."

Her mother caught the wheels of the chair and spun it to face Suzanne and Alexa. With a strength that shocked Suzanne, she rolled herself directly into their pathway. She stared at Alexa. "You . . . Did you call my Suzy 'Mom'?"

"Yes, ma'am, I did." She tipped her head inquisitively, her ponytail swishing across her shoulder. "Are you my grandmother?"

Mother's mouth dropped open. Her face turned ashen. Then, before Suzanne had a chance to react, her eyes rolled back in her head and she slid from the chair onto the floor in a dead faint.

CHAPTER 7

Paul

Paul opened the screen door to the enclosed porch at the back of the Zimmerman farmhouse. The door scraped along the floor, following the path it had carved in the tongue-and-groove boards. He shook his head. Stubborn woman. Why wouldn't Mrs. Zimmerman allow someone to repair the things that needed fixing? A readjustment of the hinges and the door wouldn't drag along the floor anymore. This fine old house would fall to ruin in another few years at the rate it was going.

He stepped around the wringer washing machine, which had drifted to the center of the sagging porch, and lifted his hand to rap his knuckles on the kitchen door. Scuffling noises along with the high-pitched chatter of a worried voice escaped from the other side. Instead of knocking, he called, "Hello in the house! Is everything all right?"

The pound of approaching footsteps gave a reply, and then the door swung wide. Clete's wife gestured him inside, gasping, "Oh, Paul, thank goodness you're here. Mother Zimmerman passed out!"

Paul jogged to the opposite side of the kitchen, where two women knelt on either side of Mrs. Zimmerman's inert frame. "Move aside. I'll pick her up for you."

"Don't touch her." The woman on the far side kept her head low, seemingly examining Mrs. Zimmerman's colorless face. "Given her previous back injury, it isn't wise to move her. When she awakens, I'll do an assessment, and then I'll decide whether to lift her myself or summon EMTs."

Her voice — low, sure, authoritative — held a smidgen of familiarity. Paul frowned, trying to place it. Then she raised her head, and although she didn't even glance at him, her blue eyes raised a wave of remembrance so strong he nearly staggered.

She spoke to the young woman kneeling close to Paul's feet. "Get a cool rag, Alexa. No, two. We'll place them on her wrists."

Paul shifted backward to give the woman — actually he realized she was a girl now that he got a good look at her smooth, youthful face — room to move. Tanya followed on the girl's heels, and Paul turned

96

his attention back to Suzy Zimmerman. So the rumors he'd heard buzzing through town were true. She had returned, and apparently she had been serving as a nurse over the past years. Although she seemed unaware of his presence, he couldn't stop staring at her. Tanya whimpered and wrung her hands, nearly hysterical, yet Suzy maintained a calm demeanor. Admiration filled him. Whatever she'd been doing since she left Arborville, she'd changed. He saw no evidence of the bashful girl he remembered.

Alexa scurried over with dripping cloths in her hands. "Here, Mom."

Mom? Paul examined the pair who worked together to rouse Mrs. Zimmerman. Suzy's coil of dark-blond braids with its few escaping wavy wisps contrasted sharply with Alexa's smooth brown ponytail. Both were slender, although it appeared Alexa might be an inch or so taller than Suzy — her legs, hidden modestly beneath a straight skirt made of blue jeans material, seemed longer as she knelt next to Mrs. Zimmerman and held a cool cloth over the woman's limp wrist. In their profiles, he saw little resemblance between them. Maybe he'd misunderstood.

Alexa jolted. "I think she's rousing. Should I hold her down?"

Suzy responded promptly. "Yes. Gentle pressure on her shoulder, honey. Not too hard, but with enough force to keep her from trying to sit up. We don't want to take any chances."

"Okay, Mom."

So he'd heard correctly. Alexa was Suzy's daughter. He supposed he should be more concerned about Mrs. Zimmerman, but he couldn't help observing Alexa instead. How old was she? Fifteen? Sixteen? It was hard to judge. He searched his memory for references to Suzy's marriage and motherhood, but he found none.

Mrs. Zimmerman moaned softly, twisting her head from side to side. Her mesh cap had come loose and sat askew on her gray hair. She lifted her hand toward her head, but Tanya caught it, and drew it back down.

"Please lie still, Mother," Tanya said.

Suzy leaned in, her lips close to Mrs. Zimmerman's ear. "Mother, can you hear me?"

A soft *yes* eased from the woman's lips. Tears trailed down Tanya's cheeks, but both Suzy and her daughter remained dry eyed. However, concern etched a line across Suzy's brow. She wasn't as detached as she tried to appear.

One hand held her mother's shoulder, and

the other seemed to pinch her wrist. "Mother, I need you to listen carefully. Do not try to move. Not yet. I know you aren't comfortable, but we need to give you some time to fully awaken and tell us if anything hurts. All right?"

Mrs. Zimmerman's eyelids lifted to half-mast. "Wh-what happened?"

"You fainted."

Mrs. Zimmerman frowned. "Nonsense." Her voice, although still quavery, gained in volume. "I'd never be undignified enough to faint."

To Paul's surprise, Suzy chuckled. "Every woman is entitled to one dramatic swoon in her lifetime. There's no reason to be embarrassed." She patted her mother's shoulder. "Now, since you seem to be awake enough to talk, let's see if we can determine if your dramatic swoon caused damage to anything more than your pride."

Suzy asked a series of questions, presenting both a professional and warm front. He watched her face as she appeared to mentally compile the information and form a conclusion. At last she released an airy sigh and offered Tanya a smile. "I believe it's safe to lift her now. Alexa will help me. Please set the brake on the wheelchair so it doesn't slide out from underneath her."

Tanya hurried to follow Suzy's instructions, and once again Paul scooted out of the way. He'd come in expecting to be the rescuer. Instead, he became the observer, watching Suzy and her daughter expertly bring Mrs. Zimmerman from the floor to her chair in one smooth motion. Suzy settled her mother's feet on the footrests, adjusted her skirt, and then placed her hands on her knees. "There you are. Better now?"

Mrs. Zimmerman's lips pinched into a scowl. "I'll be better when everyone stops fussing over me."

"Of course you will." A hint of bitterness seemed to creep into Suzy's expression, but it disappeared when she turned to Tanya. "She needs to be hydrated. Is there a water glass in her bathroom?"

Tanya nodded.

"Good. I'll make use of it."

"I want coffee," Mrs. Zimmerman said loudly.

Suzy acted as though she hadn't heard. "Also, I think it's best if she rests this morning. She likely pulled muscles in her fall, and some aches and pains will emerge. Until we've identified all of those spots, her bed is the best place to be. So . . ." She moved behind the wheelchair and released the brakes. "I'll take her in and get her settled. Alexa, you can help me. Tanya, just a light breakfast for Mother, please — some toast or oatmeal? If you need me, you'll know where to find me. Come along, Alexa." And without so much as a glance in Paul's direction, she wheeled her mother out of the room. Her daughter followed like an obedient puppy.

Paul stared after them, both amused and aggravated. Had he become invisible? He'd never been so thoroughly ignored. The teen-age boy he used to be reared his head, and he fought the urge to teasingly taunt, "Hey, Suzy Zimmerman, why're you being so stuck-up?"

Tanya darted across his pathway on her way to the cupboard, pulling his attention away from Suzy. "Oh, my heart and soul, what a fright Mother Zimmerman just gave me! I wish Clete had been here when his mother fell out of the chair."

Paul had known Tanya, the younger sister of one of his good friends, her entire life. Once she started talking, it was pointless to try to stop her. So he stood silently and let her yak.

She poured water into a small pan and set it on a burner. "I'm glad Suzanne knew what to do, but I think we made a mistake in bringing her here without talking to Mother Zimmerman first." She removed a canister of rolled oats from a cupboard and popped the lid. "After all, the shock of seeing Suzanne caused her to lose her senses. She's never done anything like that before today."

Tanya dumped a cupful of oats into the water and followed it with several heaping spoons of brown sugar and a dash of cinnamon. She swirled a wooden spoon through the mixture, but then her hand froze midstir. "Or was it seeing Alexa that made her faint?"

He started to ask what Alexa had done to cause such a reaction, but Tanya set the spoon to work again and continued talking. "Either way, the shock was too much for her. We should have warned her about Suzanne's return. But I suppose it's too late to change that now. We'll just have to make the best of it."

Suddenly she huffed out a breath and slapped the spoon onto a little ceramic plate. She turned a penitent look in his direction. "Mercy sakes, Paul, here I am jabbering like a magpie and I didn't even bother to ask what you wanted."

I want to talk to Suzy. But of course he couldn't make such a bold declaration. The last thing he needed was to get the rumor mill grinding about him and the girl he'd hoped to marry when he was a boy of eighteen. "I came to see Clete so we can finalize plans on the renovations around here."

Tanya turned back to the pan of oatmeal. "He took the kids to town and planned to stop by the hardware store before coming back out. He should be here soon, though, if you can wait. Would you like some coffee? There's still plenty in the percolator."

He'd already had two cups at the diner when he took his son for breakfast before school, but Paul eased himself into one of the kitchen chairs. "That sounds good if it's not too much trouble."

"Not at all." She poured a mug and placed it in front of him, smiling. "Especially for the one who's going to fix this house for Mother Zimmerman. Maybe when it's easier for her to get around and to reach things, she'll be less grumpy." She removed the pan from the stove and carried it to the counter, where she emptied the contents into a bowl. "We're all very patient with her, knowing how hard it is for someone who has been so independent to have to lean on others to meet her most basic needs. But I confess, there are days . . ." She stared into space for a moment, seemingly lost in thought.

Paul cleared his throat. "Should you take that oatmeal in before it gets cold?"

Tanya gave a little start, then grimaced. "Yes, I should. And if I know Mother Zimmerman, she'll find some reason to keep me in there for a while. So please help yourself to another cup of coffee if you want it. It shouldn't be too long before Clete returns." She folded a spoon inside a napkin, then departed, the scent of cinnamon wafting in her wake.

Paul sipped, listening to the mumble of voices and waiting for Tanya to return. But, as she'd forewarned, she stayed in the bedroom. He was swallowing the last bit of his coffee when the kitchen door opened and Clete came in.

With a huge grin, he sauntered straight to Paul. "Hey. I saw your truck and thought I'd find you in here working. But instead you're taking a break."

Sometimes Paul wondered how Clete and Tanya had gotten together. Tanya was as high strung as Clete was laid back. Maybe it was true that opposites balanced each other. He and Karina had been so like-minded she could finish his sentences for him, but he and Suzy —

He shook his head. He shouldn't be thinking about Suzy. He forced a laugh. "I was just waiting for the foreman to come tell me what to do."

Clete plucked a thick mug from a pegged rack on the wall and poured himself a cup of coffee. "You're the builder, not me. Where do you want to start?"

"I'd say outside, except the ground's so mushy right now from our rains that I need to put off building the concrete ramps." Paul placed his cup in the sink, then ran his hand along the clean countertop, imagining the work involved in carving the cabinets down a good six inches to accommodate Mrs. Zimmerman's reach. "The biggest jobs will take place inside. And they'll make the most mess and commotion. So I need to be sure your mother and . . ." How long would Suzy be here? She'd acted as though she was taking charge, but Tanya's comments made him wonder if they'd ask her to leave. "And everyone else who comes and goes out here is ready for it."

Clete drained his cup and set it on the table. "We're ready for it. We've waited long enough. Even if it's messy and noisy, it's got to be done. So feel free to get started wherever you think is best. We trust you, Paul."

Somehow it stung to be trusted. If Clete knew what Paul had done twenty years ago, would he still be his friend? He headed for the door. "All right then. Cabinetry in the kitchen first and then the bathroom cabinet and roll-in shower. I'll take a break from interior work to build the ramps as soon as the ground is dry enough to pour concrete. All-in-all, plan on me being around for eight weeks — maybe closer to seven if I work on Saturdays."

"Do you want to work on Saturdays?"

Paul shrugged. "I'm open to it, but I'd have to bring my son with me." Without meaning to, he flicked a glance toward the room where Mrs. Zimmerman now held her daughter, daughter-in-law, and grand-daughter captive. "Would Danny be . . . an intrusion?"

Clete laughed lightly. "Do you mean will Mother run him off?"

Paul's face heated at Clete's candor.

"Danny's a good kid. He'll be here with you, and Mother will stay far away from the mess. It's fine if you want to bring him along."

"I'm glad to hear that since summer vacation will likely start before I'm done out here. As big as he is, he isn't keen on being stuck with a babysitter. You might be seeing quite a bit of Danny."

"No problem."

Paul started for the door to collect his toolbox, but then he paused, curiosity overcoming good sense. "Hey, Clete, I found out this morning that Suzy's here."

A crooked smile — a nervous smile? — quirked Clete's lips. "Yeah. Shelley, Sandra, and me asked her to come help take care of Mother. She's got that nursing training, you know."

He knew. He'd seen it in action. He took hold of the doorknob, needing something to keep him steady. "Is she home for good, or . . ."

Clete rubbed his chin with his knuckles. "I'm not sure. I want her to stay. It's too much for Tanya, Shelley, and Sandra since they've got kids to raise. But it'll be up to her, I guess. She took a two-month leave of absence from work. So she'll be here at least that long."

Two months. For as long as he'd be out here working. Given their history, being together every day might prove awkward. He clamped his jaw tight and headed for his truck with the too-familiar ball of shame and regret rolling through him. He'd wronged Suzy. Badly. In the worst way. She'd trusted him, and he led her down a pathway of ruin. It didn't matter that he'd only been eighteen and so deeply in love he lost all will to resist temptation. It didn't matter that she'd carved a good life for herself elsewhere — the entire town lauded the Zimmermans for having a missionary nurse in their family. It didn't matter that he'd gone on to fall in love with Karina Kornelson and followed the sect's and God's courting mandates to the letter. All that mattered was he'd wronged Suzy. And out of fear or shame or desperation she'd left her home and family. For good. How did a man forget perpetrating such pain on another soul?

As Paul reached into the bed of his truck for his tools, awareness struck. For years he'd prayed for the chance to seek Suzy's forgiveness. Now she was back. God had given him his opportunity to absolve himself of this weight of guilt. He felt lighter already.

Thanks, Lord. It'll be good to set things right.

Abigail

Abigail lay reclined against a pile of pillows and pretended to doze, but she watched her daughter through barely slitted eyelids. Suzy was the epitome of efficiency. Tucking sheets just so, even while Abigail weighted the mattress, fluffing pillows, arranging pill bottles in a neat row on the dresser top, pausing every fifteen minutes like clockwork to gently pinch Abigail's wrist, count, and record whatever she deemed worthy of recording on a little pad of paper. Suzy might not have been honest about everything in her yearly letters — most notably her failure to mention Alexa — but she'd been honest when it came to her vocation. She wore her title as nurse as blatantly as if someone had painted the title on her forehead.

How many times had Abigail imagined her daughter performing duties as a nurse? More times than she'd bragged about Suzy's ministry, and she'd bragged plenty. She'd comforted herself with the knowledge Suzy was faring well despite being tossed out by her mother. Such pleasure — the only pleasure she'd allowed herself — she'd found in envisioning scenes just like the one being played out in her bedroom.

But of course, she'd never imagined Suzy nursing *her.*

Abigail gritted her teeth and stifled a moan. What had possessed her children to bring Suzy here? Clete should know better. He must have taken leave of his senses. Suzy belonged in Indiana. In the hospital where she cared for people who deserved her tender ministrations. Having her daughter under her roof again brought back all the pain, the regrets, the self-recrimination and stirred them to a boiling point.

If she had two sturdy legs, she'd take Suzy by the arm and march her out the door. Then she'd tell Clete she didn't need him farming her land — she'd do it herself. She'd chase everyone away and live out her last days alone, as was fitting given the harm she'd inflicted.

Lying there, silent and tense, she railed against the accident that had left her an invalid. She couldn't get her legs and her independence back, but she could do one thing. She could send Suzy back to Indiana. Of course, the girl wouldn't just go. She was too dedicated to serving those in need and, if she was anything like the Zimmermans who'd come before her, too stubborn to give up.

But there were ways to get people out from underfoot. Abigail had scared off more than a few with deliberate ungraciousness. She'd have to do the same to Suzy. A deep ache settled itself in her heart as she considered more long years without her oldest child in her life. But she'd been selfish twenty years ago, thinking of what was best for herself instead of Suzy. Keeping Suzy here now would be even more selfish.

Abigail would make her go. It might shatter what remained of her withered heart, but she'd do it. As quickly as she could. It was the only way to appease her conscience.

CHAPTER 8

Alexa

Her patience was slipping away. When would Mom leave Grandmother's room? Aunt Tanya had gone out half an hour ago, declaring her plans to wash sheets and towels and then run some errands in town. From the sound of things, she was banging the sheets with rocks to get them clean — there'd been a steady succession of thuds and bumps coming from the kitchen ever since she stepped out of the room. But even though Grandmother claimed she was fine and wanted everyone to stop mollycoddling her, Mom refused to budge from the edge of the mattress. Was she using Grandmother's fainting episode as an excuse to avoid conversation with her daughter?

Alexa had deliberately waited until Uncle Clete and the children drove away before coming downstairs. She'd intended to take Mom aside, tell her what she'd overheard, and then ask why she'd never told her family she had a daughter. It had taken her all night to gather up enough courage to approach Mom, but then Grandmother had fainted, and the chance slipped away. But as soon as she got Mom alone again, she'd ask. And she wouldn't accept anything less than the truth.

She sat on a chair in the corner of the bedroom and watched her mother tend to her grandmother. Mom was so patient. Kind. Gentle. All of the things the Bible said people should be, that was Mom. Alexa had grown up admiring her mother, wanting to emulate her. And she'd always accepted Mom's various excuses about not visiting Arborville. It was too expensive to travel so far, it would take too much time away from work, her family was so busy on the farm they wouldn't have time for a visit . . . Always an excuse. A plausible excuse. Not even when the excuses frustrated her did she suspect her mother of being dishonest. But now?

I just wish she'd come alone. Her uncle's words taunted her. As did remembering how Mom initially intended to leave Alexa behind. Because Mom hadn't wanted her family to know she had a daughter. Because she was ashamed to have borne an out-of-wedlock child. What other reason could there be for keeping her a secret from them? *Oh, please, let there be some other reason, God. I don't want to be Mom's shame . . .*

Pressure built in her chest, a painful weight of sorrow and confusion. Unable to sit still a moment longer, she bolted from the chair and crossed to the bed. "Mom?"

"Not now, sweetheart."

Alexa considered defying her mother. She'd only done it once before — when she was twelve and boldly applied makeup one of the other girls from school brought in her purse. Mom hadn't gotten angry. First she'd warned Alexa about being sneaky. Sneaky people couldn't be trusted, she'd said. Then, using verses from the second chapter of First Timothy about a woman's proper adornment, she'd explained why she chose to leave her face clean of makeup. And finally she had suggested Alexa would be wise to concern herself with making her insides beautiful and reflective of God rather than painting her outsides with worldly ideas of beauty. Mom's kind response had extinguished the flame of Alexa's rebellion.

She bit down on her lower lip. Being forceful now, being impatient and selfish, wouldn't reflect God. But how much longer did she have to wait? Grandmother's eyes — blue like Mom's but a paler shade — bored into Alexa's face as if she could see the storm brewing within Alexa's heart. Uncomfortable beneath the woman's scrutiny, Alexa started to turn away.

"I want some coffee."

Grandmother's brusque statement seemed to be sent to Alexa. She paused, looking uncertainly at Mom. Then Grandmother spoke again.

"I've sipped enough water. I want coffee."

Mom pinched her lips together for a moment, then nodded. "All right. I suppose you've had enough water that a cup of coffee won't hurt you. Alexa, would you go pour your grandmother a cup?"

"I want fresh coffee. By now the morning's pot will be stale."

Back in their apartment they had an automatic brewer as well as a French press, and Alexa knew how to use both. But she'd gotten a look at the old-fashioned percolator on the stove. "Um, I'll go ask Aunt Tanya to make another pot."

"Tanya's busy. Suzanne can do it. Surely she remembers how to operate a percolator." Was Grandmother challenging Mom? She added, "And while you're out there, find out what all that banging is. It sounds

115

like someone's tearing the house apart."

Mom rose. "All right, Mother. I'll see to it. But you lie still." She rounded the bed and touched Alexa's hand. She lowered her voice. "Don't let her get excited. I'll be back soon."

"No need to rush, Suzanne." A sly smile climbed Grandmother's cheek. "I'll be in good hands with my granddaughter."

Mom froze for a moment, her lips forming a grim line, but then she nodded. "You're right. Alexa is very capable." She gave Alexa a look that seemed to communicate caution, then she hurried out of the room.

The moment she departed, Grandmother patted the mattress beside her hip. "Sit down here, Alexa. Let's get acquainted."

If she'd been given the invitation two days ago, she would have leaped at the opportunity to become acquainted. But after hearing Uncle Clete's comment and witnessing her grandmother's surly treatment of Mom, she hesitated.

"Come on. I won't bite."

Alexa wasn't so sure. Resting against a jumble of pillows, her hair hidden beneath a white cap with trailing black ribbons and a patchwork quilt pulled to her chin, Grandmother resembled the dressed-up wolf from the children's picture book about Little Red Riding Hood. Alexa perched on the edge of the bed near Grandmother's feet, careful not to bounce the mattress.

Grandmother linked her wrinkled hands over her belly. "Your mother calls you Alexa, but I'd like to know your full name."

Her congenial tone — the kindest she'd used since Alexa had come downstairs — raised a flag of apprehension in the back of her brain. She answered warily. "Alexa Joy Zimmerman."

"Hmm. Alexa . . . Joy . . . Zimmerman." Grandmother seemed to sample its sound. "We have the same initials, then. I am Abigail Jantz Zimmerman. How old are you, Alexa Joy Zimmerman?"

"I turned nineteen last December third." She'd shared a cake she baked herself with Mom, Linda and Tom, and some of the young people from church. She'd also given her mother a bouquet of flowers in appreciation for nineteen years of being such a great mother. Mom had cried, and Alexa had thought it her happiest birthday ever, but now she couldn't help but remember all the birthday cards and greetings she'd never received from this woman lying on the bed.

Grandmother chuckled — a rusty sound. "Well, I will be sixty in June. Sixty. Can you believe that?"

No, she couldn't. She would have guessed her grandmother to be much older. But she wisely only smiled.

"If you're nineteen, you're finished with school, yes?"

Alexa shrugged. "Well, yes and no. I graduated from high school a year ago, and I've been saving to attend college, but I'm not completely sure what degree to seek. So I'm waiting."

Grandmother's thick brows descended. "I only attended up through ninth grade. Our school here only goes that far — one year past what the government requires. Then our young people find jobs. They get married and build families. You obviously aren't married, so do you have a job?"

It occurred to Alexa that for every question she answered, Grandmother answered it, too, sharing a little piece of herself. Was she playing a game? Alexa began to feel like a mouse to Grandmother's cat. "Yes, ma'am. I work at an elementary school near our apartment, in the cafeteria. I help cook the lunch and then serve it to the students."

"I never had a job." Another dry chuckle rasped from Grandmother's throat. "At least not one that paid me a wage. I finished school and then helped in my aunt's home.

I only had one sister who was a few years older than me, but my aunt and uncle had a dozen children. They needed help, so I stayed with them and helped them until I got married. Then I helped my husband." She frowned and shook her finger at Alexa. "But just because I didn't draw a wage doesn't mean I was lazy or my work didn't matter, young lady. I've always worked heartily as for the Lord."

Alexa nodded. "Yes, ma'am."

Grandmother sighed, losing her stern expression. "So you want to go to college . . ." She linked her hands together and held them beneath her chin, as if praying. "Your mother is the only one of my children to get schooling beyond ninth grade. She chose to become a nurse."

Alexa already knew this, but she listened respectfully.

"I was happy to know she was studying to be a nurse. A worthwhile vocation. Ministering to people in need. Something a good Mennonite girl would want to do." Grandmother's voice turned so reflective, Alexa wondered if she'd forgotten she was speaking to someone besides herself. "And when she said she was working in a Mennonite hospital — a hospital that offered services for free or little cost to those in need — I was proud. Yes, proud. What mother wouldn't be proud to have a missionary nurse for her daughter?"

If Grandmother was so proud of Mom, why hadn't she ever let Mom know? Why did she only send a letter once a year? Why hadn't she ever come to visit and see what Mom did? So many questions. But Grandmother had seemed to drift away to somewhere inside herself. If Alexa spoke she might startle her into another fainting episode. So she bit down on the end of her tongue and held her questions inside.

"Everyone in town knew I was the mother of a missionary nurse. No one else could make such a claim. They admired me for raising a daughter who would serve so unselfishly. And I held up my head and let them admire me." Abruptly she lowered her hands and fixed Alexa with a rueful smile. "I would have been wise to remember, Alexa, the admonishment from Proverbs 16:18, 'Pride goeth before destruction.' " She set her lips in a firm line and turned her face away.

A chill made its way across Alexa's frame. Did Grandmother see her arrival as destruction? A series of bangs and thuds, the loudest yet, came from the other side of the door as if to underscore her thoughts. She stood, ready to flee the room and the ugly idea her grandmother had put in her head.

Mom stepped in holding a mug. Steam rose from the plain blue mug, bringing with it the rich aroma of coffee. Although Alexa had always loved the smell of brewed coffee, queasiness attacked. She scurried to the opposite side of the room.

Mom held the mug to Grandmother. "I'm afraid this is reheated coffee from the morning pot."

Grandmother scowled at the contents as if flies were doing the backstroke in the liquid. "Why not fresh?"

"All that noise you're hearing? That's the contractor tearing out your cabinetry." Mom's cheeks bloomed a rosy hue. The steam from the coffee must have overheated her. Or maybe Grandmother's grumpiness caused a blush of frustration. "He'd taped up a big sheet of plastic across the middle of the kitchen — I suppose to keep the dust mess to a minimum — and while the stove is accessible, the sink is on his side so I couldn't get water. Luckily he stacked everything from the cabinets on the kitchen table so I could make use of a saucepan to reheat the coffee. You don't have to drink it if you don't want to."

Alexa's patience wore out. She took a step

forward. "Mom?"

Mom shifted her attention. She must have sensed Alexa's tension because she frowned. "Is something wrong?"

Alexa folded her arms across her chest. Many things were wrong. "I need to talk to you."

Grandmother waved her hand. "Give me that coffee. I've waited all morning for it."

Alexa released a soft snort. For someone who claimed to be proud of her daughter, she sure didn't treat her very well. Mom might as well have been a minion and Grandmother a reigning despot. "Mom, I need to talk to you."

"Suzanne!" Grandmother raised her voice, nearly shouting. "I want my coffee."

Mom placed the mug in Grandmother's waiting hands. "Here you are, Mother. Be careful. It's hot."

"It's supposed to be hot. Don't treat me like an imbecile." Grandmother took a sip, grimaced, then shrugged and finally looked at Mom. Alexa expected her to offer a thank-you, but she said, "My legs are cramping. Do you know how to massage cramping muscles?"

"Of course I do."

"Then do it. My toes are starting to curl." She zipped her glare at Alexa. "There's no need for you to stay in here and watch your mother play nurse. Go explore. Read a book. Hang towels with Tanya."

Alexa had never been so rudely dismissed. Her face burned.

Grandmother added in a surprisingly gentle voice, "You've spent enough of your day stuck in a room with a crotchety old lady. So go."

Alexa looked at Mom, asking with her expression, *Should I?* Mom gave a slight nod. Alexa sighed. She headed for the door, then stopped next to her mother. "When you're finished here, please come find me. I really do need to talk to you about something important."

"Your mother will be spending her day with me, Alexa, so you'll have to entertain yourself." Grandmother sipped her coffee, her bearing as regal as a queen's. "Before you go, though, do you see the small drawer on the right-hand side of my dressing table?"

While sitting in the corner earlier, Alexa had admired Grandmother's antique dressing table with its oval mirror, tiny side drawers, and teardrop door pulls. She nodded.

"Open it and take out what's inside."

Alexa slid the little drawer open. The space was empty except for a wadded handkerchief. Puzzled, she picked it up. The layers of linen held an oddly shaped lump that gave it a heft she didn't expect. Alexa carried the little package to the bed and held it out.

Grandmother shook her head. "I don't want it. I want you to take it. Call it a . . . belated birthday gift."

A rumpled old handkerchief? Somehow it seemed an appropriate gift.

"Your mother is going to massage my legs now, so go on." Grandmother raised her mug again and shifted her gaze toward the window.

Cradling the handkerchief in her hand, Alexa left the room. Mom closed the door behind her, leaving her in the dining room with the mutter of voices behind her and continuing bangs and thumps waiting in the kitchen. She scuffed her way to the front room where a shaft of sunshine poured through the window and highlighted thousands of tiny dust particles. She passed through the sunlight, sending the particles scattering, and sank onto the sofa.

Curiosity overcame her. What had Grandmother stored all by itself in the little drawer? She peeled back one flap of the handkerchief. A chain made of thick links slipped from the wadded fabric and drooped all the way to her lap. *What on earth . . .* She pinched the end of the chain and pulled it free of the handkerchief. The wispy square of cloth with its tiny pink embroidered flowers fell to the floor, and she gasped.

Suspended on the glistening chain, a round gold locket as big as a quarter caught the light and tossed it back. The shiny disk rotated on the chain, giving Alexa a glimpse of etching on the other side. She laid the locket flat on her palm and examined the filigreed markings. She recognized the letters, the center one representing Zimmerman larger than those flanking it — AZJ. Her grandmother's monogram. Her monogram.

Her heart turned a flip inside her chest. She covered her mouth with her trembling fingers. What kind of game was Grandmother playing?

CHAPTER 9

Paul

Paul pried the final cabinet loose with a downward thrust of his crowbar. Nails screeched like angry cats and released their hold on the wall. He dropped the crowbar onto the floor to catch the sturdy box before it fell onto the countertop. He carried it to the porch and set it on the floor with the others. Straightening, he wiped his brow with his shirt sleeve. Crisp air eased through the porch's screened walls, and he paused for a moment to enjoy what Karina used to call the kiss of spring.

His gaze drifted across the row of cabinets. He'd been pleased to discover they were identical in size, each fifteen inches wide by twenty-eight inches tall. Reassembling them on the floor as one large unit — four across and two high — would allow Mrs. Zimmerman to have access to every shelf. Clete had readily accepted the suggestion to reuse the existing cabinetry. And why toss them out? They were solid yellow pine, built by a craftsman who took pride in his labor. Once Paul placed them on a short platform and added decorative molding, no one would ever guess they were made-overs.

Of course, he'd need to apply another coat of paint to make the cabinets look truly new. Unfortunately his crowbar had left some scratches and dings in the wood. But a little filler, sanding, and paint would fix them up again. He found great satisfaction in taking something worn out and giving it new life. Additionally, refurbishing old-but-still-usable items saved money and time, which made him a good steward. Being a good steward earned respect in his community.

He turned to go back inside, but he caught sight of someone walking along the clothesline. Tanya had driven away in Clete's truck only a few minutes ago, so who was out there? The sheets waving gently on the line hid all but the person's feet. He watched the steady progress of white-and-pink tennis shoes worn over anklet socks until the wearer emerged on the other side of the clothesline. Ah, Suzy's daughter, Alexa.

The girl moved slowly across the yard toward the barn, her head low. She seemed to be examining something she held in her cupped hands, but Paul couldn't tell what it was from this distance. And what did it matter? He had a job to do — he'd best get to it. He aimed his feet for the kitchen door, but a shriek from outside changed his direction. He dashed into the yard as another shrill scream, accompanied by wild barking, pierced the air.

He rounded the corner of the house to find the Zimmermans' black-and-white border collie, Pepper, giving Alexa an exuberant welcome. Muddy paw prints decorated the girl's skirt. She held her hands in the air as if under arrest while the dog joyfully leaped around her, tongue lolling and tail wagging. Although Pepper meant no harm, the girl was clearly terrified. He called out sternly, "Pepper, sit!"

Without a moment's pause, Pepper plopped down on her furry behind and panted up at the girl.

Alexa gave Paul a look of pure relief as he closed the distance between them. "Thank you so much. I was afraid he'd knock me flat."

Paul hid a smile. He put his hand on the dog's head. "Pepper's really a friendly old girl. And she responds well to commands, so the next time she charges at you, just tell her to sit, and she'll do it." Pepper whined, wriggling in place. Paul gave her head a pat to encourage her to stay put, then he stuck out his hand. "We haven't met. I'm Paul Aldrich."

"It's nice to meet you. I'm Alexa." She gave his hand a quick, polite pump and then shot the dog a sour look. "I'm glad to know how to control that hairy beast in the future, but I'm afraid you told me too late. When she jumped on me, I dropped my locket." Pepper followed Alexa's movements with bright eyes as she began searching the ground. The dog poised, as if to leap.

"Pepper, stay," Paul said before joining Alexa in the search. He chuckled when he spotted the glint of gold in the thick grass about six feet behind her. "You didn't just drop it — you must have launched it." He stooped down and picked it up. Although he wasn't an expert when it came to jewelry, he knew an antique when he saw one. The weight of the chain and its pendant spoke of solid gold, not the cheap gold-plated necklaces available today.

He released a soft whistle as he handed it to Alexa. "I'm glad we found it. You wouldn't want to lose that."

She cradled it to her chest. "No, I wouldn't. My . . . grandmother gave it to me."

"Was it her betrothal locket?"

The girl blinked at him, confusion marring her face. "Her what?"

"Betrothal locket." Obviously Suzy no longer lived the Old Order lifestyle. Her clothes, though modest, didn't match the caped dresses worn by the women of their sect. But why hadn't she told her daughter about their traditions? He pointed to the round pendant. "You see, when a young man in our sect wishes to become published —"

Alexa's brow crinkled.

Paul added, " 'Published' means becoming engaged."

Sincere interest replaced her expression of confusion.

"He gives the girl a locket. If she wears it in public, then he knows she's accepted the invitation. After the wedding the wife usually puts a picture of her husband inside. I bet if you look, you'll find a photo of your grandfather in that one."

Alexa gazed down at the locket for several seconds. Then she gave him a hopeful look. "Do you know how to open it? I couldn't find a latch."

He needed to return to work, but for reasons beyond his comprehension, opening the locket for Alexa took priority over cleaning up his mess in the kitchen. He held out his hand, and she slipped it into his palm. He turned the locket this way and that, seeking a means of releasing the catch, and then smiled. "Here it is. See?" He pressed a tiny knob concealed beneath the decorative link connecting the locket to the chain, and the two halves popped open as smoothly as they probably had the day it was purchased.

Her face lit up. She took the locket and stared at the black-and-white image tucked into the bottom disc. "So that's my grandfather . . ." Tears shimmered in her eyes. She blinked quickly, clearing the moisture. She grinned. "He was very handsome."

Paul couldn't comment on that — what did he know of handsome? But he shared what he knew to be true. "Cecil Zimmerman was a good man. Quiet, gentle, hard working." He'd always thought Suzy was natured more like her father than her outspoken mother. "I had a lot of respect for him. Our community suffered a great loss when he went on to his eternal reward. God surely welcomed Cecil into heaven with accolades for being a good and faithful servant."

Alexa seemed to drink in his words. "He died when I was very young. All I really remember is that Mom cried a lot and I felt bad because she was so sad."

Why hadn't Suzy come home for her father's memorial service? Or for anything else, for that matter? Indiana and Kansas were far apart, but not so far the distance couldn't be traveled. She'd missed her father's memorial service, her brother's and sisters' weddings, the birth of nieces and nephews, all events worthy of a visit home. He considered asking Alexa what had kept them away, but he didn't want to be nosy.

She looked at the picture again and released a wistful sigh. "I wish I could have known him."

Paul couldn't hold back a question. "Hasn't your mother told you about him?"

Alexa bit down on her lower lip, consternation creasing her face. For a while he thought she wouldn't answer, but then she spoke in a rush. "Mom doesn't like to talk about her life before she moved to Indiana. The few things she's told me were shared with such apprehension, I almost felt guilty asking. I'd hoped when we came here I'd learn everything about my family, but —" She stopped as abruptly as she'd started.

Holding up the locket, she offered a wobbly smile. "Thanks so much for finding this and showing me how to open it. I better go inside and wash the mud from my skirt before it sets in for good." She sidestepped gingerly around the dog and then dashed off.

Pepper whined and rose, but Paul said, "Pepper, stay." The dog lay down and rested her chin on her paws, staring after Alexa and twitching in eagerness to get up and follow. Paul stayed next to Pepper until Alexa disappeared around the corner of the house. Then he shook his finger at the dog. "Next time, behave yourself. No jumping on people."

Pepper leaped up and batted the leg of Paul's work trousers with one paw. He chuckled and gave her neck a scratch before turning toward the house. Pepper trotted alongside him, her tongue hanging from her mouth and her ears flopping. Paul frowned. Although he'd never been one to stick his nose into other people's business, he couldn't deny the desire to understand why Suzy had been so secretive about her past with her daughter and why she'd never come home. Yet at the same time he resisted uncovering the reason.

He wasn't naive. What he and Suzy had done in the barn loft was wrong. His parents had lectured him about remaining pure because giving in to temptation once made it easier to give in a second time, and then a third. Had his indiscretion led Suzy down a path of promiscuity, which in turn caused her to hold her daughter away from her grandparents and other family members? If so, he needed to seek forgiveness for more than he'd imagined.

Suzanne
"All right, that's enough."

At her mother's brusque statement, Suzanne arched backward and pressed her hands to the small of her back. After leaning over the bed and rubbing her mother's calves for the past half hour, she needed a back massage. And a hand massage — her fingers were cramping from working Mother's muscles. She made a mental note to add *able to massage cramping muscles* to the list of qualifications for the replacement nurse.

"Isn't it close to lunchtime by now?" Petulance laced Mother's tone.

Suzanne silently prayed for patience as she checked her wristwatch. "It's a little after eleven. You didn't have much breakfast so we can have an early lunch if you like."

"No, no, if I eat lunch early, I'll want an early supper, and then I'll be hungry at bedtime. I can't eat at bedtime. I get heartburn."

Suzanne already had heartburn. *Dear Father, how will I last two months?* But she smiled. "All right then. We'll wait until Tanya gets back from town. Do you know what you'd like?"

"Yes." Mother narrowed her gaze and stared fiercely at Suzanne. "I'd like to know how you have a daughter when, right now in Sommerfeld, your cousin Andrew and his wife are planning a wedding for the baby I thought you gave up for adoption."

Her baby girl was getting married? So many feelings swept through her at Mother's blunt announcement — regret for having given her baby away, desire to know her, fury at her mother for the demands she'd made twenty years ago — she couldn't decide which took precedence.

"Alexa told me she turned nineteen on the third of December. The same birthday as Andrew and Livvy's Anna-Grace." With each statement, Mother's voice grew softer in volume yet harsher in tone. She nearly grated out a question. "So what I want is to know, is Anna-Grace your daughter or not?"

An acidic taste flooded Suzanne's mouth. She swallowed. "Yes, Mother."

"Then how do you also have a daughter with you?" Mother pressed her palms to the mattress and sat upright.

135

Suzanne's answer came easily, the words having been uttered to Alexa countless times as assurance of her place in the world. "God gifted me with Alexa."

Mother's eyes widened. "Twins?"

Suzanne closed her eyes for a moment, gathering strength. Then she turned a pleading look on her mother. "In all honesty, this conversation is pointless. Discussing something that happened twenty years ago doesn't change a thing. I did what you asked me to do — I gave Andrew and Olivia the chance to be parents. Can't you simply accept Alexa's presence with me and let it go?"

For long seconds Mother stared into Suzanne's face, her expression unreadable. Then she released a noisy huff and tossed her covers aside. "I want out of this bed. It's ridiculous for me to have to stay here all day just because I had a little fainting spell. I've taken worse tumbles in my lifetime and didn't take to bed over them."

Suzanne could have argued that in the past Mother had possessed two good legs to support her, but why argue? Mother won every battle. Fighting her was useless. And if she was willing to drop the conversation concerning Alexa and Anna-Grace, Suzanne would humor her. She hurried to the corner and retrieved Mother's wheelchair.

She reached to assist her into the chair, but Mother slapped her hands away. "I'm not helpless. I can do it." She transferred herself from the bed to the chair, landing at an awkward angle on the padded seat. Grunting a bit, she pressed her elbows on the armrests and righted herself. Once she was settled, she fired a smug I-told-you-so look at her daughter.

Suzanne responded with a tight smile. She released the brakes on the chair and aimed it for the doorway. But before she rolled the chair through the opening, Mother held up her hand and barked, "Stop!"

She shifted around to look into Suzanne's face. Scowl lines marched alongside her mouth. "I gave Alexa my locket. You're the oldest daughter, so it should have gone to you before being passed to the oldest grand-daughter. But it would eventually be hers anyway, and her initials match mine, so I gave it to her."

Although Mother's face and tone were angry, Suzanne found the gesture touching. The gift indicated Mother had already accepted Alexa as a member of her family. But it could cause problems with her siblings. She placed her hand on her mother's bony shoulder. "Are you sure that's what you want to do?"

Mother snorted and faced forward again. "In this life, more often than not, we do what we have to instead of what we want to. You should know that by now." She gripped the rolled edges of the armrests. "Take me out on the porch. I need some air."

CHAPTER 10

Suzanne

The morning proved so pleasant, Suzanne remained on the porch with her mother and Alexa. Mother sat in her wheelchair, and Suzanne and Alexa shared the old swing. The chains' creak and the wind's gentle whisper offered a peaceful accompaniment to their quiet conversation.

Tanya returned shortly before noon. She came up the walk with two pizza boxes balanced on one hand, a lumpy plastic bag hanging from the other, and an apologetic look on her face. As she plopped the pizza boxes onto Alexa's lap, she said, "They're only from the convenience store on the highway south of town so not nearly as good as homemade, but with the kitchen such a wreck we can't cook."

After the challenge of reheating coffee in the torn-up kitchen, Suzanne had wondered how they would prepare lunch. "Tanya, you're a genius. Thank you."

Alexa lifted the lid on the top one. A wonderful aroma escaped. "It sure smells good. What kind are they?"

Tanya wrinkled her nose. "Super Deluxe, I think they called it. I didn't know what kind you liked, so I got the ones with everything. Just pick off what doesn't please you."

Alexa laughed. "I won't pick anything off. Unless I find an anchovy."

Tanya grinned. "I also stopped by the grocery store and picked up bread —"

"Store-bought?" Mother made *store-bought* sound like something poisonous.

Tanya grimaced. "I'm sorry, but I can't imagine baking until Paul is able to put the kitchen together again. Remember, Clete and the girls said you'd have to make do while he worked in there."

Mother snorted.

Tanya went on, "Bread, lunchmeat and cheese, boxed cereal, fruit, and bags of chips so you can prepare simple breakfasts and lunches. As for supper, Sandra, Shelley, and I will take turns bringing something out so you'll have one good meal a day. Oh!" She held the plastic bag aloft. "I also got a good supply of paper plates, napkins, plasticware, and Styrofoam cups." The look of apology returned. "I know it's considered wasteful, but I didn't know what else to do. Paul said he'd have to turn off the water in the kitchen, which means no washing dishes, so . . ."

Suzanne stood and took the bag from Tanya. "It'll be fine. You thought of everything."

Tanya shrugged. "We've had time to plan. It took nearly three months for Paul to clear his schedule." She released a short laugh. "Of course, he'd have to find the time to work out here just as you arrived! And speaking of Paul, I'm going to ask him to join us. He brought a lunchbox with him, but he'd probably rather have pizza."

Suzanne had secretly celebrated escaping a face-to-face encounter with him that morning — thank goodness for that plastic sheet! — and her stomach rolled over as she considered sitting with him on the porch where he used to join her for long talks in the evenings half a lifetime ago. She sought an excuse to avoid inviting him to eat pizza with them. "Won't his wife be offended if he doesn't eat the lunch she packed?"

Tanya shot her a startled look. "Didn't you know? Paul lost his wife to cervical cancer several years ago."

Pain stabbed Suzanne as if an arrow had

impaled her heart. Paul was a widower? Her discomfort was whisked away, and sympathy flew in to replace it. How tragic, to be left alone at his young age.

Tanya went on. "So he packs his own lunch. I doubt he'll mind saving it for tomorrow." She trotted off the porch, swinging a glance over her shoulder. "Alexa, want to help me put these groceries away?"

Alexa set the boxes aside and followed Tanya. Suzanne, her movements slow and clumsy given her inner turmoil, opened the bag and removed the paper plates.

"Don't use those," Mother snapped. "Tanya can take them back to the store. We'll have water in the bathroom so we can wash dishes in the bathtub. I won't have the town whispering about me using paper products. More than wasteful, it's lazy."

Within the Old Order sect, being accused of laziness was a terrible insult. But Suzanne would not wash dishes in a bathtub. She popped open the package of plates and forced a light tone. "Paper plates are perfect for a picnic, Mother. I'm sure people have more important things to worry about than whether or not you're using paper products." In all likelihood, Paul used paper products more often than not with no wife to see to the housekeeping chores.

142

Mother released a disgruntled huff and set her lips in a firm line, but when Tanya, Alexa, and Paul joined them, she didn't refuse a plate holding two slices of pizza. Suzanne's hands trembled slightly as she served Paul, her awareness of his loss still strong. He mumbled a thank-you, but he looked to the side rather than meet her gaze. As soon as he had the plate, he moved to the far end of the porch steps, sat, and leaned against one of the pillars. His long legs stretched across the risers.

When everyone had a plate, Tanya turned to Paul. "Would you bless the meal for us?"

He immediately bowed his head. Sawdust decorated the dark strands of his hair, and a few bits fell onto his pizza. Suzanne kept her eyes open, watching more sawdust drift onto his plate while he offered a simple thank-you for the meal. When he raised his head, Suzanne cleared her throat.

"Um . . ." She couldn't bring herself to use his name. She pointed. "You lost some sawdust from your hair into your pizza."

He angled the plate toward the sunlight and made a face. "I sure did." He set the plate aside, stepped into the yard with one lithe leap, and bent over. Lifting both hands, he ruffled his thick hair with his fingers. A shower of wood bits rained into the yard.

Suzanne found herself mesmerized. As a teenager Paul had exuded confidence, and his simple, unconcerned manner of dealing with the sawdust in his hair let her know he hadn't lost his sense of self-assurance. For some reason, the realization both rankled and pleased her. He straightened, leaving his short-cropped hair standing in disheveled ridges that begged to be smoothed into place. Suzanne quickly turned her attention to her pizza.

Out of the corner of her eye, she watched Paul plop down on the porch, flick the bits of wood from his pizza with his finger, and lift the triangle to his mouth. His first bite encompassed a good third of the slice and left a smear of tomato sauce on his mouth.

Suzanne yanked a napkin from the package and carried it to him. "Here." She tapped her own mouth to indicate where he needed to mop.

He took the napkin, wiped the spot clean, then flicked a hesitant glance at her. "Did I get it?"

She nodded.

He looked at her, this time holding her gaze. A sheepish grin pulled up one side of his lips. "Thanks, Suzy."

With one simple word — *Suzy* — her discomfort returned in an overwhelming whoosh of emotion. She whirled toward the porch swing and caught her mother staring at her. Mother's scowl of disapproval skewered her in place for several seconds. Heat filled her face. "I believe I saw a pitcher of tea in the refrigerator. Would anyone like some?"

All but Mother expressed interest, so Suzanne hustled into the house, allowing the porch door to slam behind her. She heard her mother scold, "Gracious, Suzanne!" But she pretended not to hear and went straight to the refrigerator. She opened the door and leaned in, willing the cool air to remove the flush of embarrassment from her face.

Tanya's comment about the timing of Paul working at the farmhouse while Suzanne was there replayed through her memory. Why had God allowed their paths to collide this way? *I can't face him every day and keep my secret, God. Alexa and I have to go home. Let me hire a nurse quickly so my daughter and I can leave.*

Paul

He observed Suzy's mad dash into the house, chased there by Mrs. Zimmerman's condemning glare. He'd seen that look before. She'd aimed it at him from her bench in church the day he'd married

Karina. The woman's obvious displeasure had made both him and his new bride uncomfortable. Hunkering over his plate and eating as quickly as possible, he recalled when Mrs. Zimmerman had seemed to like him. As a kid, he'd been in and out of her house regularly, spending time with Suzy. They'd been best buddies before they were old enough to consider courtship. But the woman had changed. People blamed it on her accident, but it seemed to him she'd adopted a bitter attitude long before the hay bale crushed her pelvis.

As he finished his last bite, Suzy stepped onto the porch with the pitcher of tea. She poured a cup for each of them, including her mother, who took it without a word of appreciation. It bothered him, seeing how coldly Mrs. Zimmerman treated Suzy. Sure, she'd given up being openly demonstrative with her other children, but shouldn't she be grateful to have her oldest daughter home? Shouldn't she appreciate Suzy's willingness to set aside her job and take care of her? Couldn't she say "thank you" instead of frowning as if being served a cup of tea was an insult?

He downed his tea, trying to tamp the rising frustration. But it remained. He crushed the empty cup in his hand. Why did he care so much? He wasn't part of this family. He had no right to form judgments. But he wanted to tell Mrs. Zimmerman to stop being so selfish and critical and offer her daughter a little bit of the mercy God had given her.

He tossed the cup and wadded napkin onto his grease-smeared plate and rose. "Mrs. Zimmerman . . ."

She looked at him. A dot of tomato sauce decorated the peach fuzz above her lips. Thin lips set in a grim scowl. A scowl that matched the heavy lines turning her forehead into a series of furrows. At first glance she looked fierce, but as he stood gazing at her, he suddenly recalled his father telling him that whatever a person carried on the inside would show on his outside. And on Mrs. Zimmerman's face he saw a deeply imbedded misery.

An unexpected wave of compassion swept over him. Of course she was miserable. Widowed young, stuck in a wheelchair, separated from her oldest child for two decades . . . Her sadness was years in the making. He hung his head. He'd played a part in inflicting misery on the woman. Instead of extending anger, shouldn't he be merciful? The words he'd planned to say drifted away like bits of sawdust on the breeze. *Thank You, Lord, for holding my tongue. I want no other regrets where Mrs. Zimmerman is concerned.*

He said, "I know the morning was pretty noisy and the afternoon won't be much better. But I'll clear out by three. I've got to be home when Danny gets there. So you'll have a quiet evening. And I'll be sure to clean up after myself so you won't have to worry about sawdust being tracked all over the house." He shifted his gaze to Tanya. "Thanks for the pizza." Then he turned to Suzy. His throat tightened, but he said, "And the tea." Turning once again to Mrs. Zimmerman, who maintained her stoic expression, he offered a smile. "Enjoy your afternoon."

He trotted off the porch and across the yard to the burn barrel, deposited his trash, then jogged around to the kitchen. By the time he got there, he felt winded, but it wasn't from the short run. No, his shortness of breath came from the heavy weight of remorse he carried. He stepped into the kitchen and picked up his electric jigsaw, ready to return to work, but his finger rested on the trigger rather than pressing down.

His chest ached. For Suzy. For Mrs. Zimmerman. Even for himself. He needed to dispose of this long-held burden. Before he went home, he'd take Suzy aside and beg her forgiveness. The thought of experiencing freedom gave him a lift, and he returned to work.

But he didn't have a chance to talk to Suzy alone before leaving that day. Or the next day since he had Danny with him. On Sunday after the worship service, other fellowship members crowded around her, keeping him from carving out a minute of time with her. Monday morning Danny awakened with a slight fever so Paul stayed home with him both Monday and Tuesday. By Wednesday he was nearly on tenterhooks. He'd rehearsed the request for forgiveness so many times, he had it memorized. If only he could deliver it.

To his surprise, when he arrived Wednesday morning the house was empty. His heart set up a *boom-boom* that rivaled the strike of his hammer on a block of wood. She hadn't decided to return to Indiana already, had she? Clete's truck was parked beside the barn, so he headed out there and found his friend working on the engine of his dad's old tractor.

Clete looked up and smiled as Paul approached. "Hey. You can bang to your heart's content in there today without bothering anybody. Mother and the girls are in Wichita."

Paul's mouth went dry. "At the airport?"

Clete applied the wrench to something inside the tractor's belly, his face crunching in concentration. He sighed and pulled his arm free. "I tell you, when Dad tightened something down, he intended it to stay. I might have to borrow a power wrench from the mechanic in town."

He shifted his attention to Paul. "Nope. The fabric store. Mother's lost so much weight, her clothes are all too big. Shelley offered to modify Mother's dresses, but she wants her skirts longer so they cover more of her legs when she's in the chair. So they went shopping. I think Suzanne plans to take Mother out for lunch and maybe go to the zoo while they're in town — take advantage of this nice weather."

Paul resisted heaving a sigh of relief. "All right then. I'll get to work." He headed out of the barn with a determined stride. He'd keep an eye out for the women's return. He would not go home tonight without setting things right with Suzy.

But when three o'clock rolled around — time for Danny to be out of school — she still hadn't returned. And Paul went home with the burden dragging on him like a ball and chain clamped on the foot of a prisoner.

CHAPTER 11

Alexa

Alexa woke as the car jolted and bounced her head lightly against the window. She opened her eyes and caught Mom's grin.

"Pothole."

Alexa rolled her eyes. "Yeah. Sorry excuse." She yawned and flicked a glance into the back. Grandmother sat in the middle of the seat, her head back, dozing. A soft snore emerged from her slack mouth. Alexa stifled a snicker and faced forward.

"This was a good day." She spoke quietly to keep from disturbing Grandmother. "The best so far." She'd actually seen Grandmother's lips curve into a small smile twice — once at the restaurant when the server brought her a slice of chocolate cake for dessert, and once at the zoo when an adorable chimpanzee came right up to the glass barrier and stared cross-eyed at her. And now, with Grandmother sleeping, Alexa had

Mom's full, undivided attention.

She nibbled her lower lip. She hated to ruin the day, but she hadn't had Mom to herself for more than two minutes since they'd arrived at the farm. Her uncle's comment still festered in her soul, and she needed to excise the wound by talking about it with her mother. Should she bring it up now? Mom looked so relaxed — more relaxed than she had since she received the letter asking her to come to Arborville. Her question would surely shatter Mom's calm.

But it might be days before she got another chance. They were almost to the farm — maybe another five miles. Her wristwatch showed 5:10. Either Tanya or one of Mom's sisters had been arriving at 5:30 every day with supper and their families in tow. By the time they cleared out, Mom would need to help Grandmother prepare for bed. Alexa had no idea what was involved in readying her grandmother for bed, but Mom always came out of the room exhausted. She hadn't had the heart to bother her when she was so tired.

So now was her chance. She sent another quick look into the back to be sure Grandmother wasn't awake. She no longer snored, but her mouth still hung open. She was out. Alexa gathered her courage, leaned toward the center of the front seat, and whispered, "Mom, can I ask you a question?"

Without taking her eyes off the road, Mom nodded.

"Are you . . . ashamed of me?"

The car jerked, then slowed. Mom held tight to the steering wheel but sent a startled look at Alexa. "Am I — No! Never!"

Grandmother stirred. Alexa put her finger against her lip and stared at Grandmother. The older woman smacked her lips a couple of times, shifted on the seat, and went on snoozing. Alexa turned back to Mom. "Then why didn't you ever tell your family you had a daughter?"

Mom's face paled. "Oh, Alexa . . ."

The pain in Mom's voice pierced Alexa's heart. But she needed to know the truth. The hurt that had sprouted her first night in Arborville poured out in a raspy torrent. "In nineteen years you never found a way to let them know about me? I took everybody by surprise. Grandmother, Clete, Shelley, and Sandra — all the people in the town where you grew up." Their startled expressions played through her mind, flaying her anew. "You've always told me I was your gift, and I believed you, but if I was such a gift, why keep me a secret? Were you ashamed to tell them you had an illegitimate child? Instead of being your gift, am I really your shame, Mom?"

Mom released the steering wheel with one hand and gripped Alexa's hand. "Alexa, you are not my shame. You are my precious child. I love you more than you can imagine." Her voice caught, and she swallowed twice before continuing. "When I discovered I was expecting a baby, my mother was mortified. And so angry. Good girls didn't do . . . what I'd done."

Alexa could imagine all Grandmother had said. She squeezed Mom's hand in silent empathy.

"She forbade me to tell anyone else, and she arranged for me to go to a home in Indianapolis where a midwife would deliver the baby. Then I was to give it to my cousin and his wife who weren't able to have children. Mother said by doing so, I would be able to redeem myself."

Alexa frowned. "And no one wondered why you left?"

A sad smile played on the corners of Mom's lips. "It isn't uncommon for our young people to spend time in another Mennonite community when they reach courting age. Mother said people would assume that's why I'd gone. After the baby was born, I could come home again and no one would have to know about it."

"But you kept me instead." Warmth flowed through Alexa's middle. Mom had defied her mother and abandoned her family . . . for her. Tears stung. "No wonder you couldn't go home or say anything about me. Mom, I'm so sorry."

Mom placed both hands on the steering wheel and turned into the farm's lane. She spoke so softly Alexa had to lean close to hear her. "You don't have any reason to be sorry, honey. You didn't do anything wrong. I committed all the wrongs." She pulled to a stop next to the house, put the car in Park, and left the engine rumbling. Turning to face Alexa, she reached for her hands. Alexa clung. "But with all the wrongs, I hope you know how much I love you. I am not ashamed to have you for a daughter. Do you believe me?"

A tear slipped free and rolled down Alexa's cheek — one warm rivulet that helped wash away the deep pain she'd held. "I believe you."

Mom sighed and bowed her head. "Thank you."

"But, Mom?" Alexa paused, debating with herself, but in the end she needed to know. "Is my father here . . . in Arborville?"

Mom kept her head low for several seconds. Then she lifted her face and looked into Alexa's eyes. "No, honey, he isn'"

Alexa started to ask if she knew where he'd gone, but Mom clicked off the ignition, curled her fist around the keys, and opened the door. "We'd better get inside. Sandra's bringing supper tonight, and I need to get the dining room table set up. Please get your grandmother's wheelchair from the trunk and help her into the house." She took off across the grass.

Alexa reached into the backseat to awaken Grandmother, but her eyes were open. Only to slits, but open. And fury seemed to smolder in her narrow gaze.

Of all Mom's siblings, Sandra was the one Alexa liked the best. Partly because she was the youngest. At twenty-five she was only six years older than Alexa, seeming more like a friend than an aunt. Partly because she was so cute with her round belly and swaying waddle. But mostly because she exuded happiness. Sandra smiled all the time, unlike Shelley who seemed to have forgotten the muscles in her face were capable of forming a smile. The nights Shelley brought supper were tense, uncomfortable evenings. But when Sandra came, joy came with her. After her serious talk with Mom, Alexa needed a splash of joy, so she welcomed Sandra warmly when she and her family stepped into the house.

Sandra and Derek's three-year-old son, Ian, pulled free of his father's hand and plowed into Alexa's knees. " 'Lexa!"

The little boy had attached himself to Alexa within minutes of meeting her the first time. She didn't understand why he'd chosen her, but she loved it. She scooped him from the floor in a hug, relishing the feel of his little arms around her neck. "Hi, Ian. Do you want to sit by me?"

"Yup." His blond curls and dimples gave him a cherubic appearance. Alexa hoped the new baby would have Ian's blond curly hair and adorable smile. He took Alexa's face in his pudgy hands. "But not on a dixenbary."

Alexa burst out laughing. "On a what?"

Derek shook his head. He plucked Ian from Alexa's arms and put him on the floor. "He's trying to say *dictionary*. We don't have a highchair or booster seat out here, so we had him sit on a dictionary last time. He didn't like it."

Ian said, very seriously, "I sit on my bottom." He sent a hopeful look upward. " 'Kay?"

"If you sit very still." Derek headed for

the dining room and Ian followed.

Watching the father and son, Alexa couldn't help smiling. They looked nothing alike. Ian had inherited his mother's coloring and soft features rather than Derek's ruddy complexion and square jaw, but their mannerisms were so similar it was almost comical. Derek walked like a cowboy who'd just vacated a saddle. Ian moved with the same wide-legged gait. When they ate the ham and vegetables casserole Sandra had provided, Derek surreptitiously pushed the lima beans to the side of his plate. Ian forked up the ham, zucchini, tomatoes, and carrots but, his little nose wrinkling, refused the lima beans as well. The two even wiped their mouths in exactly the same way — one swish of the napkin from left to right.

Alexa shifted her gaze to Mom, who sat between Sandra and Grandmother. Grandmother's hair was almost solid gray, her face lined with age and years of worry, but Alexa could see the similarities in the three women. If Shelley were sitting there, too, it would be clear to anyone they were all related.

She thought about her appearance — straight brown hair, brown eyes, her face heart shaped rather than oval like the three Zimmerman women sitting in a row on the other side of the table. And her differences went beyond looks. Mom enjoyed reading or knitting in her spare time, but Alexa would rather garden or ride a bike than sit and read a book. Mom cooked because they had to eat, but Alexa found pleasure in creating tasty recipes. She and Mom, even though they loved each other, had little in common. Apparently she was more like her father . . . whoever he was.

Deep down she'd hoped she might find her father when she came to Arborville. Thanks to Tom, Sunday school teachers, and other men from their church, she'd never lacked for male role models, but she still wondered about her father. Just like Mom's family, he didn't know she existed. If he found out about her, would he welcome her enthusiastically, the way Sandra had, or would he hold his distance, like Shelley? There were no guarantees.

Alexa scooped up the last bite of casserole on her plate and looked again at Mom. Gratitude swelled her heart. *God, I might not have a father who loves me. I might not even have a big ol' family that loves me. But I have Mom, and she gave up so much for me. If I'm her gift, then she's mine. Thank You, God, for letting me be hers.*

Sandra pushed from her seat, her bulk

making her clumsy. "I baked a pie for dessert. Cherry. Who wants some?"

Ian waved his fork in the air and nearly clunked Alexa on the side of the head. "Me! Me!"

Alexa, laughing, lowered the little boy's hand. "You can give Ian my slice."

Sandra's face fell. "You don't like cherries?"

Alexa cringed. "I'm afraid not. Sorry."

"What are your favorites, then, so I'll know for next time?"

Mom chuckled and began gathering up the used plates. "Alexa likes anything with chocolate."

Sandra grinned. "Except cherries?"

Sheepishly, Alexa shrugged.

Grandmother shuddered. "I like cherries and I like chocolate, but I don't like cherries with chocolate. Every year, Clete gets me a box of chocolate-covered cherries for Christmas, which I never eat."

The thought of sticking one of those gooey candies in her mouth made Alexa want to gag. Knowing she and Grandmother had even such a silly little thing in common pleased her. "Maybe he's giving you an opportunity to share, Grandmother," she said, hoping to earn a smile.

Grandmother didn't scowl, but neither did

her face reflect amusement. She opened her mouth as if to speak, then snapped it closed. Curling her hands around the wheels on her chair, she backed herself from the table. "It's been a long day and I'm tired. I'm going to my room to read a bit before turning in."

Sandra touched her mother's arm. "Are you sure you don't want a piece of pie first? I used your recipe."

Grandmother shook her head. She jerked her face toward Alexa. Something — was it obstinacy or orneriness? — glinted briefly in her eyes. "Now, if you'd baked a chocolate cake instead of the pie, Alexa and I would both have a piece. There's always room for chocolate cake. Am I right, Alexa?"

Grandmother was teasing. With her. The thought of being in cahoots with her grandmother made her want to wriggle out of her skin in delight. She nodded. "Of course. Always."

"So now you know, Sandra." Grandmother shifted in her chair to look at her youngest daughter. "Who is bringing dinner tomorrow night?"

"It's Shelley's turn," Sandra said.

"Tell her Alexa and I want chocolate cake for dessert."

Sandra and Mom exchanged a look, their

faces wearing matching expressions of puzzlement.

Derek cleared his throat. "Mother Zimmerman, Shelley probably already has tomorrow's dinner planned. You know how she likes to stick to her calendar."

Alexa had only been around Shelley twice, but she understood the warning in Derek's statement. If Sandra was the sunniest person she'd ever met, Shelley was the most structured. Already Alexa felt as though Shelley saw her as an intrusion. She wouldn't make it worse by expecting her to accommodate her dessert preference.

"Don't worry about bothering Shelley. Since Grandmother wants chocolate cake tomorrow, I'll bake one for her."

"You bake?" Derek and Sandra chorused the startled question.

Alexa swallowed a giggle. If they only knew how much time she spent in a kitchen! "Yes. It'll be a challenge, given the shape the kitchen is in, but I can get to the stove, so I can do it. Let me make dessert." At that moment, the most important thing she could do was to bake the best chocolate cake her grandmother had ever eaten.

Sandra looked at Mom, who looked at Derek, who looked at Sandra. The three of them shrugged. Sandra said, "If you want to bake a cake, Alexa, I'll tell Shelley not to bring a dessert."

The third smile of the day twitched on Grandmother's cheek. "It's settled then. I'm going to my room. Suzanne, give me an hour of peace before coming in to help me dress for bed." She wheeled around the table and through the doorway to her bedroom. With a flick of her wrist, she closed the door behind her.

Alexa turned to Mom, ready to express her delight in being able to contribute to the next evening's dinner, but the look on her mother's face stopped her. Mom was staring after Grandmother with the same simmering fury Grandmother had shown earlier in the day.

CHAPTER 12

Suzanne

Before going in to help her mother prepare for sleep, Suzanne slipped out to the barn. With the sun's departure, the air had turned cool, but the sturdy walls of the century-old building would keep her warm. Alexa had given her a funny look when she'd stated she'd be out in the barn, but she knew she wouldn't be overheard out there. She needed a private place to use her cell phone. Beyond a quick call to let Linda and Tom know she'd arrived safely, she hadn't taken the time to phone. But tonight she needed her friend.

She entered the barn and pushed the heavy, rolling door closed behind her. The old knob-and-tube wiring still worked well, and light flooded the interior with her twist of the switch. A gray-striped barn cat, apparently startled by the light, leaped from the stacks of hay bales in the corner and dashed beneath a bench. A variety of smells, some pleasant and some pungent, met her nose, bringing with them a strong sense of stepping backward in time. As a child, she'd loved to visit the barn and watch her father work.

Melancholy struck — she missed Dad. She automatically moved to the tractor, which had been her father's pride and joy, and perched on one of the tractor's rubber tires. She took out her phone. The cat, apparently deciding she needed observation, crept out to sit nearby and wash its paw while keeping its gold eyes pinned on her. Beneath the cat's round-eyed scrutiny, she punched in Linda's number.

Linda answered on the second ring. "Well, hello, girl! I was sure happy to see your name pop up on the caller ID. We miss you around here. How are things in Kansas?"

Suzanne released a sigh. "Things are confusing. Do you have a few minutes?"

Scuffling noises carried through the receiver, letting Suzanne know Linda was settling in for a long chat. "Absolutely. Tell me all about it."

Suzanne spilled everything, starting with how difficult she found it to feel comfortable in the small community after her lengthy time away, how Clete and Shelley

165

seemed to hold her at arm's length, and finally how hard it was to deal with her mother. "She's so unappreciative and gruff. Nothing I do pleases her. It's almost as if she thinks if she's unhappy, then everyone has to be unhappy, too."

Linda's throaty chuckle filled Suzanne's ear. "Reminds me of a little painted shingle I saw at a gift shop. It said, 'If Mama ain't happy, ain't nobody happy.' "

Despite her frustration, Suzanne laughed. The cat shot back under the bench. "Send that to me and I'll give it to her for her birthday." She sobered. "To be honest, Linda, there are times I want to snap at her. I know it won't do any good, and I know it isn't respectful, but she tries my patience so badly. I'm afraid one of these times I'm going to lose patience completely and say something I'll regret."

"Aww, Suzanne . . ." Linda's tone, soft and soothing, delivered as much comfort as a hug. "Lemme ask you something. Do you think maybe some of your frustration with your mama is leftover resentment from all those years ago when she made you go away?"

Suzanne considered her friend's question. Although she and her mother had exchanged yearly letters, they'd always been dutiful missives lacking any hint of their thoughts or feelings. She and Mother had never discussed the pain of that time or the subsequent months at the unwed mothers' home when Suzanne pined away with loneliness and felt weighted beneath a burden of guilt larger than her swelling belly. She'd never received her mother's advice on how to comfort a colicky baby or been able to share her delight in all the little milestones Alexa conquered. Over the years, the pain of being sent away in anger and condemnation had become secondary to the imbedded hurt and regret of being isolated from the ones who should have been her support and encouragement. In her heart, she'd forgiven her mother. But she hadn't forgotten.

She swallowed a lump of sadness. "I don't know. Maybe."

"Seems to me you ought to examine yourself then, make sure you aren't reading more into your mama's behavior than what's really there because you're still mad at her."

Suzanne wanted to defend herself — Linda hadn't seen Mother's scowls or heard her harsh words — but she respected her friend too much to argue. Besides, as much as she hated to admit it, Linda was usually right. "I'll do that."

"Good. Now tell me how our Alexa is getting along. She was so excited about meeting her uncles and aunts and cousins. Is she happy there?"

Mixed emotions rolled through Suzanne. Hesitantly, she shared her family's reaction to meeting her daughter and Alexa's attempts to fit in. Linda expressed pleasure that most of them, after their initial shock, had been kind to Alexa. Suzanne didn't mention the conversation she'd shared with her daughter earlier in the day, though. She still felt raw from Alexa's question and couldn't bring herself to repeat it even to her dearest friend. But she did divulge a big concern.

"My mother seems taken with her. Our very first day, she gave Alexa a precious heirloom. Her betrothal locket. Traditionally, it should go to the oldest daughter." Hurt tightened her throat, making her words come out huskier than usual. "But as Mother said, the locket would have been passed to my daughter eventually anyway, and Alexa was so touched by it — the locket meant even more to her than it would have to me. So I shouldn't complain. But —"

"Why would you complain? Isn't it good to have your mama and Alexa getting along?

What's the matter, girl?"

The worry that had risen up and wrapped its tentacles around her heart at supper returned, squeezing with such intensity Suzanne found it difficult to draw a breath. "I think Mother is trying to win Alexa away from me."

"Oh, Suzanne . . ."

"Don't 'Oh, Suzanne' me." She clutched the phone with shaking hands. "She's asked to spend time alone with Alexa, and she won't tell me what they discuss. She has this secretive smile she only gives to Alexa. And tonight, she coerced Alexa into baking her a chocolate cake."

Linda's laugh blasted out. "Are you listening to yourself? Honey, you're getting yourself all worked up over nothing. Nobody has to coerce that girl into baking. She'd do it for a stranger as much as she enjoys it."

Tears stung Suzanne's eyes. She leaped up and paced back and forth, scaring the cat from its spot beneath the bench to the opposite side of the barn. "You don't understand. She wanted me to give up my baby twenty years ago. Now she's doing it again — trying to come between my daughter and me. I won't let her take away another child, Linda. I won't."

A long silence fell on the other side of the

conversation. Then Linda released a soft huff of breath. "So what are you gonna do?"

Suzanne eased back onto the tire. The inquisitive cat slunk across the floor and leaped onto the tractor seat where it kept a furtive watch on her. "I can't leave until I've secured a nurse for Mother. It's clear my siblings can't keep coming out day after day to take care of her. But I can't do it, either, no matter what Clete thinks. So as soon as I've managed to find a caretaker the family can afford, I'm coming back to Indiana."

"You sure that's what you want to do?"

Suzanne had asked Mother the same question about giving the locket to Alexa. She gave the answer Mother had given. "It's what I have to do."

"Well, all right then, honey. Tom and I will pray you through it."

Suzanne drooped forward, tiredness stealing the strength from her bones. "Thank you."

"I just hope you won't look back someday and wish you'd stuck around — made things work. Family . . . that's not something you can pull out of thin air. Seems to me you've been without them too long already."

"Alexa is all the family I need." But even she heard the lack of conviction in her voice. Before Linda could dispute her statement, she said, "I should probably get inside. Believe it or not, I'm out in the barn. It's the only place I could be alone."

The cat yawned, showing a pink tongue and pointed teeth.

"Well, except for a cat. But I don't think this whisker-faced mouser will repeat anything I said."

Linda gave the expected chuckle. "You take care of yourself in between taking care of everybody else, you hear? You want me to mention to Administration you might be back before your leave is up?"

She started to say yes, but something held the word from escaping. "Not yet."

Alexa

The squeak of the backdoor hinges caught Alexa's attention, and she looked up from scrubbing the drop-leaf table to see Mom push aside the plastic curtain and enter the front half of the kitchen. Eager to show her mother what she'd accomplished in the past half hour, she straightened and held her arms wide. "Ta-da!"

Mom sent her a puzzled look. " 'Ta-da' . . . what?"

Disappointed, Alexa allowed her arms to droop to her sides. The cloth in her hand dangled limply, reflective of her aching muscles. Despite the plastic tacked from one side of the room to the other, dust from the carpenter's demolition had coated every surface and crept into tiny cracks and crevices. But thanks to her zealous use of dust rags, broom, and scrub cloth, the space was now sparkling clean. How could Mom not notice?

"Mom, really . . ." Releasing a brief huff of laughter, Alexa shook her head. "It's clean in here. And since it's clean, I can bake in here." The thought of mixing up one of her rich, gooey chocolate cakes erased her weariness. These past few days, occupying herself by reading some of the books she found on a shelf on the upstairs landing or exploring the property — she especially loved the barn loft — had passed so slowly. She needed something more to do, and she liked baking more than nearly anything else.

She moved to the little washtub she'd set up on the edge of the old-fashioned gas stove and plopped the rag in it. She paused for a moment, gazing into the plastic tub. "If my chocolate cake makes Grandmother smile, maybe Shelley will be pleased, too."

Cool hands descended on her shoulders and turned her around. Mom pulled her into a brief hug. "Honey, you don't need to try to please Shelley."

Yes, she did. She needed to win favor with her family. With all of her family. Soon they would be glad to know her instead of being embarrassed by her. Alexa began gathering mixing bowls, spoons, and measuring cups from the boxes lining the wall. As she arranged the items on the table, she gave a cavalier shrug and grinned impishly. "It's more for me than anyone else. You know how much I love chocolate."

Mom leaned against the corner of the table and folded her arms. "Yes, I know you love chocolate, and I also know you wouldn't have even attempted to bake in this disaster area of a kitchen if you didn't think it would score points with your grandmother and aunt. I don't want to see you setting yourself up for disappointment. They aren't worth it."

Alexa's hands froze midtask. Mom's voice had become hard. Bitter. So unlike her. She turned slowly toward her mother, almost afraid to look in case she saw a stranger standing in Mom's place. "How can you say such a thing about your own mother and sister? Of course they're worth the effort. Haven't you always taught me to serve others the way I would serve Jesus? Isn't He worth the effort, Mom?"

Mom sighed and hung her head. "That came out wrong."

"I guess so." Alexa nibbled her lower lip, uncertainty binding her in place. For a few brief seconds, Mom had seemed to turn into Grandmother. Alexa didn't like the change.

Lifting her head, Mom met Alexa's gaze and spoke kindly — more like the mother she'd always known. "I only meant we don't really know them. And we won't be here long enough to get to know them. So even though we want to do our best to get along while we're here, you don't need to expend endless energy on building relationships that will likely be short term."

Alexa frowned. Something didn't make sense. "Two months is enough time for us to build relationships. I already feel as though Sandra and I are friends. The same with Tanya. Grandmother even seems to like me. And why can't we continue our relationships with your family when we go back to Indiana? I know you've stayed away because you didn't want them to know you'd kept me, but the cat's out of the bag. There's no reason for us not to stay in touch now, right?"

Mom set her lips in a pained grimace and didn't answer.

Alexa took a step toward Mom, her pulse tripping into double-beats. "Mom? Is there something else that's kept you away from Arborville all these years?"

CHAPTER 13

Abigail

In the little hallway between the dining room and kitchen, Abigail sat in her wheelchair and listened for Suzy's reply. When she'd left her room and overheard Suzy and Alexa talking, she only intended to let her daughter know she was ready to change for bed. She hadn't meant to eavesdrop. But then she heard Alexa's question, and Abigail wanted answers as much as Alexa did.

Her Suzy had secrets — lots of secrets — and she suspected her daughter would clam up tighter than the joints of the cabinetry Paul Aldrich was building if she knew Abigail was listening. So she stayed put and strained her ear toward the opening, hoping to satisfy her curiosity.

After several long, silent seconds, Suzy's breath whisked out on a sad sigh, and she spoke in a defeated tone. "Honey, can we let the past remain in the past? I can't change any of the choices I made twenty years ago, and rehashing it serves no useful purpose. We've done well on our own, haven't we?" Abigail envisioned Suzy embracing Alexa the way Abigail had once pulled her children to her breast to offer comfort. Suzy's tender voice continued. "Be satisfied that you've had the chance to meet my family. Let it be enough to have . . . put names to faces, so to speak."

"So what you're telling me," came Alexa's voice, low and controlled yet with an edge of belligerence, "is there are other reasons, but you want to keep them to yourself."

Abigail held her breath.

Suzy's blunt answer came. "Yes."

Blowing out her air, Abigail pushed the wheels on her chair forward and rolled into the kitchen. Alexa and Suzy jumped apart as if they'd been caught with their hands in a cookie jar. Abigail shook her head and forced a soft chuckle. "If I didn't know better, I would say you two were up to no good. Did I really startle you that much?"

Alexa busied herself with the supplies scattered over the table and didn't answer. Suzy hurried behind Abigail and caught hold of the wheelchair handles. "I'm sorry I kept you waiting, Mother. I imagine you're ready to turn in."

Abigail chuckled again as Suzy pushed her chair through the hallway and dining room toward her bedroom. "And now you change the subject. Mm-hm, I interrupted something for sure."

"Don't be silly." Suzy pushed the chair to the edge of the bed and set the brakes. "What nightgown do you want? Your pink one or the blue one with the yellow daisies on it?"

"It makes no difference, Suzanne. Just get one." While Suzy headed for the closet, Abigail lifted her transfer board from its spot between the bed and nightstand and positioned it as a bridge from her chair's seat to the mattress. She then shifted herself to the edge of the bed, grunting with the effort it took to drag her useless limbs. Her left hand slipped, and she flopped across the bed. With another grunt of aggravation, she righted herself, then sat with both palms pressed to the mattress, panting. How she hated the clumsy person she'd become. Why couldn't that bale have stolen her life instead of only taking the use of her legs? God had chosen a special punishment for her. And after what she'd done, she supposed she deserved it.

Suzy returned with the pink gown draped over her arm. "Here you are, Mother. I like this one best. Let's get you undressed and then —"

"Why are you here?" Abigail blurted the question, surprising herself as much as Suzy.

Suzy blinked twice. "I'm here to help you." She laid the nightgown aside and reached for Abigail's cap.

Abigail slapped her hands away. "I can do it myself. And you didn't answer my question. You know what I meant. Why did you come back to Arborville? And don't tell me because Clete asked you to." She yanked the pins holding her cap in place with such force she pulled hairs from her head. Each yank stung, but she didn't care. At least she felt something besides fury for a few moments. "You stayed away for twenty years. Twenty years!" She clutched the pins in her fist and glowered at her daughter. "An absence like that isn't accidental. You never meant to come back." She lifted her cap from her hair and wadded it in her hand. "Why didn't you just tell Clete no?"

Anger glinted in Suzy's eyes, and Abigail gloried in it. Finally a real spark of emotion instead of the nicey-nice sweetness she'd showered over everyone since her arrival. When Suzy replied, sarcasm colored her tone. "How could I say no to the only invitation I received in twenty years?"

Abigail narrowed her gaze. "Don't turn it back on me, Suzanne. When I put you on the bus, I told you to come home after the baby was born. You chose to stay away."

"You chose to —" Suzy snapped her mouth shut and closed her eyes. For several tense seconds she stood in silence, repeatedly clenching and unclenching her fists. At last she relaxed her hands, opened her eyes, and pinned a calm look on Abigail. "Mother, I refuse to fight with you. Maybe one day we can sit and discuss my leave-taking, but I will not do it in anger. So I think it's best if we set the topic aside for now."

Abigail blew out a derisive breath and began unbuttoning her dress. Her fingers trembled uncontrollably, complicating the simple task. Before Suzy could offer to help, she snapped, "If you won't talk to me, then get out. I can put on my gown, take myself to the bathroom, and put myself to bed. I'm not a little child who needs your help."

Suzy hesitated.

Abigail screeched, "I said get out!" Hurt flickered in Suzy's eyes, but Abigail ignored it. As her daughter moved stiffly toward the door, Abigail called after her, "Don't think you have to stay here for me. I can take care of myself. I don't want to be your Christian duty, Suzanne." The door slammed on Suzy's exit. Abigail's manufactured fury seeped out of her in a rush. She sagged forward and whispered, "I just want to be your mama again . . . and I can't be. So go home, Suzy. Please — go home."

Suzanne

Suzanne stepped into the kitchen Saturday morning and found a young boy sitting at the table with a bowl of cereal in front of him and a spoon in his hand. The boy shifted to look in her direction, and as she looked into his face she was whisked backward in time. She gave an involuntary jolt. A single-word query escaped on a breathy note: "Paul?"

The boy's forehead crinkled. "Paul's my dad. I'm Danny."

The boy was a carbon copy of his father from the cowlick in his thick dark hair to the shape of his ears and the dimple in his chin. She hadn't realized she'd carried such a strong memory of Paul as a boy. The discovery disconcerted her. It took a full minute to bring her thoughts to the present. In the meantime, Danny sat gazing at her with his spoon gripped in his hand, his cereal turning soggy.

She located her senses and said, "I'm

181

sorry I disturbed your breakfast. Go ahead and eat."

Danny dipped his spoon, but he watched her out of the corner of his eye as she moved to the stove to start the percolator. He swallowed a bite and scooped up a second. "Are you Mrs. Zimmerman's daughter? The one who left a long time ago and is a nurse?" He stuck the spoonful of shredded wheat in his mouth and chewed while gazing at her.

Of course community gossip would be overheard by children, too. Suzanne forced a smile. "That's right."

"Seems like Mrs. Zimmerman sure could use a nurse. She can't walk, you know. Dad says she never will. You gonna live here now?"

Suzanne feigned great interest in measuring coffee into the aluminum basket. Since the evening Mother had ordered her out of her room three days ago, the two of them had barely exchanged two civil words. Mother refused to let Suzanne help her ready herself for bed, and she'd chosen to go unbathed rather than have her daughter assist her in and out of the tub. Danny was right. Mother most definitely needed a nurse. But Suzanne would not be filling the role.

The queries she'd sent online via Alexa's

smartphone — thank goodness she'd agreed to let her daughter purchase a phone with more bells and whistles than her own simple little flip phone — should produce a candidate soon. At least, she hoped so. She didn't know how much longer she could bear Mother's snarls and contempt.

She settled the lid on the percolator, adjusted the flame beneath the pot, then glanced at the wall clock. Eight fifteen. She frowned. Mother should have come out of her room by now. She turned to Danny. "I'm going to go check on Mrs. Zimmerman. Do you need anything before I go?"

The boy gazed at her for a few seconds, unblinking, then he shrugged. "I'm okay. Thank you."

Danny possessed the guilelessness of a youngster but was also polite. His parents had done well with him. For one fleeting moment she pondered if she'd had a boy instead of a girl, would he have looked like Danny? She pushed the reflection aside, offered him a smile, and then quickly aimed herself through the hallway to the other side of the house.

Once outside her mother's bedroom she paused to send up a petition for patience. She'd exhausted her own supply days ago. *Your strength is sufficient, Lord* . . . The prayer complete, she tapped on the door. "Mother? Are you awake?"

"It's after eight, Suzanne. Of course I'm awake. I've been awake for over an hour already."

"May I come in?"

"Yes, and be quick about it."

Suzanne bit the end of her tongue, drew in a deep breath, and opened the door. Her mother had donned a dress and sat in her wheelchair, but her thick gray-streaked hair lay in flattened strings across her shoulders. She held a hairbrush in one hand and a pair of flesh-toned support hose in the other. As Suzanne entered the room, Abigail thrust the hose at her.

"I'm dizzy this morning, so I can't put these on myself. When I lean forward far enough to reach my toes, I'm afraid I'll fall out of the chair. Hurry and get them on me. My feet look like sausages." She pushed the command through clenched teeth, clearly irritated at having to admit needing help.

Suzanne battled irritation, too. She bit back a sharp comment, knelt before her mother, and rolled the hose to slip over her feet. She stifled a gasp when she looked at her mother's swollen ankles. Her feet shouldn't look this way so early in the morning. Any number of calamities could befall someone who'd lost the use of a limb. Blood clots were one of the worst and often caused the kind of swelling Suzanne now witnessed. Aggravation fled before the tide of worry. When she'd finished helping Mother dress, she'd call Clete and suggest a trip to the doctor for an MRI or sonogram of Mother's legs.

As she tugged one hose leg over her mother's foot, she suddenly realized Mother was wearing the same blue print dress she'd worn yesterday. She glanced at the end of the bed — the neatly made bed — and spotted the folded nightgown she'd set out for Mother last night. Sitting on her heels and loosely clasping her mother's thick ankles, she looked up in astonishment. "Did you spend the night in your chair?"

Mother's lips pursed into a sullen line. She looked away.

"Mother! You did, didn't you?"

Mother whacked the arm of the wheelchair with her hairbrush. The *crack* reverberated from the plaster walls. "What difference does it make if I want to sit up all night or not?"

"It makes a difference because of this." Suzanne lifted one of her mother's feet. Mother turned her face away and set her

185

jaw in a stubborn angle. Suzanne sighed. "Mother, listen to me. The chair doesn't allow enough circulation. You need to be out of your wheelchair at least eight hours of the day so the blood can flow." She pulled the hose free and examined her mother's toes by turn. They were cold to the touch, but to her relief she found no evidence of gangrene.

She tugged the hose into place and then rested her hands on her mother's knees. "You're going to need to keep your feet elevated today. Do you want to lie in your bed with a pillow under your feet, or would you rather go out on the porch and sit in the lounger?"

Mother huffed a mighty breath. "I want to stay in my chair."

"That isn't an option."

"Do not treat me like a child, Suzanne."

"Then stop acting like one."

Her mother glared at her for several seconds as if trying to wish her away, but Suzanne remained on her knees, quietly waiting for her to choose where she would spend the day. Mother was stubborn, but Suzanne was, too, and she would win. Her mother's health depended on it.

Finally Mother threw her hands in the air, the hairbrush nearly clipping Suzanne on the chin. "Fine! I won't stay cooped up in here."

Suzanne rose, hiding a smile. "The lounger it is."

"I want breakfast first. At the table, not outside where bugs will bother me. And when I go to the porch I want Alexa to sit out there with me. If you want to be helpful, you can do laundry."

Pain stabbed at the blatant rejection, followed by a fierce prick of apprehension. But Suzanne decided to choose her battles carefully. She gave a brusque nod.

Mother jammed the hairbrush at Suzanne. "Since you're determined to treat me like an invalid, you can do my hair. But hurry up. I want my morning coffee."

Suzanne gritted her teeth as she wove Mother's hair into a bun. Another battle would surely ensue when she gave her mother a cup of herbal tea instead of coffee. Caffeine wouldn't help flush the excess fluid from her body. As soon as she had Mother settled on the porch, she'd take Alexa's telephone and check for messages. Another nurse couldn't arrive soon enough.

CHAPTER 14

Suzanne

Suzanne entered the back porch and layered her mother's sheets in the barrel-shaped belly of the wringer washer. She'd been surprised by the presence of the electric washer, which was considered a "modern convenience." All through her childhood, a hand-operated tin tub had lurked in a corner of the basement, and from the time she was six or seven years old, she had helped Mother turn the crank that operated the beater paddles. Having a plug-in machine with no hand crank was a huge step up but still a far cry from the automatic machines she operated at the Laundromat in Franklin. She hoped she wouldn't do something wrong and render the washer inoperable.

As she turned the faucets to fill the tub with water, Paul came around the corner pushing a wheelbarrow. His son followed on his heels, whistling. The boy caught Suzanne's eye through the screen and ceased his tune to smile and wave at her. Self-consciousness attacked with Paul so near, but she couldn't ignore the gregarious boy. She offered a quick wave and then turned her attention back to filling the washer.

"Um . . . Suzy?"

Paul spoke, sounding as self-conscious as she felt. Slowly she turned to look at him through the gauzy wire.

"Do you have to do laundry today?"

Considering Mother's adamancy, she did have to see to the wash. Rather than share her mother's blunt orders, Suzanne formed a question of her own. "Is there a reason I shouldn't?"

He grimaced. "Danny and I are pouring the wheelchair ramp. Now that the ground's dried up and the *Farmers' Almanac* predicts sun for the next several days, it seemed a good time to get it done. I closed up Pepper in the barn so she won't get her paws in the wet cement, and you won't be able to use the back door until the cement dries. Probably tomorrow evening at the earliest."

That explained the absence of the affable pooch and the presence of the odd wooden framework built over the porch steps. She'd meant to ask Clete about both when he

189

came by the house.

Paul went on. "So if you intend to hang clothes on the line, you'll need to go out through the front door."

Suzanne had no desire to lug baskets of wet laundry all the way through the house, past Mother on the porch, and then around to the backyard. "We used to hang our wet clothes on lines in the basement during the winter months or on rainy days. I'll just hang everything down there today." She hadn't been in the basement since her return. Were the lines still up? She swallowed a laugh. Why wouldn't they be there? It didn't seem as though much else had changed in the past two decades.

She stepped closer to the sagging screen and peered at Paul through a sizable tear in the mesh. "I know you're remodeling the kitchen and bathroom and putting in ramps to accommodate Mother, but are you planning to do any other work out here?"

Paul's brow crinkled. "Such as?"

She hurried to the washer, turned off the faucets, and flipped the switch to activate the rotator. The machine chug-chugged to life. She returned to the screen and raised her voice to be heard over the washer's loud motor. "Well, painting for one thing. It's all peeling and looks awful."

Suzanne frowned, looking from the four-inch lap siding to the mesh screen enclosing the porch. She touched the ragged tear. "The porch screen needs to be tightened or replaced. And the floor slopes downward. The entire place has fallen into serious disrepair."

"I know."

His regret-filled voice pulled her attention from the house. As she looked him full in his face, she realized the years had also weathered him, adding crow's feet to the corners of his eyes and etching a sharp V between his eyebrows. A few strands of gray at his temples caught the sunlight, turning silver against his dark brown, short-cropped hair. Despite the changes, she still glimpsed the handsome boy he'd been. The man he'd become was no less appealing.

She took an awkward step in reverse.

Seemingly unaware of her discomfiture, he said, "I've only been hired to make modifications. Clete said he had to fight your mom pretty hard just to get her to agree to the changes we're making. But I'm concerned about the condition of the house, too. I'm afraid it'll fall apart if someone doesn't give it some care. Maybe you'll be able to change your mom's mind about fixing things up out here."

Mother wouldn't listen to anything Suzanne said. But she would talk to Clete.

Paul continued, his tone musing. "I don't think the windows have even been washed since your dad passed away. But the disrepair started even before he died. It's as though they just quit caring how the place looked. Very sad. She's a grand old house." He gave a little jolt, as if coming awake. "I better get to mixing this concrete. Get me that shovel, will you, Danny? And Suzy, please hook the latch on the porch door so nobody accidentally comes out before the cement is dry."

Why did being called Suzy by Paul make her feel young and girlish again? With a quick nod, she set the little hook into its eye, then turned back to the washer. The machine had vibrated its way from the wall. If it continued, it would eventually unplug itself and could go through the screen. Paul had made a neat pile of scrap lumber left over from the kitchen demolition. She chose a sturdy length and positioned it in front of the washer's wheels so it couldn't roll any farther. Then she hurried inside, giving the kitchen door a solid slam behind her. But the resounding *crack* didn't chase away the strange feelings coursing through her heart.

Paul

Paul showed Danny how to use the shovel's blade to push the mixture of concrete and water back and forth until it resembled thick, gray pudding. He hid a smile at his son's serious expression and firm grip on the shovel handle. While Danny mixed the second batch, Paul used a trowel to smooth the load they'd already dumped into the frame. Pouring cement was a mindless task. Too mindless. It allowed his thoughts to drift to places they probably shouldn't go.

If Danny hadn't been standing next to him, he'd have finally voiced that apology he'd been holding on to since Suzy's arrival in Arborville. But he couldn't say anything with Danny close by. What nine-year-old boy needed to know the man he claimed as his hero had fallen so far from grace as a youth? Someday he would confess his shortcomings to his son in the hopes Danny would learn a lesson and not make the same mistakes himself. But not yet. The boy was still too young to fully understand.

Holding back the words, though, was getting harder and harder.

"Dad? I think it's done."

Danny's call pulled Paul from his reverie. He rose and crossed to the wheelbarrow, gave the shovel an experimental swirl, then smiled and rubbed his hand over Danny's sweaty head. "You're right. It's ready. Good job. Let's get it poured and then you can mix up one more batch, huh?"

Danny wrinkled his nose. His mother had made a face just like that when she was teasing Paul about something. The reminder created an ache in the center of Paul's chest. "Another one? My arms are about to fall off."

Paul laughed, the brief pang of melancholy dissipating. "All right. I'll mix the next one while you rest your arms, okay?"

Danny smiled his approval, and the two of them pushed the wheelbarrow to the form. Paul tipped the bed on its nose. The concrete oozed out like thick cake batter, and Danny used the shovel to scrape the edges and bottom of the wheelbarrow. While Paul mixed the next batch, Suzy entered the porch, wrung the sheets into a basket, then started a load of what looked like dresses. She didn't even glance in their direction, which bothered him. And then he got aggravated at himself for being bothered. He turned his focus to his work.

The third wheelbarrow-full completely filled the form, and Paul troweled it smooth, then used a stiff-bristled broom to rough up the surface of the ramp.

"What're you doing that for, Dad?"

Paul continued working as he answered his son. "Think about the sole of your sneakers. Are they smooth or grooved?"

Danny balanced on one foot to check the underside of his shoe. "It's got lines and circles."

"What are they for?"

The boy dropped his foot and then scratched his chin the way Paul often did when he was deep in thought. "So I don't fall down?"

"That's right. Smooth soles will let you slip around, but ridges give you traction and help you hold your footing."

"So those ridges in the cement are for traction?"

Paul grinned and gave the concrete one final sweep. "Yep. You figured it out. Mrs. Zimmerman won't go sliding down the ramp in her wheelchair, thanks to the traction."

Danny stared at the wet concrete for a moment. "But wouldn't it be more fun to go *zi-i-i-i-ing*?" He swooped his arm.

Paul chuckled. "Maybe for you, but I doubt Mrs. Zimmerman would enjoy it." He dropped the broom and shovel into the wheelbarrow and headed for the water pump to clean his equipment.

Danny trotted alongside him. "I talked to Mrs. Zimmerman's daughter this morning. You know, the one who's staying here — the one who's a nurse."

Paul's pulse sped at the mention of Suzy, but he hid it by giving the pump's handle several emphatic thrusts up and down. "Yeah. What about her?"

"I asked her a question and she didn't answer me."

Water spurted from the rusty spout. Paul flicked a glance at his son while sloshing water through the wheelbarrow bed. "What did you ask?"

"I asked her if she was gonna live here now because Mrs. Zimmerman needs help. And she acted like she didn't hear me, but I know she did." He angled his head and peeked at his father through thick eyelashes. "Was I nosy?"

Paul was pleased Danny would worry about being rude. He was a good boy. "Maybe a little," Paul said as he emptied the wheelbarrow and watched the water paint the grass a grayish hue. He filled the wheelbarrow a second time. "Or maybe she just isn't sure yet."

Danny offered a look that said, *Really*? "Seems like she ought to know, Dad."

According to Clete she'd taken a leave of

196

absence rather than quitting her job. Although Mrs. Zimmerman needed a nurse, he'd seen how the woman treated her daughter. He wouldn't blame Suzy a bit for catching the earliest flight back to Indiana, but a part of him wished she would stick around, make Arborville her home again. He just wasn't completely sure why he wanted it — for her, her family, or for himself.

He finished swishing the side of the wheelbarrow and tipped out the water. He placed his damp hand on Danny's shoulder. "Whether she stays or not is her business, and we shouldn't pester her about it."

His son's eyes widened. "I didn't pester her!"

Paul smiled and squeezed Danny's shoulder before curling his hand around the wheelbarrow handle. "I didn't say you did. One question isn't pestering." He headed for the barn, Danny at his side. "But asking a second time would be nosy. So don't ask, okay?"

Danny sighed. "Okay. But Jay sure hopes she stays. He was tired of having to come out here all the time with his mom. He said his grandma is real grumpy, and he doesn't like to be around her."

"People who are sad are usually grumpy."

Paul often reminded himself of that truth to keep from snapping at the crotchety woman. "Tell Jay he needs to practice compassion."

"All right."

They stopped outside the barn doors. Pepper's whines begged him to let her out, but Paul turned to Danny. "And something else . . ."

Danny looked upward, his expression attentive.

"Talking about people isn't a very kind thing to do. I know you're curious about Mrs. Zimmerman's daughter. It's hard not to be, considering how few new people come to Arborville." Paul spoke kindly yet firmly. He didn't want Danny establishing a habit of talking behind others' backs. "But instead of talking to Jay or your other friends about Su— about the Zimmermans, you should just come to me if you have questions. All right?"

Danny toed the grass with his sneaker, his head low. "Um . . . Dad?"

"What is it?"

"Do you . . . A long time ago, did . . ." His son squirmed in place.

Paul caught Danny's chin and lifted his face. "Speak plain. What is it?"

Danny swallowed, his wide eyes pinned on Paul's face. He blurted, "Jay said his dad said you and his aunt were gonna get married, but then she went away and you married Mom instead. Some of the bigger girls thought maybe you'd want to court her again since Mom's gone."

Paul lowered his hand with a jerk. The kids at school were discussing Suzy and him? They were all too young to know he'd once wanted to marry her, so their parents must be talking. His face burned.

Danny went on, his innocent voice stinging Paul. "So would you want to, Dad? Court Jay's aunt, I mean?"

CHAPTER 15

Alexa

"Did you leave a beau behind in Indiana?"

Alexa looked up from the Alcott novel she'd selected from the shelf in the upstairs landing. She and Grandmother had sat on the porch in silence — Grandmother in the lounger and Alexa on the swing — for nearly two hours. Not that she hadn't tried to engage her grandmother in conversation. She'd asked several questions about the farm, the town of Arborville, chitchatty topics. But Grandmother's clipped answers had discouraged her. So the sudden question, a question one might consider to be personal, took her by surprise.

"Um . . . no." She laughed softly. "Actually I don't date much."

Grandmother's eyebrows rose. "A pretty girl like you? Why not?"

Alexa wasn't sure how to respond. All through school, she'd had several friends, both girls and boys. Rather than breaking into couples, they'd gone as a group to sporting events, the theater, or the bowling alley. One boy, Trevor Key, had taken her to the junior and senior proms, and once they'd gone out for pizza and a movie by themselves, but she hadn't felt anything special for Trevor. Apparently he'd felt the same because he never asked her again.

She finally shrugged. "I guess the right boy hasn't come along yet."

Grandmother released a little *humph.* Alexa waited for a few minutes, but when her grandmother lay with linked hands over her belly, gazing across the yard, she returned to reading. She'd nearly finished another chapter when Grandmother suddenly spoke again.

"What about your mother?"

Confused, Alexa frowned. "What about her?"

Grandmother huffed. "Dating. Does your mother date?"

Alexa set the book aside. "I'm not sure I should answer that."

"Why not?"

"Well, because it's Mom's business, not mine."

Grandmother rolled her eyes. Alexa found the gesture annoying. She vowed not to do it anymore. She reached for the book.

"I'd ask your mother, but she doesn't talk to me." Grandmother sounded bitter. And maybe a little hurt. "That's why I asked you. But if you want to keep secrets . . ."

Alexa sighed. "Grandmother, I'm not keeping secrets. I just think it would be better if you talked to Mom about her dating life."

Grandmother's face lit up. "So she has one? A dating life?"

How had she gotten herself backed into this corner? Alexa tucked a loose strand of hair behind her ear and gathered her thoughts. She could only recall two times when Mom had gone on dates. Both times Alexa had stayed with Linda and Tom, and both times Mom had come back before Alexa's bedtime. As a kid she hadn't seen any significance in the early return, but now it spoke volumes.

Alexa chose a careful answer. "Mom is busy with her job at the hospital, with church, and with friends. She doesn't go out on dates, but I don't think she minds. She's happy with her life."

Grandmother gazed at Alexa, her lips pressed tight and her forehead crinkled into furrows. Several seconds ticked by before she snapped, "She's happy? You're sure?"

"Yes, Grandmother. I'm sure."

"She's happy. That's good." Grandmother turned her face and stared outward. She seemed to forget Alexa was there. "Yes, it's good. But even so, she could have had so much more . . ." She fell silent again, blinking so slowly Alexa could count the sweeps of her short, straight eyelashes. After seven blinks, her eyes slid closed.

Alexa waited a little longer for her to speak again. When Grandmother remained silent, Alexa reached for her book. But as her fingers brushed the novel's cover, she noticed one lone tear trailing from the corner of her grandmother's closed eye downward where it disappeared in the peach fuzz on her jaw.

Suzanne

When Clete's pickup pulled into the yard, Suzanne was waiting. As soon as he turned off the ignition, she scuffed tiredly across the yard. All the treks up and down the basement stairs with baskets of laundry had exhausted her. Or maybe she should blame the many trips down memory lane her brief conversation with Paul had inspired.

Tanya slid out first and came at Suzanne with open arms. She bestowed a hug, the ribbons from her cap tickling Suzanne's cheek, then pulled back and smiled.

"We brought fried chicken, potato salad, that Jell-O fruit salad with the little marshmallows Mother Zimmerman likes so much, and biscuits. Picnic fare! We thought we'd spread blankets on the ground and enjoy this nice May weather before it gets too hot to be outdoors."

"That sounds fine," Suzanne said.

The truck's back door popped open, and the children spilled out, whooping in excitement. Pepper, still locked in the barn, barked in response. After listening to the pound of Paul's hammer all afternoon, Suzanne's senses were in overdrive. The cacophony pierced her ears. She winced.

"Jay Cletus Zimmerman!" Tanya caught hold of her son's arm. "Julie and Jana, you too, stop that hollering. You'll upset your grandmother."

Laughing instead of yelling, the trio took off for the barn. Suzanne cupped her hands and called after them, "Don't let Pepper out!" They waved in response.

Tanya turned an apologetic expression on Suzanne. "They've been wound up like this all day. I think being cooped up for so many rainy days has left them with pent-up energy."

Suzanne forced a smile. "It's all right."

She moved around to Clete, who was lifting a large wicker basket from the truck's bed. "I need to talk to you."

He set the basket on the ground and reached for the second one. "Sure. We can talk while we eat."

"I mean in private."

Tanya stepped close. "Alexa can help me set up for supper. You two could go to the summer kitchen. No one will bother you there."

Clete glanced at Suzanne. "That okay with you?"

Suzanne had loved the old summer kitchen when she was growing up. Using it for a playhouse rather than its intended purpose, she'd wiled away many days in the cheerful little building. She nodded.

Clete handed Tanya the basket. "All right then. Come on, Suze."

They walked side by side behind the house where Paul's truck still sat beneath a towering cottonwood tree, its back hatch down and tools scattered across the bed. Clete slowed when they neared the newly poured ramp. Splotches of lighter gray showed where the cement had started to dry.

Suzanne pointed. "You'll want to keep the kids off the ramp. Paul said we shouldn't use it until tomorrow evening."

Clete stopped and frowned at the ramp for a few moments, then he set off for the toolshed at the corner of the yard. He returned with a hammer, two wooden stakes, and a coil of rope. He pounded the stakes into the ground, then used the rope to create a barrier around the ramp. He stepped back and nodded at his handiwork. "That should tell the kids to keep away." Hooking the hammer in the loop on his work pants, he set off again in the direction of the summer kitchen.

Suzanne followed, taking in the appearance of the small building as they approached. Weeds had grown up all around the foundation, but she noted places where the old concrete blocks were crumbling. The screen door hung by one hinge, so Clete opened it flat against the lap siding. Weeds anchored it in place.

Suzanne turned the doorknob, but the door didn't budge. "Is it locked?"

Clete stepped forward. "There's never been a lock on it. The old wood is probably swollen from the rain." He gave the door a solid push with his shoulder, and it groaned open. An unpleasant odor — mildew, mice, and neglect — wafted out. He made a face. "You sure you wanna go in there?"

Suzanne shrugged. "Is there someplace else we can be alone?"

"Probably not."

"Then let's go." She entered the room, experiencing another strange sensation of stepping back in time. How many mud pies had she baked in the old cast-iron stove in the corner? She'd loved doing her homework out here, with all the windows open and a sweet breeze washing through. Now rusty patches dotted the majestic old stove and its pipe lay across the floor. A once-white painted wood table and two Windsor chairs remained in the middle of the floor.

Suzanne crossed to the table and pulled out a chair. It was coated with dust, but she sat gingerly on the cracked seat. The joints popped but held. Clete left the door open and took the second chair, sitting as carefully as she had. Once seated, he braced his palms on his thighs. "Will this take long? Mother likes to eat promptly at 5:45."

"I'll try to make it brief." But as she gazed into her brother's unsmiling face, her carefully prepared speech fled, leaving jumbled, disjointed thoughts in its stead.

Clete frowned. "What is it, Suzanne?"

She pulled in a breath, gathering her courage. "It isn't going to work for me to stay and care for Mother long term. She resists everything I do. I think she even resents me being here. I know you're concerned about the cost, but if all four of us pool our resources, we should be able to afford a night nurse. Because Mother's injury is permanent, there are programs available to provide part-time care. I've already put out some queries, and I'm gathering information. As soon as I have replacements available, I will return to Indiana. I wanted to let you know what I was doing."

Clete stared at her for a few seconds, his expression blank. Then he rose. "Okay. Is that it?"

Suzanne released a soft, humorless laugh. She'd expected an argument. Or a series of questions. She didn't know what to think of his emotionless acceptance. "Not quite."

With a sigh, he sat again.

"Clete, the house . . ." She chewed her lower lip for a moment, seeking the right words, but there was no kind way to say what she thought. "It's a mess. I realize Mother can't do much now from her chair, but the disrepair is much older than her injury. Obviously it's been neglected for years. Even Paul expressed concern that it might fall to ruin if something isn't done soon." She glanced around the dim interior of the summer kitchen. The cracked windows, peeling wallpaper, and sagging tin ceiling with exposed patches of lath where plaster had fallen away made her sad.

She turned to Clete again. "Mother and Dad taught us to take good care of our belongings, to see them as gifts from God. I don't understand why everything looks so run-down and unkempt. Dad wouldn't have let things go this way."

Clete stood so quickly he nearly tipped the chair. "How would you know?"

She drew back in confusion. Although the light was muted, the dirty windowpanes blocking the sun, she read anger in his square face. "Know . . . what?"

"What Dad would have done. You've been gone for twenty years, Suzanne. People change in twenty years. How could you possibly know Dad? Or Mother, or me or Shelley or Sandra, or your nieces and nephews?" His voice grew more harsh with every additional family relationship mentioned. He shook his head, his forehead crunching into stern lines. "I'm not trying to hurt your feelings, but I resent you telling me what should and shouldn't be done when you haven't even been around to share in this family for so long."

Her brother's blunt comment hurt her deeply and raised defensiveness, but she tamped down both emotions and chose a reasonable tone. "I'm not trying to tell you what to do, Clete. I was only asking *why* things look the way they do. It doesn't make sense to me."

"And what you plan to do doesn't make sense to me." He curled his lips into a contemptuous snarl. "Shelley told us we were crazy, but Sandra and me hoped —" He released a low growl and swept his hand across the tabletop. Dust flew in a glittering arc toward the floor and peppered the toes of his boots. He stared at his feet for a moment, his frame stiff, and then he faced her again. His anger had faded, but Suzanne couldn't determine whether sorrow or simple apathy replaced it.

"You wanna know the truth? The deacons offered to give us benevolence funds to pay for a nurse. But I told them no. I told them to save those funds for somebody who really needs them. We have a nurse in our family, and she'll come help. After all, that's what families do for each other — they *help.*" He blew out a short huff and turned toward the window. Leaning forward, he braced his hands on the windowsill and gazed outward. "Don't I look the fool."

Guilt — a far-too-familiar emotion — flooded Suzanne. She moved slowly to her brother and placed her hand on his arm. "It isn't that I don't care. But —"

He jolted upright and stepped away, dislodging her hand. "Of course you don't care. How could you? As I said, you don't know us. You've been gone for so long, you probably don't even remember teaching me to play checkers. Or how many times you rode bikes with me down to the pond to skip rocks." His gaze narrowed into a challenging glare. "Do you remember that baby sparrow I found under the bushes? Do you remember arguing with Dad about taking care of it? He didn't want you to — said it was just a sparrow and you should let the barn cats eat it. But you said it was one of God's creatures and it deserved a chance to grow up and fly. So he let us keep it in an old rabbit cage, and we fed it worms and beetles and whatever else we could catch. When it was big enough, we took it out to the cornfield and let it loose."

Tears swam in Suzanne's eyes, distorting her vision, but her memories were clear. She nodded. "I remember. We even prayed for it before we set it free, for God to keep it safe."

"Uh-huh." Clete's gaze shifted to somewhere beyond Suzanne's shoulder. He seemed to drift away into his memories. "We held hands while we watched the bird fly off, and I thought then my big sister could fix anything." He gave a little jolt and shot a resentful look at her. "When you're eight, you're pretty gullible. By the time you're in your thirties you should know better."

She whisked away her tears with her fingertips. "I'm sorry for letting you down. But Mother doesn't want me here. And I —"

He clomped past her and paused on the threshold. Sunshine lit his serious face and brought out the bronze of his skin. He looked so much like their father, more tears spurted into Suzanne's eyes. He flicked a loose curl of paint from the doorjamb with his fingertip and shrugged. "Don't worry about it. As I said, people change. It's my fault for thinking you were still the sister I remembered." A tight smile formed on his face. "We've managed this long without you. I guess we don't need you after all." He strode off without a backward glance.

CHAPTER 16

Abigail

Abigail felt a bit like a Roman goddess reclining in her lounge chair while Tanya, Alexa, and the children sat in a circle on a tattered quilt spread on the grass. Although they tried to include her — Tanya was especially ingratiating, continually asking her questions and offering her another scoop of fruit salad, more jam for her biscuit — Abigail was still apart, separated by the height of the lounger and her own self-imposed isolation.

She nibbled at a crisply fried chicken wing, listening to Julie and Jana squabble and Tanya referee. Tanya was so diplomatic. So patient. Abigail remembered being patient that way with her children. When she was young. Before the weight of guilt and the entanglement of lies had taken control of her. People blamed her ill temper and intolerance on her widowed state or the accident. But she knew better. Even before she'd lost Cecil and then the use of her legs, she'd lost her happiness. She had no hope of regaining any of them. So why shouldn't she be bitter?

Closing her eyes, she allowed herself to drift away. She'd always loved picnics. The children's merry chatter, the fresh spring breeze, and the aromas from the food teased her senses and carried her back to other days, other picnics, when she'd knelt on the blanket and doled out chicken legs and sandwiches and fruit to her children. Her lighthearted voice rang in the recesses of her mind — *"Careful, Clete, don't spill your lemonade or the ants will come marching two by two."* The days were sweet in her memory, and longing to return to those simpler, carefree times nearly turned her heart inside out.

"Daddy!"

The happy, childish voice reminded Abigail of her Sandra as a five-year-old greeting Cecil when he returned from his work in the fields. She opened her eyes, expecting to see Cecil amble across the yard, a wide grin on his tanned face, and little Sandra with yellow braids bouncing on her skinny shoulders race to leap into his arms. A square-jawed man approached, and a golden-haired child went running, but reality crowded out the tender remembrance. Cecil was gone. Sandra was grown. And she was a foolish old woman, pining for something that could never be.

Clete caught Jana's hand, and the corners of his lips even tipped up in a smile as he led her back to the quilt, but deep lines marched across his forehead, speaking of an inner torment. Questions rolled through Abigail's mind, but she kept them to herself as Clete sank down on the quilt next to his wife.

Tanya handed him a filled plate. "I'm sorry we didn't wait for you. The children were hungry."

"It's all right. I didn't expect you to wait." Clete extended one leg off the quilt into the grass and balanced the plate on his thigh. He held a fork in his hand, but he didn't dip into the food. "By the way, I asked Paul and Danny to join us. I figured we'd have enough to share with them, too."

Abigail stifled a groan. Wasn't it enough to bear Suzy's presence? Did she have to be subjected to the other one from whom she'd stolen something irreplaceable?

Jay waved his fists in the air. "Woohoo! I get to eat with Danny!"

"You won't have anything left to eat if you

don't settle down," Tanya chided. "You almost dumped your plate. Please be careful."

Jay whisked a sheepish look at this mother. "Sorry." He hunkered over his food.

Alexa frowned at Clete. "Where's Mom? She needs to eat, too."

He barely glanced at his niece. "She'll come when she's ready." Clete appeared to want to say something more, but then he jammed his fork into the potato salad and carried a large bite to his mouth.

Alexa set her plate aside and rose. "I'm going to find her. Sometimes she gets so busy she forgets to eat." She started around the blanket, but then she stopped. A smile lit her face. "Oh, here she comes. And Mr. Aldrich and his son are with her. I'll get them some plates."

Abigail wanted to ignore Suzy, the way she'd been doing all day. But something — maybe her reflections of past days or maybe something undefined — pulled her gaze in the direction of her daughter's approach. Suzy, the Aldrich boy, and Aldrich himself moved across the thick, greening grass. Soft, early evening sunlight bathed them in a gentle glow and combined their shadows into one large undulating form. The boy, who walked between them, was jabbering, his hands flying in wild gestures, his face turning to his father and then to Suzy. The adults laughed softly, and the man curled his hand around his son's neck while sending a smile at Suzy.

Abigail's breath caught in her throat as an idea formed. She'd thought it impossible to regain what she'd lost. But might there be a way to redeem at least some of her former happiness? She'd sent Suzy away from the one she'd claimed to love. If she brought them together again, might some of this heavy burden of guilt be lifted?

Although she'd vowed to scare Suzy back to Indiana as quickly as possible, a second plan now took shape in her mind. Suzy had taken a two-month leave of absence. Six weeks still remained of that time. Six weeks to rekindle what Paul and Suzy had once felt for each other. Six weeks to restore a portion of what she'd stolen from them.

Paul and Danny dropped onto the quilt next to Jay while Suzy sat next to Alexa. On opposite sides from each other. Abigail tightened her jaw in frustration. Six weeks . . . would it be enough? She'd better start *now.*

"Mr. Aldrich?"

Abigail didn't realize she'd screeched his name until all conversation around the quilt stopped and everyone stared at her in surprise. Heat filled her face, but she covered her embarrassment with a frown and a harsh command. "I was speaking to Mr. Aldrich only. The rest of you pay attention to your plates."

A grin toyed on the edges of the carpenter's mouth while the others ducked their heads and flicked glances at one another from the corners of their eyes. Satisfied she'd cowed them, she addressed Paul again.

"I don't know what Clete is paying you to work out here, but it probably isn't enough."

"What? Mother!"

She chose to ignore her son's disgruntled outburst. "So from now until the work is done, I want you to be our guest for meals on working days and also on Sunday noon. And of course, your son is welcome, too."

Tanya bounced a panicked look at Abigail. "Mother Zimmerman, tomorrow after service we're going to Shelley's. She might need more notice if —"

Abigail waved her hand, dismissing Tanya's concern. "Shelley always fixes enough for a small army. There will be plenty. If you're worried about it, Alexa here can always bake up a couple of cakes to take along, right, Alexa?"

She gave a slow nod, her expression wary. "Well, sure, Grandmother, if that's what you want."

"Good." Abigail smiled at Mr. Aldrich, feeling smug. "You just consider my family your family for the duration of your job." *And possibly beyond* . . . She plucked a piece of meat from the half-eaten chicken wing and stuck it in her mouth, hoping the others would follow her example and return to eating. After a few uncertain moments, they picked up their forks and soon conversation resumed, although a bit more restrained than it had been prior to her proclamation.

Abigail, pleased with herself, found a giggle threatening. The desire took her by surprise. She couldn't recall the last time she'd felt so giddy and hopeful. Surely she'd stumbled upon the perfect means of making restitution for the harm she'd inflicted on Suzy, Paul, and their daughters so many years ago . . . and at the same time, restoring her own happiness.

Paul

He shouldn't have come. Paul leaned into the sofa cushions and cringed as Shelley slapped two more plates on the table. He couldn't recall ever feeling as out of place as he did at this moment. Her husband,

Harper, had welcomed Paul and Danny exuberantly, giving no indication he viewed them as an intrusion, but Shelley's actions screamed otherwise. Yep, he should have refused Mrs. Zimmerman's bold invitation. Everyone in the fellowship knew not to disrupt Shelley Unruh's regimented schedule.

The women — except for Mrs. Zimmerman, of course — buzzed back and forth between the kitchen and the dining room like bees zipping between a flower bed and the hive. They carried bowls of vegetables and salads, platters of ham and baked pork chops, baskets of rolls, and so many relish plates Paul lost count.

Danny sat as still as a mouse beside him, his wide eyes watching as the center of the extended table became crowded with the bounty of food. Was Danny thinking of Sundays when he was small, when Karina was alive and healthy and able to host dinners in their home?

Back before Karina got sick, they'd enjoyed Sundays with lots of food and lots of guests. Paul had bantered with the men in the living room, just as Clete did now with his brothers-in-law, while Karina and the women prepared the table and the children chased in and out, earning reprimands from every direction. Although Shelley's behavior raised a prickle of unease, the remembrances were sweet. And the smells drifting from the dining room were wonderful. His stomach growled in anticipation. He wanted to enjoy the meal, to fellowship with this big, boisterous family. But he wouldn't linger. As soon as they'd finished eating, he'd leave.

Finally Shelley stepped into the wide doorway and sent an unsmiling look at her husband. "Harper, we need the piano bench. Everyone, gather around. Hurry now before the food is cold."

The men leaped to action as if given an order from an army sergeant. Clete pushed Mrs. Zimmerman's chair to the table while the others all slid into chairs without a moment's pause. Paul, his hand on Danny's shoulder, waited until the others were settled so he didn't accidentally take someone else's assigned spot.

Harper carried in the piano bench and placed it at the end of the table. Shelley pointed at the leather-upholstered bench. "Paul and Danny, have a seat."

"Shelley . . ." Harper grimaced. "They aren't going to fit on that thing together."

"Where else can I put them? We've used up everything including the rickety folding chairs putting everyone else around the table." Shelley lowered her voice to a raspy whisper, but it still carried clearly across the room.

Mrs. Zimmerman spoke up. "Put Ruby and Pearl on the bench. They're small enough to fit."

Shelley scowled. "I have Ruby and Pearl near me so I can help them with their plates."

"I'm right here close. I'll help them."

A collective, startled gasp rose from half of the adults. Paul gawked in surprise at Mrs. Zimmerman, too. Normally she was telling the youngsters to go somewhere else — they were grating on her nerves.

"Ruby and Pearl, come sit by Grandma," Mrs. Zimmerman went on, seemingly oblivious to Shelley's seething and the others' shock. "Shelley, you can sit there next to Harper now, and Danny and Paul can take the remaining two chairs. Danny, sit next to Mrs. Unruh so she and your father aren't bumping elbows. She's left-handed and tends to swing her elbow out too far sometimes."

Harper coughed — if Paul wasn't mistaken, the man was covering up a laugh. Shelley set her lips in a tight line and glared at her mother for several tense seconds while the people around the table from Sandra and Derek's three-year-old son all the way up to Clete sat like stone posts, waiting.

Then Harper moved to the chairs where his twins perched side by side. "C'mon, girls, go sit by your grandmother. Paul, Danny, have a seat."

The girls, Danny, and Paul followed Harper's directions while Shelley remained rooted in place, irritation pulsating from her stiff frame and steely expression. Harper took his wife by the elbow and guided her to the empty chairs at the head of the table. He seated her in one, his hand resting briefly on her shoulder in silent communication, before sliding into the last open chair. A stiff smile formed on his lips. "Shelley, do you want me to say grace, or should we ask our guest?"

She shrugged, her movement jerky. "Whatever you prefer."

Harper's smile seemed a bit more relaxed when he turned it on Paul. "Do you mind?"

Although right then Paul would have rather been burned at a stake than deliver a prayer with Shelley listening, he said, "Not at all."

Without a word of instruction, the Zimmerman family members joined hands.

Danny grabbed his father's right hand, and Paul automatically reached for the hand of the person on his left. And he found himself — for the first time since he was eighteen years old — holding hands with Suzy Zimmerman.

CHAPTER 17

Abigail

It was improper and even irreverent to keep one's eyes open during a prayer, but Abigail remained wide-eyed and watchful as Paul Aldrich delivered a prayer of gratitude. She'd inwardly cheered the serendipitous seating arrangement that put Paul and Suzy next to each other. When they linked hands, she'd hoped for some glimmer of reaction — of rekindling — between her daughter and her one-time beau, but to her disappointment the pair only seemed uncomfortable. A worry struck. Had too much time passed for them to remember the deep affection they'd shared?

"Amen."

As bowls and platters were passed around the table and conversation began to flow, Abigail contemplated how to ignite the old spark. She recalled some of the activities Suzy and Paul enjoyed with the other young people in the community, but she couldn't just blurt out a random topic that held significance only to the two of them. It had to occur naturally. So she cut up slices of ham for Ruby and Pearl, poured gravy over their potatoes, and buttered their rolls, all the while keeping her ear tuned for an opportunity to interject some snippet that would take Suzy and Paul back to the days of courtship.

After waiting nearly fifteen minutes, she nearly wiggled out of her wheelchair in delight when Sandra created an opening. "Derek and I took Ian fishing at Heidebrecht's pond yesterday, and Ian caught his first fish — a little sunfish."

"Oh, his first catch!" Abigail's voice blared out. She patted her lips with her napkin, bringing herself under control. She aimed her face at Sandra but watched Paul and Suzy out of the corner of her eye. "That pond has given youngsters their first fishing experience for years. It seems like only yesterday Suzanne came home, filthy dirty and smelling like she'd rolled in a half-dozen dead fish on a riverbank. She had a string of perch in her hand and a grin on her face. She was eight. No, nine. And she'd spent the afternoon fishing with . . ." She pretended to search her memory, then turned her smile on the pair of now grown-up fishermen. "With you, Paul, am I right?"

Neither Suzy nor Paul smiled. In fact, it appeared they ceased to breathe for several seconds. Then Paul swallowed, offered a brief, stiff semblance of a smile, and nodded. "Yeah, probably. Suzy — Suzanne and me . . . we did some fishing at the pond."

"Oh, not just some," Abigail corrected, a genuine chuckle rumbling at his sheepish look. "I recall a couple of summers when you two went fishing nearly every day."

Alexa sent her mother a speculative look. "You liked fishing, Mom? You've never seemed all that outdoorsy to me."

"Well, I suppose —"

Abigail cut off Suzanne's reply. "When your mother was a girl, she was half tomboy. Always running off to climb trees or ride bicycles or drop a fishing line. And more often than not, she was with Paul. The two of them were a little Tom Sawyer and Becky Thatcher all the way through junior high school." She sighed, true regret giving it a heaviness that surprised her. "Those were good days." She pinned Suzy with a firm look. "Weren't they?"

Her daughter's cheeks flamed red. "I . . . I suppose they were." She glanced at Paul, who glanced back, then they both ducked their heads.

Abigail tamped down another chortle. She'd managed to get their memories rolling. But she shouldn't push. She'd be quiet now. She cleaned her plate — Shelley was an excellent cook — while the grandchildren shared their stories about fishing, some of which were no doubt more fiction than fact, but the adults laughed and encouraged the tales anyway.

Shelley, who'd remained quiet throughout the entire meal, rose. "Suzanne, would you help me cut the cakes Alexa brought? It's time to serve dessert."

How dare Shelley interfere with Abigail's matchmaking scheme by pulling Suzy away from Paul! That girl was far too self-centered for her own good. Abigail snapped a suggestion. "Why not have Sandra help you?"

Shelley raised one eyebrow and met Abigail's glare with one of her own. "Because Suzanne doesn't have a toddler and isn't seven months into a pregnancy." She headed for the kitchen, calling over her shoulder, "Keep your forks, everyone, but stack everything else off to the side. Suzanne, hurry, please."

Abigail seethed in silence as Suzy and Alexa both followed Shelley into the kitchen. If Shelley said something hurtful and forced Suzy to turn tail and run, she'd never forgive the girl.

Suzanne

Suzanne's hand trembled as she pressed a knife through the layers of one of the two matching chocolate cakes. If she wasn't careful, she'd make a mess of Alexa's beautiful creation. But her stomach churned in intense nervousness, making her quiver from head to toe. What had compelled Mother to talk about the time she'd spent with Paul when she was younger? She'd seen Alexa perk up, taking in every word and giving her questioning looks. She didn't want ideas planted in her daughter's head.

"Cut half servings for the children," Shelley instructed as she clanked plates onto the counter next to Suzanne, her strident voice sounding like Mother's. "They don't need so much sugar."

Suzanne glanced at her younger sister. Her sour expression matched the one their mother usually wore. Mother was older, widowed, and confined to a wheelchair, all reasons to be irritable. Shelley was still young — not yet thirty — but she behaved like an embittered old woman. What had happened to the bashful, sweet-natured little girl Suzanne remembered? Thinking of the little sister she'd once known, she answered kindly. "I will. Should I slice larger pieces for the men than for the women?"

"I don't care. But don't cut one for me." Shelley poured water into the coffee percolator. "Chocolate gives me indigestion."

Alexa looked up from the cake she was cutting. "I'm sorry, Aunt Shelley. I wish I'd known. I made chocolate because Grandmother likes it so much."

Shelley sniffed, plopping the percolator on the stove. "It doesn't really matter." She wiped her hands down her starched apron, her chin high. "As long as Mother and everyone else is happy with chocolate, I'll be fine." She marched out of the kitchen into the dining room, calling, "Who will want coffee with their cake?"

Alexa whispered, "Why didn't you tell me Aunt Shelley doesn't like chocolate? I could have made a carrot cake or strawberry tarts instead of the second chocolate cake. Now I feel bad."

"Don't feel bad." Suzanne sensed Shelley wanted them to feel guilty. Why play into her childish tantrum? "To be honest, I didn't know chocolate gave her indigestion." *How could you possibly know . . ."* Clete's words came back to haunt her, and despite her determination not to give way to guilt, the emotion washed through her. But she wouldn't let it touch Alexa. "You made two beautiful cakes with no motivation other than kindness and complete sincerity. If Shelley can't appreciate the effort, it's her problem, not yours."

Alexa smiled weakly. "Thanks, Mom."

Another thought occurred to Suzanne. "In fact, go peek in the refrigerator."

With a puzzled expression, Alexa crossed to the refrigerator and opened the door.

"Is there anything that looks like a dessert?"

Alexa leaned down, and the sound of aluminum foil being peeled back reached Suzanne's ears. Then Alexa giggled. "There's a whole pan of lemon bars in here."

Suzanne grinned. "Bring them out. Shelley will have dessert after all."

Alexa carried the pan to the counter, her smile wide. "I might have one, too. They look great."

Suzanne peeked into the pan at the crumbly bars. "Mm, they do look good. And I bet a couple of others —" She froze, suddenly recalling Paul's preference for lemon meringue pie. She'd baked him one for his sixteenth birthday, and he told her she could bake a lemon meringue pie every week for the rest of his life and he wouldn't complain. Had his wife baked him lemon meringue pies?

Alexa nudged her. "Mom? You didn't finish your sentence."

Suzanne gave herself a mental shake and forced a smile. "Sorry. I got lost in thought there for a minute. I think some others might like a lemon bar, too. Let's serve both." A different kind of tremble attacked as she followed Alexa into the dining room with the plate of lemon bars in her hand. She sucked in a steadying breath, determined not to react to Paul's face lighting in pleasure at the sight of the treat. But her concern was unfounded. The chairs where he and Danny had been sitting were empty.

An odd disappointment gripped her, but she pushed it aside and smiled as she held the plate high. "Shelley had lemon bars ready, and Alexa baked chocolate cake. Pass these bars around while Alexa and I serve the cake."

The children finished their dessert quickly and asked to be excused. They darted out to the backyard to play while the adults savored cups of coffee with their sweets. As soon as the back door slammed behind the last child, Shelley turned to Suzanne.

"Since we're all here and our guests have gone, can we clear the air?"

Harper touched his wife's hand, glancing toward Alexa. "This might not be the right time."

Shelley jerked her hand free. "She's nineteen — all grown up. I think she can handle it."

Sandra cupped her swollen belly and looked from Shelley to Suzanne and then to her mother. "What are you talking about?"

Mother caught the wheels of her chair and rolled it away from the table. "Shelley, if you are going to start one of your tirades, I want to go home. I'm not in any mood for it."

Shelley gawked at Mother. "You're the one who started it, berating us for bringing her here! Well, you need to know she doesn't intend to stay." She turned a condemning glare on Suzanne. "Isn't that what you told Clete? You're leaving?"

Alexa's jaw dropped.

Mother, her hands still curled around the wheels, froze in place. "You're leaving, Suzanne? When?"

Suzanne sent Clete a helpless look, but he angled his face away, his jaw clenched. Had he told Shelley with the intention of starting a family feud, or had he only needed to vent with someone? She wished she knew him well enough to understand his motives. She rounded the table and placed her hand over Mother's arm. "I told Clete I would be leaving as soon as I made arrangements for another nurse."

"Which she expects *us* to pay for," Shelley inserted.

Apparently Clete had left out part of their conversation. As kindly and straightforwardly as she could, Suzanne shared with her mother everything she'd told Clete about locating qualified people. Sandra and Alexa looked stricken, Shelley seemed to simmer with contained fury, and Tanya hung her head. The men shifted in their chairs, their gazes aimed anywhere except at Suzanne. Their discomfort would have been comical had the situation been different.

Suzanne finished, "I think it's best, Mother, to hire someone else."

Mother glared at her. "You think it's better for me to be with strangers?"

"You and I . . ." Suzanne swallowed a knot of anguish. "We're strangers, too."

Derek cleared his throat. "Suzanne?" He slipped his arm around his wife's shoulders. "I won't say I'm not disappointed. Ever since I met Sandra, she's talked about the sister who left when she was very small and how much she wanted to know you. She's been so happy to have you home."

A single sob broke from Sandra's throat. She turned her face into her husband's chest. He patted her back as he went on. "But I also think I understand. After all, you've established yourself in Indiana. That's your home now, and we pulled you out of it. We were all thinking about what was best for us. Not what was best for you. So . . ." Derek glanced at the Zimmerman siblings one by one, as if waiting for one of them to confirm or deny what he'd said.

Tanya grimaced, her expression contrite. "Maybe I was being selfish, wanting someone else to take care of Mother Zimmerman. With our kids still so young, I have my hands full already. It seemed overwhelming, going out to the farm so often. Not that I don't love you, Mother Zimmerman, but . . ." Her voice trailed off, too.

Shelley tossed her head, making her black ribbons dance on her shoulders. "Well, I'm not going to make some grand speech about being selfish. I haven't been selfish. I've done more than my fair share, having to grow up overnight and become Mother's helper when Suzanne left, then being nurse after Mother's accident. I've put in plenty of time to this family. Just as Clete and Sandra have done. It's Suzanne's turn, and that's all I have to say about it."

Harper leaned close and whispered something to her, but Shelley shook her head and folded her arms over her chest.

Tension tingled in the room. No one spoke. Suzanne waited for Shelley to explode, for Sandra to beg, for Clete as the man of the family to take charge and say something that would settle everyone's nerves. But they all remained closemouthed.

The back door slapped open and a child called, "Mama! Ruby fell and scraped her knee. She's bleeding and needs a bandage."

Shelley bolted out of her chair, mumbling, "She better not have gotten blood on her dress." She charged around the corner and the door slammed again.

Another bout of silence fell. Finally Alexa stood. Everyone looked at her, and something in her daughter's eyes made Suzanne's pulse speed up. Alexa turned slowly, her gaze meeting Suzanne's, and so many emotions that Suzanne couldn't identify them all glittered in her dark eyes.

"I know when you asked Mom to come you weren't inviting me here." She looked at Sandra. "But I've wondered about all of you ever since I was little. I've wanted to meet you, to know you." Turning to Clete, she continued in a quiet voice. "We never had the chance because you didn't even know I'd been born."

Alexa shifted again, this time looking at her grandmother. "I'm sorry I was the reason Mom had to go away. I'm sorry that keeping me meant she couldn't come home. And mostly I'm sorry that you're all so angry with each other. It's just been Mom and me, so I can't pretend to know what it's like to be a big family, but I don't think being mad is the way it's supposed to be."

Alexa drew in a big breath and faced Suzanne. Tears shimmered on her lashes. "Mom, I don't blame you for wanting to go back to Indiana. If you want to go right away, I won't stop you. But I . . ." She lowered her head for a moment, as if gathering courage. When she looked up, her expression seemed to entreat Suzanne for understanding. "I want to stay here. With my family."

CHAPTER 18

Paul

"Dad?"

Paul jerked, roused from a place of semi-sleep. "What?"

Danny plopped the Sugar Creek Gang mystery he'd been reading onto the sofa cushion and scowled. "Why couldn't we have stayed longer over at the Unruh's? I bet Jay and his cousins are having a lot of fun right now, and I could be playing with them instead of sitting here listening to you snore."

"Was I snoring?"

"Yeah." Danny huffed. "We didn't even get dessert, and Jay said it was gonna be chocolate cake his cousin made. He said Alexa's the best baker ever — even better than his mom." He slapped his hand over his mouth, his eyes wide. "That was supposed to be a secret."

Despite the weight of discomfort still resting on his chest, Paul couldn't hold back a short laugh. Although usually done in innocence rather than spite, Danny had never been able to resist repeating what he heard. All the more reason to have bustled him out of Harper and Shelley's house quickly this afternoon. Given time, Mrs. Zimmerman might have shared more stories about Suzy and him, and Danny would have eventually blabbed them on the school playground or, worse, the churchyard. He'd been wise to leave early.

"It's all right. I won't tell Jay's mother what he said."

Danny slumped in relief. Then he aimed a squinty-eyed look at his father. "But why didn't we stay? When we go to other people's houses for the Sunday meal, we always stay longer." He chewed the corner of his lip. "Is it because Ruby and Pearl's mom was so grumpy?"

"In part." Paul pushed the footrest down on his recliner and rested his elbows on his knees. "The Zimmerman family is big, so there were a lot of people to feed. I thought we might be in the way." He hadn't lied to Danny, but he'd withheld a portion of the truth. He had no intention of telling his son how hard he'd found it to listen to Suzy Zimmerman's mother reminisce about their

Tom Sawyer–Becky Thatcher days. "I tell you what, when I go to work in the morning I'll ask Alexa if there was any cake left over, and if there was, I'll ask if I can bring you a piece for tomorrow's supper. Okay?"

"Okay." Danny didn't sound cheered.

"Now what's wrong?"

Danny sighed. "It's not just the cake. I'm bored. I thought I'd get to play with the kids for a while. I know they're all younger than me, but still . . ."

A familiar regret gripped Paul. He and Karina had wanted and prayed for a large family but they'd only had one child. As much as he thanked God for his son, there were days when he wished he'd been blessed with, as his father would have put it, a full quiver. Especially now with Karina gone, Danny often spoke of loneliness. He would have been an attentive, loving brother.

"Well, then," Paul suggested in his brightest voice, "how about you get out the Parcheesi board?"

Danny bounced up, flipping the book onto its face. "Really?"

"Sure. See if you can skunk your ol' dad."

"Okay!" He took off at a trot for the hall closet where their games were stored.

Paul and Danny played three rounds of Parcheesi with Danny winning two to Paul's one and gloating all the while. Paul laughed, teased, chatted with his son, but underneath a lingering sadness refused to leave. Danny was lonely not having any brothers or sisters. And Paul was lonely, too. Sitting at dinner tables with families, watching husbands interact with their wives, had been painful during the first months of his widower status. But now when he saw a man slip his arm around his wife's shoulders or lean in to whisper something meant only for her ears, he only felt deep envy. He missed having a wife. Karina had been gone for over three years already — sufficient time for the fellowship to approve Paul seeking another marriage partner.

He watched Danny roll the dice and tap his little game piece across the board. A prayer formed in the back of his heart. *Lord, guide me to the woman You would choose to become part of our family. Bring me the one who will love Danny as her own and be the partner I need. I'm ready.* Maybe, if he were very blessed, another child or two would one day call him Dad.

Suzanne

Suzanne parked the car as close to the house as possible and turned off the motor. The silence that fell with the engine's hushed rumble nearly smothered her. None of the car's occupants — not she, Alexa, or Mother — had spoken one word on the drive from Shelley's to the farm.

Words hovered on her tongue. Statements of protest, declarations of worry, heart-wrenching queries. But she gritted her teeth and kept them inside because her emotions were too raw, her anger and hurt too intense to allow them to escape. She'd inflict damage if she gave her tongue free rein. So instead she silently prayed and waited for the tidal wave of hurt and confusion to pass. When she felt in control, she would talk to Alexa. But not until then.

From the backseat Mother said, "Do you suppose the ramp Paul built to the porch door is ready for use? I'd like to try it out rather than making you carry me up the front stairs."

"Mom, do you want me to go back and check on it?" Alexa asked.

Her overly sweet tone offered evidence of how troubled she was by her mother's stony silence, but Suzanne couldn't find the strength to reassure her. She felt bruised and battered. And Alexa, her precious daughter, had inflicted the blows with her spoken desire to remain here in Arborville rather than return to Indiana.

Suzanne sighed tiredly. "Go ahead. I'll get the wheelchair from the trunk."

Alexa darted off, leaving the passenger door open. Suzanne did the same, ignoring the car's beeping signal that the keys were still in the ignition. The *beep . . . beep . . . beep,* shrill and obtrusive against the peacefulness of the late Sunday afternoon, should have raised a complaint from Mother, but she sat quiet and patient in the backseat. But then why shouldn't she be happy now? She'd won. Alexa wanted to stay.

Suzanne slammed the trunk and unfolded the chair with stiff, jerky motions as Alexa trotted across the yard. An uncertain smile hovered on her lips.

"I walked up and down it twice, and it seemed firm. So I took down the ropes." She paused, as if waiting for affirmation.

Suzanne gave the chair a push toward the car's back door. "Fine." Then she remembered securing the porch door. "I'll need to unlatch the door or we won't be able to get in through the back. Wait here."

By the time she unlocked the front door and made her way through the house to the back porch, Alexa had already pushed Mother around the yard and was waiting at the base of the ramp.

Suzanne pulled the door inward and

frowned. "How did you get her out of the car by yourself?"

Alexa sent her mother a puzzled look. "I did an assist-transfer. I know how it's done. I've watched you plenty of times."

"I told you to wait."

Alexa drew back as if she'd been slapped. "I . . . I'm sorry, Mom. Grandmother was eager to see the ramp, so —"

Suzanne held up one hand. "It isn't important. She's here now. Bring her in."

"I'm sitting right here listening," Mother said, but instead of snide she sounded almost playful, "and I want to bring the chair up the ramp by myself." She chuckled. "Or at least try. So move back, both of you, and let me see what I can do."

Alexa didn't release the wheelchair's handles. She looked at Suzanne questioningly. Suzanne doubted Mother would be able to make it all the way on her own — she'd only propelled her chair on flat surfaces — but she didn't have the energy to argue with her. She gave a brusque nod, and after a moment's hesitation, Alexa stepped away from the chair.

Suzanne wrung her hands and watched her mother take hold of the rubber grips and push. The chair rolled forward half a foot. Mother slipped her hands backward

244

on the grip, and the chair inched backward half the distance. With a little grunt, Mother pushed again, repeating the forward six inches, backward three progress.

Alexa hovered behind the chair, her hands upraised and her lower lip pinched between her teeth. She caught Suzanne's eye, asking silently, *Should I help?* Although Suzanne was tempted to nod — Mother's face glowed bright red and the veins in her neck stood out — she shook her head. Mother wanted to be independent. They should give her the chance.

Ten minutes after she applied her hands to the grips, Mother gave the chair a final push and crossed the porch's threshold. Alexa bounded up the ramp and wrapped her grandmother in a hug from behind. "You did it, Grandmother! You did it!"

Mother, sweat rivulets rolling down her temples, patted Alexa's arms and turned a grin of triumph on Suzanne. "I did. I sure did."

Suzanne didn't add her congratulations. Because she wasn't envisioning her mother's success at mastering the ramp. No, her mind filled with ugly images of her mother stealing away her child. She couldn't even muster a smile.

Mother's broad grin faded. She gave

Alexa's arm a slight push, and Alexa straightened. Once again taking hold of the grips, Mother aimed her chair for the kitchen doorway. She rolled past Suzanne slowly, her shoulders slumped as if a load had been strapped to her back. When she reached the threshold, she said with her face aimed forward, "Someone give me a little boost over the hump and take me to my room. I want to rest. And as soon as I'm settled, I think you two should talk."

Once again Alexa bustled forward, usurping Suzanne's position as helper, and gave her grandmother's chair a push over the threshold and then through the cleared pathway in the midst of the construction mess. Suzanne trailed behind and watched Alexa roll the chair through Mother's doorway. Then Alexa closed the door.

Soon the sound of soft voices and scuffling noises crept across the room to Suzanne's ears. She should go in and help. She'd vowed to be Mother's assistant until she found a full-time nurse. But her feet refused to budge. She did not want to see Mother and Alexa working together, talking together, growing together. Her chest ached. Why hadn't she refused Clete's request to return? She could not give up her daughter all over again.

The bedroom door opened and Alexa stood in the frame. "Have a good rest, Grandmother. I'll wake you by five so you don't miss supper." Mother mumbled something in reply to which Alexa offered a light laugh, then she closed the door behind her, turned, and spotted Suzanne. The smile died on her lips.

The look of apprehension on Alexa's face pierced Suzanne's mother-heart. She'd put it there with her silence. Mother had suggested they talk, and as difficult as it would be to share her hurt with her daughter without divulging more than she was ready to share, they needed to talk. *Lord, let me convince her to come home with me. Please don't let me lose her. Please, please . . .* The sting of tears accompanied her plea, and she blinked rapidly.

Alexa hadn't moved.

Suzanne forced a wobbly smile. "Did you get her settled in?"

"Yes." Alexa glanced at her wristwatch. "I'll wake her in an hour."

Had she offered the time as a hint? How Suzanne hated this feeling of uncertainty, as if she'd somehow lost her connection with her daughter. "Then . . . how about we . . ." Would Alexa understand?

After a moment's pause, Alexa nodded. "I

think we should." She angled her head, almost seeming to give a challenge. "Can we go outside, though? So we don't bother Grandmother."

Apparently Alexa expected a noisy argument. Suzanne didn't have the energy for a noisy argument. She hoped she'd be able to muster enough strength to speak plainly. But the afternoon was pleasant, and the porch swing provided a good spot to sit. So outside was fine. "Of course."

"Good." Alexa took off toward the kitchen, moving past Suzanne in a determined stride. "Grandmother was just telling me I should visit the old summer kitchen where you played house when you were a little girl. Let's go there."

CHAPTER 19

Alexa

She'd thought the exterior of the house was dreary, but it seemed well kept compared to the dilapidated appearance of the building Grandmother had called the summer kitchen. For a moment Alexa questioned the wisdom of entering it. Would the roof cave in? But Mom didn't seem concerned. She forced the door open and stepped into the dim interior. So Alexa followed.

She glanced around the dusty space, trying to envision what the room might have looked like when Mom was a little girl. Her active imagination allowed her to paint the woodwork bright white, hang flowered wallpaper on the walls, and decorate the space with cheerful curtains, furniture, and a rug made of braided strips of rags. Her lips twitched into a grin, picturing Mom busily stirring up pretend soup at the iron stove and serving it to her dolls.

"Alexa?"

Mom's quiet voice chased the cheerful images into hiding. Alexa turned slowly and met her mother's gaze. Very little light made its way past the filthy windows, but even in the shadows Alexa recognized sadness in Mom's eyes. No amount of imagination could change that reality. And what she needed to say would only make Mom sadder, but she had to say it. She had to *do* it. She'd spent too many years wondering and hoping to give up on gaining her family now.

"Mom, I know you're upset with me." She dove into the subject without preamble, still standing in the middle of the dusty floor with cobwebs swaying over her head like a jellyfish's stingers. "And I'm sorry that I upset you. But I'm not ready to go yet. I don't know them yet. They don't know me. I want more time here. I need it."

Mom reached out and caught the arched back of a chair frame as if she needed something to hold her upright. "I'm sorry I haven't been enough family for you, Alexa."

Anger stirred in Alexa's chest. Mom's comment felt manipulative — too much like Grandmother had been when they'd first arrived and how Aunt Shelley was all the time. She expected better from Mom. "Don't."

Mom arched one brow.

"Don't try to make me feel guilty."

Mom lowered her head. "You're right. I shouldn't have said it that way — like a petulant child." She looked into Alexa's face again. "But I'm frightened. Your entire life, it's been you and me . . . and God. I put my focus on raising you and loving you. Every day I prayed that I would be able to fill your need for mother and father and brothers and sisters. So it hurts to realize how much I failed."

"You didn't —"

"I must have, or you wouldn't choose them over me."

"I'm not choosing them over you, Mom. I'm choosing them in addition to you." Alexa crossed the floor, kicking up dust as she came, and grabbed her mother's cold hands. "Why does it have to be one or the other? Now that they finally know I was born and that you kept me, why can't I have both you and them? It isn't a competition."

"Not to you maybe, but —" Mom's voice broke. She squeezed Alexa's hands so hard her fingers ached. "I don't want to lose you."

"You aren't going to lose me." Alexa felt as though she were the grownup comforting a child. Although she didn't understand her mother's fear, she recognized its depth in

Mom's frantic grip on her hands and in the pallor of her face. "You're my mother. Nothing can change that."

Mom let go of Alexa's hands and grabbed her in a fierce embrace. Mom's shoulders shuddered with silent sobs and Alexa clung hard, offering assurance with her hug. "Promise me, Alexa." Mom choked out the words. "Promise you'll always be my daughter."

Confused and more than a little frightened by her mother's desperate plea, she managed to speak firmly. "I promise, Mom."

Mom held tight for several more seconds before finally relaxing her grip. She stepped back and quickly wiped the tears from her face. Then she cupped Alexa's cheeks. A sad smile tugged at her lips. "I'm so sorry. Will you forgive me?"

"Of course." Alexa answered promptly, but she wasn't entirely sure why Mom needed forgiveness.

Mom seemed to wilt. She took a step back and pulled in a long, slow breath. As she expelled the air, color returned to her cheeks, making her look more like herself. Her before-coming-to-Arborville self. "I think I'll go in and lie down. Will you wake me when you wake your grandmother? Then I'll make sandwiches and cut up some fruit for supper."

"Sure." Alexa watched her mother until she disappeared inside the house, then she sank onto one of the rickety chairs to replay their conversation. Given Mom's fear, even though it seemed irrational, maybe she should change her mind and go back to Indiana when Mom went. Her heart hurt as she considered forfeiting the chance to really know and become a part of the extended Zimmerman family.

She was much older than her cousins, so she couldn't be their playmate, but she could be something like an aunt or older sister to them. Sandra had already begun treating her like a younger sister, and Shelley might grow to accept her. Eventually. With time. As for Clete . . . She chewed her lip. She wasn't sure what to make of Uncle Clete. He was pleasant, never gruff or rude to her, but he held himself apart from Mom and from her. How did one break down a man's barriers? Not having any other male relatives, she really wanted to know Uncle Clete.

Grandmother, in spite of her snappishness and complaints, had found a place in her life for Alexa, and she didn't want to give up the newfound kinship. But if it was so hurtful for Mom, should she? Alexa rose and ambled around the room, idly running her fingers over torn edges of wallpaper and the dust-covered surfaces while her thoughts continued to roll.

They'd only been in Arborville eleven days. Eleven days was not enough time, given the years of separation, to develop or rebuild relationships. She didn't want to hurt her mother, but she didn't think Mom was being fair to her family, her daughter, or herself. Whether Mom wanted to admit it or not, she needed her family as much as Alexa wanted them. She'd been alone and on her own long enough. It was time to be a true Zimmerman again.

Alexa paced back and forth, planning what she would say to Mom when she went to wake her. She whispered the words, sampling the right vocal inflection to be kind yet convincing. "You have enough leave to stay here for the whole two months, so why not use it? Think of it as one month for every decade of absence — that's a small price to pay to make up for lost time, isn't it? The longer you're here, the more comfortable your sisters and brother —"

She shook her head. She should mention Grandmother first. "The more comfortable your mother, brother, and sisters will become with you. And, of course, the more comfortable you'll become with them." Her feet sped in their journey back and forth, and she began gesturing, her hands stirring the musty air. "As you told Grandmother, you're really strangers right now. It'll take time to get to know each other again, but it'll be time well spent. Life is short. Family is important. Take the time, Mom. Take the time . . ."

She paused, her brow furrowing, as she imagined her mother's response. Linda always called Mom determined, but Alexa knew it was pure stubbornness. Once Mom set her mind to something, she followed through. An admirable trait most of the time, but right now? Alexa wanted her mother to tuck her obstinacy in a drawer. She might need to offer a compromise of sorts to change Mom's mind.

At once an idea struck. She hugged herself and giggled as the idea grew. She'd need help. Tanya would help, and Sandra would, too. It might take some real pushing to get Clete and Shelley involved, but Sandra — cute, sweet, pregnant Sandra — would be the most likely one to win them over.

Tomorrow was Sandra's turn to bring supper out to the farm. As soon as her mother's youngest sister arrived, Alexa would take her aside and share her plan.

She smiled, envisioning Sandra's happy laugh and quick agreement. With a light step, Alexa headed for the house. She *would* reunite Mom with her family, and she *would* secure a place for herself in their affections. Once she'd accomplished those goals, then she would be willing to go back to Indiana. Then everyone would be happy.

Paul

Monday morning, instead of parking in the back, Paul pulled his pickup up, tailgate first, to the front of the house. He'd loaded the bed with treated lumber, a post-hole digger, paint, and everything else he needed to complete the second wheelchair ramp.

As much as he disliked leaving the kitchen in such a mess, he couldn't resist taking advantage of the pleasant late-spring days to work outside. The back-porch ramp had been a one-day project given its simple concrete slab construction. But the one in the front would include two long stretches running parallel with the porch and turning at a landing. The front-porch floor stood three feet higher than the ground, so a single ramp with a 1/12 pitch would extend too far into the yard and look, as Danny had laughingly said, like a long tongue sticking out.

After making several sketches on graph paper, he finally created a design that would be functional but would also blend in with the porch. Clete hadn't said anything about making the ramp pretty, but the old farmhouse with its wraparound porch surrounded by a railing and sawn balusters possessed a charm Paul didn't wish to destroy. Mrs. Zimmerman might actually allow someone to repaint the house and repair the broken decorative brackets. When that day came, he didn't want someone pointing at the ramp and complaining about its ungainly appearance.

The front ramp would take at least two days to build. Maybe more. He wanted to have it done by the time school let out the twenty-second of May. After that, he'd have Danny with him every day. He could keep his son busy inside with sweeping sawdust, collecting nails, and the other little tasks that stole Paul's construction time. None of those activities were potentially dangerous or too difficult for a nine-year-old. But the ramp? It involved cutting and fitting two-by-fours, securing balusters into a frame, careful measuring and focus. With Danny underfoot, he'd be distracted and the boy might try to use some of the power tools out of curiosity. It was better to finish the ramp on his own.

As he unloaded his pickup, the front door opened and Suzy's daughter stepped out on the porch. She held a cup of coffee in one hand and a plate with some sort of crumbly cake and a fork in the other. She moved to the edge of the porch and held both items toward Paul. "Would you like some breakfast? Cinnamon-apple streusel coffee-cake . . ."

He'd already eaten a bowl of cold cereal before taking Danny to school, but who could resist an invitation like that one? Paul dropped the load of lumber he'd lifted from the truck's bed and brushed his hands on his pant legs as he crossed to the bottom of the risers. The closer he got to the plate, the richer the smell of cinnamon and nutmeg became. He grinned and took the cup and plate. "According to Jay, you're a better baker than Tanya, and she has a reputation for being one of the best in Arborville."

The girl blushed. "Well, lucky for you, Mom made the coffee. I can't figure out the percolator. Ovens are pretty standard, though, and anyone can operate one."

Paul wouldn't know. He tended to purchase frozen casseroles and canned vegetables. Maybe he and Danny didn't eat as healthy as most families in Arborville, but they hadn't starved, either. He sat on the lowest riser, set the coffee cup beside his hip, then bowed his head over the plate. When he lifted his head after praying, he discovered Alexa had sat on the top riser on the opposite side of the stairs. Having her so near, with no one around as chaperone, left him with an uneasy feeling. Would Suzy approve?

Before he could suggest she go back inside, she said, "Mr. Aldrich, may I ask you a question? It's about the Old Order religion."

Paul forked up a bite of the moist cake, giving himself a moment to contemplate her request. No one would consider talking about religion unseemly. He nodded.

"Do you celebrate birthdays?"

Paul almost choked on his bite. He'd expected her to ask about doctrine or why the women wore caps or . . . something. The subject of birthdays hardly seemed religious in nature. He held back a laugh and answered as seriously as she'd asked. "Yes, we do."

The girl blew out a big breath, a smile breaking over her face. When she smiled, her brown eyes sparkled, bringing out their golden flecks. She was pretty even though she didn't look anything like Suzy or the other Zimmermans. "I'm so glad. You see, I have this idea, but last night I woke up wondering if it was even allowed. Some religious groups, like the Jehovah's Witnesses, don't celebrate birthdays, you know. And even though Mom and I were here on Mother's Day, nobody brought Grandmother flowers or a card or anything. So I didn't know if I should even mention it to Sandra, which I planned to do this evening, until I knew for sure. So your answer makes me very happy."

Paul teasingly reamed his ear with his fingertip and squinted at her. "Huh?"

She laughed again, seeming no older than Danny's age. "I'm sorry. Mom scolds me all the time about getting carried away. But when I'm excited about something, I just get, well, gung-ho!"

Paul took another bite of the cake, enjoying the way the cinnamon lingered in his mouth. "So . . . what are you all gung-ho about?"

Alexa looked right and left before leaning forward slightly and whispering, "A surprise party for Grandmother."

Paul swallowed the last of his cake and drowned it with coffee. He wasn't one to put a damper on someone's excitement, but he wasn't sure hosting a surprise party for

Mrs. Zimmerman was a good idea. The surprise might end up being on Alexa when the woman spouted in irritation and sent everyone out of the house. She hadn't welcomed visitors in years.

He cradled the coffee cup between his palms, trying to decide whether he should mention his concern or not. He didn't know Alexa at all, and it wasn't his place to advise her, but someone needed to at least give her a warning. "You said you're going to talk to Sandra about it?"

The girl nodded.

Sandra was a sweetheart — everyone said so — and she'd be too kindhearted to tell Alexa to forget the idea. "Why not Clete?" He didn't mention Shelley. Shelley would set Alexa straight, but she'd crush the girl in the process. He often pitied Harper Unruh, who spent a great deal of time apologizing for his wife's critical behavior.

Alexa wrinkled her nose. "I can't see Uncle Clete wanting to help blow up balloons or attach streamers all over the room. No, parties are really women's things."

"Then why not your mom?"

The girl sent a furtive glance over her shoulder. She whispered again. "Because part of the surprise is for Mom. Kind of a welcome-home-again party. Mom left when

261

she was so young, she missed a lot of birthdays with her family. I want this party to help make up for that." Her brow pinched into lines of worry. "Does that make sense?"

Paul handed Alexa the empty plate and cup, rising as he did so. "It makes sense. And I wish you well with it." In other words, he hoped it wouldn't blow up in her face. "Thanks for the coffeecake. Jay was right — that was delicious. You're quite the accomplished baker for someone so young." Old Order girls had conquered cooking by the time they were fifteen, but Alexa hadn't been raised Old Order.

She shrugged. "I like doing it."

"Maybe you should open a bakery. I bet lots of people would line up to buy your cakes."

She ducked her head, and pink crept across her cheeks. "Thanks."

For reasons he wouldn't explore, pleasing her with his comment gave him a lift. "And speaking of buying your cakes . . . Danny was very disappointed he didn't get a piece of chocolate cake yesterday for dessert. Do you have any left?"

"More than half of a cake. Several people ate Aunt Shelley's lemon bars instead."

His mouth watered. Maybe he should have stuck around. It had been a long time since he'd enjoyed a lemon-flavored dessert. The store-bought frozen lemon pies always fell short in his estimation. "So can I buy a slice or two from you?"

With another crinkle of her nose, she shook her head. "Nope. I don't run a bakery, so I don't sell my baked goods. I'll wrap up two big slices — one for you and one for Danny."

"Thanks."

"Thank you for being willing to answer my question." She paused. "May I ask one more?"

He needed to get busy, but the girl was so polite, he couldn't refuse her. "Sure."

"This house . . ." Alexa's gaze made a sweep across the house's front. "It sure needs a paint job. How much do you think it would cost to make it look nice again?"

Although Paul wasn't a painter, he'd purchased enough cans for smaller projects to be able to give an idea. "For the primer and paint, I'd say around fifteen hundred dollars."

Delight bloomed on her face. "Is that all?"

Paul stifled a laugh. *All?* Of course a teenager wouldn't recognize that fifteen hundred dollars was a significant amount of money. "For the paint. Hiring someone to do the painting adds another five to seven thousand."

"So sixty-five to eighty-five hundred might cover it?"

"That'd be a close estimate, I'd say."

The girl seemed unaffected by the amount. "And how long would it take?"

Paul scratched his head. "A house this size? If you had a crew on it, less than a week probably."

"And are there painting crews for hire in Arborville?"

She *was* gung-ho. She reminded him of Pepper holding tight to a choice steak bone. "Pratt or Wichita are the closest big cities, so they would be your best bet for hiring a crew." Of course, professional crews were probably already booked for spring and summer. He didn't want to trample her plans — she was a nice kid and seemed sincere in her desire to do something kind for her grandmother — but someone needed to give her a dose of reality. "If you're serious about getting this place painted, don't put off calling. The good crews schedule well in advance, so . . ." Would she understand?

She nodded. "All right. I'll make some calls today. Thanks. Bye now, Mr. Aldrich." Alexa headed inside, moving gracefully, her long dark ponytail swishing across her shoulder blades.

Paul stood for a moment gazing after her. She was a pretty girl, polite, giving, and surprisingly mature for one so young. Suzy'd done a good job raising her. But why had she raised her all alone? Where was Alexa's father?

CHAPTER 20

Suzanne

With Alexa seeing to Mother's needs, Suzanne found herself with a free morning. After a restless night in her old bed — tossing and turning, praying and crying — she'd determined the best thing for everyone was for her to depart as quickly as possible. She'd beg Alexa if she had to, but she wouldn't leave her daughter behind. Once they were gone, Mother and her siblings could fall back into their own routines and everyone would be happy. Or at least be satisfied.

Because Mother and Alexa were in the dining room and Paul was making a racket out front, Suzanne chose to return to the summer kitchen to use the Internet connection on Alexa's cell phone to finalize hiring a caretaker. Notepad and pen in hand, as well as a bucket of cleaning supplies — she intended to at least remove the grime from the tabletop and chairs before making use of the furnishings — she headed across the grass, still damp from the morning's dew.

So many scents filled the air. Spring in Kansas in the country was a glorious time, and she inhaled deeply of the rich aromas of soil, grass, and lilacs. If the scents could be bottled, she'd choose to surround herself with the fragrance of a Kansas spring every day of the year. The hardy winter wheat was already knee high, and she paused for a moment to gaze across the field. The green tips swaying in the breeze gave the appearance of ocean waves. The rain had been a gift to the area farmers, giving their crops the moisture needed to grow strong and full. Clete should enjoy a good return this year.

As a child, she'd always loved harvest time. All the men of the community would move from farm to farm, working together to bring in the wheat, then the corn and soybeans. When she lived in Arborville, she'd taken their cooperation for granted. She'd known no other way. But after being away from the small Old Order community for so many years, she understood the uniqueness of their cooperation — everyone doing his share, each patiently waiting for his turn to host rather than demanding to be first. Having witnessed the world's "all about me" attitude, the fellowship — the true camaraderie displayed by the community members — took on a deeper significance.

Standing there in the shade of the giant cottonwood, gazing across the wheat field, Suzanne missed those days of fellowship with an ache that took her by surprise. Should she stay long enough to see one more harvest before returning to the city and the busy, faster-paced life she now considered her norm? Then she gave herself a little push that set her feet in motion. She couldn't turn back time. Those days were in the past and needed to stay there.

She cleaned the table and chairs in the kitchen, then sat and worked her way through the applications that had arrived in Alexa's e-mail box. Surprisingly, more than a dozen people had indicated interest in the job. By the end of an hour's careful examination and prayer, she'd eliminated all but the two she considered the most likely to meld with Mother and the town of Arborville. Suzanne called each of them to arrange face-to-face interviews. Neither answered their phones, but she left voice mails with instructions to call in the early evening hours. Then, her task complete, she stood and gathered her belongings to return to the house.

As she pushed the chair under the table, leaving tracks in the dust with the chair's legs, she experienced a rush of frustration. She couldn't quite identify its root, but she needed to expel it somehow. Without a second thought, she snatched up the cleaning rags and attacked the windowsills, then the old freestanding cupboard, the work counter, and the stove. Her rags became filthy, so matted with dust they were no longer effective. The spigots in the rusty old sink squeaked but offered up not even a drop of water, so she hurried to the back porch for a bucket of water and fresh rags. She also grabbed a broom.

Back in the summer kitchen, she worked with a vengeance. Sweat poured down her face and trickled between her shoulder blades. She started to open the windows to allow a cross breeze, but their dingy windowpanes demanded a wash first. After retrieving a fresh bucket of water and another bundle of rags, she scrubbed away the years' accumulation of grime and cobwebs, then shoved the panes upward, the old ropes groaning in protest at being used once again.

As she cleaned, she hummed between coughing, sneezing, and stomping on spiders. With every section that emerged free of dust and filth, her heart felt lighter, and her tune became merrier, less restrained. By noon her muscles ached, she needed a bath, and her throat was so parched and raw from breathing in dust, she would have thought she had tonsillitis if she didn't know better, but she couldn't deny a deep satisfaction at what she'd accomplished.

Of course, the bright sunlight pouring through the clean windowpanes also illuminated just how much more needed to be done to bring the little summer kitchen back to its former glory. Suzanne stood in the middle of the floor and bemoaned the sorry state of the once-cheerful building. Dad had always been so careful about upkeep. How patiently he'd taught her to take care of her belongings, giving them the same careful attention she should give her spiritual life. *"If you ignore things, Suzy, they fall apart. A fallen-apart house or a fallen-apart life — both are sad things, indeed."*

The feeling of satisfaction washed away on a wave of regret. So many things — the farm, relationships, her own peace — were falling apart. She looked from the drooping tin ceiling to the cracked plaster walls to the rusty stove. What would it take to restore this place completely? What would it take to restore her broken relationships with her brother, sisters, and mother? A band wrapped itself around her chest and squeezed, making drawing a breath painful. What if she made the effort with her family only to discover worse problems underneath, much the way all her cleaning had revealed the more complicated issues of the summer kitchen?

Approaching footsteps crept through Suzanne's inner reflections, and she turned to spot her daughter stepping over the threshold. Alexa looked around, her eyes widening. "Wow, Mom, look at this place!"

Alexa's startled exclamation brought another stab of sadness. *Yes, look at it. Look at the cracks and crumbling plaster and warped floor . . . Look and see how very sad it all is.*

"It looks fantastic!"

Suzanne shook her head, certain she'd misunderstood.

Alexa darted around the room, examining the old cupboard with its enamel top and the ropes with weights holding the windowpanes open. She ran her hand over the scarred table, slid the sole of her tennis shoes across the cracked linoleum floor, then grinned. "Now that all the dirt's out of here, you can sure see what needs to be done. And phew." She chuckled. "It's a lot."

Suzanne nodded sadly. The summer kitchen was a lost cause. Her heart ached.

"But look at the potential. This could be so cute if it was all fixed up."

Suzanne gawked at Alexa. "You think so?"

"Yeah." Alexa began circling the room again, as if measuring it. "Haven't you ever seen pictures of summer cottages or mountain cabins? This is just the right size to be a little getaway. A person could put a daybed or sleeper sofa along this wall" — she gestured as she spoke, outlining the items with her hands — "and install a curtain track so you could separate the two halves when you wanted some privacy. If you pushed the table and chairs out of the middle of the room, there'd be space here for an armoire with a pull-down desk and maybe a bookshelf. Oh!"

She scampered to the cupboard and opened the doors wide, revealing a mouse nest and lots of droppings. She made a face over her shoulder. "You missed cleaning this. Yuck! But if you put some lace on these shelves — you know, let it droop down over the edge a bit — and stacked vintage dishware in here, it would make a great display and have everything you needed for a meal. If, of course, you could get that old stove functional. But even if you couldn't make it work again, it's so interesting I wouldn't want to take it out. You could just use it to hold plants or . . . or something."

Spinning to face Suzanne, Alexa clapped her hands together and beamed. "Mom, let's do it!"

Suzanne, still trying to envision the old stove covered in potted plants, frowned. "Do . . . what?"

"Fix this place up."

Suzanne nearly groaned. "Oh, Alexa . . ."

"No, think about it." Alexa darted close and grabbed Suzanne's hands, swinging them to and fro. "We'd have our own private space — a little home away from home when we come to visit. There's already plumbing out here —"

"It's not connected."

"— and electricity —"

"Knob and tube, Alexa. Probably a fire hazard."

"— and enough space to create separate sleeping and relaxing areas. All it needs is some TLC."

Suzanne stiffened her arms to bring an end to the gentle motion. "I'm not saying there isn't the potential for this being a very sweet little cottage. But it would take weeks and quite a bit of money to whip this place into shape. I don't have either to commit to it."

Alexa yanked her hands free and stepped back. The look of betrayal on her face cut Suzanne to the core. "Just like you're not willing to commit time to rebuilding your family."

Her daughter's words too closely lined up with the thoughts that had tortured her earlier. Suzanne winced. "Honey . . ."

"Fine. It's no big deal if we don't fix this place up. There are bedrooms in the house we can use." Alexa folded her arms over her chest, her stance defiant. "But I hope you aren't going to be in a great big hurry to get back to Indiana, because Grandmother's birthday is June 13, less than four weeks away. It's her sixtieth. And I intend to be here and help her celebrate it. I also intend to invite her son, her daughters, her grand-children, and her church fellowship to join in the celebration. And for a present, I'm getting her house painted."

Suzanne's jaw dropped open. "Y-you're doing what?"

"You heard me. It needs it, and I've got enough in savings to cover it. Mr. Aldrich said so."

How had Paul gotten tangled up in this? Suzanne spluttered, "That's your college money."

"Yes, it's *my* money, and if I want to use it to paint Grandmother's house instead of taking classes, then that's what I'll do."

"Oh, but, Alexa —"

Tears winked in her daughter's eyes, and her stiff pose faded. She held her hands toward Suzanne, as if in supplication. "Don't argue with me, okay? I want to do this. I want to give her something . . . worthwhile. I want to *fix* something for her. She's so broken, Mom, and I'm not talking about her legs. Her spirit is broken. And I just think if I can make the house beautiful again, then something inside of her might be restored to beauty, too."

Suzanne feared Alexa was expecting too much from a fresh coat of paint, but she couldn't find the wherewithal to say that. So she stood in mute agony while her daughter went on in a wistful tone.

"And I really want you to help me do it. I want you to celebrate with Grandmother, too. You missed so many of her birthdays by living so far away, keeping your secret." The tears spilled over Alexa's lashes, giving her face a dew-kissed appearance that was both heartbreaking and heart stirring at the same time. "Can you stay long enough for her birthday? One day of celebration with your whole family. Just one. Please?"

CHAPTER 21

Abigail

Shouldn't matchmaking be easier than this? Abigail speared a bite-size chunk of lettuce with her fork, wishing she could use it to skewer Paul into one of the dining room chairs instead. Even though Alexa had invited him, very kindly, to sit at the table and eat lunch with them, he'd taken his chef salad out to the porch. He used the excuse that he was too sweaty and dirty to sit at the table, but he seemed no filthier than Suzy. What on earth had that girl been doing?

Suzy pushed the pieces of lettuce, eggs, tomatoes, and ham around without carrying anything to her mouth. Abigail stayed quiet and let her play with her food for over five minutes before she lost her patience and snapped, "Are you going to eat that or not?"

Suzy looked up from her bowl, surprise on her face. "I'm eating."

Abigail snorted. "Eating requires chewing and swallowing. All you're doing is re-arranging the salad. And the clink of your fork on the side of the bowl is annoying." If Suzy or Alexa would talk instead of sitting there like a pair of bookends, Abigail probably wouldn't even notice the *clink-clink.* "Eat it or put it away for later. Stop playing with it."

Suzy sighed and set the bowl aside. "I suppose I'm not hungry." She wiped the back of her hand across her forehead, creating a grimy smear that matched the one on her jaw. "I wore myself out this morning."

Alexa shot a quick frown in her mother's direction before she bent over her salad bowl again. Whatever Suzy had been doing, Alexa didn't approve. Curiosity got the best of Abigail. "What did you do to make yourself so tired?"

Suzy acted as if she hadn't heard, but Alexa answered. "She cleaned the summer kitchen."

Abigail stared at Suzy. "That old wreck? What for?"

Alexa turned her frown on Abigail. "It's not a wreck. It's charming. All it needs is a bathroom and it could be a wonderful little retreat cottage."

Abigail laughed. The old building needed

much more than indoor facilities to be deemed a wonderful anything. "Oh, Alexa, the things you say . . ."

She put down her fork. "So you're siding with Mom?"

"Siding with —" Abigail looked from Alexa to Suzy to Alexa again in confusion. "Your mother spent the entire morning cleaning out there. It seems to me she's the one who sees value in it, not me." She lowered her fork as well and sat up straight, her enjoyment of the salad gone. "What is the matter with you two? Do I have to tie your tails together and throw you over the clothesline until you work out your differences?"

Alexa bowed her head. "No."

Suzy looked off to the side. "Of course not."

Abigail picked up her fork again and poked the tines into a grape tomato. "Then stop arguing and let me eat in peace."

"We're not arguing." They chorused the remark in the same vocal inflection and with the same stubborn expression.

Abigail burst out laughing. "Well, that's the first similarity I've seen between mother and daughter." She used the speared tomato as a pointer and bobbed it at each of them by turn. "Alexa might not possess the

Zimmerman coloring, but I see she inherited the Zimmerman hardheadedness." She popped the tomato in her mouth, chewed, and swallowed while the pair across the table exchanged a sheepish look. "I thought I told you two yesterday to talk. Are you still feuding?"

Suzy sighed. "Mother, we aren't feuding. We never were. But . . ." She glanced at Alexa, who seemed to hold her breath. "I might not be leaving as soon as I'd thought."

Abigail's heart gave a hopeful leap. "Oh?"

Alexa's eyes flew wide.

"No." Suzy toyed with her fork, her head low. "Even if I get a nurse hired soon — and that's a real possibility because I have found two strong candidates for the position — I might . . . stay . . . a little longer." She looked up, meeting Abigail's gaze but appearing to avoid Alexa's. "I could help the new nurse . . . settle in."

The reason sounded flimsy, but Abigail wouldn't say so. If Suzy stayed longer, it would buy her time to put her and Paul together. Assuming an indifferent air, Abigail said, "Whatever you want to do, Suzanne."

Alexa rested her elbow on the table, leaning toward her mother. "Do you mean it? You'll stay?"

"I said I *might,* Alexa."

"Why not just do it? You have the time."

"I want to think about it. And pray about it. Decide what's . . . best."

"You already know it's the right thing to do. You're just being hardheaded, like Grandmother said."

Had they forgotten Abigail was still in the room? She cleared her throat. Loudly. They both looked at her. "Am I going to have any say-so about who is hired to help take care of me?"

"Well . . ." Suzy fiddled with a straggly length of hair falling along her temple. "I hadn't thought about you wanting to be involved in the hiring process."

"Of course you hadn't. No one seems to include me in decisions anymore." Abigail tried not to sound too irritated, but Clete and the younger girls had invited Suzy here without asking her. They'd put Paul Aldrich to work tearing apart her house even though she told them repeatedly she didn't want those things done. Sitting in this chair didn't make her stupid, but her children acted as if they believed she'd lost her ability to think and make decisions. If she was going to be dumped on some stranger who would help her bathe and dress and all the other things her useless legs kept her from doing on her own, she should at least be able to choose the stranger. She aimed a firm look at her daughter. "I want to pick the person."

"All right, Mother. After I've interviewed them and assured myself they are qualified, I'll have them speak with you."

Suzy spoke in a syrupy voice she probably used on agitated patients in the hospital. It only increased Abigail's irritation. She narrowed her eyes into a glower. "I said *I* want to pick the person. Not from your leftovers, but from the applicants. How many are there?"

"Thirteen people submitted applications, but —"

"Then let me see them."

Suzy shook her head. "Mother, not all of them met the qualifications I requested. That happens sometimes — people see an opening and apply without bothering to follow the requirements. We don't want someone who isn't familiar with lift techniques, muscle massage, and recognizing signs of blood clots or tissue death. A patient with paralysis requires a different type of care than someone who is elderly or has some sort of diminished capacity. We need to find the person who can meet your specific needs."

Abigail rolled her eyes and released a disgruntled huff. "I know all about my 'specific needs,' and I think I'm the most qualified to choose a helper. I'm the one who will be stuck with this person, after all. Give me the applications."

"They're on Alexa's phone."

"What?"

"They were submitted online. I read them on Alexa's phone."

Abigail wasn't sure why Suzy's knowledge of the technological device bothered her so much, but it did. She snapped, "What's wrong with using paper and pencil?" To her further aggravation, Suzy laughed.

"You just reminded me of a nurse at the hospital in Franklin. Only she is constantly complaining about our continued use of paper files rather than inputting data on computers. Maybe I should have you send her a letter expounding all the positive aspects of written forms." Suzy's smile faded and she seemed to drift away.

Abigail stared at her daughter, wishing she knew what Suzy was thinking about in those moments of quiet. Her fellow employees at the hospital? The patients? The church family she and Alexa had claimed? Guilt nibbled at the edges of her conscience. Derek had called Sandra, Shelley, and Tanya selfish for

283

pulling Suzy away from her life in Indiana. Hadn't Abigail initially been furious with Clete and the girls for the same reason? Suzy was settled out there, obviously good at her job and happy with it. She hadn't wanted to be responsible for taking something more from her daughter and had only wanted to send her straight back. But now she was trying to hold her here. Confusion rolled through her.

As the mother, she was supposed to know the right thing to do for her children. She'd failed Suzy so badly when she'd come to her, scared and tearful and begging for understanding. Abigail had reacted in anger and embarrassment rather than seeking God's wisdom. Now she had a second chance, but what was best — trying to give Suzy and Paul an opportunity to bloom what had once been only a bud, or allowing the past to remain in the past and letting Suzy keep what she'd built for herself in Indiana?

The uncertainty bore down on her, and Abigail shifted her gaze away from Suzy to Alexa. Even more guilt attacked when she considered all Alexa had been denied. Did the girl want to stay here and connect with her family because she'd been separated from the sister with whom she shared her mother's womb? Did she yearn for the father she'd never known?

Another question rose from Abigail's mind, a question that had bothered her since the day she, Alexa, and Suzy went to the Wichita zoo. If she knew the answer, it might help her know what was best for Suzy in the future.

"Alexa." Her voice blared out loud and intrusive in the otherwise quiet dining room. "I'd like a piece of that chocolate cake. And a big glass of milk. Or no — not milk. Whip some cream. Cake and fresh whipped cream would be perfect."

Without a word of complaint, Alexa picked up the salad bowls and left the room. As soon as she disappeared through the butler's pantry, Abigail leaned forward and whispered, "Suzanne, I need to know something. I want you to tell me the truth."

Suzy's eyebrows descended briefly. "What is it?"

"When we came back from the zoo — remember that day? — I thought I heard you tell Alexa her father isn't here in Arborville."

Panic flickered in Suzy's eyes. She sent a quick look over her shoulder.

Abigail waved her hand. "She's busy and can't hear us." As if to prove her words, the sound of a whisk being exuberantly swished against the sides of a glass bowl carried from the kitchen. "Did I hear you correctly?"

"Mother . . ."

The single word groaned from her daughter's throat, nearly silencing Abigail. But the need to understand was too great. "Did you let more than one man touch you when you were seventeen years old?"

Suzy's lips trembled. She shook her head.

"Paul Aldrich is the one who . . . who . . ." Even after all these years, Abigail couldn't bring herself to say it out loud.

One quick bob of her head affirmed the unspoken statement.

Abigail frowned. "Then you lied to Alexa."

Again Suzy nodded, this time her nod slow and agonized.

Abigail slumped back in her chair. The commandment concerning truth given by their Lord and Master played through her mind. She'd borne false witness for years, letting people believe Suzy had gone away to become a missionary nurse. Now Suzy was bearing false witness, withholding the truth of Alexa's parentage. Such a mess. Such a big, big mess.

"Do you ever intend to tell her the truth?"

Suzy stared at Abigail, her face pale and her lips set in such a grim line they nearly disappeared from view. From the kitchen, the swishing noise stopped and Alexa began to hum, a sweet and lilting tune unfamiliar to Abigail's ears. In a few more minutes she'd come in with the cake topped by whipped cream. The sweet dessert would probably make Abigail sick to her stomach, but she'd eat it anyway. Every bite. As penance.

"Suzanne?"

Suzy finally answered. "Mother, I didn't want to go away and give my baby to my cousins to raise. I did it because you said I had to. But Alexa is *mine*. I won't give her up. The subject of her paternity is closed. Don't ask me about it again."

Alexa entered the dining room with a tray in her hands. Instead of plopping a dollop of whipped cream on top of the slices of cake, she'd done the opposite. The wedge of cake became a castle suspended on a cloud. The presentation was delightful, almost too pretty to desecrate with a fork.

"Here you are, Grandmother." Alexa placed a dessert plate in front of her. "Mom, you get one, too, even though you didn't eat your lunch." Her light-hearted statement seemed to erase a portion of the tension hovering in the room. Two more plates remained on the tray. "I'm going to take one to Mr. Aldrich, and I think I'll eat mine out there."

Suzy jerked, as if zapped by a lightning bolt. "Alexa —"

Alexa headed for the front door without a pause. She called over her shoulder, "Enjoy!"

Suzy stared after her, worry knitting her brow.

Abigail wanted to tell Suzy she was wrong to keep Alexa from her father and wrong to keep Alexa's father from knowing he had a daughter. It was wrong. *Wrong.* But Abigail couldn't reprimand her. She'd set the example of fabrication herself. Her daughter was only perpetuating what she, the mother, had begun. Such a web they'd woven, and after all these years, it was probably foolish to think they could free themselves. She might as well reconcile herself to going to her grave with this burden on her heart.

CHAPTER 22

Alexa

As soon as supper was over, Grandmother settled on the sofa with a book. Mom took over cleanup in the dining room. Derek caved to Ian's begging to visit the litter of barn kittens Alexa had discovered earlier that day, but when Sandra started to follow Derek, Alexa commandeered her with a whispered, "Can we talk?"

Sandra agreed, and Alexa took her to the porch. Sandra lowered her cumbersome frame into Grandmother's lounger, and Alexa perched on the edge of the swing. She shared her plans for surprising her grandmother with a party and a house makeover, watching Sandra's face for signs of disapproval. None appeared.

"I love your ideas, Alexa."

Sandra's response sent a burst of joy through Alexa. She gave the porch floor a push with her feet and set the swing into motion. Her heart soared with the sway of the wooden swing. "Then you'll help me? I want to invite everyone — all the people from church and members of your family who don't live in Arborville but are close enough to drive over." Wouldn't Mom be surprised to have her cousins and other relatives in attendance?

Sandra lifted her hand to her brow, casting a shadow across her upper face. Mr. Aldrich had cut down several large bushes to make room for Grandmother's ramp, and the evening sun now fell across the porch. "I'm willing to help with the party, of course, but the house painting?"

Alexa stopped the swing with a downward thrust of her toes. "What?"

Sandra stretched out her hand and brushed Alexa's knee. "It's a wonderful plan, but I'm not sure Mother would be in favor of a bunch of strangers coming out here and working. We had to fight with her to let Paul in, and she's known him since he was a little boy. She's rather . . . reclusive."

"But you have to agree the house needs it. Think how beautiful it would be with a fresh coat of paint." Alexa pulled out her phone, which she'd wrestled away from Mom after letting Grandmother examine each of the nursing applicants, and opened the photo gallery. "Scoot over a bit. Let me show you something."

Sandra shifted slightly, opening a slice of space next to her hip. Alexa eased into the spot. The lounger's metal legs squeaked, and Sandra grimaced. "I hope this thing will hold all three of us." She cupped her belly. "This one sure makes me bulky."

Alexa gazed for a moment at Sandra's round, tight belly. What must it feel like to carry another life inside your body? Derek was so solicitous to Sandra, holding her arm as she went up and down stairs, helping her from her chair, gazing at her tenderly as if he thought her the most precious thing in the world. Poor Mom had been all alone. Little wonder she clung so tightly to her daughter.

Guilt tried to weasel its way into her thoughts, but she refused to give it sway. She wasn't abandoning Mom. She was only bringing her back to the family who should have been there for her all along. She was doing *right*.

She punched the screen on her phone and brought up a photograph she'd downloaded from the Internet. "Look. This isn't your farmhouse, but it's similar in style, see? It has a third-floor attic with dormers and a porch that wraps around. There's a lot more gingerbread on this one than on your house, but still . . . it gives you an idea how the house would look if it was painted something besides white-white-white." She grinned to let Sandra know she wasn't being critical.

Sandra took the phone and frowned at the image. "I won't deny this house is lovely. I like the colors, too. But why so many?"

Alexa had chosen this image because of the color scheme. Soft saffron made a perfect background for the accent colors of dark ocher, slate blue, and bright white. Peaceful colors, yet eye-catching. The Zimmerman farmhouse's unique window frames, corbels under the eaves, and fishscale siding on the dormers would be showcased beautifully with the varied palette. "What's wrong with having so many colors?"

Sandra sent Alexa an apologetic look. "Shelley would say the house looked like a peacock's tail. Mother might, too. She isn't one to be showy."

Alexa hit the sleep button on her phone and the screen went black. So did her enthusiasm. She returned to the swing and sank down, defeated.

"Let me talk to Derek, okay? And maybe even Clete. I think it's wonderful how you want to gift your grandmother. It's a very extravagant gift! A party and her house painted? If you do all this she will never forget her sixtieth birthday, that's certain."

Alexa slipped her phone into her pocket. "Mr. Aldrich told me I'd need to make arrangements quickly because professional painters get very busy fast. So please talk to them soon."

"How about now?" Sandra struggled to stand, and Alexa took hold of her hands to pull her upright. Sandra grinned a thank-you. "I'd like to see the kittens, so I'll send Derek to you." She started for the stairs in her waddling gait.

Alexa trailed behind her. "I'll go with you. I want to see the kittens again, too. They're so cute right now — so big-eyed and clumsy."

Sandra laughed. She looped elbows with Alexa as they ambled across the lawn. "I'm going to ask a nosy question, and you don't have to answer if you don't want to, but where will you get the money to pay to have the house painted? I know what we're paying Paul to do the remodeling needed. It's a lot, and he's giving us a discount since we're from the same fellowship."

Alexa didn't mind being asked. Sandra wasn't snoopy and critical like Shelley, who had asked questions and then berated her for the answer. "I started working a part-time job when I was a sophomore in high school. Mom taught me to give ten percent to the church and encouraged me to put twenty-five percent in savings. I usually put closer to fifty percent in my savings account. When I graduated, I took a full-time job at the elementary school, working in the lunchroom, and I did the same with my salary. I've had enough to give Mom some for rent and utilities on our apartment, but Mom really wanted me to build my savings. So I've got more than enough in there to have the house painted."

"Weren't you saving for something special?"

Remembering Mom's aghast outburst, Alexa hesitated. Would Sandra react like Mom? She stopped, drawing Sandra to a halt with her. "Is it against the . . . I don't know what to call them . . . *laws* of the church for Old Order Mennonites to go to college?"

"I think the word you're seeking is *ordinance.* And our fellowship doesn't strictly forbid college attendance. After all, there are some jobs — such as nursing, like your mother has done — that require more training than our local school provides. So if one of our young people believes God wants him to continue school for training in a specific field, he talks to the deacons. They all pray together and seek God's guidance. Then the deacons either approve or disapprove the request based on what they think is best for the person and for the fellowship as a whole."

"So the church operates like a family, in a way."

Sandra smiled. "I like that description. A loving family should have each member's best interest at heart."

"Did Mom get approval to become a nurse before she left?"

Sandra's smile faded. "I was so little when your mother left, I honestly don't remember a lot about it. As I recall, Mother and Dad sat us younger children down and told us Suzy was going away for a while, we weren't to worry, and she would come back by Christmastime. Christmas came and went, but Suzy didn't come home. Mother again said not to worry — she'd be home soon. By the next Christmas, she still hadn't come, and Mother began telling people Suzy was studying to become a nurse."

A sad smile lifted the corners of Sandra's mouth. "I thought that was wonderful, and I told my mother I wanted to be a nurse someday, too. Isn't that what little girls do — try to emulate the ones they admire? Then, of course, we were told Suzy was working in a church-run hospital and was too busy to come home. And I finally stopped asking about her because every time I did, Mother would be so sad. And grumpy."

Sandra's image blurred as Alexa gazed through a mist of tears. Mom had given up a lot to keep Alexa, but the rest of the family had given up something, too — their daughter and sister. The realization made her all the more determined to bring everyone together.

"Of course," Sandra's tone held a hint of melancholy, "now I understand why Suzy left and why she didn't come back. So to answer your original question, she probably didn't receive approval from the deacons to go for training. However, she obviously found her calling even without their approval, and just as I did when I was a six-year-old, I think it's wonderful that my big sister is a nurse."

Alexa blinked away her tears. "Me, too."

"I also think it's wonderful to have a niece so close to me in age. I only wish —" Sandra captured Alexa in an impulsive hug, nearly squeezing the breath from her lungs. "Never mind. You're here now, and that's all that matters." She pulled back and smiled brightly. "Let's go ask Derek about your idea to surprise Mother, okay? Then we'd better head back in before Mother and Suzy wonder what happened to us."

Derek seemed reserved about hiring a paint crew, but he promised to talk to Clete and Harper and possibly the deacons if Clete thought it necessary. He said they'd give Alexa an answer as quickly as possible.

While she waited for the men to make a decision, Alexa kept herself busy. On Tuesday she took the telephone directory and her mother's old-fashioned flip phone to the summer kitchen and called every paint crew in both Wichita and Pratt and even some of the smaller surrounding cities. As Mr. Aldrich had speculated, most of them were already booked and couldn't commit to a "maybe" job, but two expressed interest and one offered to drive out, look the house over, and give her an estimate. Although Alexa wasn't sure what would happen, she decided an estimate was a good idea, and she asked him to meet her on Thursday morning when Mom would take Grandmother to a doctor's appointment in Wichita.

She handwrote invitations to Grandmother's surprise sixtieth birthday party and hid them away in the drawer of the summer kitchen cupboard. She planned the menu and made a list of grocery items as well as décor items so she could make the dining room as festive as possible. The house needed some cheer, and Alexa intended to make the place pulsate with color and life both inside and out.

Shelley brought supper Tuesday evening, and Alexa came close to taking Harper aside and asking if he, Clete, and Derek had come to any conclusions concerning the house. But fear of Shelley overhearing and adding her opinion, which Alexa was certain would be negative, kept her quiet. He made no effort to speak to her privately, either, so she could only surmise the men were still contemplating whether or not she could, or *should,* do it.

Wednesday, feeling fidgety, she borrowed her grandmother's car and drove to Wichita. The GPS on her phone led her directly to a huge arts and crafts store with a vast selection of party goods. After browsing up and down the aisle three times and examining the options, she selected plates with a bright yellow center and a border of overlapping bold pink, orange, purple, and blue flowers. She considered using yellow for the napkins and decorations, but on a whim instead loaded her cart with pink napkins, yellow plastic tablecloths, and balloons and streamers in orange, purple, and blue. With a giggle, she added a disposable helium tank to the cart. Why not make the balloons float? The children would love it.

In the floral department she located clusters of silk daisies in every color of the rainbow. She chose three bunches in each of the colors in the plates, then grabbed several bags of clear marbles and some simple clear glass vases to hold the flowers, inwardly picturing the vases with two or three balloons tied to the necks. That thought led her to the ribbon department. Wouldn't it be nice to add big bows to the vases as well as the corners of the tablecloth and maybe the back of each chair? She tossed in six-yard rolls of both one- and two-inch ribbon in the same colors as the flowers, planning to mix them for a more exuberant display.

As she headed for the checkout counter, she glanced at the tumble of items in the bottom of the cart and couldn't help smiling. Such an explosion of colors! Grandmother's party would be a feast for the eyes. Even if her uncles told her she shouldn't have the house painted, at least the interior would be bright and cheerful for Grand-mother's celebration. *But, God, I really want to make the old house look alive again. Please let them say yes. Please, please, please . . .*

The prayer rolled in the back of her mind all the way home. When she reached the lane leading to the farmhouse, she noticed Clete's pickup pulled up next to Mr. Aldrich's. The men were both busy applying white paint to the newly constructed wooden ramp. Alexa parked beside Uncle Clete's truck, left her purchases in the trunk, and trotted across the grass to the men.

"It's done already? It looks fantastic!"

"Thanks." Mr. Aldrich continued applying the paintbrush while he spoke. "Its main purpose is functional, but I wanted it to look nice, too."

"Oh, it does." She took several backward steps to admire the ramp from a bit of a distance. Mr. Aldrich had matched the railing and spindles to the porch, making the ramp seem like a natural extension. Once they planted flowers or some low bushes in front of the ramp, it would look as though it had always been there. Unconsciously, she grimaced. As wonderful as the ramp looked, the fresh coat of glossy white paint served to make the rest of the house look even more run-down in comparison.

She darted forward again and moved close to Uncle Clete. "White's exactly what I wanted for the porch posts, railing, and spindles. It's clean and crisp looking. So I'm glad you're using that for the ramp. It'll blend in . . . with the porch." Would he catch the hint?

He glanced at her, letting her know he'd heard her, but he didn't say anything.

Alexa waited a few seconds, debating with herself about tossing out another hint or letting the subject go for the moment. But in the end, she couldn't stand it. Taking a step closer to her uncle, she clasped her hands tightly at her waist. "What have you decided? About the house, I mean . . . me hiring a crew to paint it?"

Uncle Clete paused with one elbow on his bent knee and his head hanging low. Alexa waited, nearly squirming in place, as he set the paintbrush on the edge of the can and stretched to his feet. "I was going to talk to you after supper, but I guess now's as good a time as any."

She searched his face, hoping for some sign of what he was thinking. She'd never met a more stoic person in her life. *Please, please* . . . The simple prayer repeated itself with every beat of her pulse. "So . . ." She held her breath.

He spoke in a flat tone that matched his expression. "Derek and Harper and me decided no."

Alexa's breath heaved out in one mighty whoosh of discouragement. Hardheaded men!

CHAPTER 23

Paul

From the look on Suzy's daughter's face, Clete needed to prepare for a storm. Paul continued applying paint to the ramp while observing the girl out of the corner of his eye. Children in his community were taught to respect their elders. None of the youth from Arborville's Mennonite fellowship would dare argue with an adult. But how would Alexa react?

Before the girl formed a word, Clete went on in his usual straightforward manner. "It's too much money for you to spend."

"It's my money, Uncle Clete. Shouldn't I be able to use it the way I want to?" She'd argued, but in such a respectful tone Paul couldn't find fault with her.

"We appreciate what you want to do. But we can't let you do it."

Alexa blinked several times. Paul recognized the attempt to hold tears at bay —

Karina had used the same method. His heart lurched in sympathy. A woman in tears always affected him. He came close to speaking in Alexa's defense.

"Not all by yourself."

Alexa gave a little jolt, and Paul did, too, splotching his knee with white paint. He stood and reached for a rag as Clete continued.

"Derek and Harper and me talked it over, and we agree the house needs painting. Since we are already paying Paul for his work out here, we can't buy paint. So . . ." Clete looked away from Alexa, his tanned cheeks streaking with red. Paul already sensed what he planned to say, but the big man wasn't finding it easy to ask for help. "If you'll use your money to buy paint, we'll bring the fellowship men together to paint the house."

A beaming smile broke across Alexa's face. "Like the picture I showed Sandra? With all the different colors?"

Clete frowned, but he offered a brusque nod. "Sandra said it was . . ." He scratched his ear. "Colorful but tasteful. I trust her judgment. So you and me can drive to Wichita one day soon and buy paint. If all the men help, we should be able to scrape and prime the house in one day, then paint it on another day."

"Thank you!"

"Mm-hm. Er, you're welcome. Thank you for buying the paint." He still angled his gaze to the left.

Alexa reached toward Clete, her movement hesitant. She placed her fingertips on his sleeve and looked up until he finally turned and met her gaze. Sincerity glimmered in her dark eyes. "Your idea is better than mine, letting Grandmother's church family have a hand in making the house beautiful again. I think it will mean even more to her knowing how everyone came together to do the work."

"Yes, well, speaking of work . . ." Clete stepped away from the girl's touch. "I need to get back to painting. I'll let you know when we can go after paint."

"All right. I'll call the contractor in Pratt and tell him I don't need an estimate after all." Alexa inched backward, her smile as bright as the sun. "Remember, though, it's supposed to be her birthday present, so we can't wait too long."

"I know, I know." Clete bent down and dipped his paintbrush in the can.

Alexa clattered up the porch steps and stepped through the door, calling, "Mom, Grandmother! I'm home!"

Clete gazed after her, his hand still and his forehead pinched into furrows.

Paul couldn't resist a bit of teasing. "That paint won't jump from the can onto the wood. Get busy over there."

Clete made a face but he put his hand to work.

Paul finished carefully coating another spindle before speaking again. "It's a nice thing Suzy's daughter is doing — buying paint for the house."

"Yeah." Clete grunted the word.

"It's good of you to let her. It obviously means a lot to her, to be able to help. She's a nice girl."

Clete set his lips in a stern line and applied paint in stiff, jerky motions.

Paul sent a puzzled look in Clete's direction. "What's the matter?"

"Nothin'."

Paul laughed. "Clete, I've known you since you were a snot-nosed four-year-old spying on Suzy and me from the bushes, and I know when something is bothering you." When Clete's expression remained dour, Paul sobered. "You could've told Alexa no. If you're that worried about painting the house, why'd you agree to do it?"

Clete blew out a big breath. "Because the house needs it. It needed it even before Dad died. Another season with the wood exposed and we'd probably have to replace boards because of rot. It's got to be done."

"Then why so glum?"

Clete pinned Paul with a glare. "Because it's taken an outsider to do what I should've done years ago. Before Dad died, he talked about getting the house painted, but Mother threw a fit — refused to let him touch it. Dad decided to wait a year, see if she'd be more receptive to it, but he died before he could ask again. So I asked. She screeched so loud I was afraid the neighbors would think I was killing her."

He painted as he spoke, his hand moving faster and more stiffly with each sentence. "Every time anybody's said anything about the house — painting it, moving the furniture, buying something new — Mother has gone into what Shelley calls conniptions. I don't know why she's so determined to let the place go to ruin, but that's the way she is. Then here comes Alexa . . ." The man suddenly ceased all movement. "She seems to like Alexa. So maybe, since it's her idea, Mother won't . . ."

Paul's can was empty, which gave him an excuse to get up and move around the ramp to where Clete bent on one knee. He put his hand on Clete's shoulder. "It's got to be done, Clete. We all know it. Can't let this fine old house fall apart."

"I know."

Something Clete had said earlier whispered through Paul's memory, and he frowned. "Why'd you call Alexa an 'outsider'? I know she's not from our fellowship and you've only just met, but she's part of your family."

"Yeah, I know." Clete took Paul's empty can and poured half of his paint into it. "I just can't get comfortable around her. Because she's" — he thrust the can at Paul and finished gruffly — "illegitimate."

Cold chills erupted across Paul's arms. Unexpectedly, defensiveness rose along with the chills. "That's not her fault. If you come right down to it, we ought to call the parents illegitimate rather than the child because they're the ones who chose to engage in intimacy outside of marriage. The child is innocent of wrongdoing."

His bold words echoed in his mind, stinging him with the truth. He'd taken Suzy in ways a man shouldn't with anyone except his wife. They'd only done it that one time, but even so, he'd been wrong. Remembering how awful he'd felt afterward about being so selfish, he'd kept himself pure right up until the day he married Karina. But he couldn't help worrying that his indiscretion opened a pattern of promiscuity in Suzy's life. How else could he explain Suzy having a child but no husband?

"Look, Paul, I don't want to talk about this." Clete rose, thumping his paintbrush into his can as he straightened. "I've heard enough of it from Tanya."

Paul hid a smile, imagining lively, enthusiastic Tanya jabbering in Clete's ear.

"And I'm praying about it. Plenty. But it's gonna take time. Having a teenage niece dumped on me by my sister who ran off and got herself in trouble when I was just a kid isn't exactly easy. To be perfectly frank, it embarrasses me."

Bitterness carried heavily in Clete's voice. Paul, as an older man in the fellowship, should advise or admonish lovingly, but what could he say that wouldn't be hypocritical? He had no business lecturing Clete for his actions when his own had been so questionable. Were *still* questionable. He hadn't asked Suzy's forgiveness yet.

He searched for something to say that might soothe Clete without sounding like a criticism. "Well, try to remember Suzy's choices were her own. You aren't responsible for what she did." *But I am.* "So you don't need to be embarrassed." *But I do.*

"Yeah." Clete removed his ball cap, ran his hand over his sweaty hair, then settled the cap back in place. "Easy for you to say, not so easy for me to do." He stepped around the paint can at his feet. "This is almost done. Can you finish up alone? I have some work in the barn."

"Sure, go ahead." Paul watched Clete trudge toward the barn, his shoulders slumped and head low as if weighted by a mighty burden. Paul became aware of a dull ache between his shoulder blades from today's labor. Or was it from the weight of guilt?

He'd eaten the lunches Mrs. Zimmerman insisted on giving him, but he'd eaten in the yard rather than in the house, trying to distance himself from Suzy and the old memories that wanted to pummel him every time she was near. But he'd put off his talk with her long enough. He had to leave by three to be home when Danny got there. Which meant he had an hour to finish the ramp and catch Suzy for a short, private conversation.

Lord, open the door, and then give me the courage to march through it. Just as the old house is due for a good scraping and repaint, I'm due to shed these regrets from the past and start new with Suzy. Praying helped ease the tension in his shoulders. He set to work with the paintbrush again, keeping one eye on his wristwatch so he wouldn't miss his self-imposed deadline to issue that too-long-held apology.

Suzanne

Suzanne held a clothespin between her teeth and, with a few deft snaps of her wrist, flipped the last wet sheet over the clothes-line. She quickly pinned it at one end, then scurried to the other to secure it before it slipped from the line. The wind wasn't roaring across the plains today the way it could in Kansas, but she never knew when a sudden blast might surprise her. She wanted the sheet secure just in case.

With the sheet safely clipped, she grabbed the basket and moved farther down the line to hang towels. The laundry waved gently in the breeze, releasing the scent of soap — a fresh scent that pleased her senses. Tonight she'd lay her head on air-dried sheets carrying the smells of wind and grass. She smiled, thinking about it. Maybe when she returned to Indiana, she'd run a line across the little balcony of her apartment and hang her towels and pillowcase. The sheets wouldn't fit — the balcony was too small —

but a clean-scented pillowcase would be nice.

Then she shook her head. What a silly thought. The fabric would pick up the odors of neighbors' charcoal grills, garbage bins, and car exhaust. Did she want to fill her dreams with those aromas? Absolutely not. She clipped the last towel to the line, scooped up the basket, and turned to go back to the house. As she stepped from between the sheets, someone moved into her pathway and startled her so badly she dropped the basket. The remaining wooden clothespins scattered across the grass.

"Whoops!" Paul stooped down and began gathering the pins. "I didn't mean to scare you."

"Well, for not meaning to, you did a good job." Suzanne clutched her chest, willing her pounding heart to calm. She'd avoided the front porch so their pathways wouldn't cross, and here he was anyway. "What are you doing back here?"

He lifted the basket and stood, his lips twitching into a weak grin. "I came looking for you."

"I came looking for you." Her pulse scampered, and her stomach danced, and half of her gloried while the other half moaned in despair. How could such a simple statement

312

bring such a strong reaction? "Why?" The word blasted out more tartly than she'd intended, but he didn't back off.

"There's something I need to say to you. Something I've needed to say for a long time. And I told myself I wouldn't leave today until I'd said it."

She wished he'd hurry up and get it over so she could go inside. With Mother constantly singing his praises and the reminder of his presence all over the house in his handiwork, she'd spent far too much time thinking about him than was healthy for her. She took the basket from him and hugged it tightly against her ribs. "Well, what is it?"

"I'm sorry."

She drew back, uncertain.

"For . . . what I did." Color climbed his cheeks all the way to his temples, as bold red as the misshapen ball cap covering his hair.

She needed no further explanation. His blushing face and stuttered words spoke with eloquence. Heat filled her face. Trapped between the damp sheet, which slapped against her bare calves, and his sturdy frame, she could only stand there gripping the basket, too embarrassed to speak.

"We were young, but that's no excuse. I

knew it was wrong and I did it anyway. And then you left, and you never came back, so I couldn't ask your forgiveness. But I'm asking now. Will you forgive me, Suzy?"

Her tongue felt stuck to the roof of her mouth. She wanted to speak — to assure him he had no reason to beg forgiveness, she'd been wrong, too — but no words would come out.

He sighed, hanging his head. "I know it's a lot to ask. If it hadn't been for me, you would've stayed here in Arborville and . . . and . . ."

Suzanne's ears began to buzz — a stress-induced reaction. She had to get inside. "Paul, it's all right." Her voice came out shrilly, as if a stranger were speaking. "As you said, we were young. We made a mistake. But it was a long time ago, and we don't need to worry about it anymore."

His head lifted and he gazed into her eyes. "So you forgive me?"

She recognized his deep need for absolution. She nodded.

His entire body seemed to relax, his shoulders straightening and his lips curving into a smile. "Thank you, Suzy."

Clearly he'd found freedom from his burden. But what of hers? She needed forgiveness, too, but asking for it would only reveal things she wanted to keep secret. So she said, "I'm Suzanne now," and then darted for the house.

CHAPTER 24

Suzanne

Suzanne had just finished asking the blessing for breakfast when the slam of the back screen door alerted her to someone's arrival. Her mother looked up, a piece of buttered toast in her hand, and frowned.

"It's not even seven thirty yet. Is that Paul already?"

Suzanne considered asking if she should go check, but if it was Paul battling his way through the kitchen — judging by the scrapes and bumps, whoever it was must be shifting things right and left — she didn't want to see him. Their brief encounter at the clothesline last night had haunted her dreams. He'd apologized to her and asked her forgiveness, but he had no idea how much she needed his forgiveness. And she couldn't ask for it.

Mother continued to frown toward the doorway leading to the kitchen. "What is going on in there? It sounds like someone set loose a herd of buffalo."

Alexa dabbed her mouth with her napkin and rose. "I'll go see." But as she rounded the table, Shelley charged through the little hallway. Some sort of cloth flapped over her bent arm as she came. Alexa quickly moved aside, and Shelley passed her without acknowledging her presence. She crossed directly to Mother's chair and thrust the items — dresses, Suzanne now realized — forward.

"I got them done. And they'd better fit because now that the girls are home from school for the summer, I can't get out the machine without them pestering me. Don't plan on me doing any alterations."

Mother offered Shelley a wry grin. "Good morning, Shelley. Would you like a cup of coffee?"

Shelley blew out a little breath that stirred the black ribbons trailing from her cap. "I had a cup at Clete and Tanya's when I dropped the twins over there." She rolled her eyes and continued, keeping her focus fixed on Mother as if Suzanne and Alexa were invisible. "Would you believe Tanya asked to keep the girls for the day? To have some sort of first day of summer celebration. Who celebrates something like that?

317

Celebrating the first day of school, that I would understand. Getting those two out from under my feet is reason to cheer. The summer can't go fast enough to suit me."

Suzanne experienced a pang of regret. She wished she could caution her sister about willing time to fly. Children grew up so quickly — the childhood years were fleeting and precious. She glanced at Alexa, and tears stung. If only she could turn back time and enjoy her daughter's growing-up years again.

Shelley headed for Mother's bedroom, her stride as rigid as a soldier on parade. "I'll put these in your closet. I hope you have some extra hangers because I didn't bring any."

"Leave that peachy-colored one on the end of my bed," Mother said to Shelley's retreating back. "I'll wear it to my doctor's appointment today."

Shelley paused in the doorway, looking over her shoulder with her brow pinched into a scowl. "What doctor's appointment?"

Mother broke off a bit of toast and carried it to her mouth. "My six-month checkup with the neurologist."

Shelley marched back to the table and balled her hand on her hip. "Why didn't you tell me you had an appointment today?"

"You were with me when we scheduled the visit."

"Well, it isn't as if I haven't had anything else to think about since then." Shelley glowered for a moment, then released a heavy sigh. "Do you need me to take you?"

"Suzanne is taking me." Mother took another bite of the toast, ignoring the crumbs that dotted her dress front. "Suzanne and Alexa."

Shelley whipped a short look in Suzanne's direction but didn't quite meet her gaze. "I see." She sounded grim.

Suddenly a sly glimmer entered Mother's eyes. "You could come with us."

Shelley's scowl deepened. "I wouldn't want to intrude."

Although she wouldn't have thought to include Shelley — mostly because Shelley didn't seem to want to be included — Suzanne was glad Mother suggested it. They'd lost so many years, they might never be close, but if they spent time together maybe they could at least learn to be civil. "You wouldn't be intruding. Why don't you come along?"

Alexa piped up. "Sure! The car will hold us all, and your girls are celebrating the first day of summer. You can celebrate, too, with a trip to Wichita."

319

Suzanne squeezed Alexa's hand in silent appreciation for her support. Alexa could have argued about including Shelley and with good reason — Shelley treated her niece as if she had leprosy. Pride in her daughter brought a smile to her face and a lift in her heart. "After we're done at the doctor's, we plan to go to lunch at the restaurant Mother likes so much out on the highway — the one with the gift shop attached. They have such unique items there and a great menu. I'm sure you'd enjoy it."

Shelley snapped, "Eating out is extravagant. Don't you have food in the cupboards?"

Mother answered. "I'm tired of sandwiches for lunch every day. Eating out once in a while won't hurt anything."

Shelley gawked at Mother. "But you've always said —"

"Do you want to come or not?" Mother glared at Shelley as if daring her to keep arguing. "As Alexa said, there's room in the car. You don't have to worry about the girls. Suzanne wants you to come."

Suzanne watched various emotions — anger, indecision, perhaps even desire — play across her sister's face. Shelley could be pretty if she would drop her stern demeanor. She was far too young to already have deep grooves etched between her eyebrows from constantly scowling. Suzanne wanted to give her sister a day of fun and relaxation, to see those lines diminished and a smile grace her face instead.

Unconsciously she leaned forward slightly, narrowing the distance between herself and Shelley. "Please come with us. I've had some one-on-one time with Sandra, but you and I haven't had the chance yet. Spend the day with us."

For a long time Shelley stood staring at her as though searching for hidden motives. Finally she blew out another little huff. "We'll have to stop by the co-op and let Harper know what I'm doing, but all right. I'll go."

"Well, help me change my dress." Mother pushed away from the table and aimed her chair for the door. "But try not to mess up my hair. Suzanne got my bun just perfect this morning, and I don't want her to have to redo it."

By the time they reached Wichita, Suzanne questioned the wisdom of inviting Shelley along. She'd given her the front passenger seat so they could talk on the way, but even though Mother and Alexa kept up a steady stream of chatter in the backseat, Shelley kept her lips so tightly closed only grunts could escape in response to Suzanne's attempts at conversation. Eventually Suzanne fell silent, too, and let her sister stare broodingly out the window.

During the doctor appointment, they both accompanied their mother to the examination room, but Shelley abruptly cut off Suzanne when she tried to ask the doctor questions. She tried not to be resentful. After all, Shelley had been Mother's caretaker long before Suzanne returned to Arborville, but there were things she wanted to know so she could pass the information along to the new nurse who would be caring for Mother. Rather than embarrassing the doctor by participating in a power struggle in the office, she jotted down the things she wanted to know and left the note with the receptionist along with a request for the doctor to call her at his convenience.

Shelley glowered at Suzanne all the way through the parking garage as if she thought Suzanne had left a terroristic threat with the genial woman at the desk. At the car Suzanne suggested Shelley ride in the back with Mother — she needed a respite from her sister's stony silence — and to her relief Mother seconded Suzanne's request. Shelley climbed in with Mother, but she continued her refusal to converse as they drove to the restaurant.

When Suzanne parked the car, Alexa retrieved Mother's wheelchair and Suzanne assisted her into its seat. She reached for the handles to push Mother across the parking lot, but Shelley crowded in front of her.

"I'll do it."

Mother chuckled. "Don't fight over me, girls."

Shelley snorted.

Suzanne sighed.

They formed a tense parade with Alexa in the lead and Suzanne bringing up the rear. She battled the urge to deliver a swift kick to her sister's posterior, but fortunately a prayer for patience alleviated the temptation.

White rocking chairs lined the long porch in the front of the restaurant, and Alexa paused to set one in motion. "I love these," she said, sending a grin across the group. "Wouldn't a pair of them be pretty on your porch, Grandmother?"

Shelley said, "She already has a porch swing, two folding lawn chairs, and a lounger. It would be cluttered with those things there, too."

Alexa's smile dimmed momentarily, but it rejuvenated so quickly Suzanne was certain she was the only one who noticed the lapse.

"You could replace the folding lawn chairs with these. The rockers are so much prettier, and they're a lot more comfortable, too. Try one, Aunt Shelley, and you'll see."

Shelley raised one eyebrow. "It would be a foolish waste of money to buy chairs when the ones we have are still good."

The ones on the porch had been used for so many years, the straps sagged and the metal frames were rusting, but it would be pointless to say so. Suzanne linked elbows with Alexa and steered her toward the door. "Let's get inside, huh? I bet Mother is hungry. I know I am. I'm looking forward to chicken pot pie. Theirs is as good as any I've ever made at home."

Shelley's derisive snort blasted from behind Suzanne. "No restaurant pot pie could ever be as good as homemade. At least, not *my* homemade."

Alexa shot Suzanne a frustrated look, which Suzanne returned before tapping her finger against her lips. A hostess led them to a square table next to the windows giving them a view of flowering gardens and a tiny fountain.

Shelley grimaced. "The sun is shining in too much here. It hurts my eyes. Can we sit over there instead?"

"Of course." Without breaking her stride,

the hostess seated them in the corner Shelley had indicated. Not even one finger of sunlight reached them. She handed out menus, informed them Patricia would be their server, and finished brightly, "Enjoy your lunch!"

Shelley snapped her menu open and scowled at the pages. "How are you supposed to read this thing? It's so dark in here."

Mother angled a disbelieving look at her. "Gracious sakes, Shelley, you're the one who didn't want to sit in the sunshine. Stop your fussing and find something to eat!"

Shelley set her lips in a grim line and examined the menu in steamy silence.

Suzanne stifled a sigh of relief and savored the brief quiet. As much as she'd anticipated time with Shelley, she now regretted inviting her along. What should have been a pleasurable outing had turned into a day of tension. She could hardly wait to return to Arborville and separate herself from her sister. The realization saddened her.

Their server approached and flashed a beaming smile. "Hello, ladies! I'm Patricia, and I'll be taking care of you today. What can I bring you to drink?"

"Water with lemon, please," Alexa said.

Suzanne nodded. "Water with lemon

would be great, thank you."

Mother requested coffee, and Patricia turned to Shelley. "And you, ma'am?"

Shelley turned her unsmiling gaze upward. "Do you have brewed sweet tea?"

"Sweet tea." The girl jotted it onto her pad.

"Wait." Shelley held up her hand like a traffic cop stopping cars. "I asked if you have *brewed* sweet tea."

Patricia's forehead puckered. "Yes, ma'am, we brew our tea."

"Do you add the sugar while you're brewing it or after, to make it sweet?"

The server now puckered her lips in addition to her forehead. She was beginning to look like a prune. "I'm not sure what you mean."

Shelley sighed. A long, dramatic, laden-with-irritation sigh. She spoke slowly, emphasizing each word. "At what point is the sugar added to the tea — during the brewing process, or do you stir in a few teaspoons to regular brewed tea right before you serve it?"

Patricia's confused expression remained. "Um . . ."

Shelley waved her hand. "Never mind. Just bring me a glass of water with lemon."

Patricia took off as if someone had fired

her from a cannon.

"You'd think they'd know how things are prepared," Shelley groused, bending over the menu again. "Now I'm half afraid to order something to eat."

Alexa gave Suzanne another can-you-believe-her look, but Suzanne was careful not to respond to it. She had to pray again — twice — to keep from kicking Shelley under the table when her sister launched into questions about whether the tilapia was sautéed in butter, oil, or margarine and whether the cook used instant rice in the pilaf. Suzanne secretly vowed to double Patricia's tip. The poor girl was earning every penny.

The food was good, as Suzanne had come to expect, but the stilted conversation and Shelley's continued critical comments about everything from the cornbread being too crumbly to the piped music being too fast paced cast a negative light over the meal.

By the time they finished eating, Suzanne had a tension headache at the back of her skull. "I know we usually browse the shop, but it's pretty crowded in here today. So let's just head home, okay?"

Neither Alexa nor Mother disagreed, so Suzanne set off for the front doors. Shelley grabbed her arm. "I need to use the ladies' room before we go." She bustled in the direction of the restrooms, leaving Alexa, Suzanne, and Mother in a little group near a display of T-shirts. Alexa held one up that said "I always wear fur thanks to my cats."

Suzanne gave the expected chuckle and picked up another shirt, but Mother tapped her on the elbow. She set the shirt aside. "Do you need to use the ladies' room, too?" Suzanne asked.

Mother shook her head. She quirked her finger, beckoning Suzanne to lean down. She bent over and put her ear near Mother's mouth. Her mother's warm breath touched her cheek as she whispered, "While she's in the bathroom, let's get in the car and sneak away."

Suzanne straightened, staring at Mother in shock. She received her second surprise when she witnessed mischief dancing in Mother's eyes and her lips twitching with a suppressed grin. Mother had just joked with her! Happiness rolled through her and emerged in a flood of laughter.

Alexa flicked a curious look across them. "What's so funny?"

Mother repeated her comment in a stage whisper, and Alexa clapped her hand over her mouth, her eyes wide. Then she, too, broke into laughter. The three of them laughed until tears rolled down their faces, but a sharp hissing voice stilled their merriment.

"What is the matter with you? People are staring!"

At Shelley's admonishment, Suzanne looked around. Other customers were looking at them, but none seemed offended. In fact, they smiled, as if approving the display of mirth.

Mother sighed. "Stop being a stick-in-the-mud, Shelley." She gave the grips on her wheelchair a thrust that sent the chair forward, muttering, "We waited too long."

Suzanne bit down on the tip of her tongue to prevent another spill of laughter from escaping as she followed her stiff-lipped sister out of the restaurant. Perhaps it had been unkind to share a joke at Shelley's expense, but the laughter had erased her headache. As she settled behind the wheel, she sent a secretive smile over the seat, and Mother winked. Winked!

Every frustration, every disappointment, every moment of embarrassment she'd suffered during the day disappeared in the space of one flick of an eyelid. In that moment, Suzanne was happy she'd come back. Happy she'd taken Shelley along for the day. Happy. The teasing wink rekindled every pleasant memory of the mother she'd known before her fall from grace. Why Shelley's irascibility had brought it out, Suzanne couldn't imagine, but she was grateful for it.

She found it easy to aim a smile — a genuine smile — in her sister's direction as she said, "Everybody ready? Okay. Let's go home."

CHAPTER 25

Abigail

The house was quiet. Like a tomb. Abigail lay in her bed in her dark room, eyes open, staring at nothing. Although the windows were cracked to allow in the cool night air — something she did year-round because she couldn't bear a stuffy room — her body was bathed in sweat. She gave the covers an awkward toss, and they slid halfway off the bed with the tangled sheets and light blanket draping across her knees. She wanted to kick them free, but of course she couldn't kick. She waited for anger or bitterness to swell at her helplessness, but the old emotions refused to come. Instead she only felt sad. Lonely. Dead inside.

Today she'd laughed. Laughed so hard tears rolled. And her comment hadn't even been that funny. It was as though years of bottled-up laughter had been waiting for an excuse to pour out, and Suzy's wide-eyed reaction gave her permission to pop the cork. The laughter had felt so good, so cleansing, so *freeing*. Why had she denied herself the expression of merriment for so long?

She knew why. But she wasn't ready to admit it. Not even to herself.

She deliberately turned her thoughts to Shelley, who hadn't joined in the laughter. Who berated them for making a spectacle of themselves. Who criticized and condemned and nitpicked until Abigail wanted to screech at her in frustration. But she hadn't. Because in her daughter's behavior she'd been given a glimpse of herself.

Tears flowed down Abigail's cheeks for the second time that day. She pawed at the moisture with her hands, but new torrents replaced the ones she batted away. "I've failed them, Lord." The prayer rasped from her aching throat — the first nonrote prayer she'd uttered in longer than she could remember. She was almost sixty years old. Her children were grown. She couldn't go back and try again to be understanding instead of judgmental, loving instead of unforgiving, tender instead of harsh. She saw her shortcomings now — she saw them far too clearly — but her reckoning had come too late.

Lifting her arm, she muffled her sobs with the bend of her elbow. She cried until her nightgown sleeve was soaked and even her hair was damp. She cried to the point of exhaustion. As sleep finally claimed her, one fleeting thought drifted from the recesses of her consciousness. *I can't change yesterday, but can I change tomorrow?*

Suzanne

Although she'd attended worship services each Sunday since her return to Arborville, on this last Sunday in May Suzanne finally felt relaxed. Mother's spot was in the back corner where a shorter bench created a little space for her wheelchair. How marvelous to settle next to Mother with a sigh of contentment rather than sitting stiff and uncomfortable, worrying about what others might be thinking. Somehow others' opinions had ceased to matter after last Thursday's trip to Wichita and the time of laughter with her mother. Mother had accepted her, seemingly wholeheartedly, and that was all that mattered.

Mother's change in attitude along with her dissatisfaction with either of the candidates she'd chosen to interview — funny how someone could look so wonderful on paper but fall far short in person — made

Suzanne less impatient to return to Indiana. She wouldn't have believed it possible for Mother to change. But she had, and it gave her a small flicker of hope that, perhaps, Shelley and Clete might eventually soften toward her, too.

She still intended to find a nurse for Mother. Her Indiana friends, church family, and coworkers tugged at her. Her life was there now. But Alexa's comments about the importance of family had left an impression. If it meant being restored to a right relationship with all of her family, she was willing to stay as long as necessary to secure a nurse who would provide excellent care for her mother. And for now it was sweet bliss to sit between her mother and her daughter in the church of her childhood.

The small building became crowded as benches on both sides of the aisle filled, the men sitting on the north and the women on the south. Suzanne watched the others move to their places without exchanging any of the chitchat to which she'd grown accustomed at the church in Franklin. Although the silence had seemed cloying her first Sunday back, now it helped establish her heart for worship. Perhaps she wasn't as separated from her Old Order roots as she'd initially thought.

As a child, Suzanne had sat on the third bench from the front, first beside Mother and then, with the arrival of little sisters, beside Shelley. Mother had moved farther toward the center to open up space for the younger girls. Sandra, Shelley with Ruby and Pearl, and Tanya with Julie and Jana now occupied the familiar bench. Clete, Jay, Harper, Derek, and little Ian filled the bench directly across the aisle where Dad had always sat with Clete during Suzanne's growing-up years.

Behind the Zimmerman bench was Paul's family bench. He still sat on the aisle. Back in her teens, she'd found it easy to peek over her shoulder at him. Every time she looked, she found him focused on her rather than on his Bible or the one preaching.

From her place in the back, she had a view of Paul's broad shoulders and short-cropped hair. His suntanned neck looked even darker against the thin band of his crisp white shirt sticking up above the collar of his suit coat. Memories carried her backward. How many times had she been scolded for sending smiles in his direction during worship? Maybe if she'd heeded her parents' warnings about flirtation, she wouldn't have ended up in trouble. But then, if she hadn't gone with Paul that night, she wouldn't have been sent to Indiana, wouldn't have been gifted with Alexa, so how could she wish away that evening?

As she sat, gazing at the back of his head, he turned and caught her looking. Her face flooded with heat, and red streaked his fresh-shaven cheeks. For several seconds they stared past everyone and everything else into each other's eyes as if they'd turned into blocks of ice. Or pillars of salt.

Rattled, she forced her gaze aside as the song leader stepped to the front and invited everyone to rise for the opening hymn. She stood but she didn't join when the others began an a cappella rendition of "Just as I Am" in four-part harmony. Her throat felt tight and raw. No words would escape it. Like a magnet, Paul's sturdy form once again drew her attention.

Although others blocked her view, if she shifted her head slightly, she could glimpse him standing with his hand on his son's shoulder, his chin high as he sang. He sang tenor, and she'd always loved listening to his clear, resonant voice, but she couldn't detect it above the others all joined together. The realization disappointed her.

" 'Just as I am, though tossed about, with many a conflict, many a doubt . . .' "

Although the beautiful music reverberated from the rafters, her chest began to ache. The words stung, their meaning far too accurate. She looked at Mother and then at Alexa. They both sang — Alexa in a sweet soprano and Mother in her familiar alto. They appeared content, the way she'd felt when she first settled onto the bench this morning. But one lengthy exchange of glances had pulled the rug of contentment from under her feet and left her floundering again.

How, after so many years, could Paul still affect her? He'd asked for her forgiveness. She'd given it. Shouldn't she be able to set her memories aside and let go? If she couldn't move past the memories — if they would always haunt her — how could she remain here in Arborville?

The congregation sang two more hymns, and then one of the deacons presented an hour-long message. Suzanne listened respectfully, keeping her focus on the man at the front or following along in her Bible when he read Scripture. She didn't allow herself so much as a peek in Paul's direction. When the sermon ended, everyone except Mother shifted to kneel at the benches for prayer. The same deacon who'd delivered the morning's sermon led them in prayers of gratitude for blessings, confession of sin, and finally petitions.

All across the room, whispered voices mingled, prayers finding their way from the lips of men to the ears of God. Suzanne prayed, but she kept her words inside rather than allowing them to escape even on a whisper. She wouldn't risk either Mother or Alexa overhearing the burden of her heart. *Let me forget, Lord. You've forgiven me. You've forgiven him. I've forgiven him. Now please . . . please, let me forget.*

With the deacon's resounding "Amen," the service ended. The quiet ended, too, as people rose and began visiting. Suzanne shook her head in wonder at the cacophony of voices. If she didn't know better, she'd think they hadn't had opportunities to catch up with neighbors during the week. But she did know better.

Being out away from town, Mother was isolated from the town's interactions. On the other Sundays Suzanne had attended, Mother demanded to be rolled out of the church immediately following the service, claiming the clatter made her head pound. Suzanne automatically reached for the handles of Mother's wheelchair to take her outside.

Mother reached back and patted her

hand. "See if you can push me over there to Fonda Loepp. I want to talk to her about the quilting group."

Suzanne searched the milling throng for Mrs. Loepp. She located her near the front of the church in the center aisle, speaking with Paul and his son. Suzanne gulped. "Um . . . Alexa?" She shifted aside and gestured for Alexa to take hold of the handles. "Your grandmother wants to talk to Mrs. Loepp. She's the one —"

"Don't tell me, she's the one wearing a white cap with black ribbons," Alexa said, a teasing grin on her face.

So many times her daughter's humorous comments had pulled her from the doldrums or moments of worry. Had Alexa sensed her gloomy thought and chosen impishness to erase it? Whatever the reason, the tension in Suzanne's shoulders eased as she released a short laugh. "Very funny. She's the one in the orange-and-green-flowered dress, talking to Mr. Aldrich."

"All right."

Mother grabbed the rubber grips on the wheels and held tight. "Suzanne Abigail Zimmerman, I didn't ask Alexa to take me to Fonda, I asked you. Why are you dumping me on Alexa?"

"I'm not dumping you!" Suzanne's conscience pricked. The prick became a stab when Mother turned a knowing look on her. She sighed. "All right, I admit, I was dumping you."

"Why?" Alexa asked the question. Given Mother's smirk, she already knew the answer. Before Mother could contribute her thoughts, Suzanne answered.

"Never mind. Here." She plunked the car keys into Alexa's hand. "Bring the car around so we can load Mother when she's finished talking to Mrs. Loepp. We'll be out soon." At least she hoped it would be soon. Mother had been using every excuse imaginable to put her in proximity with Paul over the past week and a half.

She inched Mother's chair between people, excusing herself as she went. Was Mother really interested in the quilting group, or was she only trying to throw her into Paul's pathway again? Although she didn't want to destroy the fragile peace they'd established with each other, she needed to have a talk with Mother concerning letting the past remain in the past.

Suzanne eased Mother within a few feet of Mrs. Loepp and Paul, intending to let them finish their conversation rather than interrupt. But Mother caught the rubber grips on the chair's wheels and closed the gap between them. Suzanne scurried along behind, uncertain what else to do. But she kept her gaze on Mother's mesh cap. No sense in locking eyes with Paul while Mrs. Loepp looked on. The quilting circle had loved to gossip back when Suzanne lived in town, and she didn't imagine the practice had changed.

"Fonda," Mother blared, pulling the woman away from whatever she was saying to Paul. "Do the quilting ladies still meet on Tuesday mornings?"

Mrs. Loepp tipped her face toward Mother. "We do. Why?"

"I'd like to join you."

Mrs. Loepp bounced a look of surprise at Suzanne. "You would? But — but —"

Mother laughed. It seemed a bit forced, but no one else appeared to notice. "I know my legs don't work, but my hands still do. Do you need another quilter?"

"Well, Abigail, of course we never turn down a pair of willing hands." Mrs. Loepp turned businesslike. "We want to finish two more quilts before the Relief Sale quilt auction in September. But . . ." Color climbed the woman's cheeks. "We meet in the basement. How . . ." She looked pointedly at Mother's chair.

"Suzanne knows how to get me down the

stairs, don't you, Suzanne?" Mother cast a glance over her shoulder, beaming.

Suzanne, aware of Paul's steady gaze on her, swallowed. "Yes, I do, although I'll need some help."

"Alexa can help you."

"Yes, she can." Suzanne spoke calmly even though her pulse raced as if she'd just finished a marathon. "But I'm not sure how long we'll be in Arborville. So you can't depend on us indefinitely."

Mother laughed again. The same oddly strained laugh she'd emitted a few minutes ago. "Well, now, we know you'll be here at least another month, yes? Didn't you take a two-month leave of absence? So you'll be here four or five more weeks."

Suzanne came close to groaning. Fonda Loepp had no need for the information, so obviously Mother wanted someone else to know how long she'd be in town. And that *someone else* and his son both seemed to be listening intently. She would definitely have that talk with Mother.

"So plan on me being with you Tuesday. I'll even ask Alexa to bake a treat to share with everyone. She's a marvelous baker." Mother blathered on, almost sickeningly cheerful. "Just ask Paul and Danny here — they've sampled some of her baked goods."

Mrs. Loepp looked at Paul, who nodded. She turned back to Mother. "That sounds wonderful, Abigail. Of course we'll be happy to have you . . . and your daughter and granddaughter . . . join us." She offered a brief, warm smile to Suzanne before looking at Paul again. "Will you let me know when your schedule is clear? Ted and I are eager to make use of that shed again."

"Of course, Mrs. Loepp." Paul curled his hand loosely around the back of Danny's neck and aimed him for the front doors.

Mother jerked her wheelchair directly into Paul's pathway. "Lunch at Sandra's today, remember?"

Paul rubbed his chin, his dark-eyed gaze flitting in Suzanne's direction, then landing on Mother. "I remember, but I think Danny and I are going to go home instead. Be lazy this afternoon." He released a laugh that sounded as tight and forced as Mother's had been. "We've earned it after the hours we put in at your place the past few days."

With Danny out of school, Paul had changed his working hours from eight in the morning until five or six in the evening instead of leaving at three. He had reason to enjoy a day of rest, but Suzanne suspected he had another reason for avoiding lunch with them.

"But, Dad —"

Mother cut Danny off. "I thought we agreed —"

"I appreciate the invitation very much, Mrs. Zimmerman." Paul spoke firmly, aiming a stern look at his son. "But you've been providing too many meals for us lately. I've nearly forgotten how to make a sandwich. So thank you, but we're going home. Come on now, Danny." He ushered his reluctant son up the aisle.

Mother scowled after him. "That is a stubborn, stubborn man."

Suzanne raised one eyebrow and peered at her mother. "And you are a stubborn, stubborn woman." She bent down and chose a gentle tone. "You can't force something that no longer exists, Mother. It's over. You need to accept it."

Her mother stared at her for several silent seconds, her lips pursed tight. Then she huffed and gave the wheels of her chair a push. "Let's get to Sandra's before Shelley throws a fit. You know how she has to keep to her schedule." Suzanne, relieved to drop the subject, followed Mother.

Clete and Harper were waiting on the porch, the brims of their hats blocking the noonday sun. Clete frowned. "What took you so long?"

"Don't fuss at me," Mother snapped, sounding like Shelley again.

Clete set his lips in a firm line and gestured for Harper to grab the other side of her wheelchair. The men carried the chair down the stairs and set it gently in the grass. Clete pushed Mother across the yard to her car, which Alexa had running with the air conditioning on high. Suzanne sent up a silent thank-you for her daughter's consideration. She and Mother both needed to cool down.

"I'll transfer her — thanks, Clete." Suzanne smiled at her brother, but he only grunted in reply and strode off toward his pickup truck where his family waited. Suzanne helped Mother into the seat, fastened her seat belt, then started to back out.

Mother grabbed her hand, holding her in place. In a voice so whisper soft Suzanne might have imagined the words, she said, "You two created life together. It will never be over. *You* need to accept *that.*"

CHAPTER 26

Paul

Until that morning if someone had asked him, "Paul, are you a coward?" he would have emphatically answered, "No." But now? He wasn't so sure.

Danny scuffed along beside him, his head low and his toes kicking up dust as they walked home. His son's dejected pose made Paul regret his decision to eat sandwiches at home rather than joining the Zimmerman family, but not enough to change his mind. He needed some distance between himself and Suzy — no matter what she said, he couldn't think of her as Suzanne — until he managed to sort out his feelings toward her.

Strange that he still had feelings for her. Marriage to Karina, raising Danny, building a business, just the act of living — shouldn't all of that have erased those old feelings? Especially since she'd forgiven him? She'd said they were young, it was so long ago, they didn't need to think about it anymore. And he'd agreed. So why had he found himself staring at her this morning? He sure wasn't a teenager, but he acted like one, getting lost in the depths of Suzy Zimmerman's crystal-blue eyes.

Danny kicked a rock and it bounced against a mailbox post and ricocheted into the street again, sending up a tiny puff of dust. Paul frowned at his son. "Careful there. You don't want to hit someone's vehicle or house."

Danny poked out his lower lip and didn't say anything.

Paul nudged his shoulder. "Stop pouting. You're too big for that."

Danny squinted upward. "Not trying to pout, but I'm mad. Can't I be mad? God made emotions, so why can't I use them?"

Paul swallowed a chuckle. He would've asked the same kind of question when he was Danny's age. He draped his arm across his son's shoulders as they ambled along together, Danny stretching his stride to match Paul's. "You're right that God made emotions, and being mad is an honest feeling. So, yes, you can be angry. But remember the Bible tells us, 'Be ye angry, and sin not.' In other words, it's okay to feel angry, but you shouldn't let anger make you say or do things that would be hurtful."

"So I shouldn't have kicked the rock."

Paul nodded.

"Well . . . I'm sorry. I guess."

Paul coughed to cover another chuckle. At least Danny was honest.

"But I don't want to spend my whole summer with just you."

This time Paul let his laughter roll. He snagged Danny against his hip and chafed his son's shoulder with his open palm. "Thanks, buddy. That really makes my day."

Danny grinned sheepishly. "That didn't come out right. But I go with you to work at the Zimmerman farm where there aren't any kids. And then on Sunday, we go home instead of going to somebody's house where there'd be kids." His scowl returned. "Did I make you mad when I asked you about Jay's aunt? Is that why you won't go eat with his family?"

Sweat trickled down Paul's temple. From the sun or from an inner heat inspired by thoughts of Suzy? He swept the dribble away with his fingertips. "I'm not mad at you. But I hope you haven't spent any more time talking about Jay's aunt." He aimed a warning look at Danny. "Have you?"

His son shook his head.

Paul blew out a breath of relief as he

guided Danny up the sidewalk to their house. "Good. As I said, I'm not mad at you, so don't worry."

"Then are you mad at Jay's aunt?"

Paul paused at the base of the porch steps. "Why would you ask that?"

"Well, Jay says —"

"I thought you weren't talking to Jay anymore about his aunt."

"I haven't been talking, I've only been listening."

Paul closed his eyes, gathering patience. A child's reasoning . . .

"And Jay says his dad and his aunt Shelley are both really mad at his aunt Suzanne. But he doesn't know why for sure. Something about her going away and causing trouble." Danny angled his head. "So is that why you want to stay away from the Zimmermans except when you have to work at the farm? Because you're mad at her, too?"

Paul's heart sank. He'd asked Suzy's forgiveness, but it seemed there were a few other people who would benefit from his apology for playing a role in Suzy's leave-taking. He rubbed his hand over Danny's short hair and left it standing in sweat-stiffened ridges. "I'm not mad at her. As I told you before, the Zimmermans have a big family and extra people just get in the way."

"Okay."

Thankfully, Danny seemed ready to rest the topic of eating with the Zimmermans. Paul started up the steps.

"Dad, can I ask you something else?"

Paul opened the front door and ushered his son over the threshold. "What's that?"

"Jay thinks his aunt and his cousin Alexa are pretty nice. He doesn't like his dad being mad, and he wants to find out what kind of trouble his aunt caused so he can help fix it. Do you know what happened? So I can tell Jay, and he can help his dad not be mad anymore?"

Paul offered a silent prayer for wisdom before answering. "Danny, the 'trouble' isn't anything Jay can fix, and it isn't something he should worry about. You tell him I said so. You can also tell him I'll talk to his dad — see if I can help him not be mad anymore, okay?"

Danny nodded, his face serious. "Sure, Dad. I'll tell him."

"Now . . ." Paul forced a smile. "Go change out of your church clothes. I'll make up some sandwiches and grab a couple bananas or apples and those cupcakes Alexa sent home with me yesterday, and we'll take our lunch to the park. Sound good?"

Danny galloped off, releasing a happy shout.

Paul retrieved bread, lunchmeat, cheese, and mustard, and laid it all out. But instead of assembling sandwiches, he propped the heels of his hands on the edge of the counter and bowed his head. *Lord, I wish I'd known how one mistake can create so many issues. I wish I'd been wiser back then, less selfish.* It hurt to know that even Jay — who wasn't born when he and Suzy suffered their lapse of judgment — was affected by the choice made so long ago. *Help me set things right again. With all the Zimmermans. Amen.*

Paul left Danny with one of his school friends for the day. Partly to make up for denying him the company of friends yesterday, and partly to keep him from overhearing what he planned to tell Clete. He'd given his son a message to deliver to Jay, but he didn't want any added embellishments.

When he arrived at the Zimmerman farm, Clete's truck was already parked beside the barn, so Paul shut off the engine of his pickup, said another quick prayer for courage — he might as well be wearing a yellow stripe down his back the way he quivered inside — and then headed for the barn.

Clete was at the workbench in the back corner, tinkering with . . . something. Paul knew carpentry tools as well as the ABCs, but anything mechanical left him scratching his head. He sidled close. "Hey."

Clete glanced at him. "Hey yourself."

"Can we talk for a minute?"

Clete thunked the wrench onto the worktable and swished his palms together. "Might as well. I think this is a lost cause."

Paul frowned at the clump of metal pieces held together with bands and screws. "What is it?"

"Carburetor from the riding mower. I hoped to overhaul it, but I can't even get it apart. Some of the pieces are rusted together."

Paul looked at the engine part again and chuckled. "I think I'll stick to overhauling kitchens."

Clete released a snort of amusement and shook his head. Leaning against the sturdy workbench, he folded his arms over his chest. "Did you have a question about the kitchen?"

"No." Paul pulled in a deep breath. "I wanted to talk to you about Suzy."

Clete clamped his teeth together, the muscles in his jaw twitching.

Paul pressed on. "You're mad at her. For leaving and staying away. Maybe even mad at her for trying to find a nurse to take care of your mom instead of sticking around to do it herself."

"Yeah."

"Well . . ." Paul rocked back on his heels. "I think maybe you're mad at the wrong person. Instead of being mad at Suzy, you should be mad at me."

Clete's forehead crunched into a series of furrows. "Why you?"

"Suzy left Arborville to get away from me."

Clete shook his head. "That doesn't even make sense. I was just a kid, but I remember you two going off fishing or bike riding or catching frogs. I remember because you were always telling me to scat. I always kind of figured you two would end up together."

Paul had always kind of figured that, too. But he'd had a good life with Karina — he loved her, and they had Danny. He didn't regret the life he carved after Suzy left. "I know. We were close. Maybe . . . too close." He hoped Clete might read between the lines so he wouldn't be forced to come right out and say what he'd done. It was hard enough just to hint. At least the morning sun hadn't lit the barn's interior too much

353

yet. Paul's face was on fire, but hopefully Clete wouldn't notice the telltale flush of embarrassment.

"What do you mean by that?"

Paul ducked his head. So much for hints. He met Clete's gaze again. "Suzy and I . . . we went too far one night."

Clete's eyes widened. "You . . ."

Paul nodded. "After that night she wouldn't talk to me or see me. And then she left for Indiana. I'm pretty sure she went because she was ashamed of what we'd done, and being in the same town with me was too hard for her." He couldn't bring himself to share his other fears about how Suzy must have conducted herself when she reached Indiana. Clete didn't need to form the kind of pictures in his head that tormented Paul late at night.

Clete stared at Paul in silence for several tense minutes, his expression unreadable. Suddenly he jerked upright. "When?"

"When . . . what?"

"When did you" — Clete ground the words past gritted teeth — "lay with my sister?"

Could Paul's face get any hotter without him spontaneously combusting? "I don't remember."

"Think!" He barked the order, his neck

and cheeks mottling with bold red. He might combust before Paul did. "January? June? March? When was it?"

Paul thought back. He'd tried so hard to bury the details of that time, recalling specifics proved difficult. He raised his shoulders in a slow shrug. "I can't be sure, but . . . early spring, I think."

"You think? Or you know?"

Paul thought hard. The snows had melted, but it was still pretty cool. He remembered Suzy shivering and him offering her his jacket as they walked to the barn. He nodded. "Early spring."

Clete's expression turned hard. He balled his hands into fists. "You got my sister —" A growl covered whatever else he'd started to say. With a roar, he lunged at Paul and knocked him flat on his back on the hard ground.

The air whooshed from his lungs, and he couldn't even defend himself when Clete straddled him and plowed his fist into his jaw. Clete cocked his arm to deliver a second blow, but someone shrieked. He leaped up and strode to the corner, leaving Paul lying on the barn floor gasping for breath.

Alexa darted close and leaned over him. "Mr. Aldrich, are you all right?"

"Yeah. I'm fine." He lied. His jaw ached so badly, speaking was torture. He needed to get up, but he wasn't sure he should move yet.

"Should I get Mom?"

"No!" Both Paul and Clete barked the reply.

Alexa looked from one man to the other, confusion clouding her face.

Paul cupped his cheek and rolled sideways. With some struggling, he managed to sit up. His tailbone hurt as badly as his jaw. For a farmer, Clete sure packed a wallop. Paul hoped he hadn't suffered any broken bones. How would he explain to the doctor how he'd gotten hurt? Mennonites were nonviolent. Or so everyone thought.

Alexa held both hands to Paul, and although it stung his pride, he allowed her to tug him to his feet. Concern glimmering in her dark eyes, she kept a grip on him even after he'd proven his legs would support him. She sent curious glances toward both men and sucked on her lower lip. Paul almost laughed, observing her obvious attempt to stifle any questions. What must she be thinking behind those big eyes of hers?

Clete stalked across the floor, and Paul instinctively tensed, preparing for another assault. But Clete pounded past, growling over his shoulder, "Let's go get that paint, Alexa, so I can be back here by noon." He stormed out of the barn.

Alexa gawked after him. Her hands, still holding on to Paul, trembled.

"You better go."

She looked up, her mouth slightly ajar. "Why were you fighting?"

"It's nothing important. Just something that happened a long time ago."

"It must've been something awful for him to go after you like that. I know Uncle Clete isn't exactly Mr. Sociable, but I've never seen him so angry."

Paul replayed the brief exchange with Clete, trying to recall exactly why his friend had turned on him. His head pounded, making it difficult to think, but slowly both spoken and unspoken communications came together. Could it be . . . Squeezing Alexa's hands, he rasped a question. "Alexa, how old are you?"

"Nine . . . teen." She drew the word out slowly, her expression wary.

Nineteen. He'd done a lousy job of guessing. A sick feeling flooded his stomach. "And" — he gulped — "when were you born?"

"Wh-why?"

He gave her hands a little tug. "When?

What month?"

"December."

"December . . ." *April, May, June . . .* Paul silently counted the months in his head. *Dear God in heaven, no . . .* How had he not realized the truth before now? He jerked free of her hands and clutched his temples, taking a backward step. His breakfast oatmeal threatened to make a return appearance.

"Mr. Aldrich?"

Alexa sounded afraid and appeared on the verge of tears. He had to get control of himself. He couldn't traumatize his daughter. *His daughter!*

Swallowing the gorge filling his throat, he forced his lips into what he hoped was the semblance of a reassuring smile. "I'm sorry. I'm holding you up. Clete's waiting. I know you want to pick out the paint colors. So go on now."

Her fine eyebrows pinched into a frown. "Are you sure? You look awfully pale. I think I should ask Mom to —"

He wanted nothing from her mother. He shook his head, wincing against the throb in his jaw. "No need for that. Scoot now. And don't worry, okay?" She bit her lip again, clearly uncertain. What a caring girl she was.

Tears swam in his eyes, distorting his vision. A man should be strong in front of his child. He turned away and faced the corner. Soon the scuff of feet against the ground followed by the firm click of the barn door's latch told him Alexa had left. Slowly he peeked over his shoulder, confirming he was alone. Then he sank onto one of the back tires on the faithful old tractor Clete's father had used in his fields. The man had given him and Suzy rides on it when they were elementary school kids. Carefree, happy, innocent days, those . . . But now?

With an anguished moan, Paul buried his face in his hands. He had another child. A daughter. A beautiful, compassionate, giving daughter. And she'd grown up without his love, without his support, without his prayers. He bent forward and gave vent to the fierce emotions rolling through him. His body shuddered with the force of his dry, wracking sobs. Sobs of heartache, yes, but also of fury. How could Suzy have kept Alexa from him?

He'd come out to the barn to help Clete release his anger at Suzy. Instead Paul discovered a rage more intense than any he'd known before. He understood why Clete had attacked. Everything within him yearned to strike out, to pummel something until it resembled nothing more than pulp.

But he couldn't, so he poured out his fury in hot tears and indistinguishable moans masquerading as prayers.

Something nudged his leg. He opened his eyes and found a small, striped kitten batting at a loose thread in the seam of his pant leg. Drawing in a shuddering breath, he stretched one hand toward the furry little creature, intending to scoop it up and give it some attention. Receive some attention from it. But it scampered away with its short tail sticking straight up like a poker. Disappointed, Paul rested his elbows on his knees and let his head hang low.

The sunbeams slanting through the high windows had inched across the floor until they touched his feet. The morning was slipping away into another day of separation from the child he should have been given the opportunity to claim and raise. Swiping his sleeve across his face, he cleared his vision and bolted off the tire. His back ached and his jaw throbbed, but he ignored the pain and stomped across the floor in the direction of the house. He'd find Suzy. He'd demand the reason why she'd stolen his child from him. And then he'd —

Yesterday's advice to Danny drifted through his memory. *"Be ye angry, and sin not."* He stopped as abruptly as if he'd collided with the barn door. He couldn't talk to Suzy. Not in his present state of mind. He'd surely say or do something sinful. He needed to wait until he calmed himself. Assuming he would be able to calm himself.

Pressing his fists to his eye sockets, he groaned. *I have a daughter, God.* Such a realization should be cause for joy and celebration. But Suzy had stolen that from him, too. He'd asked her forgiveness. Now he wouldn't be able to rest until he heard her beg for his.

CHAPTER 27

Alexa

Alexa huddled as far into the corner of the truck seat as possible without sticking her head out the open window. Wind blasted her face and twisted her ponytail into knots. For a while she'd held the thick tail along her neck to prevent it from blowing, but eventually her hand began to tingle, the blood flow slowed by the awkward position. So she just let her hair wave and slap against the seat's headrest. She'd probably tear half of it out, detangling it later, but she wouldn't ask Uncle Clete if she could roll up the window.

He hadn't said one word since he thumped the paint cans in the back of the truck, then slammed himself in behind the steering wheel. She sent a quick, sidelong glance at his stern profile. His firmly clamped jaw and narrowed eyes communicated his anger. She'd never been so uncomfortable in her life. She turned her face toward the wheat fields covering the landscape and willed the miles to pass quickly so she could separate herself from the taciturn man on the other side of the cab.

She bit the inside of her lower lip and blinked rapidly to hold back the tears threatening to escape. She'd so looked forward to this day, spending some one-on-one time with her uncle and choosing the paint for Grandmother's house. She'd anticipated a joyful, relaxed day, a time of nurturing a relationship with Uncle Clete. But his terse comments peppered between long, stony silences had made her so nervous her stomach churned. Not even finding the perfect paint colors to make Grandmother's house as beautiful as any posted in the *Better Homes and Gardens* magazine she read in the doctor's waiting room could lift her spirits.

She wished she'd gone to the paint store with Mom instead. Or Sandra and Derek. Or even Mr. Aldrich. What was Uncle Clete's problem, anyway?

Her ears rang from the constant wind noise and the tinny clatter of the cans bumping against each other in the truck bed. Her chest felt heavy from the weight of disappointment. Her throat ached — dry from the wind and tight from tamping down the desire to cry. And curiosity tangled her insides even more than the wind tangled her hair. Why had Uncle Clete and Mr. Aldrich, two men who'd known each other their entire lives and appeared to be friends, come to blows that morning?

She looked at her uncle again. He gripped the steering wheel so tightly his fingers were white. He seemed to glare at the highway rolling out in front of them. Didn't he ever get tired of being so uptight and growly? His thick eyebrows crunched together into a unibrow with his dark scowl, and for a moment an image of the grouchy *Sesame Street* character who lived in a garbage can flashed in her mind's eye in place of her uncle. A short huff of laughter escaped.

Uncle Clete shot her a quick frown. "What?"

Alexa looked out the window. "Nothing."

They rode in silence for several more minutes, Alexa counting off the mile markers and silently praying the turnoff for Arborville would magically appear.

"You don't need to tell anyone what you saw this morning."

She shot him a startled look. "You mean about you pounding Mr. Aldrich into the barn floor?" Sassy? Maybe a little. But he deserved it after his long morning of broodiness.

To her surprise he didn't berate her for being impertinent. He nodded. One brusque bob of his head. "It's nobody's business. So just pretend you didn't see it."

Alexa laughed again. A humorless laugh of surprise. "That's a little hard, I'll admit." Where she found the courage to speak when she'd felt so cowed earlier, she couldn't know, but the release of words eased the heaviness in her chest. "I'll keep it to myself if that's what you want. It probably would upset Grandmother to know her son and the carpenter were going at each other like two junior high boys on a playground. But I'd really like to know what the fight was all about."

She waited for several seconds, but her uncle didn't speak. "Uncle Clete?" Her ponytail whipped around and several strands caught in her mouth. With a disgruntled huff, she tossed the hair over her shoulder and gazed at her uncle. He acted as though he hadn't heard her.

Raising her voice, she said, "Mr. Aldrich said you were fighting over something that happened a long time ago."

Uncle Clete jolted. "Oh, yeah?"

So he could hear her. Alexa hid a smile.

"Yes. He said it was nothing important, but I don't believe him. Grown men don't generally resort to fighting each other for no good reason. So what was it all about?"

He hit his blinker and slowed the truck to turn onto the dirt road leading to Arborville. The tires stirred dust that billowed through the open windows. He made a face and cranked his window up. Alexa did the same. With the wind noise gone, the cab felt claustrophobic. Her ears closed, and she forced a yawn to open them.

Her uncle still hadn't answered her question, but oddly she lost the desire to know in the thick, cloying silence. Clinging to the door handle with one hand and the edge of the seat with the other, she held tight. The truck seemed to hit every pothole in the road. She couldn't wait to get out.

Uncle Clete turned into the lane, pulled the truck up beside the barn, and put the vehicle in Park. Alexa reached to open the door, but he put out his hand. "Wait."

She froze, and her heart set up a patter she could actually feel against her ribs.

"I changed my mind. You can tell one person about the fight Paul and me had this morning."

Puzzled, Alexa frowned. "Who do you want me to tell?"

"Your mother." Uncle Clete's eyes glinted like steel, and his harsh tone made the fine hairs on Alexa's arm stand at attention. "Ask her what the fight was all about. It's her place to tell you, not mine."

Suzanne

Suzanne snipped the tip of the peony's stem and quickly inserted it into the Mason jar of water. Smiling, she fingered the pink petals of the half-opened bloom. The flowers should last for several days before wilting. She reached for another blossom, which she'd cut from the huge bush behind the summer kitchen. Two tiny red ants fell from the thick cluster of petals and crawled across the table.

"The door's open," she said, watching them go. "Go back to the garden where you belong." It was a long journey to the door and freedom for such small creatures, but they'd make it eventually.

She returned to filling the jars she'd collected with buds and blossoms, noting more of the ants hardly bigger than a grain of salt weaving in and out of the tight centers of the flowers. Was it Dad's mother who said God created the peony plant to give the tiny creatures a home? Probably. She'd possessed a deep faith and spoke of God as

367

naturally as some people breathed.

Suzanne intended to put one of the jars of flowers on Grandmother Zimmerman's grave. The others would decorate the resting places for Dad, Grandfather Zimmerman, and Dad's brother who'd died before she was born. She wasn't sure yet what she would do with the fifth jar, but she'd cut enough flowers to fill five jars and she wouldn't waste them.

"Mom? Mom, where are you?"

Apparently Alexa had returned from her excursion to the paint store. Maybe she'd accompany Suzanne to the cemetery. It would be nice to have her along. Suzanne zipped to the doorway and stuck out her head. "I'm in here, honey!"

Moments later Alexa entered the summer kitchen and crossed to the opposite side of the table. She made a face and flicked an ant onto the floor. "What are you doing?"

"Making arrangements to put on graves." Suzanne slipped the last bloom into a jar, then stepped back and admired the row of bright-colored bouquets. "Mother didn't want to visit Dad's grave. She said he isn't there so why bother." A shaft of sadness pierced her heart. She wished she could see and talk to her dad one last time. "But I really want to go. It is Memorial Day, after all, and I want to . . . remember."

Alexa gazed at her for several seconds, her face puckered up as if uncertain how to respond.

"Do you want to go with me?"

"I'd like that."

Alexa's quick, positive response warmed Suzanne. She reached across the table to squeeze her daughter's hand. "I was hoping you would." She winked. "You can hold on to these things in the car so they don't spill."

Alexa gave the expected chuckle although it seemed to lack real heart.

Suzanne tipped her head. "Are you all right?"

"Oh, sure." The answer came quickly. Brightly. Maybe too brightly. "Just a little worn out from my morning excursion."

"Were you able to get the paint you wanted?" Suzanne still didn't completely approve of Alexa spending her hard-earned money for something Clete should have done a long time ago, but she wouldn't squelch her daughter's desire to give.

"We got it." Alexa helped Suzanne transfer the flower-filled jars to a slatted crate. "But the store was really crowded. I guess Memorial Day sales brought everybody out. So it was a little stressful. And Uncle Clete —" She clamped her lips together.

Suzanne sent her a worried look. "Uncle Clete . . . what?"

Alexa shrugged and formed a stiff smile. "He's not exactly the best person to take shopping. You know, he doesn't talk much or get excited or anything. So it kind of took the fun out of it for me."

Genuine sympathy flooded Suzanne. She wrapped her daughter in a hug and planted a quick kiss on her temple. "Don't let him steal your joy. Just because he wants to be Mr. Crabby Pants doesn't mean you have to be."

Alexa nodded, but she still looked sad.

Suzanne lifted the crate. "Come on. Let's go to the cemetery, put these flowers on the graves, then you and I can stop by the convenience store and grab some pizza. I bet you haven't had lunch." Clete wouldn't think to feed his niece.

"That sounds good, Mom."

Alexa remained quiet as they drove to the cemetery. Suzanne chose not to interrupt her daughter's inner reflections. Visiting graves affected people in different ways, and perhaps Alexa was preparing herself for her first encounter with the grandfather she'd never met. Suzanne only wished they could have met in person. Alexa would have adored Dad, who had been the favorite of every fellowship child for his friendly teasing and kind heart.

Tears stung, and she blinked the moisture away to clear her vision. She parked behind the church in the shade of the overgrown cedar tree wind block, then stacked her arms on the steering wheel and gazed out the window. The iron gates to the cemetery stretched wide like the wings of a swan welcoming its young to draw near. Beyond the gate, gray headstones — either rectangular slabs or square, tall pillars — formed a silent, disorganized army holding sentry on a bed of freshly mown grass. White clover and tiny purple flowers shaped like bells dotted the carpet of green. With flat stones creating curved footpaths and century-old trees sending dappled shade across the graves, the cemetery seemed a peaceful place. Even as a child, Suzanne had never been hesitant to wander the grounds the way some children were. Eagerness to revisit this place of childhood memories now tugged at her, and she swung her car door open.

Alexa had held the crate of jars in her lap on their drive, and she stayed in the seat while Suzanne rounded the hood and opened the passenger door. She took the crate and set it in the grass. Alexa stepped out, batting at the wrinkles in her skirt.

"Let's leave the crate here and each take two jars." Suzanne lifted out two jars and held them toward Alexa.

"What about the fifth one?"

"I don't really need it. I just hated to waste the flowers. We'll figure out something to do with it." Suzanne grabbed two more jars and headed into the cemetery. According to Mother, Dad's stone was in the southeast section near his brother's and parents' graves, so she aimed herself in that direction with Alexa moving gracefully beside her.

Suzanne glanced at the names on stones as she moved past, each name raising an image of people from the small community where she'd been raised. Odd how strong the memories were, considering how long she'd been away.

When she came upon the stone with *Cecil E. Zimmerman* etched into its face, so many remembrances attacked she couldn't sort them all. She stood with the cool, moist jars in her hands, breathing in the scent of peonies and letting the images wash over her in waves. *Dad . . . Oh, Dad, I miss you so much . . .*

She set one jar off to the side, then moved directly to the base of the stone and knelt.

She wriggled the base of the Mason jar until she flattened a patch of grass enough to hold the jar upright. Then she sat back on her heels and placed her fingertips on the sun-warmed top edge of Dad's headstone.

More memories flitted through her mind, and she smiled even though a tear trickled down her cheek. "I really think I had the best dad in the world, Alexa."

Alexa squatted beside her with the jars of flowers still in her hands. She rested the jars on her knees and aimed an attentive look at her mother. "Tell me about him."

How to encapsulate her father into a few simple sentences? She wished she were a poet so she could do justice to his life. "For one, he had time for me no matter what. For all of us children. I was the only child until Clete came along, so I had Mother and Dad's full attention up until then. But I was never jealous of Clete, or Shelley or Sandra when they were born, because Dad made me feel important by taking time for me."

Alexa's smile encouraged Suzanne to continue.

"For another, he taught me to trust and love God. He read the Bible to us every day — at breakfast before he went out to work and in the evening before we went to bed.

In between, he lived what he believed. All those biblical fruits of the Spirit? Dad had them imprinted on his life. He was loving, patient, kind, gentle. When he got angry, he didn't lose his temper and holler or strike out but practiced self-control. Oh, he wasn't perfect." Suzanne chuckled, remembering a time Dad kicked the tractor tire when the machine's engine refused to start. "But he was as close to perfect as a human could get. He was a wonderful example for my brother, sisters, and me to follow."

Alexa nodded, her expression thoughtful. "I see him in you, Mom. All those things you just said? You're that way, too."

Suzanne's heart swelled in appreciation even as her conscience reminded her just how imperfect she really was. "Oh, honey . . ."

"No, really, Mom. You've been that kind of example to me." Alexa set the two jars aside and shifted to sit on her bottom. "Now I know where you learned it, and I'm glad. But I wonder . . ." She toyed with her ponytail, her expression thoughtful. "How did you — and Sandra, too — pick up those traits when Clete and Shelley didn't seem to get it? They're both so . . ." She made a face.

"Negative?"

"I was thinking more like perpetually disagreeable." Alexa sighed and plucked a blade of grass. She twisted it gently between her fingers, seeming to examine the play of sun on the tiny blade as she went on. "I want to like them. They're my family. But sometimes I don't think they want to be liked. At least, not by me. They're nothing like what you were just saying about your dad. It doesn't make much sense, how two of you are so nice and two of you just aren't."

Alexa tossed the bit of grass away and shrugged. "I guess Clete and Shelley are like Grandmother instead of Grandfather. Although she's getting better. So maybe there's hope for Clete and Shelley, too, hmm?"

Suzanne smiled. "There's always hope."

Alexa smiled back.

Suzanne rose. "Let's put these other jars out and then get you that pizza I promised. I don't want you to collapse from starvation."

Alexa laughed lightly — a more genuine laugh — and they placed a jar in front of each of Suzanne's grandparents' headstones as well as the one for the uncle she'd never met. Then they walked slowly toward the car with the late-spring sun warming their heads and the light breeze kissing their cheeks with its delicate perfume.

Alexa's gaze shifted back and forth, and suddenly she stopped and grabbed Suzanne's hand. "Mom, look." She pointed to a newer headstone set off the path in a little space by itself. It looked lonely. "Is that Mr. Aldrich's wife?"

Suzanne stepped closer and, shielding her eyes from the sun with her cupped hand, read the stone aloud. " 'Karina Anne Kornelson Aldrich. Beloved wife, mother, daughter, sister, friend. Gone but not forgotten.' "

"Oh, how sad." Alexa's tone held deep sorrow. "She's been gone three years already. She was so young when she died."

Suzanne slipped her arm around Alexa's waist. "We never know when death will knock at our door, so it's wise to always be ready."

Alexa nodded somberly. "Poor Danny, growing up without a mom. I feel for him."

Suzanne's heart caught.

Alexa turned an eager look on Suzanne. "Mom, could we put that last jar of flowers in front of her grave? We don't know her, but it just seems the right thing to do. Please?"

Once again, Alexa's compassionate spirit

touched Suzanne. Maybe God had prompted her to bring the extra jar so Alexa could perform this small act of kindness. "Sure, that's fine."

Alexa retrieved the jar, placed it next to the stone, and then tenderly fluffed the flowers. She turned, a smile of satisfaction on her pretty face, and swished her hands together. "Done. Now, how about that pizza?"

"Let's go." Suzanne looped arms with her daughter and headed for the car.

Alexa climbed in while Suzanne tossed the empty crate into the trunk. When she settled behind the steering wheel, Alexa spoke again. "By the way, Mom, I need to tell you something. Something important."

Had her voice held a hint of foreboding, or was it only their silent surroundings giving Suzanne the feeling that something unpleasant was about to occur? She shrugged off the odd sensation — silly to develop an aversion to cemeteries now that she was grown up when they'd never frightened her in childhood — and turned the key in the ignition. "Okay. But food first. I might even eat a slice myself. And then . . ." She waggled her eyebrows at her daughter. "I have an idea I think you'll like."

"What is it?"

"Never mind." Suzanne reversed the car and then aimed it for the road. "It's a surprise."

CHAPTER 28

Paul

Paul crouched on his haunches and twisted a screw into the pre-drilled hole to secure the first cabinet door in place. He winced, turning the screwdriver as quickly as possible so he could stand and stretch again. Every time he bent forward or picked up something, his tailbone let him know it was not happy. For two cents he'd go home. Today was a holiday, after all — weren't the post office and the bank closed? If he'd taken the day off, he could've avoided being knocked on his backside and clopped in the face by the kid who used to pester him to play catch or bait his fishing hook or take him on in a game of checkers.

Even more than his back and jaw hurt, his heart hurt.

The front screen door slapped into its frame with a sharp *crack.* Startled, he jerked, and the screwdriver jumped from the screw's slot and created a deep gouge in the new paint job. He gritted his teeth, then regretted it because the action intensified his jaw pain. Hissing through his teeth, he repositioned the screwdriver and started again.

"Mr. Aldrich?"

This time he yanked backward and nearly knocked himself on his seat. Catching hold of the cabinet's door frame, he steadied himself and then looked up into Alexa's curious face. The morning's frustrations rolled away in one rush, and a smile formed on his lips without an ounce of effort. He stretched upright, battling against the stiffness and continued pain in his back. "Hi, Alexa. What do you need?" Whatever it was, he'd do it.

"Mom said when she left, Grandmother was reading in the living room, but she isn't there now. Do you know where she went?"

Disappointment struck. He wished she wanted something more complicated. The desire to gift her, to please her, tangled him in knots. "She headed to her bedroom shortly after Su— your mother left the house. I haven't heard any noise from in there, so she might be napping."

Alexa chewed her lower lip, something he already recognized as her habit when she was thinking. "I'll go peek in at her. Thank you." She turned and scurried off, the stiff fabric of her modest, mid-calf-length skirt snapping softly with her stride.

Rather than returning to work, Paul remained frozen with the screwdriver gripped in his fist, his gaze on the opening leading to the dining room. Only a few moments later she returned, and he greeted her with another smile. The action hurt his jaw but lifted his spirits. "Was I right? She's napping?"

"Out like a light," Alexa said with a nod that bounced her brown ponytail. Several strands of hair had come loose and formed sweat-damp squiggles around her face. If she were six years old and if she had grown up calling him *Dad,* he would take his comb and smooth the strands back into place. He fought a sharp pang of remorse at what he'd missed.

She continued, oblivious to his inner turmoil. "Would you please tell her Mom and I decided to make a quick run to Wichita to see if they're having Memorial Day sales at the mall? We'll be back by suppertime, but if she needs something before then, Tanya said she'd be on call."

"Sure, I'll tell her." His first real favor for his daughter. He wanted to shout for joy.

"Thanks, Mr. Aldrich. Enjoy your quiet afternoon." She turned to leave.

"Just a minute, Alexa." At once, she stopped. Cringing against the pain shooting through his lower spine, he took a step toward her. "I'm sorry about this morning. About what you saw."

She sent him a sheepish grin. "To be honest, it looked like you were on the receiving end. You don't need to apologize."

"Yes, I do." He hadn't been given the privilege of teaching her from childhood, and maybe it was too late to interject instruction now, but he needed to share what he believed. "Violence isn't a way to solve problems, and allowing anger to take control of a person doesn't glorify God. So regardless of what it looked like, Clete and I were both involved, and we're both at fault. So I apologize, and I ask you to forgive me." *Please, Alexa, forgive me for not being there for you when you were a baby and a little girl. Forgive me for not being there for you now . . .*

Her eyes grew wide, and she nodded solemnly. "Of course, Mr. Aldrich."

He smiled, ignoring the ache in his jaw. "Have fun shopping."

"Oh, we will. Mom and I always have fun together."

His smile faltered. Why did her cheerful

382

statement irritate him?

Once again she turned as if to leave, but then she spun back to face him. "May I ask you something?"

"Sure." He folded his arms over his chest and locked his knees, giving her his full attention.

"My uncle wouldn't tell me what you two were fighting about. He told me I should ask Mom, because it's 'her place' to tell me." She caught her lip between her teeth again, her forehead crunching. "I'd rather not ask Mom. She's had kind of a sad day, visiting the cemetery and doing some reminiscing. So I wondered if you would tell me instead."

Although he'd longed to do something for her, he couldn't bring himself to divulge the reason Clete had attacked him even if it would make things easier for her. "You know what? I think Clete is right. Your mom is the best one to answer your question." Had he passed the responsibility to Suzy out of spite? Just in case his motives weren't as pure as they should be, he added, "But you don't have to ask her today if you don't want to. Pray about it. I'll pray for you, too. You'll know when it's time."

She gazed at him for several seconds without moving, without even blinking, as if trying to read beneath his skin. Then she nodded very slowly and walked backward, her gaze still locked on his. "All right. Thank you. Good-bye, Mr. Aldrich." She grabbed her purse from the shelf beside the hallway and dashed off.

Paul returned to the cabinet and squatted, but then he sat with the unused tool in his hand. He'd planned to stay out here and work until five before going after Danny, but what would it hurt to cut his day short? Mrs. Zimmerman had been asleep for over an hour already. She wouldn't nap much longer. He'd stay until she roused so he could deliver his message from Alexa — he wouldn't fail to honor the first promise he'd made to his daughter — and then he'd pick up Danny and they'd go together to Karina's grave. He had the need to do some reminiscing of his own.

Danny leaped out of the pickup and galloped toward the cemetery as exuberantly as if he were joining a game of baseball. And that boy loved playing baseball more than eating, sleeping, or anything else Paul could think of.

Paul grabbed the cut bouquet of dyed daisies he'd picked up from the barrel at the convenience store and followed more slowly, shaking his head indulgently at his son. Wouldn't Karina be proud of Danny? Although reckless at times and maybe a little lacking in tact — he was young, after all — he followed his conscience when it came to truthfulness, and he was openly loving. His teacher called him a good-hearted boy. Karina, who'd been the sole caretaker when Danny was small, had planted those seeds of goodness in him. Even though she was gone, her influence continued in their son's mannerisms and behavior. She'd been a loving, diligent mom.

Just like Suzy must have been to Alexa, based on his daughter's kindheartedness.

Blowing out a breath of aggravation, he pushed aside thoughts of Suzy. He had come to spend time remembering Karina.

Danny leaped from steppingstone to steppingstone, taking a meandering journey all the way around the cemetery. With one final burst, he raced directly to the little plot where Karina's body rested. He came to a halt in front of Karina's unpretentious, knee-high stone, and a look of surprise broke across his face. "Dad! Dad, come here!"

His son's frantic call sent Paul into a clumsy trot even though every thudding footstep sent a new shaft of pain through his spine. The daisies shed petals with his jarring movements. Had someone desecrated his wife's grave? There'd been some trouble a couple of years back when high schoolers from a neighboring community drove over late one night and vandalized the cemetery. He glanced around, seeking evidence of damage, but saw nothing out of place.

His heart pounding, he rounded the stone and followed the line of Danny's pointing finger. Surprise replaced his worry. A jar, one like the ladies used for canning vegetables, sat at the base of Karina's stone. Peonies tucked into the jar created a plump, pink mushroom.

Danny yanked at Paul's hand. "Lookit that, Dad. Mom's already got flowers!"

"She sure does." Paul frowned at the bouquet. The flowers didn't upset him — it was a kind gesture to decorate his wife's grave — but who would have put them there? The first year after Karina's death, several of her friends had left little bouquets or notes at her grave, but as time went by and focus shifted, he'd been the only one to visit. So why now?

"Betcha Alexa and her mom did it."

Paul jolted. "What?"

Danny pointed to the far corner of the

cemetery. "I saw flowers just like these over there. Where Mrs. Zimmerman's husband is buried. So I betcha they did it."

Paul didn't know whether to be pleased or perturbed. Before he could decide, Danny took the daisies from Paul and squatted with his bottom hovering several inches above the close-cut grass. He placed the cut flowers next to the jar, fiddling with the petals as he began a casual one-sided conversation.

"Hi, Mom. Me and Dad came by to see you. We brought you some daisies, too. I wanted to bring roses, but Dad said they cost too much —"

Paul cringed. At least no one else was in the cemetery to overhear his son call him a cheapskate.

"— so we got the daisies partly because they didn't cost so much, but mostly because there are lots of colors. Dad says you like rainbows, and those daisies look like a rainbow. Well, sort of. If rainbows were scrunched up. And shaped liked daisies."

Paul hid a smile.

"I got to stay at Jeremy Theiszen's house today instead of going to work with Dad at the Zimmerman place. We had a lot of fun building a fort in his backyard. Dad says you and Jeremy's mom used to be friends.

Maybe that's why I like Jeremy so much, huh? He's my best friend in my class at school. Oh!" Danny plopped down and crisscrossed his legs, as if settling in for a long talk. "School let out, and I got mostly good marks. I did best in science. Dad says that's because I take after you — he says you liked science."

It suddenly occurred to Paul how many times Danny had used the phrase "Dad says" when referring to details about Karina. Granted he'd not yet turned six years old when Karina died, but didn't he have any memories of his own of her?

He touched Danny's hair and waited until his son looked up. "You know what I liked best about your mom?"

Danny crinkled his nose and shook his head.

"Her smile. When she smiled, it was almost like someone turned on a light bulb. That's how much she lit up. And her smile always made me want to smile back, even if I'd been having a bad day." He closed his eyes for a moment, seeking an image of Karina's face in his memory. It came — fleetingly, but it came. He grinned down at Danny. "What did you like best about her?"

"Um . . ." Danny played with the daisy petals again. Several dropped onto the grass.

He flicked them with his finger, his head low. Then he looked upward again. "Didn't she make paper airplanes and fly them with me? Didn't you say she did that?"

Sorrow pressed down on Paul. "Don't you remember?"

Danny made a face. "I'm not sure." He pushed to his feet and stuck his hands in his pockets, staring at the headstone. He lowered his voice to a whisper as if afraid Karina would hear his confession. "I *want* to remember. But when I think about her it's all kind of . . . fuzzy. I'm not sure if it's real or not." Tears swam in his eyes and he sniffed.

Paul put his arm around Danny's shoulders and pulled him close. "It's all right, son."

"But she's my mom. Shouldn't I know her?" He leaned his head against Paul's rib cage. "It makes me feel bad."

It pained Paul that his son's cheerful countenance had faded so quickly. He shouldn't have asked about Danny's memories. He leaned down stiffly and kissed the top of his head. "You don't need to feel bad. Not too many people can remember things from when they were five years old. And whenever you have questions about her, you ask me, and I'll tell you whatever you want to know, okay?"

"Okay." He didn't sound cheered.

Paul set him aside and cupped his chin, lifting his face. "Your mom loved you so much. Her biggest worry when she got sick was leaving you. She read Bible stories to you until you could recite them in your sleep —"

Danny's lips twitched into a grin.

"— because she knew she was going to heaven, and she wanted to tell you as much as she could about Jesus before she had to go. And you know what? Before she died, you came into our room and told us you'd asked Jesus to take away your sins."

Danny's face lit up just as much as Karina's had. "She was there, too? I didn't remember that!"

"Yep. And she was the happiest I'd ever seen her. Because then she knew your place was secured in heaven and she would see you again someday."

Tears shone in Danny's eyes even while he grinned. "And when I get there, I'll find her and we'll *really* get to know each other, right, Dad?"

"Right." Paul snagged Danny in a tight hug.

Danny clung for several minutes, his face pressed firmly against Paul's shirt front, then he pulled back and rubbed his nose with his fist. "I'm gonna go to the truck now." He waved at the gray stone. "Bye, Mom. See ya later." He bounded off.

Paul watched him until he climbed into the truck's cab, then he turned back to the grave. Danny had shed his despondence as easily as those daisies were shedding their petals. Maybe he should have gotten the roses, after all. "Karina, it was hard for you when I told you about my relationship with Suzy. It took some prayers, but you finally told me God had forgiven me and you shouldn't hold me accountable for something that, in God's eyes, hadn't even happened. You showed me mercy and grace. I've been grateful for it. But what would you have said if you knew I'd fathered another child?"

He closed his eyes, waiting for a reply. He heard no audible voice, but by drawing on his memories of his wife, he believed he knew what she would have advised. *"You're responsible for her being born, so you need to be responsible in all ways."*

He nodded. Pressing his fingers to his mouth, he placed a kiss on his fingertips and then transferred it to the headstone. "You're right, as usual." He drew in a fortifying breath. "You can't come back to us. Danny can't know you here on earth. But I'm here. As you and God are my witnesses, I will know my daughter, and she will know me."

CHAPTER 29

Suzanne

Suzanne bit through the crispy graham crackers. Melted marshmallow and chocolate oozed between the crackers onto her fingers, but she didn't mind. She hadn't eaten s'mores in years. The flavor transported her to childhood, to other evening bonfires, to happy places.

Stars winked overhead, the nearly full moon seeming to smile down at the group gathered around the snapping bonfire. Mother had declined joining them, claiming the smoke would bother her, but all of her siblings had responded to her invitation for an evening picnic and bonfire in honor of Memorial Day. Clete had even gathered branches and built the fire without a word of complaint, and Shelley brought an extra bag of marshmallows that she said was taking up space in her cabinet.

The children, their tummies full from

roasted marshmallows, now snoozed inside, leaving the adults to visit around the fire without distraction. Across the pit, Alexa perched on the footrest of Mother's lounger and held a straightened metal hanger with two plump marshmallows bobbing at its pointed end. She laughed at something Sandra said, her sweet face softly lit by the fire's glow. Suzanne smiled. How good to see her daughter so relaxed and happy. As a matter of fact, even Clete and Shelley seemed to be enjoying themselves — a small miracle.

Derek opened the last package of graham crackers and plopped a slab of chocolate onto a cracker. "Gimme those marshmallows, Alexa, before you charcoal them. They've gotta be done by now."

Alexa aimed the hanger at him, and Derek sandwiched the blackened marshmallows between the crackers and slid them free of the hanger. He carried the treat directly to his mouth and took a big bite. His eyes widened and he flapped his hand at his face. "Hot!"

Sandra swatted at his arm. "Goofy, you're supposed to blow on it first."

He swallowed, clasping his throat and making a comical face. "*Now* she tells me."

Sandra and Alexa exchanged knowing

looks while Harper and Clete teased Derek, and Tanya and Shelley laughed. Suzanne felt a smile grow in response. Such joy to simply *be,* with no one setting their lips in grim lines or sniping out critical comments. She memorized the moment, savoring the pleasant fellowship with her brother and sisters even more than the sweet flavors on her tongue. Caught up in her contented reflections, she nearly missed Sandra's question.

"Tanya, can Andrew and Olivia stay with you when they come for Mom's birthday? I've already claimed Anna-Grace and Sunny, but I don't think Andrew and Liv will want to sleep on the lumpy sleeper sofa in the basement at our place."

"Andrew?" Suzanne leaned forward, her heart firing into her throat. "Is his family coming to Mother's party?"

Alexa grimaced. "Aww, I wanted them to surprise you."

Sandra hunched her shoulders, a sheepish grin quirking her lips. "I'm sorry, Alexa. I forgot."

Alexa offered Sandra a smile. "It's okay." She faced Suzanne, her eyes shining. "Isn't it great? We invited Grandmother's nephews. They're all coming and bringing their families with them. Since it's a three-hour drive, they plan to spend the night. Andrew said they might even stay over on Saturday night and attend worship with us Sunday morning before going back."

Sandra giggled. "So now we're all scrambling to find places for them to sleep. It's quite the crowd! But Mother will be so pleased. She hasn't seen her sister's sons in years."

Suzanne tossed the last bite of her s'more into the fire. "I . . . I thought when you said 'family' it would be just . . . us."

A frown pinched Alexa's brow. The firelight brought out the golden flecks in her eyes, and Suzanne read confusion in her daughter's expression. "No, Mom. Sandra and I sent invitations to all of the fellowship members, Grandmother's nephews, and even two of her cousins. Quite a few have already told Sandra they're coming. I thought you'd be pleased."

Suzanne swallowed a hysterical laugh. Pleased? Soon she'd be under the same roof with Anna-Grace Braun, the infant she'd been forced to relinquish to her mother's nephew. How could she be in the same room with Anna-Grace and not dissolve into a puddle of sorrow?

"What's wrong, Suzy?" Sandra asked.

Suzanne glanced at her youngest sister,

noting that all her siblings were looking at her strangely. She forced a wobbly smile. "N-nothing. I'm . . . I'm just . . ." She couldn't find a suitable word. Surprised? Unprepared? Devastated? Yes, devastated. But she couldn't say so.

Sandra offered an assuring smile. "Don't worry. We've already decided your job is to keep Mother occupied elsewhere while we prepare for the party. Tanya, Shelley, and I are fixing the food, Alexa is baking the cake — she promised one the size of a football field — and all of us will put up the decorations while you and Mother are away, so you won't have to do much." She feigned a persecuted look and gestured to the others. "*We'll* be doing the hard part."

"And Paul said he'd work extra hours to get the kitchen finished before Mother's birthday." Tanya winked at Alexa. "I promised him the biggest piece of cake for his trouble."

Paul and Anna-Grace? Together? With her? Suzanne eased back into the creaky chair, willing her lips to form a smile. But they only quivered. "It . . . it sounds as if you've got everything figured out."

Alexa's frown deepened. "Mom, I think you need to step away from the fire for a little bit. Your face is all red and you're sweating."

Suzanne laughed — a nervous blast. "Maybe you're right. I do feel a little light-headed. Probably too much heat plus too much sweet. Oh, I made a rhyme." She laughed again, but even to her ears the sound was too shrill to hold real mirth. She pushed out of the chair and held up her sticky hands. "I'm going to go wash up. Does anyone need anything while I'm in the house?"

"Check on the kids," Shelley said, "and make sure they're still sleeping."

"Will do." Suzanne scurried across the dark yard toward the house. Her siblings' soft chatter combined with the muffled crackle of the fire created a gentle melody that contrasted with the fierce pounding of her pulse. Inside the house, she collapsed onto the sofa and closed her eyes. *Dear Lord, help me. Help me . . .*

Abigail

Abigail awakened the day after Memorial Day to the sound of bird song. A lazy smile formed on her face without effort, enjoying the bird's cheerful tune. Last night she'd fallen asleep listening to the mumble of her children's voices interspersed with laughter — a peaceful sound too long absent from the farm. As much as she'd complained and scolded, Clete had been right to bring Suzy home. They needed her here. They needed the healing her presence could bring.

She tossed aside the light covers and automatically tried to fling her legs over the edge of the mattress. Only when her limbs didn't move did the reality of her loss once again crash down on her. How long until her brain completely recognized her legs' uselessness? Every time she forgot, allowing years of habit to override her present infirmity, she suffered another bout of angry frustration and regret.

The joy of the morning's sweet awakening was whisked away, and bitterness slipped into its place. With a grunt, she pushed herself into a seated position, then grabbed her calves and shifted her feet to the floor. Her chair waited next to the bed, the transfer board lying across the arms in readiness. She needed the bathroom, but instead of reaching for the board, she sat scowling at the reprehensible chair. She wished she could kick it. Kick it hard. Knowing she couldn't only made the anger swell hotter, higher, and when someone tapped at her door, she barked, "What do you want?"

The door creaked open and Alexa peeked

in. "Would you like a cup of coffee? It's ready." Her smooth, youthful face pursed with worry and a hint of hurt feelings. But even so, she spoke kindly.

Shame flooded Abigail. She didn't deserve Alexa's kindness. But thinking of coffee made her need for the bathroom increase. If she didn't hurry she'd shame herself in another way. She waved her hand, desperation sharpening her tone. "No coffee yet. I'll call when I want it."

The door clicked closed and Abigail made use of the transfer board. To her relief, she reached the bathroom in time. She washed her hands and then her face, grunting a bit with the effort of reaching the spigots. As much as she disliked having Paul Aldrich take over her personal space, she looked forward to having the sink at a more manageable height. She brushed her teeth, dribbling foamy paste all over the edge of the white porcelain when she spat. She cleaned up the mess with her washcloth, then tossed the cloth into the tub with her used towels from last night.

She couldn't see her reflection in the bathroom's mirror, so she grabbed her hairbrush and reversed the chair through the doorway into the bedroom where Clete had set the mirror on her old dressing table at a sharp angle to catch her image. She turned the chair toward the mirror and raised her brush, but then she sat, her hand frozen in position, and stared at the person reflected in the rectangular glass.

Streaked blond and gray hair stood out in wild disarray. Purple smudges beneath the eyes and deep lines drawing from the nose to the corners of the mouth spoke of sleepless nights and the burden of worry. The neck of the loose-fitting gown sagged, exposing a patch of crepey skin. For a moment, Abigail blinked in confusion. That apparition was *her*? When had she become such an old, frazzled-looking, ugly woman?

Averting her gaze, she dropped the brush in her lap and turned the chair toward the door. Popping it open a scant inch — heaven forbid Paul should catch a glimpse of her — she called, "Suzanne? I need you!" Her words echoed through her mind. She did need Suzy. She needed Suzy to forgive her. To love her again. To somehow make her beautiful.

When Suzy entered the room, though, Abigail only said, "I want my green-checked dress. The seersucker one. It doesn't wrinkle."

With professional detachment and gentle touches, Suzy removed Abigail's rumpled nightgown and helped her into clean under-clothes and the dress she wanted. She knelt to slide Abigail's support hose over her legs before she slipped on her oxfords and tied the laces. Abigail had to close her eyes against tears as her daughter ministered to her, patient and tender. When she was dressed, Suzy brushed Abigail's hair, braided it, and twisted it into a bun. She reached for the white mesh cap resting on the edge of the dresser, but Abigail shook her head.

"I can get it. You've done enough."

Suzy handed her the cap. "All right. Alexa has coffee waiting when you're ready."

"I know. She told me."

"Toast or cereal this morning?"

"I don't care. Surprise me."

Suzy laughed, as if Abigail had a made a joke. "All right." She left the room and closed the door softly behind her.

Abigail slipped the cap over her bun and rolled close to the dressing table to retrieve the bobby pins from a little saucer on the table's wood top. Although she tried not to look at herself as she jammed pins into place, her gaze rebelliously connected with the mirror. In some ways the image was dif-ferent from the earlier one. This time a snow-white cap hid most of the neatly combed hair, and a crisp dress, buttoned to the neck, shielded the wrinkled throat. But the same old face etched with frown lines remained.

Abigail shook her head slowly, watching the black ribbons of her cap rumple against the bodice of the fresh, springtime-colored dress. Had she really thought Suzy could help? All the primping in the world couldn't change what was underneath. So why try?

With a sigh she aimed her chair for the dining room and pulled close to the table as Suzy carried in a platter of buttered toast and a fat jar of strawberry jam. Alexa bounced up from her chair and poured a cup of aromatic coffee for Abigail. She managed to push aside her doldrums enough to offer a weak smile of thanks for the coffee.

"I finally figured out the percolator," Alexa said as she sat back in her chair, "and I told Mom I want to find one for ourselves when we go home again. This percolated coffee tastes as good as any you'd pay four dollars a cup for at a coffee shop."

"Four dollars?" Abigail nearly dropped the piece of toast she'd picked up. "Who pays four dollars for one cup of coffee?"

Alexa grinned. "You'd be surprised how many people. Lots of times it's even more than four dollars."

"Ridiculous." Abigail slathered jam on the toast, shaking her head. She found it refreshing to talk about something as inconsequential as the cost of a cup of coffee after the bitter ruminations in her bedroom. "Some people must have more money than sense." She dropped the knife back in the jar and looked at Suzy. "Pray so we can eat."

Suzy obliged, and the moment she said, "Amen," the back screen door slammed and Clete's voice called, "Mother?"

"In the dining room," Abigail called back. "Grab a cup on the way through the kitchen if you want some of Alexa's good percolated coffee."

Clete entered the room with empty hands and a sullen expression. "No thanks. Just wanted to let you know Paul will be late today. He's trying to get a doctor's appointment before he comes out to work."

Alexa shot Clete a wide-eyed look. "Is he all right?"

The girl's concern seemed deeper than idle interest, igniting Abigail's curiosity. She watched her granddaughter's face as Clete replied.

"Said he hurt his back yesterday and wants to get it checked out."

Alexa chewed her lower lip. Even a fool would be able to recognize her deep concern. Worry stabbed Abigail, too. She aimed a frown at Clete. "Did he hurt himself working here or at home? If he hurt himself here, we need to pay his doctor bills."

Clete scowled. He flicked a glance at Alexa before answering — an odd reaction. "I'm handling it, Mother."

Suzy turned sideways in her chair. "If he's hurt badly and can't work for a while, who will finish the projects out here? I can't possibly hire a nurse until this mess is straightened out. It wouldn't be fair to ask someone to work in these circumstances."

Clete folded his arms over his chest and leaned against the door frame. "I'm sure he'll be able to finish the job. But if not, I'll find somebody else."

"No one else will work as reasonably as Paul Aldrich." Abigail surprised herself with her staunch statement. "You know how he gives the fellowship families a reduced rate."

Clete pushed off from the door frame. "As I said, Mother, I'll handle it." He turned to leave.

"See that you do," Abigail snapped.

He sauntered off without answering. She picked up her toast and took a bite, her thoughts rolling. If Paul Aldrich got hurt on her property, she'd have another reason to feel guilty. She hoped he'd be all right. But she didn't pray about it, because God was wise enough to know she wanted it more for herself than for him.

CHAPTER 30

Suzanne

The doctor ordered Paul to three days of rest to let his back heal. Mother's worry ended when Paul assured them he hadn't been hurt working in her house, but Alexa remained distraught over the situation. Suzanne questioned her, but she would only say she felt bad for him.

Although Suzanne wished the kitchen renovation didn't have to be postponed, she appreciated the opportunity to interview potential caretakers for her mother without having to deal with the construction noise.

Of the four candidates who drove out to the farm to meet Mother, talk with Suzanne about the position, and ask questions, the one who seemed the most interested in the job was also the one Mother liked the least. "She reminds me of an eager puppy — far too bouncy and chipper. She grated on my nerves," Mother claimed. Although Suzanne wanted to argue because the woman was qualified and willing to make the drive to Arborville, she had to agree with Mother's assessment. Her overly cheerful behavior seemed a bit over the top to be sincere and made Suzanne uncomfortable.

Both she and Mother liked another applicant named Connie. Middle-aged with an unflappable nature and calm demeanor, the woman seemed a perfect fit. But she expressed concern about the drive from Pratt and said she would have to give it some thought. They parted with the agreement she would call no later than mid-June with a decision, and if someone else came along in the meantime, she would understand.

Consequently, Suzanne was left still searching. Thursday evening after she helped Mother bathe and prepare for bed, she borrowed Alexa's phone and curled into the corner of the sofa to look through the applicants again in the hopes she'd missed one. As she squinted to read the documents on the three-inch screen, Alexa came in and plopped down next to her feet.

"Mom?"

Focused on the application, Suzanne murmured, "Hmm?"

Alexa bumped her knee. "Mom."

She sent a quick look over the top of the phone. The serious expression on her daughter's face captured her full attention. "What?"

"Is Mr. Aldrich coming to work tomorrow?"

Suzanne smiled and set the phone aside. "Honey, I'm sure his injury wasn't bad enough to warrant all your worrying. Clete said he plans to be here tomorrow, and he'll work Saturday, too, to make up for the time he missed."

Alexa blew out a sigh. "I'm glad."

Suzanne lifted the phone again.

"But, Mom?"

Lowering her feet to the floor, Suzanne shifted to face Alexa. "What is it?"

"I just wondered . . ." Alexa bit the corner of her mouth for a moment. "Did Uncle Clete tell you how Mr. Aldrich got hurt?"

Suzanne shrugged. "No. He just said it didn't happen on the job."

Alexa sat on in brooding silence, her narrowed gaze locked on something across the room.

Suzanne placed her hand on her daughter's knee. "Alexa, what is bothering you? Your concern for Mr. Aldrich is very sweet, but it seems a little out of place. After all, you hardly know the man." She didn't intend to scold, but neither did she want to encourage Alexa to develop a relationship with Paul. Nothing good could come of it.

"Maybe I don't, but . . ." Alexa tipped her head and peeked at Suzanne through her heavy fringe of eyelashes. "How well do you know him?"

"We . . ." — Suzanne forced a light laugh — "grew up together. We were friends. Of course, that was a long time ago."

"Yeah." Alexa crunched her brow, still pinning her mother with a thoughtful look. "Mom, on Monday morning when I went out to the barn to tell Uncle Clete I was ready to go to the paint store, I found him and Mr. Aldrich rolling on the barn floor, fighting."

Suzanne drew back in surprise. "Are you serious?"

Alexa nodded. "I'm pretty sure that's how Mr. Aldrich got hurt."

Suzanne covered her mouth with her hand, stunned. No wonder Alexa had been quiet. What an awful thing to witness.

"Mr. Aldrich told me they were fighting about something that happened a long time ago, but he wouldn't tell me what."

Ice water seemed to fill Suzanne's veins.

"And Uncle Clete told me I should ask you about it. That it was your place to tell

410

me. I thought that was a little odd, but Mr. Aldrich agreed and even said he'd pray for me to find the right time to ask you about it." Alexa sucked in a breath and blew it out in a noisy rush. "So what happened, Mom? What were they fighting about?"

It was Suzanne's turn to fall silent. She had no idea what to say.

Alexa waited while the steady ticktock of Dad's old key-wound clock seemed to grow louder with each second. A full minute passed before Alexa spoke again, her voice strained and low. "I've been thinking about it quite a bit. Wondering. And I kind of put things together in my mind. Can I tell you what I think?"

Suzanne, fearful of what would come next, refused to answer.

Alexa went on as if she'd received approval. "I think maybe Clete attacked Mr. Aldrich because he was the one who got you pregnant. Am I right?"

Shame roiled in Suzanne's middle, melting the ice water and bringing it to a boiling point. Although her daughter's tone held no recrimination, only a genuine desire to know, she couldn't find the strength to speak of that painful time. In lieu of words, a low moan emerged from her throat.

Alexa gripped her hand. Her fingers felt

as hot as the bonfire they'd enjoyed only a few nights ago. Such a pleasant, relaxing night — a night of peaceful settling in together with her family, giving her a false sense of security. If Alexa discovered the truth, she'd never know peace again.

Suzanne pulled loose and clutched her hands together in her lap.

Tears flooded Alexa's eyes. She leaned in, her face beseeching. "Mom, please tell me. I know you told me my father wasn't here in Arborville, and if Mr. Aldrich is the one, then you must have lied to me."

Disappointment showed in her daughter's face and voice — a disappointment brought on by Suzanne's duplicity. Pain stabbed her chest with such ferocity she could barely take a breath.

"Please tell me the truth now." Alexa's dark eyes shimmered with unshed tears. "Am I right about why they were fighting?"

The need to escape became too great to ignore. Suzanne bolted from the sofa and charged for the staircase. But something made her stop and look back at Alexa. The anguish in her daughter's expression pierced her anew. Alexa wanted the truth. The Bible instructed believers to be truthful. But the truth would hurt Alexa, hurt Paul, hurt her mother and brother and sisters and even the extended family. She couldn't tell the truth. God, who knew all and understood all, surely knew why she had to keep her secret, didn't He?

Alexa had guessed part of it. Suzanne wouldn't outright lie and tell her she was wrong. But neither would she divulge every bit of the truth she'd held to herself for more than nineteen years. Truth, yes, but the whole truth? Absolutely not. Not even in a court of law.

She held her arms open, and with a little cry Alexa dashed to her. She held her daughter close, the way she had when Alexa was a toddler in need of comforting. She stroked Alexa's hair, pressed her lips to her temple, and finally took her face in her hands. Her courage gathered, she whispered raggedly, "Yes, honey. He's the one. And I beg you . . . don't ask me about it again."

Alexa

Mom released her and darted up the stairs. Alexa stood at the bottom of the staircase and stared into the shadowy landing, too stunned to move. When she'd offered her speculation, she'd half expected Mom to say her active imagination had carried her away again. To instead have her suspicion confirmed left Alexa weak and reeling.

She didn't think she could manage the stairs, so she stumbled back to the sofa and dropped onto the faded cushions. The question that had plagued her from the time she was old enough to understand their family was different from others was now answered. She could replace the nameless, faceless image in her mind with Paul Aldrich, a tall dark-haired man with brown eyes and a warm smile.

But with the knowledge came a rush of new questions. Why hadn't Grandmother and Grandfather insisted Mr. Aldrich do the honorable thing and marry Mom? Why had they instructed Mom to give the baby away? Were they trying to protect themselves from humiliation, or were they trying to protect Mom from something else?

She whispered into the quiet room. "Did they send Mom away to shield her from . . . Dad?" She sampled the title. Somehow it didn't settle well. Not yet. It was too new, too unfamiliar. She'd need some time to adjust to it, to decide if she wanted to pursue a father-daughter relationship. Sadness sagged her shoulders. As much as she'd longed to know her father, now only uncertainty gripped her.

Her grandparents had separated Mom from the boy who'd impregnated her.

Mom's tearful instruction to never speak of the subject again, the fact that she'd lied to Alexa earlier when asked if her father was in Arborville, the secrecy surrounding her conception and birth, and her uncle's violent behavior toward Mr. Aldrich made her wonder if he'd not always been the pleasant, kind person he seemed to be today.

She pulled up her knees and wrapped her arms around them, huddling into a small ball. Had he, at one time, hurt her mother in some way?

The troublesome question followed her up the stairs and rolled through her dreams. By morning Alexa had made a decision. She wouldn't ask Mom for the details of her relationship with Mr. Aldrich. Nor would she ask Grandmother or Uncle Clete. But she would satisfy her curiosity. Somehow. No matter how long it took.

After a simple breakfast of instant oatmeal and juice, she started the percolator and then penned a note for her mother. *Spending the morning in the summer kitchen. Don't worry. I ate something and I'm fine — just feel like being alone. It's a girl thing.* She added a smiley face and left the note on the dining room table where she knew Mom would find it. Then she headed outside.

Her sandals were wet from dew by the

time she reached the summer kitchen, so she kicked them off and left them on the stoop. She propped the door open and then opened the north and south windows to allow a cross breeze. It was pleasant now, but as the sun crept higher, the temperature would rise. Eventually she hoped to cook out here, but she had no desire to cook herself. Too bad the little house was no longer hooked to a power line — she'd drag out the fan from her bedroom. Getting electricity would be the first item on her to-do list for the summer kitchen.

Armed with her smartphone, paper, and pencil, she sat at the table and began creating a renovation plan. She'd need contractors to take care of the big things like plumbing, electricity, painting, and reshingling the exterior. Those jobs would eat up most of her budget. So she'd have to be thrifty in fixing up the interior. She wasn't worried. Growing up in a single-parent household, she'd learned to shop at second-hand stores, flea markets, and garage sales. She loved scoring a good bargain, and as she sketched out her plans, her excitement grew.

Not only would the summer kitchen become a cottage getaway for her and Mom when they came to visit Grandmother —

because they *would* come to visit every year from now on if she had anything to say about it — but it would give her an excuse to spend time with Mr. Aldrich. He was a carpenter. He knew every contractor in the area. He would become her go-to guy. And as she spent time with him, asking him questions about renovations and decorating and designing a small but efficient bathroom, she would get to know him. As a worker, but also as a man. And, eventually, as a father.

In time, when they were comfortable with each other — when she felt secure enough — she would come right out and ask what she needed to know. She lifted her head from her notebook and voiced the most pressing question. "Mr. Aldrich, why didn't my mother's family allow you to be part of my life?"

The border collie, Pepper, set up a raucous barking. Alexa's pulse skipped a beat. She rose and darted to the door. Sure enough, Pepper was chasing Mr. Aldrich's truck up the lane. The pickup rolled to a stop next to Uncle Clete's pickup. Pepper, still barking, circled the truck, her tail wagging as fast as a hummingbird beating its wings.

Both the driver and passenger doors opened, and Mr. Aldrich and his son climbed out. Pepper attacked Danny, leaping and licking and barking all at once. Danny's giggles carried all the way across the yard, and Alexa couldn't help smiling.

Mr. Aldrich gave the dog's neck a few scratches before turning toward the house. Alexa ducked back in case he looked in her direction — she didn't want to be caught spying on him, but it warmed her to see his kindness toward that annoying, long-haired mutt. She gave him enough time to get inside before peering out again.

Danny had located a stick, and he gave it a mighty throw, hollering, "Git it, girl!" Pepper took off in a black-and-white blur. She snatched up the stick in her mouth and whirled, but instead of carrying it to Danny, she raced toward the wheat fields. Danny charged after her. "Pepper, you crazy dog! You come back here!"

Alexa held her breath and hid in the shadows until the dog zipped by with her ears flapping and long fur waving. Danny pounded behind her, continuing to call fruitlessly for the dog to come back. He came to a halt at the edge of the yard and plunked his fists on his hips. "Fine then! I didn't wanna play with you anyway!"

Turning, he kicked at the long wild grass growing near the field and then scuffed toward the house. As he passed the summer kitchen, he glanced up and spotted Alexa. A grin formed on his face. He ambled over. "Hi! What'cha doing out here?"

A little embarrassed to be caught spying, she shrugged. "Thinking. Dreaming." She tipped her head toward the wheat field where Pepper had disappeared. "Did Pepper abscond with your stick?"

"Abscond? What's that?"

"Steal."

"Oh." Danny's grin turned into a scowl. "Yeah. Crazy dog. It was a good stick, too. I could've used it to hit rocks. But I guess I can find another one. There're lots of trees out here, so lots of sticks." His grin returned, and he swung his arms, lightly brushing the legs of his trousers with each swing. "What're you dreaming about?"

Alexa had spent time with Danny already, but now seeing him as her half brother, not just a little boy, made her look at him differently. His thick dark hair, cut short, spiked upward above his left eyebrow with a natural cowlick. He looked a lot like his father, with eyes of brown sugar and a dimpled chin. In his button-up plaid shirt, trousers, and boots — odd summer attire for a child — he was a miniature of Paul Aldrich. And since he'd lived every minute of his life with the man, he would know him well enough to share some information if Alexa wanted to ask.

Two emotions struck simultaneously — jealousy and eagerness. She chose to push the first aside and adopt the second. She smiled and held her hand toward the table where a pair of chairs waited. "Come on in and have a seat. I'll tell you what I'm dreaming about, and you can tell me what you think of it. Okay?"

CHAPTER 31

Alexa

"Wow, you have good dreams."

Alexa chuckled. Danny's comment pleased her more than she could understand. She fiddled with the edge of the paper and shrugged. "I have a good imagination. My mom tells me I have an overly active one." Was it her active imagination that had conjured the idea of Mr. Aldrich being a less-than-stellar choice as a husband and father?

"I hope you get to do all that." Danny pointed at the drawings. "Do you think you'll get it done soon? Because I'd like to come out and play in here when it's done. My friend Jeremy and me built a fort in his backyard out of blankets and stuff, but this would be a lot better. A wall that moves back and forth?" His eyes glowed. "I like that!"

"Not a moving wall, just a curtain that

slides on a track."

Danny grinned. "Okay. It'd still be neat, though. Would it be all right with you if Jeremy and me played in your cottage? If Dad lets us come out with him, I mean?"

Another idea seemed to drop from the ceiling and clunk Alexa on the head. She gasped.

Danny stared at her. "What?"

She flipped to a clean sheet of paper and began writing furiously.

He leaned forward, squinting at the page. "What'cha writing?"

"Shh. Gimme a minute."

He froze in place, his arms folded underneath his chest and his gaze following the point of her pencil. When she jabbed a final period in place, he lifted his face to give her a wide-eyed look. "Did you have another dream?"

Alexa tapped the top of his head with her pencil. "I did. And you're the inspiration for this one."

Danny bounced in his chair, making the legs squeak. "What is it?"

"Huh-uh." Alexa rose and clutched the notebook to her chest, grinning at him. "Not yet. I need to talk to your dad first." She wanted to say *our dad*, and sadness momentarily struck. She pushed the feeling aside. If this worked out, she'd have the chance to get to know — to *really* get to know — her father.

"Aww . . ." Danny sagged into the chair. "C'mon, Alexa, tell me. Please?"

She fought a giggle. She'd loved interacting with the kids at the grade school cafeteria and had imagined having a younger sibling, but the reality was much better than her imaginings. Danny was adorably personable, and he'd already weaseled his way into her affections. Temptation to share her idea teased, but in the end she decided it wouldn't be fair to get his hopes up and then crash them if Mr. Aldrich said it wasn't possible.

"I'm sorry, kiddo, but you'll have to wait."

Danny heaved a mighty sigh.

She headed for the door. "C'mon. I baked monster cookies yesterday. We'll ask your dad if you can have one."

His face instantly transformed from melancholy to delight. "Okay!"

They walked together across the sunlit yard — Alexa cautiously, her sandals in her hand, and Danny half-skipping, half-sauntering. She couldn't help but smile at him. Danny was such a happy, well-adjusted, well-behaved, seemingly well-cared-for kid. Watching his joyful progress,

423

Alexa pondered anew why she'd been kept separated from her father all these years. Something didn't make sense.

Paul

The sound of his son's giggle preceded the slap of the back screen door into its frame. Paul paused in attaching the new handle to the cabinet drawer and watched for Danny to bounce into the kitchen. Bounce, not walk, because Danny tended to do everything with exuberance. To Paul's surprise, Alexa entered first with Danny trailing on her heels like a shadow. Seeing the two of them together took his breath away. *My children . . .*

"Dad, Alexa made monster cookies, and she said I could have one if it was all right with you. So is it all right? Can I have one? Please?"

Paul didn't intend to ignore Danny, but he couldn't seem to peel his attention away from the way Alexa smiled down at the boy. With affection and indulgence and a hint of amusement. Her expression reminded him of how Suzy used to look at Clete. Even when Paul had gotten aggravated with her younger brother, wishing he'd go away and stop bugging them, she never lost her temper with him. He'd dubbed the special look "big sisterly." Now Alexa had it, too. What a gift Danny was receiving, and he didn't even know it.

"It won't spoil my lunch. Honest. One cookie?"

Danny's begging finally pulled Paul to the present. He coughed into his hand to open his tight throat before answering. "Sure. If Alexa wants to share, that's fine."

She gave him a look he could only define as hopeful. "Would you like one, too? They're full of oats and peanut butter and chocolate chips and walnuts — really good."

Although his stomach was still full from the hearty breakfast he'd eaten at the café before coming out to work, he wouldn't decline a cookie from his daughter. "I'd love one."

Alexa put down the notebook she'd been carrying and popped open a plastic tub. She held it to Danny first, who eagerly snatched out a cookie and carried it directly to his mouth, then she offered the tub to Paul. He swiped his hand along his pant leg twice before fishing out a cookie as big as his palm. He aimed a grin at Alexa as he held the cookie aloft. "They look good."

"Mm, 'ey are good," Danny mumbled around a mouthful.

Paul shook his head at his son, frowning slightly.

Danny swallowed the bite, then shrugged sheepishly. "Sorry. I'm not supposed to talk with food in my mouth."

To Paul's delight, Alexa laughed and tweaked Danny's nose. "You're forgiven." She tucked the container back on top of the refrigerator and lifted the notebook again, resting it in the crook of her arm. "Mr. Aldrich, when you take a break, I'd like to talk to you about something."

Danny gulped, pawing at Paul's arm. "She's got an idea, Dad, and I inspired it."

"Actually, you both did," Alexa said.

Paul lifted his eyebrows, his interest piqued. "Oh?"

Alexa nodded. "I'm not sure if it will work, so I don't want to get everybody involved until I know. But I figured you would be the best one to ask. So when you have a minute . . ."

Paul took a small nibble of the cookie. "I can't work and eat at the same time. But I can eat and listen." He bit off another tiny chunk. He intended to make this cookie last. "So go ahead."

She rocked slightly, the hem of her flowered skirt swaying above her bare toes. "I was thinking about fixing up the summer kitchen — turning it into a little guest cottage for Mom and me. Then Danny asked if he could visit it, too, which made me wonder . . ." She angled her head and her ponytail slipped along her shoulder in a sleek, dark wave. "Would this farmhouse make a good B and B?"

"What's a beanin' B?" Danny asked. He'd finished his cookie, and crumbs ringed his mouth.

"Danny, go wash your face and hands." Paul waited until his son scooted around the corner before addressing Alexa. "You know, my wife once said something about this being a good spot for a bed-and-breakfast inn." He'd forgotten about the conversation until Alexa's question stirred the memory. Recalling Karina's comments made him smile. "People who go to B and Bs generally want a peaceful getaway."

Alexa nodded. "Exactly. And what would be more peaceful than a farmhouse in a Mennonite community? Of course, if they want a little entertainment, bigger cities are a reasonable drive away. There's parking space out by the barn, and you built ramps so it's handicap accessible the way places are supposed to be these days, but the house itself . . . would it work? There are enough bedrooms, I think, but they're all upstairs except for Grandmother's, and there's just that little powder room off the kitchen. So is there a way to add a tub or shower in there? And maybe a bedroom on the first floor? And how much would that cost? What about this kitchen — would it work for cooking for guests?"

Paul started to laugh. He didn't mean to, but her exuberance tickled him. "Slow down a minute. You're having one of your gung-ho moments." He liked that he already recognized when her excitement kicked into a gallop.

Danny careened back into the room, and Paul handed him the uneaten portion of his cookie. "Here, you can have the rest of this. But eat it outside. Then play for a while. I'll need your help later on." Danny grabbed the cookie and slammed out the back door. Paul returned his attention to Alexa, who stood with her head slightly downcast and her lip caught between her teeth.

She peeked at him, her eyes sparkling with mischief. "So . . . am I getting gung-ho for no good reason?"

He folded his arms over his chest before he snagged her in a fatherly hug. "I can't speak to any rules or regulations the state might have about opening a B and B here, but I can say with pretty fair certainty the house could work. Even with just the one bathroom upstairs, it could work if the guests are all housed up there and they know ahead of time they'll have to share."

Alexa listened intently, nodding slightly as he spoke.

He hated himself for what he had to say next. But a father wouldn't let his child walk into a land mine, and he wouldn't let Alexa blithely make plans that would crumble beneath her feet. "But your grandmother is in a wheelchair. She needs to be *cared for,* not to be *taking care of* guests. How would she manage it?"

"She wouldn't. I would."

Paul jolted. "You?"

In a heartbeat her enthusiasm returned. "Remember when you told me I should be a bakery? Well, not *be* a bakery, but run one. I love to cook, and I think I'm pretty good at it. And I've been praying about what I want to do for my job. My mom, being a nurse, ministers to people, and I admire that so much, and I wanted to do some kind of ministry, too. Wouldn't running a bed-and-breakfast inn be a ministry? Helping people relax, fixing them good meals, serving them . . . Jesus served His disciples, right? So isn't serving people a good thing?"

Without conscious thought, Paul reached

out and gave her a quick hug. He couldn't pull her close with the bulky notebook between them, but it didn't make the embrace any less heartfelt. When he stepped back, her cheeks wore pink stains and wonder glowed in her eyes.

He spoke huskily. "Serving people is a very good thing, Alexa, and I'm proud of you for wanting to be a servant. So many young people today . . ." He couldn't have raised her better himself. He swallowed and went on, forcing a light tone. "There would be hurdles to leap, of course, but your plan is doable. It's a matter of your grandmother approving it." His heart fell. Abigail Zimmerman wouldn't welcome guests into her home. And Suzy surely wouldn't want to let Alexa live so far away. The plan was doomed.

Alexa inched toward the doorway leading to the dining room. "I'll go talk to Mom and Grandmother. I . . ." She pulled in a breath and held it, as if battling with herself. Her air whooshed out as she said, "I appreciate you taking the time to talk to me, Mr. Aldrich. Thank you." She dashed off.

He smiled, envisioning her expression as she'd shared her ideas. He couldn't shake the feeling she intended to say something else before she left, but her sweet words of gratitude echoed through his mind.

Lord, if this is Your will for Alexa, let it come to pass. Offering the prayer erased the edges of apprehension. As he returned to work, the prayer repeated itself in the back of his heart. But he wouldn't allow himself to speculate on how wonderful it would be for him to have his daughter in the same community where he could see her every week.

CHAPTER 32

Suzanne

"Why would anybody want to come to this run-down old house?"

Suzanne cringed at Mother's question. Alexa's enthusiasm melted as quickly as snowflakes landing on a child's warm tongue. "Mother . . ." She injected gentle reproach in her tone.

Mother shifted in her lounger to scowl at Suzanne. "It's an honest question." Her expression softened when she turned to Alexa, who sat on the porch stairs and rested her chin in her hand, the picture of despondence. "I didn't mean to hurt your feelings. But, Alexa, think. People would turn in at the lane, take one look at the place, and turn around and leave. They wouldn't want to come inside."

Did Mother's voice hold a bit of embarrassment? Maybe regret for having let the house go? Suzanne hoped she interpreted correctly, because then maybe Mother wouldn't be upset when the fellowship men converged to give the house a face-lift.

Alexa cupped her hands over her knees. "We'd have to do some fixing up. I already thought of that."

Mother released a little snort.

Alexa flicked a glance at Suzanne before continuing. "But isn't it peaceful out here on the porch, Grandmother? There's always a nice breeze."

"Yes, Kansas is generally windy."

"If it's too windy, your front room is big enough for guests to sit and visit with each other or read a book."

"On my old furniture? They'd probably turn up their noses at my sofa."

"And the dining room! The table is perfect for everyone to sit around and start their day with a good breakfast and conversation."

"I'll grant you, the table can seat a small army, but it's right off my bedroom. I wouldn't want to listen to a bunch of strangers jabbering right outside my door."

Suzanne intervened before Mother could turn another of Alexa's positives into a negative. "I think what Mother is trying to say in her rather indelicate way" — Mother shot her a glare, which she ignored — "is running a B and B would be too much for her."

"Well . . ." Alexa scrunched her face into a grimace. "I wasn't actually thinking of Grandmother running it." She looked into Suzanne's eyes, her expression pleading. "I want to do it myself."

"What?" Mother exploded with the short query Suzanne held back.

Alexa launched into an explanation of using the bed-and-breakfast as a means of ministering to those who needed a place of rest and rejuvenation. Her gaze zipped between her mother and grandmother, her hands gesturing with excited little chops of emphasis. Suzanne listened, stunned, uncertain how a two-month hiatus had become a possible full-time change for her daughter.

"Mr. Aldrich says it's possible, that the house would accommodate guests," Alexa went on. "He doesn't know about regulations concerning B and B businesses, but —"

Suzanne nearly came out of her chair. She forced herself to remain seated on its edge. "You talked to Paul about this?"

Alexa nodded.

"Before you talked to *me*?" The anger — and fear — coursing through her middle shocked her even more than Alexa's announcement about running a bed-and-breakfast inn.

Mother patted her on the wrist. "Settle down, Suzanne."

Suzanne jerked away from the placating touch. "Why would you talk to him? He has no bearing on what you do."

Alexa stared at her as if she'd never seen her before. "Mom, he's a builder. He knows about these things."

Suzanne glared into her daughter's face for a few more seconds. With Mother sitting there, she couldn't say what she wanted to, but the words roared through her mind. *Don't you turn to that man as if he has all the answers. Getting a woman pregnant does not a father make, and you are not his — you are mine!* "You should have come to your grandmother and me first. After all, this affects us more than it affects Paul Aldrich."

"I'm sorry, Mom." Alexa blinked rapidly. "I just thought it was better to find out if the house could even *be* a B and B before I talked to you about it. I wasn't trying to leave you out."

Her daughter's respectful explanation did nothing to alleviate Suzanne's anger. "Well, you can just forget the idea. It would be too much work, and your grandmother isn't up to having strangers coming and going out here. You have a job and a church and friends and . . . and . . ." She avoided adding *me,* recognizing even in her anger how self-centered she would sound. "A *life* in Indiana. So just put your grand scheme out of your head right now."

Alexa smacked her notebook closed, yanked it against her chest, and clomped down the steps.

Suzanne curled her hands around the chair's plastic armrests to hold herself in place. "Where are you going?" She better not be going to talk to Paul again.

Alexa shook her head, her ponytail bobbing. "Back to the summer kitchen, Mom. I want to do some thinking. And some praying."

Some praying . . . Alexa's simple comment speared Suzanne's heart. She should have prayed before spouting off at her daughter. She'd treated Alexa like a rebellious 'tween rather than the mature young woman she was, and all because of her own insecurities.

She eased back into the chair, forcing herself to take deep, slow breaths. Her gaze drifted across the delicate fretwork decorating the porch, then to the yard with its expanse of green grass and gardens of zinnias, snapdragons, bachelor's-buttons, and roses. Mother had never wanted fussy gardens, but Dad wanted color, so he'd planted flowers that would reseed themselves and come back year after year. She understood why Alexa could envision the farmhouse as a B and B. But to stay here and run it? Her imagination was carrying her to places she shouldn't go.

"What are you thinking?" Mother intruded upon Suzanne's thoughts.

Suzanne snorted. "I don't think you want to know."

Mother chuckled softly. "I bet I already know."

Suzanne didn't want to find out. She stood. "It's nearly lunchtime. I'll go fix some sandwiches. Do you want me to take you inside, or would you rather stay out here?"

Mother caught hold of Suzanne's wrist and squeezed. Her leathery palm was warm and dry, her touch assuring, but Suzanne found no comfort in it. Mother said, "She went to him because she wants to know her father."

"Well, she can't." Suzanne snapped the words, intentionally harsh. "In or out, Mother?"

Mother sighed. "I'll stay here."

Suzanne slammed herself in the house and marched toward the kitchen. But not to make sandwiches. The sandwiches could wait. She and Paul Aldrich needed to get a few things settled.

Paul

Paul lay on his back with his head inside the cupboard. The awkward position put pressure on his lower spine, and his back throbbed like a bad tooth, but he couldn't access the drainpipes any other way. He'd just need to hurry. "Hand me the wrench, Danny."

The tool slapped into his palm, and he tightened the jam nut against the gasket. Tight enough to hold, not too tight to crimp the gasket. He didn't want any water leaking and ruining the inside of the cabinetry.

"What else do you need, Dad?"

Paul smiled. Danny was always so eager to help. He shifted his attention to the coupling nuts. "Nothing yet. I'll let you know when I'm ready for something else."

"Okay."

He finished with the wrench and thrust it out. "Flashlight and rag now."

Danny didn't take the wrench. "Dad?"

He raised his voice a bit. "I said flashlight and rag, Danny."

"I heard you. But . . ." Danny patted his knee. "Can you come out?"

He didn't want to come out until he'd

438

finished. But his son's insistent whisper changed his mind. Paul lay the wrench on the floor and wriggled his way downward until he could sit up without clunking his head. As soon as he cleared the cabinet, he understood why Danny had wanted him. Suzy stood near his feet, and her expression warned of a brewing storm. He set his lips in a grim line. She could thunder all she wanted to. He had a few lightning bolts ready to fling in return.

Paul managed to sit up. It took some doing. His back still didn't want to cooperate very well. "Danny, would you run out to the pickup and get our lunchboxes? I think I'd like to eat under the cottonwoods in the back. I'll meet you there."

Danny sidled toward the porch, his wary gaze fixed on Suzy. "Sure." He scampered out.

Paul hooked the little kitchen footstool with his foot and slid it across the floor toward Suzy. She sat stiffly on the stool. Its short height brought her down so her face was only a few inches above his. He closed the cabinet door and leaned against it, bending one knee and bracing his hand on it. "What's on your mind?"

"Alexa."

Interesting. She'd been on his mind a lot

lately, too. "What about her?"

"I want you to leave her alone."

Paul squinted at her. "Excuse me?"

"You heard me. Stay away from her. Don't talk to her. Don't even look at her."

She had a lot of nerve — he'd give her that. If his back wasn't still giving him fits, he would leap to his feet, yank her up, and shake her until her teeth rattled. "You mean like I've had to do for the past nineteen years?" To his satisfaction, her stiff pose melted a bit. "I know, Suzy. I know how you went off and had our baby girl all by yourself."

Fury roared through his gut. He'd never experienced such a fierce desire to inflict bodily harm on another human being, and the feeling scared him. He grated out, "How could you have kept something like that from me?"

Her face paled. She gripped her hands tightly over her knees and clung as if in need of a lifeline. "I was wrong to keep my pregnancy from you. I was so young, so scared, and my mother was so forceful . . . But that isn't an excuse."

"You're right." Paul growled the statement. "I spent years feeling guilty, believing I shamed you so badly you had to go away. But my wrong is nothing compared to yours. You should have come to me."

She jerked her chin upward, and steely determination entered her expression again. "And what would you have done if I'd come to you instead of going to Mother, Paul? What?"

"I would have married you. We could have raised her together."

She laughed. Actually laughed! He balled his hands into fists and willed himself to stay seated. She shook her head. "A have-to marriage? In this community? We would have lived with the stigma of our youthful indiscretion our entire lives. And our daughter would have grown up under a cloud of recrimination."

She was right, and he hated that she was right. Gripping the cabinet, he pulled himself to his feet. She rose at the same time, her movements much more graceful than his clumsy stumbling. He glowered at her. "Then I could have gone with you. I could have . . . have . . ." He didn't know what he could have done. He pointed at her, his finger trembling with the force of his anger. "You took my daughter away from me!"

"I know." She hung her head, her entire body seeming to shrink. "You'll never know how sorry I am."

A tear trailed down her cheek, but it didn't move him. He wouldn't feel sorry for her. Not after what she'd done, what she'd stolen from him. "You should be sorry."

She looked at him again through watery eyes. Defiance glinted in her narrowed gaze. "I lost something precious, too, Paul. And now all I have is Alexa. So I'm telling you . . ." She swiped her hands across her eyes, removing the shimmer of moisture, but the belligerence remained. "Leave her alone. She isn't yours, she's *mine.*" She jabbed one finger against his chest. "Leave . . . her . . . alone."

CHAPTER 33

Alexa

Setting aside her ideas about operating a bed-and-breakfast inn in her family's century-old farmhouse in the heart of Amish-Mennonite country didn't come easily, but after much prayer and thought, she chose to honor her mother. Grandmother's reticence hadn't surprised her — Grandmother was, by nature, a negative person. But Mom's reaction . . . That had surprised her good. Mom, who rarely got angry and had always been supportive, hadn't acted like herself at all.

Alexa frequently pondered her mother's strong rejection over the weekend as she and Sandra finalized the plans for Grandmother's birthday party. She came to the conclusion that Mom's anger was borne of fear of losing Alexa to Mr. Aldrich. If she stayed in Kansas, she'd spend more time with her father than with her mother. For nineteen years, it had been Mom and her against the world. Mom didn't have a husband or other children, so of course she'd be afraid of losing Alexa.

But Mom needed to understand something. Alexa was growing up. And growing up meant striking out on her own. She'd give Mom a few days to settle down, then she'd take her aside and talk with her. She had no doubt, in time, Mom would be supportive again. She loved Alexa too much to stand in the way of her pursuing the course God had planned for her.

Because the more she thought and prayed about it, the more Alexa believed opening a bed-and-breakfast inn was a God-planted seed. Maybe the seed wouldn't bloom here in Kansas at the Zimmerman farm, but that didn't mean she'd never see it blossom. She could be patient and wait for God to reveal where and how. She was young. She had time.

And in the meantime, she'd continue asking Mr. Aldrich questions. Whether Mom liked it or not, he possessed knowledge Alexa needed, and she couldn't squander the opportunity to "pick his brain," so to speak. Besides, it was her right to know her father. Something else Mom would have to accept.

After worship service on Sunday, the family gathered at Clete and Tanya's for lunch. Tanya had set up a self-serve taco bar, and the children took their plates to the backyard while the adults gathered around the dining room table. Midway through the meal, Sandra poked Alexa with her elbow — their preplanned signal to launch Operation Surprise Party.

Alexa wiped her mouth and sent a bright smile across the table at her mother. "Hey, Mom, remember that museum we saw in Wichita when we took Grandmother for her appointment? The one you said you'd like to visit sometime?" She turned to Grandmother. "We decided to do the zoo instead, but even you commented it looked like an interesting place to visit, remember?"

Grandmother nodded. "I remember. The County Historical Museum."

"That's the one!" Alexa could sense Sandra smirking and was careful not to look at her. Grandmother was sharp enough to pick up on hidden motives. Alexa kept her gaze fixed on Mom. "I was thinking . . . Grandmother's birthday is next Friday, right? Wouldn't you like to do something fun with your mom for her special day?"

Just as they'd planned, Mom agreed, but her tone lacked real enthusiasm.

Grandmother made a *tsk-tsk* sound with her tongue. "Alexa, I'm a little beyond seeing getting older as 'special.' "

Alexa laughed and shook her head. "Oh, come on. You aren't *old*. And you and Mom haven't had any real time for the two of you in . . ." She hesitated, unwilling to cast a negative light on what was meant to be a happy occasion.

Sandra rescued her. "So exactly what are you thinking, Alexa? That Suzy and Mother should take a day trip together?"

"More than just a day trip." Alexa shot Sandra a grateful grin. "A minivacation."

Tanya joined in right on cue. "What a great idea! Mother Zimmerman hasn't been away from the farm for more years than I can remember. All of us have enjoyed getaways, but she always stayed behind. Suzanne can provide the nursing care she needs, so she makes a perfect traveling companion. And you can take care of things at the house while Mother Zimmerman is away. You're a genius, Alexa."

Grandmother held up both palms, scowling. "Now wait just a minute. You're talking about me like I'm not in the room again, and you know how I feel about that." She frowned at each of them by turn. "I haven't taken a vacation because I don't like being

446

away from my home."

"But, Grandmother, it would only be for a couple of days. Maybe three."

"Three!" Grandmother's eyes widened. "Three days away from my house?"

"Well, sure," Tanya said. "There's so much to do in Wichita. Museums, and the zoo, and shopping. We took the girls to a place in the mall where you can build your own teddy bear. People of all ages were there, creating furry little friends to take home with them. I can just imagine you and Suzanne making mother-daughter bears as a memory of your time together."

Grandmother scrunched her face. "You've got to be kidding . . ."

Shelley had initially resisted being part of their team of convincers, but she suddenly blurted in her typically saucy manner, "Mother, stop being a stick-in-the-mud. How many times have you bemoaned not having your oldest daughter with you for holidays? Now she's here and she's willing to do something special *just with you,* and you're being a pill. Stop it."

Grandmother pursed her lips and glared at Shelley for a moment. She turned to Mom. "Did you know about this?"

"Yes."

"What do you think about it?"

Mom didn't even hesitate. "I approved it."

Alexa jumped in again. "Come on, Grandmother, this is meant to be my present to you." She injected as much disappointment in her tone as possible without sounding overly dramatic. "You wouldn't reject a birthday gift from me, would you?"

Silence fell around the table. If Grandmother still refused, all their careful plans would be for nothing. Sandra and Tanya had declared Alexa the most likely person to convince Grandmother to leave the farm, thus making the trip her idea rather than anyone else's. Alexa held her breath, hoping her aunts were correct.

Finally Grandmother shook her head and sighed. "I suppose it would be ungrateful to reject a gift. If Suzanne really wants to go away for three days with a grumpy old woman, I won't resist."

Alexa threw her arms around her grandmother's neck. "Thank you!"

She patted Alexa's arms, then wriggled. "You're welcome, but don't strangle me."

Alexa laughed and picked up the last taco on her plate. "I made reservations for you at a bed-and-breakfast in an 1889 Victorian house with period furnishings and a private courtyard and a library where you and Mom can kick back and read and —"

Grandmother's laughter covered Alexa's words. "All right, all right, you've convinced me. You can quit trying to sell the idea now."

Alexa grinned at Mom, who actually winked in response. Conversation rose again, moving to other topics, but Alexa didn't join in. She listened. And gloated. Not only had she convinced Grandmother to go away for enough time to get the house scraped, painted, and decorated for the party, she'd also put Mom in a place where she would have firsthand experience receiving the kind of attention Alexa hoped to provide to guests someday. *God, let this time with Grandmother not only bind Mom to her mother again, but let it open her eyes to what You're leading me to do. Let her give me approval, because I can't go ahead if she's set against it.*

Alexa caught the handle of Mom's suitcase and braced herself to toss the case into the trunk of Grandmother's older model sedan.

"Hold up, Alexa." Mr. Aldrich trotted across the yard. The bill of his cap shaded his face, but she knew he'd be smiling. Every time he looked at her, he smiled. The familiar warmth blossomed in her chest as he stretched out his hands toward her. "Let me do that for you."

Even though she was capable of lifting the suitcase — she and Mom had learned to be independent without any man around to see to heavy items or opening doors or taking out the trash — she stepped back and watched him swing the case into the trunk. He made it look a lot easier than she would have. "Thanks."

"No problem. Anything else need to go in there?"

"Grandmother's wheelchair and her suitcase. But she isn't quite finished packing yet." Alexa wasn't sure if Grandmother was deliberately delaying the leave-taking or if she just couldn't decide what to take. As she'd said, she hadn't been away from the farm in years. It might be uncertainty rather than unwillingness that slowed her progress.

Mr. Aldrich fell in step with Alexa as she moved toward the house. She liked having him walk beside her. Their shadows stretched long across the grass in the morning sunlight and seemed to run ahead as if preparing the way.

"I was pretty surprised when Clete told me his mother would be going on a trip with Suzy."

Alexa still hadn't gotten used to people calling her mother by the shortened name. In a way, it made her wish she had a nickname, too. It seemed casual, personal, affectionate. But Mom didn't seem to hold any affection for Mr. Aldrich anymore. Did he still harbor feelings for her? She wished she could ask.

Alexa forced herself to respond to his comment rather than delving into the past. "I think she surprised a lot of people, but I'm glad they're going, and not just so we can . . . do what we need to do." Better remain evasive in case Grandmother came out on the porch and overheard them talking. "Mom and Grandmother need time together. It'll be good for them."

The corners of Mr. Aldrich's eyes crinkled with his approving grin. "That's a very unselfish attitude. You're a caring young woman, Alexa."

Just as had happened when he'd said he was proud of her for wanting to enter a vocation of service, pleasure flooded her. Mom often praised her, but hearing words of affirmation from this man — from her father — awakened parts of her that had lain dormant her whole life. She swallowed a delighted giggle and quoted one of her mother's mottoes, " 'It's more blessed to give than to receive.' Mom taught me that. She's always put others above herself. If I can be half as caring and unselfish as her,

I'll be happy."

"Yes, well . . ." His steps faltered for a moment, his expression turning hard. The muscles in his jaw bunched as if he clamped his teeth down on other words. Then he pulled in a slow breath and his face relaxed. "Just be careful to never put humans — not even your mother — on a pedestal. None of us are perfect. Try to emulate Jesus instead. He won't disappoint you."

Alexa hurried to assure him — partly in defense of Mom and partly because she wanted him to know she understood what he was saying. "I always try to look to Jesus first. Mom taught me that, too."

They reached the porch, and Alexa started up the steps. Mr. Aldrich remained at the bottom. "As soon as they've gone, come out to the barn. I'm cutting down the last of the cabinetry and have my saw set up out there. It's noisy, so I won't hear you holler — you'll have to come get me. I'll stop what I'm doing and make a phone call to let the fellowship men know they can come out and get started on the house."

She hugged herself, imagining the transformation that would soon take place. She could hardly wait to see the house decked out in its new color scheme. "Okay."

The screen door opened and Mom

452

stepped onto the porch. She held a suitcase so old school it didn't even have wheels. Its weight made her list to the right. "Alexa, I think we're finally ready. I'll take this to the car. Do you want to go in and say good-bye to your grandmother?"

Alexa hurried up the steps. "How about I bring her out, and I'll tell both of you good-bye by the car."

"Fine." Mom headed across the porch and slowly made her way down the steps, the case thumping against her leg. When she reached the bottom, she angled her path to move around Mr. Aldrich.

He shifted, too, blocking her passage. He held out his hand. "Let me take that for you." It was a gentlemanly gesture, but his voice sounded clipped. Hard. Almost demanding.

Mom lifted her chin slightly and took a giant step to the side, avoiding his hand. "No, thank you. I'm capable of taking care of it myself." She scurried on across the grass.

Mr. Aldrich scowled after her for a few tense seconds before clomping across the yard to the barn.

Alexa gazed after him, chewing her lip. It hurt her heart to see Mom and Mr. Aldrich at odds with each other. Did every child want her parents to be happy together rather than uptight? Although troubled by their behavior, she also found pleasure in feeling what kids who grew up in two-parent homes probably experienced from time to time when their moms and dads had differences. For the first time in her life, she felt completely like a normal daughter. Should she go after him or Mom — or both — and play peacemaker? What would kids in traditional families do?

The longer Mom and Grandmother remained at the farm, the less time the men would have to get started on the new paint job. And Alexa, with no experience playing buffer between a set of parents, had no idea how to fix things. So she sent up a little prayer for God to repair whatever was broken between her mother and Mr. Aldrich and hurried inside to Grandmother.

CHAPTER 34

Suzanne

At the car, after settling Mother in the passenger seat, Suzanne wrapped Alexa in a hug. She clung tightly, almost desperately, and Alexa squeezed back just as hard. Suzanne took comfort in her daughter's firm embrace.

She stepped away and tried to smile. Alexa's image swam, distorted by her tears. She blinked quickly, hoping Alexa wouldn't notice, and forced a bright tone. "All right. We're off on our adventure. I'll see you Friday evening. Yes?"

Alexa nodded. She closed the passenger door, sealing her grandmother inside, and lowered her voice to an excited whisper. "By six everyone will be here, the house will be wearing its brand-new colorful coat, and the buffet Sandra and Tanya planned will be ready. I can hardly wait!" She leaned forward and planted a quick kiss on her mother's cheek. "Have lots of fun. Relax. Laugh."

"I'll do my best."

"I'll be praying for you to be safe and happy."

Alexa's sweet words brought another rush of tears. She grabbed her close again. "I'll pray the same for you."

A soft chuckle sounded in Suzanne's ear. "You're acting just like you did when you dropped me off for my first day of kindergarten. Remember? I would have been fine and not cried at all if you hadn't started crying."

Suzanne snuffled and laughed, stepping back. "I guess we both survived that separation, didn't we? And I'll survive this one, too. It's just . . ." Her gaze drifted in the direction of the barn, where Paul's power saw sent up a high-pitched hum. She caught her daughter's hands. "Are you sure you don't want to go with us instead of staying here? Sandra, Shelley, and Tanya can get the party things done."

"M-o-o-o-o-m." Alexa drew out the word, affecting a mock pout. "Stick to the plan, will you? I want to make sure the house gets decorated and painted the way I want it." She hooked Suzanne's elbow and escorted her around the car. "I'll be just fine for a few days without you. You and Grandmother are going to have so much fun you won't even miss me. Wait and see."

Suzanne sighed and popped open the car door. "All right, then. We're off."

"Good!" Alexa gave her door a push and then stepped back, smiling and waving at both her and Mother.

Mother waved back, then looked at Suzanne. "Are you sure you want to go? You look worried."

"Of course I want to go. I'm looking forward to our minivacation." She put the car in gear and backed up slowly, watching Alexa trot toward the barn. She pinched her forehead into a frown.

"Suzanne, you aren't looking forward, you're looking back."

Mother had no idea how true her words were. She sighed and aimed her gaze to the road. "Just making sure I don't hit anything, Mother. Here we go." As she pulled out of the yard, she glanced at the rearview mirror. Alexa was still in the barn. Her stomach tightened into knots. She'd commanded Paul to keep his distance from Alexa. *God, make him do it.*

Paul
Paul shut off the saw as Alexa darted across

457

the barn floor toward him. Her smile stretched from ear to ear, and his leftover grumpiness from the brief encounter with Suzy drifted away like sawdust from the saw's blade. "Are they gone?"

"Yes!" She clasped her hands beneath her chin and released a joy-filled giggle. "Let's get started!"

"Okay." Paul strode to the corner, where a black plastic rotary-dial telephone was mounted on the wall. Alexa hovered near his elbow as he called Bernie Lapp. At the man's gruff greeting, Paul said, "All's clear. C'mon out."

"For both projects?" Bernie's voice blared through the line.

Paul cringed. Would Alexa overhear? She wasn't meant to know about the second project, a surprise he'd planned for her. "That's right. I'm in the barn, and I'll point you to the right paint cans." He couldn't have the men grabbing the paint meant for Alexa's guest cottage and slapping it on the side of the house.

"All right. Be out soon." The line went dead.

Paul turned to Alexa. "Okay, your part is done. I can take it from here."

"Are you sure? You remember how I want it painted? Window frames ocher with slate on the inside trim? The fish scale —"

"Ocher with slate blue on the fascia boards." He grinned and patted his shirt pocket. "I've got it all right here, Alexa. Don't worry. You can trust me." *You can trust me . . .* Wasn't that what he'd said to Suzy the night he led her to the barn loft? *Don't worry. Nobody gets pregnant the first time. It'll be all right, Suzy — you can trust me.* And standing before him was the evidence of how wrong he'd been.

"Mr. Aldrich?" Alexa was looking at him strangely. "You're kind of spacing out on me."

He forced a laugh. "Sorry. Just thinking." He steered her toward the door. "You get the house spiffed up and ready for weekend guests." Karina always wanted fresh sheets on all the beds, everything dusted and spit-shined. The task should keep Alexa busy and out of the way. "I'll be in and out working in the kitchen so it's ready by Friday, but Clete has the paint plan, too, and if there are questions we'll holler at you, okay?"

She sighed. "Okay. I just really want to *see* it all happen. *Make* it happen."

Paul smiled. "You've done more than your fair share already." He took her by the shoulders and turned her so she faced the house. "Take a good look at the way it is now. Memorize the 'before.' Then Friday, when everything is done, I'll bring you out to this spot and you can look at the transformation. If you haven't seen the mess that has to happen in between, you'll appreciate the 'after' a lot more."

Alexa's lips quirked into a lopsided grin. "I don't know. I think I'm going to appreciate seeing that kitchen all done even though I've put up with every mess in between."

The first of the cars turned into the lane, workers arriving. Paul pointed. "Here they come. Go on now. We'll get more done if you aren't underfoot." He smiled to soften the reprimand.

She sighed again, but she hurried off. Paul removed the second paint plan from his hip pocket and headed across the yard to greet the workers.

Abigail

Who would have thought she would be jaunting off with Suzy in the middle of the week? Especially with wheat harvest in full swing. Everywhere she looked, combines cut wide swaths through fields, opening up the view to the horizon. The non-Mennonite farmers in the area each owned their own equipment so they didn't have to wait their turn with fellowship-owned machinery. They'd finish sooner but with no more success than what the men of her fellowship enjoyed.

Abigail had always liked the way the Kansas landscape gently rolled. The rich soil was perfect for wheat, and she found pleasure in watching the green shoots appear, then grow tall and slender, the cluster of kernels at the top plumping more each day. But watching the wheat come down was best. The land seemed broader, the sky bigger, and sunrises and sunsets more vibrant with the unobstructed view. Her view was usually from the porch on her house or her own yard, so witnessing the harvest in progress from the highway was more exciting than she'd expected.

Suzy drove in silence, so Abigail gazed out the window, letting her thoughts roll much the way the landscape rolled toward the horizon. Her only excursions away from the farm since Cecil's death were to attend church service or shop in Arborville and, since her accident, visit the neurologist and spine specialist in Wichita. This trip was a treat. That Alexa. She was a wily one, springing this birthday getaway on her just days before the time to leave. If she'd had weeks to consider going away for such a selfish reason, she would have talked herself out of it. But the spontaneity of the excursion — just packing up and going on what felt like a whim — was the most fun thing she'd done since she was a girl.

If Suzy had raised Alexa in Arborville, would her oldest grandchild have convinced her to take little vacations away from the farm over the years? Would she have laughed more, smiled more, relaxed more? Of course there was no way to know for sure, and it was pointless even to consider it now since one couldn't turn back time and reverse choices. But Abigail couldn't seem to stop wondering what might have been had she made a different decision when Suzy came to her and confessed her sin.

Something she knew for sure — if she hadn't sent Suzy away, her daughter wouldn't have become a nurse. She probably would have stayed in Arborville, married Paul Aldrich, and assumed the role of wife and mother. Would she have been happier? More fulfilled? Only God knew the answer to those questions, but Abigail could say with certainty her daughter was a good nurse, had carved a good life for herself. She'd given up a lot — a potential husband, a child, closeness with her family — but seemingly God had blessed her. And for that, Abigail was grateful.

She sent a sideways look at Suzy. Was the look of consternation on her face due to concentrating on traffic, did she wish she wasn't going away for time alone with her mother, or was she just missing Alexa? It was sad that she, the one who'd given birth to Suzy, couldn't determine the cause. A mother should be able to read her child. But maybe this minivacation would help bring them together again. Very soon Suzy would leave for a second time unless something kept her in Arborville.

As much as she'd tried to push Suzy and Paul together, now both seemed determined to keep their distance from each other. Abigail was sure Paul had guessed Alexa was his child, and of course Alexa had already figured it out — every time the girl looked at the carpenter, a dreamy expression drifted across her face. Wouldn't Alexa be thrilled if her mother and father became united?

Abigail turned eagerly to face Suzy. "Don't you ever want to marry?"

Suzy gave a little jolt. "Where did that question come from?"

Abigail laughed, self-conscious. Of course Suzy hadn't been privy to her thoughts so she couldn't follow the trail leading to the query. "I've been sitting here thinking. You're only thirty-seven years old, still a young woman. You could even have another child. Maybe two. Why, Mavis Troyer was forty-one when she had her last baby." Would Suzy remember Mavis Troyer? Probably not. "My point is, you're young enough to enjoy many years as a wife if . . . if you wanted."

"I suppose."

Her daughter's doubtful tone raised an unexpected wave of irritation. "Why do you have to be so stubborn? Do you want to grow old all alone?"

Suzy's brows pinched downward. She kept watching the road ahead, not even sending a glance at her mother. "I don't suppose anyone *wants* to grow old alone, but sometimes that's the way life turns out. You're alone now, with Dad gone. And sixty isn't ancient, either. Do you ever think of marrying again?"

Abigail snorted. "No man in his right mind would choose me, knowing how he'd have to take care of me. Besides, I'm too cantankerous for most. Your father was always patient, but not many men would put up with me." She hadn't spoken so forthrightly to anyone in years. She found a release in saying the words out loud. Then she realized Suzy had managed to veer the conversation from its original course. She wagged her finger at her daughter. "But we weren't discussing me. Answer my question. Don't you want to be a wife?"

Suzy sighed. A long sigh. A sad sigh. "Sometimes asking what we want isn't the best question. Sometimes we have to ask, 'What is best?' Or better yet, 'What is God's will?' I'm not opposed to marriage. Sometimes I do feel lonely and wish I had someone to share my life with. But I'm not going to marry someone out of loneliness or out of the desire to have more children. God intends marriage to be a partnership of love and trust and respect. Those feelings can't be manufactured just because I want to experience them. They need to be real."

Abigail shook her head. "You're talking in riddles."

Suzy laughed softly. "Well, I suppose the question, 'what is love?' could be considered a riddle. All I know for sure is I've not met anyone to whom I wanted to give my heart. Except Alexa. So she has been my life. And she has been enough."

Abigail squinted, searching her daughter's face for signs of untruthfulness. "Are you sure?"

"I'm sure."

Although Suzy's tone and the firm nod of her head indicated great certainty, Abigail wasn't convinced. Sorrow struck, carried on a tide of guilt. She swallowed and said gruffly, "I'm sorry you didn't have more." She wanted to add *because of me,* but she couldn't gather the courage.

Suzy must have understood, though, because she nodded again, and a sad smile curved the corners of her lips. "But they had more, didn't they? Paul enjoyed marriage and the birth of a son. Anna-Grace grew up with a mom and dad who love her. If we were to ask if they were unhappy with their lives, both of them would probably tell us they had no regrets."

"But what of your regrets?" Abigail sucked in a breath and held it.

"Wallowing in past regrets doesn't do any good." Her chin tilted up a notch. "So I won't discuss them."

Abigail released her air. She touched Suzy's elbow. "But —"

"We're almost to Wichita. We can't check in to the B and B Alexa arranged until three o'clock, so where would you like to go until then? The zoo, the museum, or the mall?"

Abigail folded her arms over her chest. If Suzy wanted to be obstinate, then she would be obstinate, too. "You choose."

"It's your birthday getaway, Mother, so you need to choose."

"I don't care."

Suzy's fingers briefly tightened on the steering wheel, but when she spoke she only sounded patient, as Abigail had come to expect. "All right then. Since it's such a pretty day, let's start with the zoo. Then tomorrow the museum, and we'll visit the mall on Friday before we go home."

Abigail didn't reply.

Suzy sighed. "Mother, when we go home, Alexa is going to ask if we had a good time, and I don't want to lie to her. So can we agree to let the past remain there and instead focus on right now?"

"If that's what you want."

"It is. I think we'll both be happier that way."

"All right." Abigail sat in silence with her arms folded. She wouldn't argue, and she'd do her best not to pester Suzy with questions. But be happy? That remained to be seen.

CHAPTER 35

Alexa

Although Mr. Aldrich had instructed her to stay out of the way, Alexa couldn't resist pausing in the yard each time she carried out a load of wash to hang on the line. She decided to wash not only sheets and towels but also all the curtains. Men swarmed the house, standing on ladders or homemade scaffolding, applying scrapers to the old paint. Even though she'd only asked to have the house painted, two men took down the shutters and removed the screen doors and set up a little workshop under the towering cottonwood. By the time they finished, Alexa was certain the old shutters and doors would look brand-new.

She fought the temptation to stay in the yard and watch them work. She knew about Amish barn raisings, of course. Growing up in Indiana with Amish communities nearby, she was familiar with the hardworking ethic and community spirit of the close-knit religious groups, but she'd never had the chance to witness it in action. The sight of the men working together, each contributing his full effort, somehow in sync with the others without even having to call out instructions, held an unexpected beauty, and Alexa wished she could set up a video camera to record it. But instead she had to satisfy herself with frequent long gazes as she hung freshly washed items on the lines.

At noon two more cars pulled onto the property — women from the fellowship bringing lunch for the workers. Alexa dashed out with a stack of paper plates and a handful of napkins, eager to help distribute the thick sandwiches, kettle-cooked potato chips, and home-baked pastries and cookies. As the men filled their plates, she thanked each one profusely, and without exception they assured her they were happy to help. Their kindness warmed her even more than the June sun beaming overhead.

The women, both members of Grandmother's quilting circle, insisted on cleaning up the mess and promised Alexa someone else would bring out a snack midafternoon. Although she'd only met them twice before, she couldn't resist giving each a hug, and to her delight, they returned the embrace without a moment's hesitation. The older one, Mrs. Lapp, even gave Alexa's cheek a soft pat and commended her for arranging something so wonderful for Abigail.

"The truth is," Mrs. Lapp said, shaking her head slowly as her gaze drifted across the house, "someone in the fellowship should have insisted on it long ago. But Abigail was so dead set against fixing anything, we didn't push the issue. Why, the house could have fallen down around her and we would have watched it happen, we were all so unwilling to force our way past her stubborn pride." She turned her smile on Alexa. "But you managed it. Good for you."

Alexa ducked her head, embarrassed yet pleased by the woman's praise. "It's a group effort. I appreciate everyone's willingness to help. And I can't wait to see the look on Grandmother's face when she comes home."

The second woman laughed softly. "Almost makes me wish I owned a camera."

Alexa grinned. She did own a camera, and even though Sandra had told her Grandmother preferred the outdated Old Order practice of no picture-taking, Alexa intended to sneak a photo or two of her grandmother's expression when she returned.

She left the pair to bag the trash and box

the leftover food, and she hurried around the house to the clothesline to remove the dried sheets and curtains. She made the beds and then started to rehang the curtains. But she decided to give the windows a good washing first. The men had said they'd wash the outside when they finished painting, so she scrubbed the glass from the inside, waving at the workers as she moved from room to room.

When the windows were clean and the windowsills free of dust and sticky little cobwebs, she dragged out Grandmother's creaky ironing board and ancient electric iron to press the wrinkles out of the curtains before hanging them again. By the time she finished three hours later, her shoulders ached, but she didn't mind. Satisfaction filled her as she surveyed the end result of her labor. Then she looked past the curtains to the faded wall coverings and vintage furniture, and she frowned. If only she could do a complete makeover so Grandmother's house would sparkle inside and out in every way.

As she stood in the middle of the living room floor, an idea bloomed. She sucked in a happy breath. She might not have time to put up new wallpaper or change the furniture, but maybe she could give the front room and dining room a new look. She giggled. Grandmother was on a minivacation, and now her living room would receive a minimakeover. With a smile on her face, she darted for the stairs.

Paul

Paul stepped back and examined the kitchen by increments, using his most critical eye. Cabinetry stretched across the east wall at a manageable height of twenty-seven inches — six inches lower than before. The retractable cottage-style doors, hinged like shutters, whispered on hidden rails. The white glossy wood looked crisp and clean against the freshly painted pale blue walls. He'd retained the old butcher-block countertops but had sanded them and applied several coats of protective oil so they gleamed nearly as bright as the polished touch-activated faucet, which arched like a swan's neck over the new stainless-steel sink. Mrs. Zimmerman had asked him to reuse the old white porcelain-coated sink, but its twelve-inch depth proved unwieldy. He hoped she'd be happy with the double-wide, nine-inch-deep sink instead.

He also hoped she wouldn't mind his relocation of the stove and refrigerator. Once tucked into the alcove beneath the back staircase, their distance a good six strides from the sink, they now stood sentry in opposite ends of the rebuilt sink base. He'd carved out a section of floor so the stove sat in a recessed box, putting its top even with the counter where Mrs. Zimmerman could reach if she chose to do any cooking.

Of course, the oven door now nearly touched the floor when it was opened, but whoever else used the appliance would just have to deal with stooping over farther. His main focus was making the kitchen functional for Mrs. Zimmerman, not for her nurse. Or for Alexa, if she decided to stick around and turn the place into a bed-and-breakfast inn.

As for Alexa, wouldn't she approve the baking center he'd fashioned by inserting the remaining lower cabinets in the alcove? He even built a pull-out cutting board on one side to increase the work space. With the old drop-leaf table tucked snug against the west wall adjacent to the alcove, she'd have plenty of room to roll piecrusts or decorate cakes.

Over the course of the day, the sounds of her bustling around and humming had carried past the sheet he'd hung to keep his mess in the kitchen. Whatever she was doing, clearly she was enjoying herself, and he'd enjoyed listening to her. Curiosity — and the desire to share his accomplishments with someone who would appreciate them — sent him across the floor. He shifted the sheet aside, stepped through the little storage passageway, and into the dining room. And there he stopped.

His mouth dropped open in surprise. When he'd told her to keep herself occupied by spiffing up the place, he envisioned her dusting, mopping, and scrubbing. But she'd done so much more. If it hadn't been for the familiar flowered wallpaper on the walls and time-aged furniture, he wouldn't have recognized the room.

The patter of feet on the stairs came, followed by Alexa breezing around the corner. She carried a folded layer of creamy lace. When she spotted him, she came to a halt, crushing the lace against the front of her plain lavender T-shirt. "Oh! Mr. Aldrich . . ." An adorable blush crept up her cheeks.

Paternal love swelled, startling in its force. He chuckled softly. "I'm sorry. I didn't mean to sneak up on you." He glanced around, releasing a whistle. "You've been busy today."

She hurried to the table and flipped the length of lace across its surface. As she smoothed the delicate fabric into place, she offered a bashful shrug. "I just figured . . . the outside of the house is getting fixed up. Maybe I should do a little something on the inside, too."

"Well, it looks great." Paul stepped farther into the room where he could peek through the wide doorway leading to the front room. He shook his head, marveling. "Where'd you get all this?"

A self-conscious giggle left her throat. She pointed overhead. "The attic. There's a treasure trove up there." She entered the front room and he followed. "These sofa covers are just sheets, tucked in and around. I made an end table with old suitcases. I like the way they look all stacked up. Vintage, right? I found a whole box of doilies, so I've had fun finding places for them. I rearranged the furniture. I thought if the sofa was at an angle, it would break up the hard lines of the room — it's just so *square* — and that allowed me to put the tall lamp behind it, where it'll help light up that whole corner."

Paul trailed her as she made her way around the room, pointing out the lamps she'd carried down from one of the upstairs bedrooms and the assorted throw pillows made by pinning portions of a moth-eaten patchwork quilt around old pillow forms. She stopped beside the battered wooden rocking chair and fluffed the quilt draped from its back and along one arm. "This one has a few tattered patches, too, but it was too good to cut up. Some careful pleating hid the rough spots. Doesn't it look inviting there?"

Paul didn't know much about interior decorating, but he liked what he saw. "Yeah. The whole place looks nice and . . ." He sought a word. "Homey." He scowled at the walls. "Is that the same wallpaper?"

She laughed. "Uh-huh. Amazing how different it looks when you break up the pattern, isn't it? I found those two paintings — they're original oils, I think — tucked under the eaves and hidden under old sheets."

Paul remembered Suzy going through an artistic stage and giving paintings to everyone one year for Christmas. He probably still had the one she'd given him tucked away somewhere. Were these gifts to her parents back then?

Alexa had crossed to the paintings and ran her fingers along the edge of the second one's frame. "Even though the scenes are very different, the colors coordinate well enough that they make a great pairing there over the sofa. I love them. They're so folk-artsy."

He didn't know what *folk-artsy* meant, but he assumed it was a good thing. "I wonder why they were hidden away?"

"I dunno." Alexa shrugged again, the gesture girlish. "But they're out now. Just like this lap quilt, which makes a perfect wall hanging, and the mirror I put over the piano. What a shame to leave it collecting dust in the attic! The crack in the corner doesn't even bother me because the shape of the frame is so pleasing — like a cathedral window. And doesn't it make the room feel bigger? Those candle sconces are perfect beside it. They were in the same box as the doilies."

She touched the empty, scrolled candle plate with her finger, tipping her head as if thoroughly examining the sconce. "I couldn't find any silver polish to buff them up, but I think I'll leave them alone. The tarnish tells a story of the years they've been in service. As time goes by, we all get a little nicked and marred, but those scars only prove we lived."

Paul shook his head. "Alexa, that was beautifully stated. You should be a poet." He glanced around again, marveling. "Or a decorator."

She grinned. "Thanks. Doing all this was so fun. It's made me realize how much I would enjoy taking an old house and renovating it to use as a retreat place."

Had she inherited this creative bent from him? He was a decorator of sorts with his woodworking and remodeling. The thought pleased him. "Obviously you have the vision and the talent to make it happen." Paul hoped his own desires wouldn't come through too much with his next comment. "Have you . . . given opening a bed-and-breakfast out here more thought?"

Alexa bit down on her lip for a moment. "Honestly? I've hardly thought of anything else. It just seems so perfect, you know? The location, the size of the house, even the little summer kitchen that could be my private quarters. But Grandmother wasn't keen on the idea, and Mom almost had a cow."

Paul sputtered. "She did what?"

Alexa grimaced. "Sorry. It's an expression the kids at the grade school use. I mean Mom pretty much told me to forget it. She —" Pink mottled her cheeks. She looked away. "Never mind. I don't think Mom would appreciate me talking to you about her."

No, she wouldn't. But what Suzy wanted wasn't important to him. What his daughter wanted was. "If it would help to talk it out, I'm listening." His heart beat a hopeful thrum. Would she share her thoughts with him? He wanted her to. He wanted her to trust him enough.

To his disappointment, she shook her head. "It's all right. I'll sort it out eventually." She offered a weak grin. "Thanks for asking, though."

He nodded. They stood in awkward silence for a few seconds, then he gave a little jolt. "Guess what? The kitchen cabinets are all in. Want to see?"

Her cheerfulness returned in the space of a heartbeat. "You bet!"

As his daughter followed him to the kitchen, he sent up a prayer for her dreams to come to fruition. For her, of course, but — admittedly — also for him.

CHAPTER 36

Suzanne

"Here we go." Suzanne gave Mother's wheelchair a push and propelled her across the mall's parking lot. The bright sun heated her head, and the black asphalt heated her soles. Sweat trickled down her temples. The weatherman had predicted the highest temperature of the month for Friday, and apparently he was right. Only nine o'clock, and already the thermostat on the mall's digital billboard showed ninety-eight degrees. She was glad they'd chosen to visit the mall today, where air conditioning would keep them cool.

A teenage boy with red dyed hair badly in need of a trim and wearing baggy cutoff jeans and a T-shirt bearing the image of a wild-eyed rock star shot past them, the strings of his untied sneakers flopping on the ground. He caught the door handle and pulled the glass door wide. Suzanne expected him to dart through and let the door close in their faces, but to her surprise he remained braced at the edge of the entrance and said, "There ya go."

Suzanne gave him a grateful smile as she pushed Mother's chair through the opening. "Thank you very much."

"No problem." He skirted around them and joined a group of teenage boys wearing similar ratty apparel. The entire gang sauntered off together in the direction of the food court.

Mother tsk-tsked.

Suzanne could imagine what her mother was thinking. "Don't be critical. He was kind to hold the door for us."

Mother angled her face so she could peek at Suzanne. "Don't leap to conclusions. I was berating myself. When I saw him, I thought, 'Oh, what a thug. Hold on to your purse.' Then he behaved like a gentleman. It was a good lesson to me not to judge a book by its cover." Suzanne, humbled, offered an apology, but Mother waved it aside. "Don't worry about it. Of course you'd assume I was being critical given how often I *am* critical."

But she hadn't been during this trip. Suzanne smiled to let her know all was forgiven. "Tell me when you want to go in to one of the stores. There's a little of every-thing here." She slowly pushed the chair across the tiled floor that formed a wide hallway between shops.

Kiosks created random islands in the center, leaving a narrow passageway. Su-zanne stopped frequently, sometimes to al-low others to pass, other times to change direction slightly to avoid bumping into benches or trash bins. Although the mall was crowded and noisy, Mother voiced no word of complaint but merely sat in her chair, hands folded in her lap over her pocketbook, gazing this way and then that.

In only a few hours, they'd be heading back to the farm. Suzanne couldn't believe how quickly the time had passed. Or how pleasant it had been. After an uncomfort-able first evening, they'd managed to relax and enjoy each other's company — some-thing that probably surprised Mother as much as it had Suzanne. Although they hadn't engaged in in-depth conversations, keeping the topics both current and light in nature, there had been no lengthy, chilly silences.

Their room at the bed-and-breakfast inn was so comfortable Mother had teasingly threatened to move in permanently. Su-zanne understood why. The innkeepers took excellent care of the guests, providing a delicious breakfast and making their library, courtyard, and television room available. She and Mother hadn't visited the television room, but they'd spent their early evening hours in the library and, as the sun slipped away, dusk in the courtyard.

Even though she'd tried not to, she imagined Alexa serving as a hostess — greeting the guests, preparing the sumptuous breakfast, making everyone feel at home. Her personality was suited to the position as were her interests and abilities. When Suzanne returned to the farm, she'd tell her daughter she would support her desire to open a B and B. But in Indiana, not in Kansas.

Mother tapped Suzanne's hand. "Look, a card store. I want to find one to give Alexa to tell her thank you for this trip."

Suzanne wheeled Mother into the shop, and they read every thank-you card on the rack before Mother made her selection. Suzanne didn't mind waiting. Mother's intention to choose the best card told Suzanne how much Alexa had come to mean to her. A hint of sadness pushed at the contentedness she'd been enjoying. Mother would miss Alexa when they left. And Alexa would miss her grandmother.

With the chosen card in hand, Mother asked to browse the store. They laughed at the silly sayings on coffee mugs and admired the intricately painted bird figurines. Mother commented that the bluebird pair would look sweet on the windowsill, so Suzanne offered to buy them as her birthday present. Mother opened her mouth as if to argue, then instead bobbed her head. "Thank you, Suzanne." They looked a little longer, fingering several items and pondering the purpose of others. Then Mother said, "All right. Let's check out."

They finished window-shopping on the first level and then rode the elevator to the second level. Just as Suzanne pushed Mother's chair from the elevator, she let out a little cry and pointed ahead. "Look! Is that the teddy bear store Tanya said we should visit?"

Suzanne wheeled the chair to the store's window. A smile tugged at her lips. She couldn't help it. Dozens of teddy bears, cats, dogs, and assorted farm and jungle animals formed a cheerful chorus line across the display window. Some wore costumes, and Suzanne pointed out the elephant in a bright pink tutu and ballet slippers.

Mother laughed. "Oh, how ridiculous! But

somehow also clever. Let's go in."

"Really?" There was nothing in the shop that would be considered practical. She couldn't imagine her mother wanting to visit it.

Mother rolled her eyes, but her cheeks twitched with a grin. "Yes, really. I want to see what all they have." She slipped her pocketbook between her hip and the chair's side and took control of the wheels. Suzanne followed her inside.

Enthusiastic children swarmed a row of bins along the longest wall. Suzanne worked Mother's chair into the midst of them, murmuring, "Excuse me." When they were able to get close enough to look, they discovered the bins contained empty shells of various animals. Mother lifted out a giraffe and wriggled her fingers into an opening in its back. She scowled at the form.

A girl who looked to be close to Alexa's age, wearing a striped cobbler's apron with *Lacey* stitched across the bib, stepped close. "Can I help you with anything?"

Mother held the giraffe aloft. "Are these puppets? If so, the opening is too small for my hand."

Lacey laughed and took the giraffe. "No, ma'am. That's where we stuff the toy." She gestured toward an odd-looking machine in the corner where several children and adults clustered with animals in their hands. "Once you've chosen what animal you want to build, you take it over there, and we can put in a heart or a little talking box before we fill it with stuffing. Then your new friend is completely personalized."

"I see." Mother took the giraffe back and examined it. She glanced toward the displays of little dresses, overalls, and other clothing items. "And then you dress them?"

"If you want to." Lacey beamed at Mother. "Would you like to build a friend to take home with you today?"

Suzanne expected Mother to toss the giraffe body aside and wheel away. The store was obviously geared for youngsters, and surely she was ready to go. She gripped the handles on Mother's wheelchair, anticipating her response.

"Yes. I would like to build a friend for each of my grandchildren."

Suzanne jolted in surprise. Then she cleared her throat. She'd gotten a peek at the price tags. Leaning down, she whispered in Mother's ears, "Um, are you sure? You'd need seven of them."

"Eight." Mother aimed a beaming smile at Lacey. "My youngest daughter is expecting another baby at the end of this month.

So I need eight."

"Congratulations! And what a fun way to celebrate." Lacey rubbed her palms together. "Let's get you started. Do you want bears, or do you prefer something less traditional?"

Suzanne felt like an interloper while Mother and Lacey formed a stack of animals in Mother's lap. For Jay she chose a black-and-white dog that looked a bit like Pepper. For Jana and Julie she selected cats — one gray and one yellow. After debating for a bit between cats or rabbits, she decided on white rabbits for Ruby and Pearl. She grabbed an elephant for Ian and a monkey for the new baby. Then she turned to Suzanne.

"What about Alexa? I'm thinking a bear — maybe that brown one there with the big nose. He looks sort of sophisticated."

Lacey held up her finger. "Let me show you something." She darted off and then fought her way back through the crowd. She showed Mother a tiny tuxedo, top hat, and bow tie. "If you want your bear to look sophisticated, you should dress him in this."

Mother laughed again. "Perfect!" She plopped the clothing items on top of the animal shells, then smirked at Suzanne. "It's so crowded in here. Why don't you go somewhere else for a little while? I'm in good hands with Lacey. Come back for me in . . ." She looked at Lacey. "How long?"

Lacey glanced around the store at the other customers. "I'd say at least an hour."

"An hour and a half then. That will give me time to finish up." Mother waved at Suzanne. "Go. Explore. Have fun. I'll see you later."

Abigail

Abigail watched Suzy leave the store, her progress slow with so many others weaving here and there, and then move past the windows. Once she was certain her daughter was gone, she aimed a conspiratorial look at Lacey. "Can we build a dozen toys instead of eight? Is that too many?"

Lacey grinned. She was a cute girl even though her brown-and-blond-streaked hair was cut in some sort of odd, spiky style longer on one side than the other. "You can build as many as you want. Are you expecting more grandchildren?"

Abigail shook her head. The black ribbon from her cap tickled her chin, and she pushed it over her shoulder. "I want one for each of my daughters and my daughter-in-law. They've all been so good to me." Tears pricked her eyes and her throat went tight.

Why had she told Lacey something she should be telling Sandra, Shelley, Tanya, and Suzy instead? Somehow it was easier to talk to this stranger than her own family. That wasn't right.

Lacey put her hand on Abigail's shoulder. The girl's touch was comforting. "Maybe you could put a little voice box in their animals with a message from you. Then they could listen to your words of appreciation whenever they want."

Abigail sniffed hard, clearing the tears. She smiled, although her lips quavered. "That's a good idea. I'll do that." Wouldn't the girls be shocked to hear words of affirmation from their mother? But she loved the idea and couldn't wait to get started. She knew just what she would say to each of them.

There were more than half a dozen styles of teddy bears, so Abigail chose a different design for each of the "big girls," as she laughingly called them. Lacey took her to a little room where the store noise wouldn't intrude and let her record her message on the voice boxes. Her voice cracked twice, and she had to start over on Suzy's because emotion tangled her vocal cords so badly she couldn't continue. But finally she got all four messages finished.

When the animals were stuffed and sewn, Lacey took her to the accessories section. The tiny clothes were all ridiculously overpriced — she could make them for a fraction of the cost — so she chose not to dress any of the animals except Alexa's. The little tuxedo and top hat were too cute to leave behind. Besides, she didn't think she could sew a top hat.

Once they had Alexa's bear decked out in his formal wear, the others looked so naked she relented and put pink hair bows on the cats, lavender tutus on the rabbits, and secured footballs on the paws of Jay's dog and Ian's elephant. Since she didn't know whether the new baby was a boy or a girl, she chose a little yellow bib with a rattle stitched in the center for its accessory. The four bears she built for her daughters each received a ruffled mobcap and a pair of wire spectacles, turning them into grandmother bears. Although the items added to the cost, she liked the way they looked, and she gave Lacey a thumbs-up signal, which made the girl laugh.

She'd just finished paying for the purchases when Suzy returned. Her daughter's eyes widened when she looked at the stack of boxes on the counter. "Are these *all* yours?"

"Yep. Lacey and I built an entire menagerie."

"It will take me at least three trips to get them all to the car." Suzy shook her head, peeking in the little cut-out windows on the boxes. A grin twitched at her cheek. "They are cute, though. The kids will be thrilled with them."

Abigail hoped all of her kids, little and big, would be thrilled.

The cashier handed Abigail her receipt, and she quickly tucked it away before Suzy got a glimpse of it. No need to send her daughter into a dead faint. The purchase was extravagant — she wouldn't deny it — but she couldn't recall the last time she'd had such fun. The price tag was well worth it.

"Do you ladies plan to do more shopping?" the cashier asked.

Abigail nearly snorted. She might window-shop, but she didn't dare spend another penny.

Suzy answered. "We plan to eat lunch in the food court and browse the other shops, yes."

"If you'd like, you can leave these here. We have a little storage room where they can wait for you. Then, when you're ready to go, one of our employees will help you take them to your car."

Suzy's shoulders relaxed as if a burden had been lifted. "That sounds perfect."

"Good." The cashier gestured for another worker to come over and instructed him to take the boxes to storage.

As the young man began to gather the boxes, Abigail waved her hands. "Wait! You can take all but . . . that one." She pointed out the box with Suzy's bear inside. "I want to keep that one with me." The worker handed the box to her, and she said, "Thank you." Then, eagerness robbing her of ceremony, she thrust the box at Suzy. "This is for you!"

Suzy drew back in surprise. "You built one for me?"

Happiness bubbled up in Abigail and spilled out in a giggle. A girlish giggle she hadn't even realized she was capable of releasing. "Yes, I did! Let's go to one of the benches in the hallway and you can look at it."

Suzy's face remained fixed in an expression of wonder. Abigail set her chair in motion, and Suzy moved alongside her with the box hugged against her chest. They had to go quite a ways from the bear store before she found an unoccupied bench, but she pulled her chair near it and then patted the seat, inviting Suzy to sit.

"There you are. Now peek. I hope you'll like it." Suddenly uncertainty struck. So many years had passed. So many opportunities had been wasted. Would the message — the carefully worded message — be too late? *Dear God, please . . .* She could find no other words, but she trusted God would read the yearning of her soul.

Suzy perched on the bench and placed the box on her lap. She peeled back the top and reached inside. Her face lit up as she pulled out the tan bear with curly fur and bright button eyes. A huff of happy laughter accompanied her smile. "Oh, Mother, she's adorable! The cutest bear I've ever seen."

Abigail wriggled in her chair, wishing she could leap up and dance with glee. She gripped the armrests. "Pinch her middle. She talks."

Suzy's eyebrows rose, and she obediently pressed her thumbs against the bear's plump tummy. Abigail's voice, carried on a rather tinny note, crackled from the little voice box. *"I am so proud of you, Suzy, and I love you very much."*

Suzy seemed to freeze, her unblinking gaze pinned on the bear. Abigail wanted to ask what she thought, whether she was pleased, if she believed her. But she couldn't find the courage. So she sat in silence, watching her daughter's face, holding her breath, hoping and praying.

Very slowly Suzy returned the bear to its box. She folded down the flaps with great care, almost reverently. With trembling hands, she slipped the box from her lap to the bench. Then she turned to Abigail. "Mother . . ." Tears flooded her eyes and spilled down her cheeks. Her lips crumpled and she lunged forward, kneeling on the floor and wrapping her arms around Abigail's neck, nearly pulling her from the chair. Then she clung, sobbing softly against her mother's breast.

Sobs pressed for release from Abigail's throat, but she held them inside, needing to assume the role of comforter rather than the comforted. For the first time in far too long, she wanted to *give,* not receive. She wrapped her arms around her daughter and rested her cheek on her warm head. She was aware of the curious gazes of passersby, and her back throbbed from the awkward position, but she ignored both and whispered soothing words to her daughter while rubbing her hands up and down Suzy's back.

Minutes passed — precious minutes, healing minutes — and finally Suzy pulled away.

She helped Abigail sit up in the chair again, her professional side emerging, and then she eased onto the bench and dug through her purse for a tissue. After mopping her face, she aimed a wobbly smile at Abigail. "Mother . . ." Her voice sounded raspy. She sniffed, then pressed the tissue to her nose for a moment. "Thank you, Mother."

Abigail sensed deeper meaning hiding behind the simple words, and she wished she could find the means to convey all her heart was feeling at that moment. But she could only nod, hoping her smile would speak what her lips could not. Suzy took her hand and squeezed, letting her know the message came through. Abigail sniffed and patted her daughter's hand — a brisk, no-nonsense pat that meant *all done, time to move on.*

Suzy plopped the box on Abigail's lap and said, a hint of teasing in her tone, "Hold tight to Abby-bear. Let's move on."

Abigail hugged the bear to her thudding heart. She caught a glimpse of her reflection in a window, and she nearly gasped in shock. That woman in the wheelchair with the shining eyes and upturned lips . . . could it really be her? Such a change had been wrought. And it came about through simple reconciliation. A prayer of gratitude winged heavenward without effort. *I'm restored, dear Lord in heaven. You've restored me. Thank You.*

CHAPTER 37

Abigail

A hand lightly shook Abigail's arm. The hazy dream into which she'd slipped shortly after leaving Wichita dissipated. She smacked her lips and raised her eyebrows, encouraging her lazy lids to open.

A soft chuckle came from the opposite side of the seat. "Wake up, Mother. We're almost home." Suzy's tender voice pulled her completely from her drowsy state.

She yawned, balling her hands into fists, and then opened her eyes. The car bounced slowly along the final dirt road leading to the farm. She sent Suzy a sheepish look. "Goodness, I can't imagine why I was so sleepy. We had three very relaxing days with more than enough rest."

"Maybe all that shopping wore you out."

Abigail glanced into the backseat. Friendly animal faces showed behind the little window holes cut in the boxes. She smiled and faced forward. "Lacey did most of the work." Maybe the effort she put into forming the messages for Suzy, Shelley, Sandra, and Tanya had worn her out. If so, it was a good kind of tired. She wouldn't complain. She sighed. "I've had my best birthday ever."

An odd look crept over Suzy's face. The car slowed a bit more and Suzy reached out and cupped Abigail's wrist with one hand. "Mother, your birthday celebration . . . it isn't finished yet."

Abigail frowned at her daughter, worry and suspicion tangling together in her thoughts. "What do you mean?"

"Well . . ." They moved past the windbreak of hedge-apple trees to the opening of the farm's lane. Suzy slowed to a mere crawl as she navigated the turn. The moment she cleared the trees, she released a gasp and pressed the brake.

The restraining seat belt held Abigail in place, but her body jolted forward against the strap with the sudden stop. "Suzy! Be careful!"

Suzy was staring ahead, her eyes wide and her mouth hanging open. Abigail turned to look forward, too, and she realized why Suzy had stopped so abruptly. They'd turned into the wrong lane. But then again, maybe they hadn't. That was her barn to the right. And wasn't that the corner of the old summer kitchen peeking from behind the house?

Her heart began to pound. Confused, she brought her gaze back to the beautiful house standing tall and proud. She recognized the ramp leading to the porch and the familiar old lounging chair settled by the big front window. This was her house, but it couldn't be her house. Could it?

Late-afternoon sun glowed against soft yellow siding and made the gold and dark blue accent colors on the window casings, fish-scale siding, and massive corbels shine like jewels. "What? How? Who?" She clamped her mouth closed on the nonsensical stammers.

"Are you upset?"

Suzy's hesitant question almost made Abigail laugh. Two months ago she would have been furious. She would have flayed whoever perpetrated this change to her house with bitter, angry words. She'd let the house go to rack and ruin as a sign of her internal failings. But somehow these past weeks and especially these past days — setting things right with Suzy again — had changed her. Although taken by surprise, she wasn't upset or angry or even resentful. The house's amazing transformation seemed to reflect the transformation she'd experienced in her soul.

Tears flooded her eyes. "I'm not upset. I'm . . . in awe. It's beautiful. It's so very beautiful." *Yes, dear Lord, being at peace with oneself is very, very beautiful.*

Suzy caught her hand and Abigail held tight. They sat in the idling car for several minutes simply admiring. Then Suzy pulled her hand free and aimed an impish smile at Abigail. "Let's get you inside. I suspect there are more surprises awaiting you."

Alexa

"Shhh!" Alexa turned to the family members crowded into the front room and dining room and waved her hands to bring their chatter under control.

They'd all donned their Sunday clothes for the party, giving them a somber appearance, but the laughter and cheerful conversation that had filled the room since their arrival was anything but somber. She hoped she could keep them quiet long enough to let Grandmother be caught unaware. "Mom's bringing her up the walk now. Get ready to yell 'surprise'!"

Shelley rolled her eyes. "If she's seen the house, she already knows something is up. So why the secrecy?"

One of Grandmother's nephews, Andrew Braun, nudged Shelley with his elbow and touched his finger to his lips. She scowled, folding her arms across her chest, but she ceased talking.

Alexa shot the man an appreciative smile before peeking through the tiny slit between the lowered window shade and the window's frame. Mom had pushed Grandmother's wheelchair up the ramp, but they remained on the porch. Apparently Grandmother was admiring the new paint job, because she and Mom were talking, pointing, smiling.

Alexa bit her lip. Couldn't they finish their examination and just *come inside*? The waiting was agony. And the fellowship members who were all gathered in the barn were probably ready to come out, too.

Anna-Grace, one of Grandmother's great-nieces who'd traveled to Arborville for the party, eased up beside Alexa and whispered, "What's taking so long?"

"The men did too good painting the house. Grandmother can't take her eyes off of it."

Anna-Grace laughed softly, shaking her head. "You could go out and get her, if you wanted."

Alexa considered the suggestion. It wouldn't seem unusual for her to be watching for her mother and grandmother's return. "Good idea. Make sure everybody stays back away from the door, though, so she won't see you all right away when she comes in."

Trusting Anna-Grace to herd everyone toward the dining room and kitchen, Alexa bounded onto the porch. "Grandmother! Happy birthday!"

Grandmother held her arms wide. "Come here, you little scamp." With a giggle, Alexa bent forward, and Grandmother wrapped her in a tight hug. "Your mother says you're responsible for all this." She released Alexa and shook her finger at her, but her shining eyes ruined the scolding effect. "It had to have cost you dearly."

Alexa shrugged, grinning. "You're worth it. But . . . do you like the colors okay?" She pulled in a breath and held it.

"The colors are perfect. Blue for my children's eyes, pale yellow for their blond hair, and gold for the wheat harvest that meets our needs."

Alexa released the breath, her shoulders slumping with the action. She should be pleased she'd chosen colors that were meaningful to her grandmother, but instead sadness pricked. None of the colors had any connection to her.

"Of course," Grandmother went on in a thoughtful tone, "that gold is also close in color to the flecks in your eyes, Alexa."

Her happiness restored, Alexa slid her hand along the porch railing, which now wore a fresh coat of bright white. "But what about this color, Grandmother? Has it no meaning?"

"It has the best meaning of all — white is for brand-new and washed clean." Grandmother reached for Mom, and the two women gripped hands and smiled at each other.

Alexa wanted to question the silent messages flowing between her mother and grandmother, but people were inside waiting. She hurried toward the door, gesturing for them to follow. "Well, come on in. I have supper waiting for you. And birthday cake, too!"

"Chocolate?" Grandmother's eyes twinkled with mischief.

Alexa laughed. "What else?"

She held open the door and stepped aside. Grandmother wheeled across the threshold, and Mom followed her in. Even before Alexa could close the door behind them, a chorus of voices exploded. "Surprise! Surprise!" Apparently those hiding in the barn heard the cry, because people spilled across the yard to the house, all calling messages of congratulations.

Within minutes the house was so crowded a person couldn't take a step without bumping into someone, but no one — except Shelley, who hid in the kitchen and busied herself refilling serving bowls and platters — seemed to mind. Some carried their plates to the yard, others sat wherever they could find a seat or leaned against the wall and ate standing up, but everyone managed to partake of the homemade chicken salad or ham salad on artisan breads, macaroni salad, cucumber salad, home-canned applesauce, and relishes.

When people approached Alexa to praise her for planning the party, she credited her aunts with helping. She intended to bake something extra special for Tanya, Sandra, and Shelley — yes, even Shelley — when she'd had a chance to recuperate.

The party lasted less than two hours, but Clete and Tanya had warned her the fellowship members would want to be in bed by a reasonable hour since Saturday was still a workday and they'd need to rise early. So she wasn't offended when shortly after singing "Happy Birthday" to Grandmother and eating a piece of cake, they began loading into the vehicles they'd parked behind the barn. Mr. Aldrich and Danny were the last to leave, and she followed them into the yard.

"Are you sure you can't stay a little longer?" She raised her voice to be heard over the rumble of departing cars' engines. "Maybe have one more piece of cake? There's still some left."

Danny affected a pleading look, but Mr. Aldrich curled his hand around the back of his son's neck. "The cake was very good, Alexa, but we need to get out of the way. It's time for your family to be alone with your grandmother."

But weren't they family, too? After all, they were her father and half brother. She wanted them to stay. Her circle couldn't be complete without them. "But —"

Mr. Aldrich shook his head, an almost-imperceptible motion. "Danny's going to help me when I start the demolition on Mrs. Zimmerman's bathroom Monday morning. If there's any cake left, he can have an extra piece with his lunch then."

Although disappointed, Alexa nodded. She shouldn't argue with her father. If the family finished off the cake — and she suspected they would! — she'd just bake another one specially for Danny and Mr. Aldrich. "All right. Thank you again for everything you did to get the house ready. It looks wonderful. And so does the summer kitchen. What a great surprise! I can't believe there was enough paint to give it a makeover, too."

Mr. Aldrich started to say something, but a second voice intruded. "Alexa?"

She turned to find Anna-Grace hurrying across the yard. When she reached Alexa, she offered an apologetic grimace. "I'm sorry to interrupt, but your grandmother asked if I would help you bring in some packages from her car. They're in the backseat."

Mr. Aldrich smiled at Anna-Grace. "Aren't you Andrew and Olivia's daughter? The one who will be getting married in February?"

Anna-Grace smiled. "That's right. I'm sorry — I met so many people this evening, I don't recall your name."

"I don't think we officially met. I'm Paul Aldrich, and this is my son, Danny."

"It's nice to meet you." Anna-Grace shook hands first with Mr. Aldrich and then Danny. "Oh, yes, you're the carpenter, right? I overheard Clete telling my dad that you remodeled Aunt Abigail's kitchen. You did an amazing job. I'm sure she will find it much easier to use now."

"That's the purpose," Mr. Aldrich said with a smile.

Anna-Grace seemed like a nice enough young woman — sweet-natured, polite — but she had lousy timing. Alexa wanted to know what Mr. Aldrich had intended to say to her. She touched the other girl's arm. "I doubt the car is locked. I'll come help you in a minute."

Anna-Grace smiled, nodded, and told Mr. Aldrich and Danny good evening. Alexa turned to Mr. Aldrich, ready to ask what he'd started to say, but he spoke first.

"You better not keep your grandmother waiting. I need to get Danny home. We'll see you in service Sunday." His hand draped over Danny's shoulder, he aimed his son in the direction of the barn.

As Alexa and Anna-Grace carried the last of the boxes and set them on the porch, Anna-Grace's parents and younger sister, Sunny, stepped outside. Her mother said, "Go in and say your good nights, Anna-Grace. Sunny is complaining of a stomach-ache."

Sunny clutched her belly. Her slanted eyes nearly disappeared with her grimace. "I ate too much applesauce."

"Aw, I'm sorry." Anna-Grace stroked one of Sunny's glossy black braids and gazed down at her with sympathy. The two sisters couldn't look more different — Sunny with her round face and straight black hair, Anna-Grace willowy with wavy hair as yellow as butter. Yet the differences didn't seem to matter. They clearly adored each other.

Alexa experienced a stab of jealousy as she watched the younger one lean briefly into her older sister's embrace. She wished it wasn't too late for Mom to adopt a little girl from China, too.

Olivia went on. "We'll drop the two of you off at Derek and Sandra's before we go to Clete and Tanya's."

Obediently, Anna-Grace headed inside. Alexa swallowed her envy and approached Anna-Grace's family. "Thank you for coming to Grandmother's party. I know it meant a lot to her to have you here."

"Thank you for the invitation," Andrew said. "We've let too much time go between visits. When your mother and I were children, our families got together every year at Christmas and at least once during the summer. But after my mother — your grandmother's sister — passed away, we quit doing it."

"Actually it was even before that, Andrew. I don't think we've come once since Anna-Grace arrived," Olivia added. The black ribbons dangling from her cap gently waved in the evening breeze, dancing across the top of Sunny's head as she turned to Alexa. "To think we never even got to meet you until today, and you're . . . how old? Eighteen?"

"Nineteen."

Andrew and Olivia smiled at each other. Olivia said, "The same age as Anna-Grace."

Alexa had assumed Anna-Grace was a little older since she was engaged — or "published," as the fellowship said — to be married. Knowing they were the same age made her wish they could have more time together, maybe just the two of them, to get better acquainted. But if the families began meeting on a regular basis, she would have a chance to grow to know this cousin.

Anna-Grace exited the house and rejoined her family. Alexa gave her an impulsive hug.

"It was so good to meet you. The next time you come to Arborville, maybe I'll have the summer kitchen finished and we can have some girl time out there."

Anna-Grace's face lit with a smile. Alexa did a double take. Odd how much she looked like Sandra and Mom when she smiled. Anna-Grace said, "That would be wonderful, Alexa. I would love that. Take care now."

Alexa watched the parents and daughters

amble toward the barn. Anna-Grace glanced over her shoulder, smiled again, and waved. Alexa waved back. How fun to have a cousin so close to her age. Maybe now that the families had gathered together again, they would do it more. She'd enjoy becoming acquainted with Anna-Grace.

Their car pulled away, and Alexa hurried inside, eager to find out whether Grandmother had enjoyed the party as much as she hoped.

CHAPTER 38

Suzanne

Suzanne sagged against the doorjamb. Thank goodness Andrew and Olivia had left early. A tension headache throbbed at the back of her skull. Maybe it would ease with their departure. Being in the same room with Anna-Grace — the sweet baby girl she'd never had the chance to hold — had nearly turned her inside out. Only by constant prayer and keeping a careful distance had she managed to resist capturing the young woman in her arms and never letting go.

She held the door open for Alexa, who carried four boxes from the porch at once. Two more trips brought all of the boxes into the house. When Alexa set the last ones on the floor, Suzanne caught her daughter in a hug, determined to push aside the images of her lost-to-her baby girl. To her dismay, hugging Alexa did nothing to ease the deep

511

pain of loss.

Her brother, sisters, and their families had all gathered in the front room at Mother's request. The adults crunched together on the sofas, and the children sat cross-legged on the floor. Mother remained in her wheelchair looking as regal as a queen on a throne. She'd parked herself below the landscapes Suzanne had painted years ago. She'd forgotten all about the paintings until she saw them hanging on the wall, one slightly higher than the other in a pleasing vignette. Alexa had done wonders in the short time she and Mother were away.

Mother patted the rocking chair. "Suzy, sit. Alexa, if I tell you who the boxes are for, would you deliver them to their rightful owners for me?"

"Of course."

One at a time Alexa held up the boxes, and Mother peeked inside and announced the recipient's name. When all the boxes were handed out, Mother said, "All right now. Open!"

The little girls pulled out their kitties or bunnies and squealed with delight. The boys, after a moment's pause, began a mock boxing match between their elephant and dog. Sandra and Tanya exclaimed over their bears, and Alexa gave Mother an exuberant hug. Shelley peered into the box but didn't remove her bear.

Jay held his dog over his head where Ian couldn't reach and looked at Grandmother. Puzzlement puckered his forehead. "Grandmother, isn't today your birthday?"

Mother nodded.

"Well, then how come you gave us presents? Aren't you supposed to *get* presents on your birthday?"

Tears stung Suzanne's eyes as a tender expression crossed Mother's face. Mother said, "Jay, my best present is realizing how blessed I am to have each of you. I gave you a little gift so you would remember this day and know how special you are to me."

Jay stared at his grandmother for several seconds as if uncertain he'd heard correctly. Then he darted across the floor and threw himself into her lap for a hug. Each of the other children followed his lead, and Mother hugged and kissed them by turn. When she'd set little Ian aside, she said, "Why don't you children take your toys upstairs. You can play in the big bedroom."

Ian darted to the piano bench where Alexa was sitting and grabbed her hand. "You come play, too, 'Lexa."

Alexa immediately rose. "Okay. We can get out the Memory game." She herded the giggling children around the corner and up the stairs.

Mother turned to Tanya, Shelley, and Sandra. "I gave Suzy hers this morning, so she already knows about this, but there are voice boxes in your bears. If you pinch its tummy, you'll hear the message."

Sandra lifted her bear as if to try it, but Mother held up her hands. "Not now! Wait until you're by yourself. It's personal."

Sandra lowered the bear to her lap. "All right."

"Clete, Derek, and Harper," Mother went on, her voice serious, "I didn't get you a toy. I figured you'd think I'd completely lost my mind." The men glanced at each other and snickered. "But tomorrow each of you can go to the hardware store and choose something you need. Charge it to my account. That will be my gift to you."

Clete frowned, clearly puzzled. "You don't have to do that, Mother."

"I know." Mother lifted her chin and pinned her son with a firm look. "But I *want* to. So you just do it, all right?"

The three men murmured their assent.

Mother leaned back in her chair and sighed. "Thank you."

Suddenly Shelley yanked the bear from her box and jammed her thumbs against

514

the toy's stomach. Mother's voice blared into the quiet room. *"You take such good care of everyone. I appreciate you and I love you."* She held the bear at arm's length and scowled at it, then lifted her scowl to Mother. "Why did you give me this?" Harper put his hand on his wife's knee, but she knocked it away and snapped, "Why, Mother?"

Mother gripped the armrests on her chair. "I already told you why. Because —"

"Because realizing how much we mean to you is your gift, blah-blah-blah."

"Shelley!" Sandra gawked at her sister. "You should be ashamed of yourself."

Shelley grabbed the bear Sandra was holding. "Let's see what yours says."

Derek reached over and took hold of the bear. His fingers must have found the voice box, because Mother's voice once again rang. *"You are pure sunshine and delight. I love you more than words can say."*

Shelley released the bear with a shove and turned to Tanya. "Want to play yours?" She swung her glare on Suzanne. "And yours, Suzy? Why not let us all hear what Mother said on *yours.*"

Harper rose, pulling his wife up with him. "Come on. You need to take a break." He started to pull her toward the kitchen.

She wrenched her arm free and moved away from him. "I'm not going anywhere until I've had my say!"

He folded his arms over his chest and glowered at her.

Suzanne trembled from head to toe, but she managed to stand. "Shelley, please don't do this. Not now." Not after she and Mother had enjoyed such a blessed time of fellowship. Not after Mother had finally lost her stern look and was trying to open herself to her family again. Couldn't they enjoy one day of peace together?

Shelley started to laugh. A bitter, ugly laugh. "Aren't we instructed not to put off until tomorrow what should be done today?" She aimed a snide look at Mother. "Isn't that what you always told me when I was growing up? 'Get it done now, Shelley. Procrastination doesn't honor God.' " She snorted. "As if you were worried about what *God* thought. You were only concerned about the neighbors finding out another one of your children didn't live up to your standards."

Tears rolled down Sandra's face, but Mother showed no expression at all. It appeared she'd shrunk inside herself, buried by Shelley's ugly accusations. Suzanne looked at Clete, waiting for him to come to

Mother's defense, but he sat with his head low, his jaw set in a stubborn jut. Someone had to counter Shelley's attack. Maybe as the oldest — even though she'd been absent for most of her siblings' lives — she should be the one.

"Shelley, I realize you're upset, but that doesn't justify being so disrespectful." She spoke softly, evenly, but firmly. "I think it's best if you follow Harper's advice and take a break before you say anything else."

"Well, you know what, Suzanne, I don't really care a great deal about what you think." Shelley's voice lost its hard edge. Instead, a deep, intense hurt carried in her tone. "Of course, I'm alone in not caring. Everyone else seems to want to cater to you. Tanya . . . Sandra . . . even Clete." She sent an accusing look across the three of them before facing Suzanne again. "You think we should hire a nurse, so we hire a nurse. You think the house needs painting, so it gets painted. For twenty years everything was one way — Mother's way — and now you prance back into our lives and everything changes."

Shelley marched around the room, flinging her hands toward items. "*Your* paintings on the wall. *Your* quilts here and there. *Your* daughter — your *illegitimate* daughter —

worming her way into Mother's affections the way my legitimate daughters never have." She whirled on Suzanne, her chin quivering. "You left and all the smiles faded from this place. From that day on, Mother didn't gently teach, she commanded. And no matter how hard I tried, I could never satisfy her. Because she was so busy holding you up as our glowing example — Suzanne, our missionary nurse off serving man and honoring God. Lies! All lies!"

Lies . . . The word echoed through Suzanne's mind, searing her with its reality.

Shelley flopped back onto the couch. She picked up the teddy bear she'd discarded and gazed at it for several seconds. Then she sighed. "I guess maybe I know how the prodigal son's brother felt when his father killed the fatted calf for the one who'd been gone. It isn't much fun to be the one who's always done right yet never gets acknowledged for it."

A soft creak — the squeak of the rubber from Mother's chair wheels — broke the tense silence. Suzanne stepped out of the way as Mother eased her chair across the floor and stopped only inches from Shelley's knees. She took the bear from Shelley, held it between them, and pinched its stomach. *"You take such good care of everyone. I ap-*

preciate you and I love you."

Shelley's expression didn't soften.

Mother laid the bear gently in Shelley's lap and then cupped her daughter's face in her hands. "The bear is meant to be your fatted calf. Your robe. Your ring. I know it can't make up for the years I should have been more loving and encouraging. I was angry with myself, and I let my feelings of failure spill over onto my children. I'm sorry. I love you, and I appreciate everything you've done to be helpful from the time you were a little girl until now."

Skepticism curled Shelley's lips.

Mother's voice dropped to a whisper. "It's the truth, Shelley."

The truth . . . Moments from the past weeks flashed through Suzanne's memory — times of sidestepping the truth, allowing misconceptions to continue. She'd held the truth in both fists and refused to let it free out of fear of hurting people, but as she watched her sister sit in selfish, bitter pride, Suzanne realized she had only been trying to protect herself. Her family deserved the truth. She deserved to be free of this heavy burden. Even if it meant facing more recrimination, she had to stop living a lie.

She headed for the door.

"Suzy, no!" Sandra called after her, panic

threading her voice. "Don't go!"

Suzanne paused to send her youngest sister an assuring smile. "I just need to run a quick errand. Don't worry, I'll be back." As she headed across the yard, she thought about Alexa's plans to make regular return visits to Arborville. If she finally shared her secrets, would she be welcome here again?

Paul

Paul turned off Danny's light and closed the door. Even though it was summer, he liked to keep the school routine — early to bed and early to rise. Stability and structure . . . it was how his parents raised him. He'd only chafed against their rules when he reached his teen years. To ill effect. More ill than he'd originally known. He prayed daily he'd be able to keep his son from making the same foolish mistakes he had. And even though Danny occasionally fussed about his dad's predictable routine, Paul intended to keep to the status quo.

He entered the living room and picked up his newspaper, ready for his nightly reading, but someone knocked on the door. Probably his neighbor, Mrs. Lapp, bringing cookies for Danny again. She always worried the boy didn't get enough home-baked treats. After tossing the paper aside, he caught the door handle and pulled it open, a smile and thank-you hovering on his lips. But instead of Mrs. Lapp, he found Suzy Zimmerman standing on his porch.

His smile faded quickly. He'd never hesitated about asking Mrs. Lapp in. After all, she was over seventy. No one would raise an eyebrow. But Suzy? Inviting her in was a good way to get the local gossip started. He stepped outside. She stood with her hands clasped behind her back. In a pink-checked blouse, her hair caught in a simple ponytail, she looked young. And uncertain. He understood the feeling.

She glanced at his untucked shirt and sock-covered feet. A blush stole across her face. "I disturbed you. I'm sorry."

He was sorry, too. Being in close proximity with her brought out emotions he didn't like to juggle. Anger, regret, frustration, confusion . . . He couldn't wait for her to return to Indiana. He would never have thought he'd attach such negative feelings to Suzy. She must have a good reason for showing up on his doorstep the night of her mother's birthday, though, so he'd do his best to be civil. "Is something wrong?"

"Yes." She straightened her shoulders and raised her chin. "It concerns our daughter."

"What about Alexa?"

Her nostrils flared slightly as she drew in a breath. She seemed to be gathering patience. "Paul, I've tried to tell you, she's *mine.*"

He squinted at her in the waning evening light. "Just because I didn't have the chance to raise her doesn't mean —"

"Paul, please . . ." The color in her face had drained, making her eyes seem darker. Haunted. For a moment she pressed her knuckles to her chin, her eyes closed. When she looked at him, she had regained her composure. She spoke in a flat, nearly emotionless voice. "Could you drive out to the house? There's something I need to tell you — to tell my family . . . and Alexa — but I can't do it twice."

"Danny's in bed."

"Is there someone who can stay with him for a little bit? This is important."

Mrs. Lapp would come over without a moment's hesitation, but he wasn't sure he wanted to ask her. Not until he knew what this was all about. "What's so important that it can't wait until tomorrow?"

A pained look crossed her face. "The truth about our daughter."

The familiar anger boiled through him. "I already know the truth."

"No, you don't. But you need to know. I

need to tell it. Please . . . can you come?"

He blew out a mighty breath. "I will not listen to another warning about staying away from Alexa. She's my daughter, and I have every right to —"

"For the last time, Alexa is *not* your child!" Suzy pressed both palms to her chest as if she needed to keep her heart from escaping. "Our child is Anna-Grace Braun."

Paul stumbled backward and slammed his shoulder blade on the corner of the mailbox nailed to the house. He felt his shirt tear, felt the metal jab into his flesh, but he ignored the pain and stared at her in shock. "A-Anna-Grace?"

Suzy nodded miserably, tears winking in her eyes. "Yes. Now please . . . will you come?"

He brushed past her, down the porch steps, and across the yard. Prickly grass poked his soles but he moved steadily toward the Lapps' house. He called over his shoulder, "I'll be out as soon as I can."

CHAPTER 39

Suzanne

"I cried the entire day after they took my baby girl away. I wanted her so badly."

The sounds of the children's laughter in the room above contrasted with the almost deathly quiet in the front room. Alexa sat next to Mother in the rocking chair Suzanne had abandoned. The two of them held hands and kept their gazes riveted on her. But Paul, who had taken the piano bench, and her siblings and their spouses angled their heads toward various spots in the room, apparently uncomfortable with Suzanne's tale.

She continued bravely, inwardly praying for strength to tell the truth, the whole truth. "I begged the midwife and the home's directors, but they all said no. Said the papers were signed, the adoptive parents had been notified. They said I couldn't change it now. So then I begged God to let me have her back. I promised I would be the best mother any child ever had if I could only have her back. But they still didn't bring her to me. Instead, the next morning, they told me a taxi would arrive soon to take me to the recovery house where I would stay for three weeks before being sent home. I didn't want to go. Not without my baby. But I knew it was useless to argue. So I dressed, and I went out to the front porch to watch for the taxi.

"It was December. So cold." She paused and sent Mother a sad smile. "I was glad Mother had insisted I take my coat. Even with it buttoned all the way up, the wind chilled me clear through, and I went around the side of the house where the wind would be blocked. I leaned against the wall and tried to plan a way to get my baby back. And that's when I heard it." She closed her eyes, reliving the moment.

"What?" Alexa's breathless query brought Suzanne's eyes open.

She looked at her daughter. Love swelled. Oh, how she prayed the truth wouldn't fracture her precious child's heart. "I heard a mewling. A sound so soft and weak, I thought it must be a kitten. I knew how cold the little thing would be, and I couldn't let it freeze, so I went looking for it. Out behind the garage I saw a box stuffed with an old towel. The towel was moving, and the mewling sound came from underneath it. I remember thinking how awful — someone had abandoned a litter of kittens. I lifted the edge of the towel to peek inside, and I nearly fainted when I saw, not kittens, but a baby."

Sandra gasped. She raised her face to stare at Suzanne and covered her mouth with her hands. Suzanne nodded somberly, acknowledging her sister's reaction before going on.

"A baby girl so tiny and new her umbilical cord was still attached. And she was hungry! I could help with that." Automatically her arms formed a cradle, and she began to rock gently from side to side. "I ducked into the garage and fed her, crying the entire time because I'd not been given the chance to nurse my own baby. But this little one didn't seem to care that I wasn't her real mother. She nursed and then fell asleep in my arms. I bundled her back up in the ratty towel and started to take her inside, to give her to the caretakers."

She stopped rocking and tightened her arms around herself. "But when I came around the house, I saw the taxi waiting. They'd put my suitcase on the porch, and the driver already had it, loading it in the trunk. He saw me and asked if I was ready to go. I didn't even stop to think. I just said yes and climbed into the taxi with the baby. But instead of the recovery house, I asked him to take me to the hospital. I didn't know how long the baby had been out in the cold. I wanted to make sure she was all right."

Her knees began to quake. Without a word Derek got up, retrieved a chair from the dining room, and set it next to the rocking chair. Suzanne sank into it, grateful for Derek's kindness. "When I walked through the emergency entrance, someone raced over with a wheelchair and asked me if I'd just given birth. I had, so I said yes. They took the baby and me to a room where the nicest nurse took care of me. She was so compassionate, so accepting."

A soft sob sounded — Mother. Alexa immediately cupped her other hand over Mother's. Satisfied Mother was being cared for, Suzanne went on.

"It didn't seem to matter to her that I was only a teenager and there was no husband with me. She just . . . took care of me. When a hospital representative came in with a birth certificate, I gave the baby the nurse's name — Alexa — because she'd been so kind. I added Joy as a middle name because the baby had brought me joy in the midst of my heartache."

Tears slid down Alexa's cheeks, but she didn't make a sound. Suzanne wished she could hold her daughter's hand, but Alexa was busy comforting Mother. She clasped her hands and tucked them between her knees.

"The representative recorded my name as the mother, and it felt so right. As if God had heard my prayers and decided to bless me for giving my own little baby to Andrew and Olivia. When she asked for the baby's father's name, I told the truth — I didn't know who he was. And because I didn't have a husband or family with me, a social service worker came in and told me about a couple who would let me stay with them for a while until I could get my feet under me. That's how I went to live with Marvin and Cecilia Martens."

Alexa smiled through her tears. "Papa Marv and Nana CeCe . . . They were so good to us. I love them."

Suzanne smiled. "What a blessing they were. They encouraged me to get my GED, and when I said I wanted to become a nurse and help people the way the nurse Alexa had helped me, they supported my decision. I stayed with them until I earned my

RN." She shook her head, recalling their tender care. "The crowns waiting for them in heaven are surely encrusted with jewels. They were my saviors — Jesus with skin on." Exhausted, Suzanne slumped against the chair back and fell silent.

Mother cleared her throat and spoke in a raspy voice. "So you didn't have twins. Only one baby."

Suzanne nodded wearily. "Yes. I've tried so hard not to tell outright lies even while withholding the truth that Alexa isn't my biological child. I didn't want to lie." She turned to her daughter and prayed Alexa would see the love she held. "The deepest truth is this: Alexa, you are my God-given gift. From the first moment I held you to my breast, you were mine. I once saw a poem written from a mother to her adopted child, and it says so perfectly how I feel about you. You didn't grow beneath my heart but *in it.*"

Tears flowed from her eyes, distorting her vision. She reached for Alexa, needing a connection with her, and to her relief she released Mother's hand and reached back. Linked with her daughter, Suzanne shared another truth. "I never told you how you came to be my child because I was afraid I would lose you."

She flicked a glance at Paul, who sat ramrod straight and silent, his gaze aimed slightly upward. "And I tried to keep you from Paul because I knew, eventually, both of you would assume he was your father. I didn't want you forming a bond because —" Her voice broke, fresh guilt skewering her. "It could only lead to another loss. I didn't want to hurt you yet again."

Releasing Alexa, she pushed herself upright and walked woodenly toward Paul. "Please forgive me. I feel as if I'm stealing another child from you."

Slowly he tilted his head until his gaze met hers. His stony expression pierced her, but she refused to look away. She deserved his condemnation, and she would accept whatever harsh words he threw at her. He rose stiffly, like a folding ruler being extended section by section. When he reached his full height, he drew in a breath. She braced herself for the verbal barrage.

"Anna-Grace Braun is the baby girl you gave up for adoption?"

She nodded.

"She is my daughter — yours and mine?"

Again she nodded. His flat tone and cold demeanor left her quivering in apprehension. The fiery glint in his eyes promised an eruption. When would it come?

"I lost her when you went away. But now she's here. I won't lose her again." He started for the door. "Now that I know the truth, I'm going to tell her. I want my daughter."

Abigail

"Paul, wait!" Abigail strained against her chair, against her useless legs. She wanted to race after him, to stop him before he made a grievous mistake. To her relief he halted a few feet from the door, but he didn't turn around. His stiff bearing pulsated with impatience. She spoke to his back. "Give me a few minutes, please?" Even though he didn't respond, she pretended as if he'd granted approval.

She sent a glance across the room. "Clete, Tanya, all of you — please go home. Alexa, go with Sandra, would you? I need to talk to your mother and Paul alone."

Alexa crossed to Suzanne first, and the two embraced. They whispered to each other, words too low for Abigail to hear, while the others collected the children from upstairs and made their way outside. Alexa skirted around Paul and joined Sandra, who put her arm around the younger girl's waist and delivered a kiss on her temple. Abigail's heart swelled. With all the things she did wrong, she must have done a few things right to see her children respect her wish and react compassionately toward the little foundling they now knew wasn't their flesh and blood.

As soon as the door closed behind Sandra, Abigail said, "Paul, Suzy, sit down." Suzy returned to the rocker, close to her mother, but Paul clomped to the farthest sofa and perched on the edge of the cushion with his hands propped on his thighs as if prepared for escape. Abigail shook her head sadly. Such heartache in this room. Such pain and regret. She carried it, too. But maybe she could keep these two from inflicting further harm.

"All right. I need you to listen." *Lord, give me strength.* "When Suzy came to me and told me she'd missed her monthly and that she had lain with you, Paul, I was very angry. My child and a young man I'd trusted had broken God's laws. I was angry and disappointed and . . ." — she swallowed — "ashamed. The shame rose above all else, and every decision I made was to hide it. I was selfish. I thought only of myself. How embarrassed I would be if the fellowship found out. How much of a failure I would appear to those I held in esteem. So I told Suzy she couldn't tell anyone else, and I sent her away to hide *my shame.* Because of *my pride.*"

Shaking her head again, Abigail heaved a regret-filled sigh. "So many scriptures warn of the pitfalls of selfish pride. I fell headlong into the pit, and I pulled so many down with me. Both of you, my dear Cecil, Clete, Shelley, and Sandra . . . So determined to cling to my pride and hide my shame, I turned bitter and ugly and harsh. I robbed both of you of the joy of raising your child, I robbed my family of the loving wife and mother they deserved, and I robbed myself of *me.*"

She snorted in self-recrimination. "What a foolish woman I've been. I didn't think about what was best for anyone except myself. I was so very, very selfish and wrong." She turned a steady look on Paul. "Don't do what I did. Before you run off to Anna-Grace and tell her you're her father, stop and ask yourself if you're telling her because it's for her good or yours." She turned to Suzy. "And consider Alexa . . . She wants to stay here and open a bed-and-breakfast inn. Oh, I resisted her. In this old house? But look at what she's done here. I can see it now — I can see her ministering to those who need refreshment. Don't deny her the pursuit of her dream out of selfishness, Suzy. You've raised her right. Now trust her to spread her wings where God leads her."

A tear slid down Suzy's cheek, but she smiled and nodded. Abigail gave her hand a firm pat and then faced Paul again. "Paul, I beg your forgiveness. I wronged you, and you have every reason to hold to your anger. If you choose not to forgive me, to remain angry, I will understand. But I also beg you not to let your anger at me trickle over on those who don't deserve to experience the sting of wrath. Be better than I was — better than I am. Learn from my mistakes."

Cecil's trusty clock, faithfully wound each Sunday morning by Alexa, ticktocked on the wall. Abigail closed her eyes and prayed for God to move in their hearts, to work His will in their lives. As she prayed, tears — warm and cleansing — poured from her eyes. The joy of her salvation, of God's amazing ability to forgive and make things clean, rolled through her in waves. Her daughter's courage to speak truth had given her the courage to share her long-held secrets, too. Now healing could come, if only they would set aside self and open themselves to His leading.

The floor creaked — someone rising. Abigail opened her eyes and saw Paul crossing the expanse to Suzy's chair. She held her breath, watching her daughter lift her face to the man who'd once possessed her heart. Would healing include new love blossoming between the two of them? Abigail began another prayer in her heart, for God to awaken romance for Suzy and Paul, but a whisper of recognition changed the prayer. *Dear Father, it would please me if my precious daughter settled here in Arborville again where I could see her daily. But not my will . . . only Yours. Plant her where You would have her continue to grow.*

Paul spoke gruffly. "We need to talk, but I can't now. It's after ten already, and I should let Mrs. Lapp go home. Can we . . . meet tomorrow? Somewhere public yet where we can talk privately?"

Suzy crunched her forehead. "I don't know where —"

Abigail said, "The cemetery."

They both looked at her as if she'd spoken a curse word.

She grimaced. Why on earth had she made such a suggestion? "It is a public place, yet no one would overhear. But maybe that's a bit . . . morbid."

But Paul shook his head. "No, I think that's fine."

Suzy said, "All right. What time? Ten

535

o'clock?"

"Let's make it nine. It won't be quite so hot then."

Suzy agreed and Paul left.

Abigail let Suzy push her chair through the house. Party reminders were everywhere — puckered balloons sagging on their ribbons, rumpled streamers, stray plates and cups, crumbs . . . The girls would have quite a chore cleaning tomorrow. She wilted into her chair, the ups and downs of the day creating an exhaustion greater than any she could recall from a day of hard labor.

Suzy helped her dress for bed, quiet and introspective yet somehow also peaceful. Abigail was grateful. Apparently her daughter's release of secrets had let her cast off a weight. Although very tired, underneath Abigail felt light and airy. Free. Suzy tucked her into bed with a kiss on her cheek and a whispered good night, tender and loving, then switched off the light and left her alone.

She lay in the dark room, replaying what she'd told Suzy and Paul. Had she said enough? She believed so. She'd done all she could do to guide her daughter. Now it was up to Suzy and Paul to forge their pathways. If she could stay awake, Abigail would spend the night praying for them. And tomorrow, while Suzy was away talking with Paul and the girls were here cleaning up the party mess, she'd take Shelley aside for a talk about the consequences of holding to selfish pride.

Dear Lord, please don't let my legacy of bitterness continue into the next generation.

CHAPTER 40

Suzanne

Suzanne pulled up to the cemetery gate at a quarter to nine. She wanted a little time alone with her thoughts before Paul arrived. To her surprise he was already there, bent on one knee in front of his wife's grave. She stayed in the car, unwilling to disturb him but unable to resist observing him. His lips remained closed, so he wasn't talking to her, but his hands were busy. Plucking weeds? Arranging flowers? She couldn't tell from this angle.

But she could see the age-carved furrows in his forehead, the unsmiling yet somehow soft line of his lips, the slight tilt of his head as if he listened to someone share a secret. He sat back on his heels and gazed at the headstone for several minutes, his eyes shifting, seeming to examine the stone inch by inch. Then his eyes slid closed, he lifted his face to the sky, and he sighed, nodded, and rose in one smooth motion. As he stood, his gaze moved outward and locked on hers.

Suzanne quickly opened her door and hurried across the close-cropped grass. Paul moved toward her at the same time, and they met on the gravel pathway weaving between stones. Neither of them spoke. Embarrassed at having been caught watching him, she didn't know what to say. Apparently he didn't either because he held his hand in silent invitation toward a cement bench tucked beneath a scraggly looking weeping willow tree in the far corner of the graveyard. She gave a brief nod, and he led the way.

They sat on opposite sides of the bench. Although in full shade thanks to the drooping, leaf-filled limbs, the cement was warm against her skin, but a gentle breeze stirred the branches and fanned her face. Somewhat secluded yet in full view of anyone who happened by, they'd found a perfect spot for a talk. If one of them finally decided to speak.

She waited several minutes for Paul to start. After all, he'd asked her to meet him. When he sat quietly, seemingly intrigued by a chip in his thumbnail, she cleared her throat and said the first thing that popped into her mind. "Where is Danny this morning?"

Paul gave a little jolt. "Danny?" He angled a look at her, squinting with one eye. "I dropped him off at a friend's house on my way over here. Said I'd pick him up before noon."

Then they needed to get their talk going. But Danny seemed a safer topic, so Suzanne said, "He seems like a very bright, well-mannered boy. I know you're proud of him. And I'm sure your wife would be, too. You're doing a good job with him on your own."

"Thanks. You've done well with Alexa, too. She's . . . she's a wonderful young woman."

Did a hint of melancholy color his tone? She smiled her thanks. "I'm grateful every day to have her in my life. She's my greatest blessing."

Paul nodded slowly, his odd one-eyed gaze locked on her. Then he looked outward and released a heavy sigh. "It's hard for me to let go of thinking of her as my daughter. These past weeks, seeing her almost every day and talking to her, getting to know her, I kind of grew to love her." He reached up to massage the back of his neck. Red splotches formed along his jaw. "I feel a little foolish now about that. Seeing how she isn't mine."

Suzanne hung her head. "I'm sorry."

He brought down his hand, swishing it through the air as if to shoo away her words. "All the apologizing in the world won't change the situation, so how about we quit doing it and focus on something else, huh?"

"Like what?"

"Like Anna-Grace."

Suzanne shifted slightly, crossing her ankles and giving Paul her full attention. "What did you decide to do?"

Paul lowered his head and scowled, scuffing the toe of one boot against the grass. "I sat up most of the night thinking about what your mother said, asking myself why I wanted her to know I was her father. I tried to convince myself she has the right to know. I kept thinking, wouldn't she wonder about her real parents? Wouldn't she worry she wasn't wanted by her real parents, and she'd be happy to find out she wasn't some castoff, rejected kid? But then I thought . . ." He clamped his jaw so tightly the muscles near his temple twitched.

Suzanne prompted gently, "You thought what?"

He looked at her. Anguish showed in his haunted eyes and the pinch of his brow. "I thought, she *is* wanted by her 'real' parents.

541

Andrew and Olivia — they wanted her. They raised her. They've loved her and taught her and cared for her since she was only days old. Just like you with Alexa. And I started thinking how I'd feel if someone came along and tried to take Danny from me. I'd fight them. I'd fight them to the death. Why wouldn't Andrew feel the same way about Anna-Grace?"

"So you're going to . . ." Suzanne chose her words carefully. "Let her go?"

"Yeah. It's hard, though."

Suzanne recalled how it had hurt last night to be in the same room with her daughter and unable to claim her. "I know."

Paul jammed his toe against the ground once more, then bent forward, resting his elbows on his knees. "But I think it's what Karina would tell me to do." He sent a brief, sidelong glance at her. The red blotches deepened and rose into his cheeks. "Back before we got married, I told Karina about you — about what I did with you when we were young. It took her a while to accept it, but eventually she said she shouldn't hold me accountable for some-thing God had forgiven, because, in His eyes, it had never happened."

He sat up, pressed his palms to the bench's flat surface, and looked at her fully. "But it did happen, and you and I have to live with the consequences of that night. Even though God forgives, we both have to live with the regrets. Am I right?"

Suzanne nodded. She would carry the regret to her grave.

"But why should we tangle Anna-Grace in our regrets? As long as she's happy with her dad and mom, why should we upset that?"

"We shouldn't."

"Yeah. We shouldn't." There was no joy in his voice, only resignation.

She dared to reach out and place her hand very lightly over his. "Paul, if I could do it over again, I'd tell you about our baby. I'd give you a chance to decide whether or not to be her dad. But now that it's over and she's grown up away from us, and our lives have gone in different directions, I can't say I regret everything. If I'd stayed, I wouldn't have found Alexa. If I'd stayed, you wouldn't have married Karina or had Danny. I realize we each lost something when I went away and allowed Andrew and Olivia to adopt our baby girl, but we each gained something, too. Something we wouldn't have had otherwise."

He turned his hand upside down and wove his fingers with hers. "I've had a good life. I can't complain."

She smiled. "Me, too."

He squeezed her hand. A soft, lopsided smile formed on his lips. "I don't want to wallow in bitterness and anger. Danny deserves better than that. I choose to forgive. I forgive you, and I forgive your mother. I'll tell her the next time I see her."

The last weight rolled from Suzanne's heart. "Thank you, Paul."

"Thank you for telling me the truth. Even if I don't have a relationship with Anna-Grace, I'll pray for her. And —" He pulled his hand free and reached for his shirt pocket. He withdrew a folded sheet of paper. "I wrote this. For her. A letter, in case she ever asks who her biological parents are and why she was given up."

Suzanne stared at the sheet, wondering what he'd said.

"I thought you might want to write one, too. Then we can put them together in an envelope and give it to Andrew and Olivia — let them decide when or if to share it with her." He blew out a breath, shaking his head. "It was tough, putting my feelings down on paper, but it felt good. I think it helped me." He pressed the square into her hand and closed her fingers over it. "I figured you'd want to see what I wrote. I'll trust you to make sure it gets to Andrew and Olivia."

She held the folded paper, its edges digging into the soft flesh of her palm. He trusted her. After everything, he trusted her. He truly had forgiven her. She whispered, "Thank you, Paul."

"Yeah." He rose and slipped his hands into his pockets. He didn't smile, but tenderness lingered in his expression. "Life . . . it sure throws a curve ball now and then, doesn't it?"

Suzanne laughed softly and nodded.

"But God . . ." Paul's face lifted, and he seemed to peek between the branches at the blue sky. "He equips us with catcher's mitts and the gear we need to keep from being too battered by it."

She'd never heard life symbolized so uniquely, but she liked it.

He looked at her again. "See you in service, Suzy." He ambled off, hands in his pockets but shoulders square and stride sure.

She waited until he climbed into his pickup and drove away before unfolding his letter and laying it flat in her lap. With the swaying branches of the willow singing a sweet lullaby and the breeze kissing her cheek, she began to read.

Dear Anna-Grace,

If you're reading this, it's because your dad and mom chose to share it with you. I pray it will bring you peace and answers rather than pain and more questions. Because I only want the best for you.

A long time ago I fell in love with a girl named Suzy. I wanted to marry her, and I convinced myself and her that because I loved her, it was okay for us to join intimately. You were conceived that night. Suzy went away after that, and I didn't get to marry her. I didn't even know you'd been born until so many years had passed that you weren't a little girl anymore but a young woman planning your own wedding. I decided then it was better not to interfere in your life but to wait until you wanted to know who I am. I stayed away not because I didn't want you but because I didn't want to be selfish. I hope you understand.

There are two things I want you to know. First of all, you might have been conceived out of wedlock — "unplanned," some people would say — but you were also conceived in love. I loved your mother, and if we hadn't made a mistake by breaking God's instruction to save sex for the marriage bed, we would have gotten married. Second of all, if you ever want to get to know me, the door is always open. You have a dad who has raised you and loves you, and I wouldn't expect you to call me dad, but if you'd like to have me as a friend or you want to know your family history, all you have to do is say so. I'll respect whatever you want.

I guess there's a third thing. The most important thing. I erred, but YOU weren't a mistake. God knew you would be born, and He loves you and has wonderful plans for your life. Seek Him first in everything you do, honor His biblical commands, and you will be able to live your life without regrets.

Lovingly, your father,
Paul Aldrich

Suzanne refolded the letter and held it in her lap. So much wisdom, so much love, so much acceptance in Paul's simple missive. She would write her own letter to Anna-Grace and seal it in an envelope with his, just as he requested. Andrew and Olivia would honor them by sharing it with her when the time was right. Just as Paul intended to pray for Anna-Grace, she would, too, that the choice she made so long ago wouldn't bring pain on her daughter's heart.

Her daughter . . . She hadn't had a chance to talk alone with Alexa yet. Mother had sent her with Sandra, and they hadn't returned by the time she left for the cemetery. But Alexa was probably at the house now, helping to clean up. Eagerness to see her precious child, to assure her how much she was loved and wanted, propelled her from the bench and across the ground. She also intended to give her blessing on Alexa's plans. Just as Paul had chosen not to be self-ish, she wouldn't be selfish either. Not even if it broke her heart to let her daughter go.

Suzanne handed Clete her suitcase, and he tossed it into the back of his pickup. Then he brushed his palms together and leaned against the truck's bed. He fixed a sorrow-ful look on her. "I can't believe it's time for you to go already, Suzy."

Suzy . . . Although she would be called Suzanne in Indiana, it felt comfortable becoming Suzy again to her family. "I know. It went fast."

"But you and that girl of yours sure got a lot done here." His gaze swept across the house, beautiful in the late-afternoon sun-light. "I still do a double take every time I look at the house. It's so different, inside and out."

Suzanne dared to say quietly, "There are lots of things that are different, both inside and out."

He nodded. Then he held open his arms, just as he had the day he picked her up at the Wichita airport, but this time she moved eagerly into his embrace rather than hesitantly. Was it only three months ago his letter had arrived, asking her to return to Arborville? Surely she'd lived a lifetime's worth of experiences in the past weeks. They'd grown together again as a family, and leaving was harder than she'd imagined it could be. But going to Indiana was right. Her job was there, her friends and church family. But she would always be welcome in her childhood home — each of her siblings, including Shelley, had emphasized the fact — and she would visit regularly now. If she wanted to see Alexa, she would have to.

"Mom!" Alexa called from the porch. She balanced a wooden tray against her ribs. The tray held a pitcher, several glasses of ice, and a plate of something Suzanne couldn't recognize from this distance. "Your plane doesn't leave for another three hours. You've got time to sample one of these. My newest creation — butterscotch-pecan-dried peach-oatmeal cookies."

Suzanne groaned and looked at Clete. "I think I just gained three pounds hearing the title."

Clete laughed and looped his arm over her shoulders. "Well, tell you what, I'll eat yours for you and tell you if they're good or not."

"Oh, no you don't!" She broke into a trot, sending a teasing grin over her shoulder. "Last one to the porch only gets crumbs!"

Clete let her win, just as he had when they were younger. They settled into the new white rocking chairs and enjoyed a glass of raspberry-infused tea and the cookies, which they all proclaimed delicious. Even though she'd already heard Alexa's plans a half-dozen times, Suzanne listened to her daughter declare her intentions to set out a plate of cookies each evening for the guests to enjoy before bed.

"And, of course, on their pillows when they arrive, they'll find a gourmet truffle — made by yours truly."

Mother chuckled. "I'll probably need to take out the seams in my dresses before she's done. She told me I'm to be her official goodie-sampler."

"But remember, you only get paid in chocolate," Alexa quipped.

Marjorie Wells, the nurse hired only two days ago, held up one of Alexa's cookies. "You can pay me in these. They're so moist. What's your secret?"

Alexa grinned. "Applesauce in place of oil and real butter instead of margarine."

She took another bite and groaned dramatically. "Oh, they're wonderful. I hope you'll share your recipe."

Alexa let out a happy gasp and spun in her chair to face Suzanne. "Mom! What if I put together a cookbook of the things I prepare for the guests? Do you think people would buy them? I could donate the proceeds to some kind of charity. Or maybe to the benevolence fund at the fellowship."

Suzanne's heart swelled. Alexa's tender compassion knew no bounds. She caught her daughter's hand and gave it a loving squeeze. "Sweetheart, I think it's a marvelous idea. When you're ready to put it together, let me know. Linda does a good job of designing the brochures and newsletters for the hospital. She'd probably jump at the chance to design a cookbook for you."

For a moment, Alexa's face clouded. "I'm gonna miss Linda and Tom like crazy."

Suzanne blinked away tears. She was going to miss Alexa like crazy. But they'd cried together, prayed together, and agreed God had opened the door for Alexa to pursue this new means of ministry. She wouldn't stand in the way of her daughter following the pathway God had carved for her. She forced a light laugh. "Linda just might clobber me when I come back without you. But I bet when I tell her what you're doing, she'll find a way for her and Tom to be one of your customers."

Alexa smiled again. "I'd love that."

Clete set aside his glass and stood. "Suze, I hate to rush you, but if we're going to get you there in time for check-in, we'd better go."

She'd said her good-byes to Tanya, her sisters, and their families at supper last night. All that remained was telling Mother and Alexa good-bye. The last time she'd bid her mother farewell, she'd been young, frightened, bearing the weight of the world on her shoulders. Although leaving was difficult, this time she left with the warmth of acceptance, and the only regret was knowing how far apart Kansas and Indiana were.

Suzanne leaned down and wrapped her arms around Mother's neck. She clung hard, her tears mingling with Mother's. Mother whispered in her ear, "You have your bear?"

Suzanne whispered back. "Abby-bear's in

the front seat with my purse. I intend to carry her all the way home so I can hug her whenever I get to missing you too much."

"Oh, my Suzy . . ." A sob broke from Mother's throat and her hands convulsed on Suzanne's back. "I've loved having you home. I don't want to let you go." She drew in a ragged breath and let her arms slip away. She smiled, her lips quavering. "But I will. Because it's what is best for you."

Suzanne kissed her soft cheek, then straightened. Alexa was standing behind her, tears glimmering in her eyes. Suzanne shook her finger at her. "Don't you dare start or I won't have any choice but to join in. I can't get on an airplane with a red nose and watery eyes."

Alexa choked out a half laugh, half sob and nodded. She slipped her arm through Suzanne's elbow, and they ambled beneath the Kansas sunshine toward the truck, savoring these last minutes together.

"Now remember, you're coming back for Thanksgiving," Alexa said, "and you'll ship the stuff from my room in six weeks, when Mr. Aldrich plans to have the summer kitchen ready for me to move in."

"Yes, yes, I remember." Suzanne feigned disgust. "You've already reminded me how many times?"

"Seven," she answered quickly, her grin impish.

"More like seventy." They both laughed. Suzanne stopped beside the truck and turned a serious look on her daughter. "You'll call me, right?"

"Every day after supper." Alexa held up her hand as if making a pledge. "At first Grandmother wasn't thrilled about getting Internet set up out here, but she finally admitted I'd need it to make reservations. So maybe we can Skype. That way we can see each other while we talk."

Suzanne had sworn off such modern technologies, deeming them unnecessary, but she couldn't refuse the chance to see her daughter's face every week. "That sounds good."

"And you can talk to Grandmother, too, if I can convince her to try it out. She can be pretty stubborn."

Suzanne laughed and caught Alexa in a hug. She rocked her back and forth and breathed in her scent. *God, let her be happy here. She means the world to me.*

"Suzy, we really need to get going."

Clete's quiet reminder forced Suzanne to relinquish her daughter. She did so slowly, holding her breath, willing the seconds to stretch longer. As Alexa stepped away, Paul

Aldrich and his son came around the side of the house. Paul carried a bundle of old lath, and Danny bent forward with the weight of a bucket. They both stopped, Paul's gaze finding hers from the distance of sixty feet.

With his hands full he couldn't wave, but he bobbed his head — one up-and-down motion accompanied by the upturning of his lips. Suzanne offered a soft smile in return and lifted her hand in a silent good-bye. After a moment's pause Paul turned to Danny, appeared to speak, and the two of them emptied their loads in the back of his pickup truck before moving behind the house again.

Suzanne turned to find Alexa watching her, a knowing expression on her face. She said, "You two made your peace, didn't you?"

Although she'd only spoken to Paul in passing since their time in the cemetery — brief exchanges pertaining to Mother's bathroom remodel or Alexa's plans for the summer kitchen — Suzanne recognized the ease with which they now conversed. No tension, no nervousness, no undercurrent of anger. "Yes, we did."

Alexa ducked her head for a moment, then fixed Suzanne with a hesitant look. "Mom?

When you left Arborville, was it to get away from . . . him?"

Suzanne widened her eyes in surprise. "Why would you ask that?"

"Because I've wondered. Because he never knew about you being pregnant. Because you didn't come back." She tipped her head. "Were you afraid of him?"

"Oh, sweetheart, no." Suzanne gripped her daughter's hands. "I loved him, and I know he loved me." His letter to Anna-Grace confirmed it. "I was never afraid of him. I was afraid of my mother and how the community would view my family after I made such a grievous mistake."

The sympathy in Alexa's eyes pierced Suzanne. She squeezed her hands and finished softly, "But I'm not afraid anymore. All is forgiven. And I'm glad I came back."

"Me, too." Alexa tipped her head, her brow puckering thoughtfully. "You know, Mom, when that thunderstorm rolled through last night, I was thinking how fresh and new everything feels after a good rainstorm. That's what we've had — a rain. A mercy rain. And when mercy rains, lives become fresh and new."

Suzanne gazed at her daughter in open-mouthed amazement. "Alexa Joy Zimmerman, when did you get so smart?"

556

Her teasing grin returned. "What did you expect? I take after my mom."

Suzanne grabbed Alexa for one final, tight hug, and then she threw the truck door open. Clete had already started the engine. The seat vibrated beneath her as she clambered in. She slammed the door, rolled down the window, and hung her head and arm out as Clete put the truck in gear and released the brake. The truck began to roll.

Suzanne waved, her vision blurred by tears. "Good-bye, Alexa! Good-bye, Mother!" Pepper raced out of the barn, barking. Suzanne laughed. "Good-bye, Pepper!"

"Good-bye, Mom! Good-bye!" Alexa trotted alongside the pickup for a few yards, Pepper leaping beside her. When they reached the lane, she fell back, but Suzanne heard her call, "I love you!"

Suzanne pressed her fist to her mouth and whispered, "Oh, sweetheart, I love you, too." Although dust billowed and filled her nose, she continued to lean out the window, reluctant to lose sight of her daughter. But as the truck increased its speed, she had no choice but to roll up the window. She leaned back, battling tears — both happy and sad tears. What a journey they'd had. A journey of ups and downs, smiles and frowns.

Despite their failings, their fumbling, and their poor choices, God had forgiven their youthful transgressions and poured out His mercy. And hearts had been changed.

Clete reached across the seat and took her hand. "She'll be fine."

"I know."

"And you'll be fine."

"I know."

"We all love you, Suzy."

She smiled at her brother. "That's good to know."

He winked, then put his hand on the steering wheel and began to whistle their dad's favorite hymn, "Come, Thou Fount of Every Blessing."

The words rang through Suzanne's memory, and she sang, " 'Streams of mercy, never ceasing, call for songs of loudest praise . . .' "

Clete sent her an approving smile. "Amen."

ALEXA'S OATMEAL COOKIES

1/3 c. butter, softened
2/3 c. packed brown sugar
1/2 t. ground cinnamon
1/4 t. baking soda
1/2 c. unsweetened applesauce
1 egg, beaten
1 1/4 c. all-purpose flour
1 1/4 c. rolled oats
1/4 c. chopped dried apricots or peaches
1/4 c. butterscotch chips
1/4 c. coarsely chopped pecans or walnuts

Beat butter until creamy. Add brown sugar, cinnamon, and baking soda and stir until well combined. Mix in applesauce and egg. Add flour in segments, mixing well with each addition. Stir in the oats, and then fold in the dried fruit, butterscotch chips, and nuts.

Drop dough by heaping spoonfuls onto an ungreased cookie sheet. Bake at 375°

Fahrenheit for 8–10 minutes until lightly browned. Allow to cool a few minutes on a cookie sheet before transferring to cooling trays. Makes 2 dozen.

Enjoy!

BAKED GOULASH
FOR A CROWD

2 lbs. ground beef (or turkey or pork)
1 large yellow onion, chopped
4 large cloves of garlic, minced
3 c. water
2 15-oz. cans tomato sauce
2 15-oz. cans diced or crushed tomatoes, undrained
3 T. soy sauce
2 T. dried oregano
2 T. dried basil
1 T. seasoned salt
1/2 t. black pepper
2 c. elbow macaroni, uncooked
shredded cheddar cheese (optional)

In a large dutch oven, cook the meat over medium heat, breaking it into small pieces as it cooks. When the "pink" is gone, stir in the onion and garlic and continue cooking until the onions are translucent. Drain the grease.

Stir in the water, tomato sauce, tomatoes, soy sauce, oregano, basil, seasoned salt, and pepper. Bring the mixture to a boil over medium heat. Reduce the heat to low, cover, and simmer for 20 minutes, stirring occasionally to prevent sticking.

Stir in the macaroni, cover, and simmer until the pasta is tender (20–30 minutes). Remove from heat, allow to cool slightly, and refrigerate overnight. The next day, pour goulash into a greased baking dish, cover with foil, and bake at 350° Fahrenheit until heated through (45–60 minutes). Remove foil, sprinkle with cheese (if desired), and return it to oven until the cheese melts.

Serve! This makes 8–10 servings.

PS — This can be eaten the day it's made, but it's much better when the flavors are allowed to marry overnight.

ACKNOWLEDGMENTS

Mom and Daddy — thank you for the strong legacy of faith you have so beautifully lived in front of me. God blessed me abundantly when He gave me to you.

Don — thank you for handling the mundane so I can disappear into my make-believe worlds. I couldn't finish these stories without you!

Kristian, Kaitlyn, and Kamryn — thanks for loving me in spite of my slip-ups. I love each of you and am proud to call you my daughters.

My wonderful critique partners — thank you for your suggestions, your encouragement, your prayers, and your friendship. So very glad we travel these writing pathways together.

Shannon and the marvelous editorial/ marketing staff at WaterBrook — thank you for your conscientious efforts to make my stories the best they can be and for putting up with my SOTP tendencies. So grateful to be part of your team.

Most importantly, *God* — thank You for the forgiveness You readily bestow on all who ask. No matter how far we've fallen or how scuffed we've become, You are merciful to bring restoration and peace to our lives. I praise You, my Father, for all of Your gifts. May any praise or glory be reflected directly back to You.

READERS GUIDE

1. One youthful indiscretion led to a host of repercussions for Suzanne and Paul. Who else was affected by their choice to step beyond the biblical mandate to save sex for the marriage bed? If God forgives our wrongdoings, in essence "wipes the slate clean," why do we have to live with the consequences of our decisions?

2. Abigail's feeling of failure with her oldest child caused her to place harsh and unfair expectations on her younger children and allowed things around her to fall apart as an outer sign of the mess she saw in her own soul. Her feelings toward herself impacted her relationships with everyone else. As humans, we all make mistakes. How can we

keep from letting our regrets turn us into bitter, unhappy people?

3. Growing up as the only child of a single mother, Alexa felt secure and loved, yet she still longed for something more. The longing led her to create pictures in her head of a big, loving family. The reality fell short of her expectations. Have you ever anticipated receiving something you really wanted only to discover it wasn't at all what you expected? How did you handle the disappointment?

4. Abigail demanded Suzanne go away, deliver her baby in secret, and give the baby to someone else to raise. In some cases, giving up a baby for adoption is the best thing for both the baby and the mother. Was that the best decision in Suzanne's case? Why or why not? How would you have advised Abigail?

5. Initially Suzanne resisted returning to Arborville because she knew her arrival would raise questions and speculations she didn't want to

face. What changed her mind? Did she go for the right reasons? Was her family's reaction to her return fair or unfair? How did Suzanne's situation resemble that of the prodigal son? How was it different?

6. Paul spent years blaming himself for Suzanne's departure from her home and family. He felt if he asked Suzanne's forgiveness he'd be able to release the regret. Have you ever sought forgiveness from someone you wronged? Have you ever needed to forgive someone else for a grievous hurt? Did forgiveness — either offering it or receiving it — bring you peace?

7. Abigail told Suzanne, "You two created life together. It will never be over." Do you agree or disagree with her statement? Why?

8. Suzanne, Abigail, and Paul all held secrets. Although none told outright lies to protect their secrets, neither did they divulge the entire truth. Is withholding the truth the same as telling a lie? Are there times when

holding back part of the truth is
more beneficial than harmful? Why
or why not?

ABOUT THE AUTHOR

Kim Vogel Sawyer is a best-selling, award-winning author highly acclaimed for her gentle stories of hope. More than one million copies of her books are currently in print. She lives in central Kansas where she and her retired military husband, Don, enjoy spoiling their ten granddarlings.